His Choice

by

Sheila Kell

HIS Series, Book 2

His Choice

Cover Art by *Lea Schizas*

The Wild Rose Press, Inc.
PO Box 708
Adams Basin, NY 14410-0708
Visit us at www.thewildrosepress.com

Publishing History
First Edition, 2024
Trade Paperback ISBN 978-1-5092-5565-8
Digital ISBN 978-1-5092-5566-5

HIS Series, Book 2
Previously Published 2015, Cunningham Publishing
Published in the United States of America

Dedication

To my sister, Valerie Hollis Habeeb.
You're always there to support me, pick me up, and
laugh with me.
I love you, sis.

Praise for Sheila Kell

Chapter One

"Who the fuck are you?" The tall man's bellow carried with the frigid, early evening wind. Dark brown eyes, the color of the fattening chocolate bar she'd scarfed down for lunch, glared at her.

In her occupation, if looks could kill, she'd have been dead too many times to count.

Adrenaline rushed through her, charging every nerve ending. Flashing a press card in front of his reddening face, she shouted over the sound of the music blaring from the passing car, "Megan Rogers, *Baltimore News First.*"

Transforming before her eyes, Baltimore City Councilman Richard Thomas squared his narrow shoulders and the corners of his mouth curved into his photogenic smile. "No comment," he stated into the recorder, aka her cell phone, she held before him.

The need to break his politician's façade burned deep inside her. She loathed him, and his actions that evening deepened her disgust. She'd caught him red-handed making an exchange with a known dealer. And she had the photos to prove it.

Front page, above the fold, here I come.

"Did you just buy drugs from an alleged Magic Shop drug dealer?" she asked bluntly.

The councilman's hard eyes narrowed into tiny slits, sending the wrong type of shiver coursing through her body.

He pointed a long, slender finger at her chest, shaking it with each word. "Look here. I don't know what you think you saw, but I did not purchase drugs. I had best not see this false accusation of yours in the newspaper," he angrily demanded.

True. She couldn't prove he'd purchased drugs. She could print the photo of the two men passing something back and forth and let the public draw their own conclusions.

Megan's ice-cold lips slowly broke into a half smile, then her heart raced when his six feet three-inch frame stepped closer. He towered over her in what she suspected was an attempt to intimidate her. She'd seen much worse in her line of work, but that didn't mean she didn't worry about the volatility of the person she was interviewing, especially when she caught them committing a crime.

Her gut told her he'd been doing something illegal. She'd followed this particular dealer, in the bitter cold for days, photographing his exchanges, hoping he'd lead her to his boss. Someone higher in Baltimore's largest drug ring, Magic Shop, must know where her brother Kevin had been taken, even if he'd died at their hands. She swallowed down the pain and fury at the thought of her brother's disappearance and centered her thoughts on the councilman.

"Then what are you doing in Washington Village speaking with Keyshawn, a suspected dealer in Magic Shop at this time of day? It's not like there's a council meeting out here. I'd think you'd avoid this area considering you once called it, and I quote, 'The Sludge of Baltimore.'"

The councilman dropped his hand, took a step back, and cleared his throat. "I like to visit all areas of our fine city to help make better decisions that impact all of our citizens."

She caught herself before she rolled her eyes. Typical political BS answer.

"Now, if you'll excuse me." He turned and walked away.

The euphoria of breaking a big story surged through her veins. She fought her instinct to chase after him. She wouldn't get anything useful, though. He'd have a great deal to say the following day when the paper published her story.

Megan's face carried a full smile.

An exclusive of this magnitude would please her editor, no, make her editor ecstatic. This scoop would allow her boss to stretch the deadline so it could appear in the morning edition. But, Megan needed to get to the newsroom soon.

She preferred to speak with Keyshawn first. She turned to find him no longer standing where he'd been. *No!* She needed him. He was her key.

After Kevin had disappeared, she'd immersed herself in his investigation of Magic Shop. If his disappearance was at their hand, she knew she'd never see him again. That didn't settle well with her.

Unmasking the Magician, the Magic Shop's mysterious leader, had been her brother's goal and it had since become hers. It'd take time, but she'd do it. She would find out what happened to her brother and break the big story he'd worked so hard to bring to light.

Megan closed her eyes against the tears forming.

The past few months had been pure torture. Her brother's investigation notes were nowhere to be found. She had located the names of his sources, but they'd refused to speak with her for fear of reprisal from the Magician. They believed that he'd done away with Kevin, and they valued their lives too much to continue speaking to the press, even anonymously.

Starting from square one, it'd taken her most of the last month to earn the trust from her new sources. Unfortunately, neither of them were in the gang. She wasn't sure how they got it, but Raven and Tyrone provided her with excellent inside information. That was how she'd found and followed Keyshawn, the dealer who brought in the most money.

She placed her phone in her inside coat pocket and zipped it. It had to be safeguarded. It held her photos, recordings, and notes on her stories. That reminded her to back up the information as soon as possible. It had to be somewhere else, just in case…. No, she wouldn't think that. She would not disappear at their hands. She would crack their group open and finish her brother's story.

She had to move forward to do that. Knowing she'd finally have to put Keyshawn's photo in print, her days of trailing him, hoping he'd lead her to his boss, Jimmy, were over. Since she had no idea what the man looked like or where to find him, she'd have to introduce herself to the dealer and hope he cooperated. Finding his boss would take her one step closer to finding her brother or his killer and expose the drug ring.

Throughout her time in the neighborhood, she'd noticed Keyshawn had quite the rapport with the local kids. She'd found it strange they all carried the same small drawstring bag. But, after she witnessed their sly swap with the dealer, she knew she'd found out how he resupplied. The children were called runners, aptly named because she had tried to follow one and he'd lost her. She decided to add more cardio to her workouts.

Megan couldn't imagine money would be in the bags since children ran them. Keyshawn would have to go to his boss and turn in his profits soon. Maybe she'd missed an exchange, not realizing it was that versus a drug buy.

That night would be the night of her big break in exposing the leaders of this criminal organization. The night she hoped to find a lead to her brother.

She sighed. If it'd been easy, the organization would've been destroyed long before. Vengeance was a powerful motivator, though. She wouldn't give up.

The beginning of dusk and deserted streets greeted her. As one of the most dangerous streets in Baltimore, no one willingly allowed himself or herself to get caught on Johnson Street at night, unless they were dealers or buyers.

She rubbed her gloved hands up and down the sleeves of her black leather jacket. But it didn't help. Goosebumps still formed. Just standing there wasn't wise. She had to get moving. Though she'd worn a purple hat, scarf, and gloves, the gang's colors, to keep from standing out, it wasn't safe.

After checking the time on her Hello Kitty watch—dang Kevin and his sense of humor—she calculated how much time before she'd need to leave. Forty-five minutes should be enough time to track down Keyshawn.

Jamming her hands in her pockets, she turned in the direction he'd fled. Her destination was where he'd ended the previous day. Could she confront him around so many people? She'd have to play it by ear, preferring not to get shot.

Rushing down the sidewalk, Megan barely managed to remove her hands from her pockets in time to windmill her arms and regain her balance on the ice before she landed on her backside. Her heartbeat raced. She needed to watch her step. No one tossed salt on the sidewalks in front of the abandoned buildings on this block.

She stepped off more carefully. Walking the familiar streets, her mind wandered. A different exchange she'd witnessed earlier in the day pushed its way to the forefront of her mind.

Two men she thought were city policemen accepted an envelope from a big, burly man she suspected was in Magic Shop. That man had scared her. He looked hard, angry and dangerous. She hadn't found the courage to follow him, though she wished she'd tried.

From the respect shown by the two men, he had to be important. Maybe he was Jimmy or another boss? Could he be the Magician? She'd photographed them and would show the photos to her sources tomorrow. Someone had to have his name.

Reviewing ideas of how she might approach that story, she didn't pay attention as she turned a corner.

"Oomph." She'd run into a wall.

The wall stepped back and a hand shot to a shoulder-holstered gun.

Danger prickled the hair on her arms, and her

scream lodged in her throat.

Oh God. Oh God. Oh God. Why had I let my mind drift, ignoring my safety?

Once she regained her composure, as best as she could, considering the situation, she gazed up, and her heart skipped a beat. The sexiest man she'd ever seen stood before her. His tight, unshaven jaw and dark, brooding look only enhanced his appeal. She slowly turned to the short, mocha-skinned, well-built man beside him. He also held his hand on a holstered gun. Could this get any worse?

"Bitch, what the fuck are you doing here? Ain't no dealers here."

She inhaled sharply. She couldn't speak to the short man, couldn't answer him. Her heart beat rapidly, seeking its escape from her chest. The blatantly hostile look displayed on his face spelled big trouble.

Panic clawed at her. Her instincts demanded she run, but her limbs betrayed her. The dream where she was unable to scream or move had become a reality.

She turned back to the tall, sexy man. Her legs weakened as his gaze raked boldly over her body. His face remained impassive, but his eyes burned with interest. The tingling in the pit of her stomach surprised her. She gulped. This was not the time to lust after a man.

Megan couldn't take her eyes off him, her wall, even after his golden-brown eyes turned cold, hard as stone. His look rattled her, frightened her. Why shouldn't it? He was a man with a gun out in the slums late at night and looked ready to murder someone.

He stared at her but remained quiet, leaving the conversation to his scary friend.

"Get the fuck off the street before I make you."

Turning back to the short man, she swallowed, attempting to find her voice. "I'm...I'm on my way home." Her breathless response betrayed her fear.

She couldn't resist looking back at the taller man once more before leaving. She searched his eyes hoping something would break through the glacial stare. She was searching for something to make her feel safe. She shivered. Apparently, that wouldn't happen. Why had she even thought that could be a possibility?

He stepped around her and walked away.

They were not wearing purple. The cold, purposeful way they moved into the night screamed for her to follow, but they walked in the opposite direction of where she'd hoped to find Keyshawn.

Observing the straightening of shoulders and respectful nods to the two men from the few people they passed, her investigative instincts fired to life. They must be important. The two men turned a corner before she moved her feet to follow. Megan hugged the walls on the opposite side of the street hoping to blend into the shadows. Her journalistic curiosity drove her. If they were important, she needed to know where they were headed. They could lead her to a boss, or maybe even to Kevin.

She furrowed her brow and froze. The image of their guns popped back into her mind. Maybe they carried them only for protection like many others. Heck, she carried one in her purse. Her intuition told her that she might be wrong, though, but finding her brother trumped everything else.

The naked desire she'd witnessed flash through the man's eyes stayed with her. Instead of repulsing her, it roused her curiosity…and her intrigue, which was a dangerous combination since she had no idea who he was and knew nothing about him.

But she couldn't put it completely aside.

She almost called it a day when they stopped. Slipping into the alley across the street, she watched one of the men knock on a door before she hid from view.

Muffled voices carried with the wind toward her. Antsy, she chanced it and peeked around the corner as Keyshawn appeared at the door.

Yes! She smiled, excited that luck had followed her. She'd have missed him if she'd traveled in the opposite direction.

One of the men grabbed Keyshawn's bicep and then pulled him down the stairs. She pressed back against the wall as they shoved him down the street. Her heart pounded loudly in her ears. Her pulse raced. What would she do if they crossed the street toward her?

Megan released the breath she held captive when they stepped into the alley across from her hiding spot. Her senses heightened. Nothing good could come from a meeting in an alley.

Her brick wall of a man stepped to the entrance of the alley, turned to the street, and crossed his arms across his broad chest in a don't-mess-with-me pose.

She immediately understood why when the man who'd accompanied him punched Keyshawn in the stomach.

Nooo! I can't lust after a criminal.

Great. Once again she craved the wrong man. First, that snake of an ex-fiancé and then, the criminal. He took bad boy to a whole new level.

Taking in the scene before her, nausea hit her hard, pummeling her gut. She closed her eyes and took several deep, slow soothing breaths.

She had to concentrate on the story, not wrap her mind around one man.

Ensuring the flash on her camera phone had been turned off, she snapped photos of them in action. This meant they were enforcers for Magic Shop, or problem solvers. Keyshawn had obviously done something wrong. She wanted to know his transgression. Had he short-changed Jimmy in money or product?

Her mother would lecture her for days if she knew Megan felt Keyshawn deserved the punishment he was getting for his crimes. He ruined the streets and his product killed people. She preferred he had jail time to being beaten though.

A thought struck her, and she stood straighter. That sexy criminal could be the man behind Kevin's disappearance, for all she knew.

More than likely one of the two new men had been involved. She shuddered. She had more to fear from them than she'd originally thought. That bucket of ice-cold knowledge froze any lust she'd felt for the man.

Anger at them bled into every cell as she considered what might've happened to her brother. Kevin had been her hero, encouraging and coaching her as she'd worked to become an investigative journalist.

It'd worked. She'd become one, and it was all because of Kevin. But she'd lost him. Baltimore had lost his brilliance, his dedication in searching for truth and justice.

And the man she'd lusted over could be the reason

her brother was missing. Rage rolled within her blood.

"Enough." Her bad boy's voice floated over to her.

The beating ended. Keyshawn lay on the ground, unmoving. The man she'd bumped into bent down and spoke to the dealer.

Suddenly realizing she'd almost left the safety of her hiding place as she'd unconsciously slipped forward to listen, Megan jolted her body to an abrupt halt and then retreated. She had to be careful to not be seen.

She flattened herself against the alley wall when they strode away. Oh, how she wanted to follow them. They'd probably lead her to a boss faster than Keyshawn.

Keyshawn. She looked across the alley and wondered if he needed an ambulance. Even though he was a criminal, she couldn't leave him to die. Maybe if she helped him, he'd reciprocate.

Her opportunity passed before she could leave her hiding spot to cross the street. Two men appeared from the house and half carried, half dragged him inside.

His being on the street the next day was doubtful.

Noting the time on her watch, urgency overtook her. She had to leave in order to get her story on Councilman Thomas in on time. Her boss was only so flexible.

Without Keyshawn, her lead to anyone of importance moved to her pending file. However, she did have two new stories to investigate—the possible policemen taking a bribe and the enforcers sending a message.

She'd pick the organization apart bit by bit if that was what it took for her to find her brother and for the Magician to reveal himself.

She nervously looked over her shoulder as she unlocked her SUV.

It was time to leave the area and her sexy enforcer behind.

Chapter Two

"Are you sure he's not going to hurt me?"

Elliott Brown's whiny voice had AJ clenching his jaw so tight he expected some teeth to crack.

"I've already told you a hundred times, no. Quit worrying and do your job." Behind the steering wheel, AJ Sands pinched the bridge of his nose, took a deep breath and released it slowly to calm his nerves before he strangled the man in the passenger seat. "Do I need to go through it again?"

Elliott nervously cleared his throat and then shook his head. "No. I've got it. It sounds simple enough."

Any moron could follow their plan, but AJ worried the idiot might prove to be the exception and screw it up, bringing down the type of trouble they didn't need.

"I'll do it." Elliott nodded.

In the backseat, AJ's partner, Hank, snorted. "You don't have a choice, fuckhead."

"No, no, I can do it."

AJ's gaze slid over the nervous man one last time. The expensive, navy blue suit covered with a gray trench coat had been tailor-made but hung a little baggy on his lean five-eleven frame on purpose. Flecks of gray had found their way through his short, dark hair. With a freshly shaven face, he looked the part he played, a high-profile attorney.

The only detraction that could be a problem was if

the wrong person noticed the redness around the new snake tattoo that peeked from under his collar.

AJ leaned close to the pseudo-attorney. "You'd best get this right. There's no room for error. Remember what's at stake should you fail."

Blackmail motivated people to do things they normally wouldn't do. They needed Elliott, and the man had made it easy for them. His greed had landed him in this situation. Elliott had embezzled millions from his employer, and instead of taking the money and running, he'd remained to steal more. Some people just weren't made to be criminals.

The agreement was that the incriminating evidence would disappear if he succeeded, plus they'd help him flee the country, help him disappear. It would go to his employer and the police if he failed.

He hadn't hesitated. He wasn't aware that his disappearing involved AJ doing away with him, not sitting on the beach in Bermuda. There never were any witnesses left who could identify anyone in the inner circle of Magic Shop.

"I'll do it. I'll do it." He reached up to scratch his neck, his new tattoo.

AJ slapped at the hand. "Quit it, or you'll make the red more noticeable."

"I understand the surgery. But couldn't I have had a fake tattoo?"

The surgery had been a success. No sight of scars. It could work. It had best work. "Suck it up."

AJ checked his watch. Timing was everything. "Ready?"

After donning a pair of leather gloves, Elliott nodded. "I'm ready."

Observing the man, who could easily land them in prison, step out in the bitter cold empty-handed, almost had AJ pulling the idiot back inside and saying, "Fuck it." But, the consequences of getting caught were preferable to the ones if they didn't complete this mission.

Easy money had lured AJ into this. It was supposed to be a quick in-and-out job. So far, there'd been nothing easy about it, mostly because of the jackass before him. And now AJ and Hank had to depend on him. They were screwed.

"Goddammit, Elliott! Your briefcase."

A gloved hand reached inside the SUV and extracted the leather case. "Got it."

AJ leaned back in his seat and watched the man walk away. No matter what they had on the whiny idiot, he didn't trust him to pull this off. Elliot had been visibly shaking when he'd left the SUV, and AJ doubted it was only from the cold weather.

AJ stretched his legs as best as he could. At six-one, there never seemed to be enough legroom in the driver's seat to fully extend them. The forest green SUV blended with the many SUVs and trucks in the small parking lot. They couldn't afford to draw attention to themselves, which meant cutting the engine and freezing their asses off.

The rectangular twenty-eight-story high-rise loomed behind them and set his nerves on edge. Although he'd abandoned God years ago, AJ sent up a silent prayer for them to succeed.

Dark snow clouds hid the sun, leaving a gray shadow hanging over the city. The temperature had plunged into single digits with a windchill factor well below zero. His black turtleneck and black leather jacket did little to protect him from the bitter cold.

Had AJ known he'd end up in fucking Chicago, he would've dressed differently. Something about this city made the hair on the back of his neck stand up, and he knew better than to ignore that feeling. The uneasiness revolved around the unexpected risks he was taking.

As Elliott disappeared around the building, AJ looked at his watch and breathed a little easier. They were right on schedule. "What do you think? Think he can pull it off?"

"Humph. He'll make it. He's too scared to fail," Hank Masters answered.

"It's a good thing they don't have to change underwear too because I think he might shit his pants before this is over."

Hank chuckled. "You're probably right." He turned and hoisted his short legs across the back seat, leaning his back against the doorframe. His large fist covered a yawn. "How long will this take?"

AJ needed his partner to remain alert. So many things could go wrong, and they needed to be on their toes.

"Not long. If we keep to the timeline, it'll be about an hour."

It would be an hour if everyone in the building who was being blackmailed or on the take didn't get cold feet and back out. They were necessary to move everything along safely, quietly, and hastily. Trusting people he didn't know left a sour taste in his mouth, though.

He hoped the man in their organization, whose sole role was to ensure the proper people assisted them, had done his job well. He supposed they'd know soon enough.

"Wake me when our boy returns," Hank muttered.

AJ swore softly. He knew better than to count on Hank.

He couldn't relax. Since he'd been a last-minute add to this job, he hadn't been in on the planning session. They'd barely even briefed him on the escape plan. Should things go to hell in a hand-basket, his gut told him they would leave him and Hank in Chicago to deal with the fallout.

The fuck if he'd let that happen.

He had the map memorized. He always had his own backup plan. Always had, always would. He couldn't count on anyone but himself when things went south.

AJ Hamilton was his real name, but there was no way he'd allow his new employer to link him with his past or his family. He preferred for them all to stay alive, himself included.

The Magician, Baltimore's largest organized crime boss, was AJ's new employer. He took care of problems that affected the success of Magic Shop, the group's street name. A death order from his boss meant the person disappeared forever at the hands of his enforcers.

The organization's leader didn't care if his enforcers chopped the victim into tiny pieces and fed them to the fish or used acid in a steel drum to eliminate all evidence. So long as no one could identify or link him to anything related to the organization.

Those on the street knew that disappearances were a message from the crime boss.

AJ had yet to meet the man, but like many others, wanted to. He didn't like working for someone he didn't know. But sometimes you had to take what you could get.

AJ reported to Damian Powell, the chief enforcer. He couldn't say he liked the man much. Thankfully, he didn't have to deal with him often. People had learned not to cross the big boss, so he had a light workload.

For some reason, he'd been paired with Hank more and more often. Hank's message was to be noticeable, bruises or broken bones. AJ's presence signified the severity of the transgression and issued a nonverbal warning of what would happen if his partner's message wasn't heeded.

He rubbed his hand over his face, the stubble of his unshaven jaw scratching it. He had to clear his mind of his little pity party over his fucked-up life, or get caught off guard.

He'd been caught unawares when he'd bumped into the little number on the street. Something had passed between them that scared the hell out of him. Her look of innocence, along with the fear in her eyes, had pulled at him to protect her and keep her safe. Her voice wavered when she'd spoken. Damn. What could he have said to calm her? *Don't fear me and oh, let's get a room?* Since his other head would've led the conversation, he'd smartly kept his mouth shut.

A smile broke out on his face. Dressed for Alaska, only her full, ivory face with a bright red nose and rosy cheeks had peeked out between the hat covering her forehead, and the scarf pulled up over her chin. He couldn't decide whether her large, dark blue eyes or the lips she'd kept wetting drew him more. Staring at her, a jolt had screamed through his body, bringing his dick to attention. He'd not even seen her body and he'd wanted her.

He knew who she was, had seen her photo in the newspaper, and that troubled him. Concern for her walking around the neighborhood, alone, late in the evening made him lose focus. He'd barely remembered leaving her and completing his job, which was dangerous for him.

He'd been unable to control his restlessness until he'd found her address and driven past her home later that evening to ensure she'd arrived home safely.

Then he'd dreamed about her.

He shifted in the seat and adjusted himself.

How long had it been since he'd been with a woman? It was before he left everything and everyone behind for this life. Way too long.

The howling wind blew the swirling snow sideways, bringing him back to the present. He hoped it wouldn't affect their return flight. The use of the private plane allowed them to leave the city before the authorities realized a crime had been committed and set up roadblocks and monitored flights.

His chest tightened at not being privy to the plan once he, Hank, and their passenger arrived at the airplane. He shouldn't worry about failure since the team worked as a well-oiled machine. They'd achieved nothing but success in their past missions. He had to trust them. He almost laughed out loud. Trust them? Not possible.

The confidence in the man's walk crossing the street assured AJ things had occurred as planned. Elliott had come through, after all.

AJ's heart rate accelerated. The usual adrenaline rush of pulling off a job filled his every cell.

He straightened in his seat and started the vehicle. "Hank, wake up. It's time to play." AJ heard a grunt and shuffling from the back seat.

Fighting a shiver when the pseudo-attorney opened the passenger door proved difficult. Damn this fucking cold weather.

"Let's go," the man sliding into the seat next to him ordered.

AJ didn't respond. They had no idea how much of a head start they'd have. He slowly exited the parking lot, turned right on S. Clark Street, and then right on W. Congress Parkway.

"Buckle up. We could be in for a dangerous ride in this weather."

The passenger begrudgingly complied. "I want to arrive at the plane safely and get the fuck out of this city."

So far, so good. Driving as fast as safely possible in the worsening weather, he picked up his cell phone and dialed. "ETA four-zero."

"We're ready for wheels up when you arrive. Any problems?" his team leader asked.

"No. We're clear so far." The man sitting next to him stared straight ahead. Most wouldn't be able to tell the difference unless they looked for it. The suit fit well, and there was no redness on his neck. This was going to work.

AJ disconnected the call and checked the rearview mirror again. Tight muscles refused to allow him to settle until this ended.

Exactly forty minutes later, they arrived at the

Chicago Executive Airport. He and Hank wiped down the SUV before they boarded the Gulfstream G650. The truck would eventually be found, but linking it to today's activities would be impossible.

AJ walked aboard and straight to the bar, grabbing a cold beer before he took a seat, where he sighed and fully stretched his legs. It was Tim's time to take over.

Tim Treymayne, the team leader, had been entrusted with ensuring the mission went smoothly. He and another man usually drove on the missions, but for some reason, they'd asked for AJ and Hank to take their place today, while they'd remained on the plane.

AJ figured since this had to be the boldest and highest profile move they'd ever made, Tim wanted sacrificial lambs in case things went wrong. They didn't realize AJ wasn't anyone's lamb.

The team bribe guy, Ted Magee, lounged in the back of the plane, a drink in his hand. "Any problems?"

AJ shook his head, wondering how much time went into preparing for a mission such as this, finding the people to blackmail or bribe. Ted had regularly bragged, "Everyone has skeletons in their closet, and I find them." Maybe it had been a threat.

This team's boss didn't accept mistakes. Every move was too important, and it took only one small error for the entire mission to fail. They'd done this many times over the past few years with nothing but success. So far, today's mission was no exception.

Each secret mission brought in more money than months of drug sales. Only this team, the bosses, and now he and Hank knew about this side business of the Magician's.

His muscles relaxed once they were airborne.

Tim made a call on the satellite phone. "It's done."

AJ let out a sigh of relief. They had successfully broken Denzel Wilkins, a high-profile drug kingpin, out of a federal prison.

Chapter Three

Applause greeted Megan's arrival at the newsroom. Joy and pride instilled lightness in her step. She'd been the people's voice in fighting the scum on the streets. She'd made a difference in the world, at least in her tiny part of it.

In the back corner, her colleagues and friends, Kelly and Victoria congregated around her cluttered desk, each holding the morning edition.

Sporting a wide, warm smile, Kelly held up the newspaper. "Megan, this is excellent! The photos leave no doubt about his activities." She swiped a loose tendril from her face.

Kelly Williams was the most strikingly beautiful woman Megan knew. While she loved the straight blonde hair she'd inherited from her mother, she did envy the natural waves in her friend's auburn hair.

"How'd you discover this?" Kelly asked.

Megan removed her coat and shrugged. She sat at her desk, then placed her purse in the top drawer. "Following Keyshawn was easier than I thought it would be. He didn't check to see if it was safe before he made exchanges, and Councilman Thomas walked around as if he owned the street."

Witnessing that particular exchange had been luck. Now the councilman would be questioned, his reputation besmirched in the media, and she couldn't be happier. Maybe they'd finally force him to resign from the Baltimore City Council.

"You have great sources to get you lined up with this dealer," Victoria said. "I've heard of him. He's notorious for avoiding the police."

A knowing grin crossed her face. "I have amazing sources." Keyshawn was only a start. With her sources, she'd catch more than the little fish.

Victoria grimaced. "I wish some of your sources could help me. I need new ones. The ones I have are useless."

She and Victoria had been paired to investigate Magic Shop. Megan was on the drug side and Victoria on the prostitution side.

"What's next for you, Megan?" Kelly folded the newspaper.

"I had hoped to continue following Keyshawn until he met up with his boss, but something happened last night that halted my plans. I do have a couple of photos of suspicious people I'd like you to look at, Victoria."

She hoped these were the photos that would help them break their stories. Something had to give, and soon.

"Actually, both of you should take a look in case you've run across them in your investigations. If you don't know, I'll take the photos to my sources. I think two of the men I captured are police officers, potentially taking a bribe."

She inwardly cringed. The police would want to talk with her. They wouldn't be happy about her article. Then she mentally smiled. It had been worth it, though.

Victoria nodded. "Good. I haven't seen anyone interesting. I followed the pimps, but they've led me nowhere except the brothel. I haven't been able to sneak in. Their security is tight."

Megan nodded. "It's okay. I think I've got a good lead for us."

"Just be careful. As you're well aware, the Magician has a reputation for being ruthless." Kelly moved closer and placed a hand on Megan's shoulder. "I'm just worried about you. We wouldn't want you to disappear. We've gotten used to our Southern belle."

"What am I, chopped liver?" Victoria asked, her hands on her hips, a silly grin on her face.

Kelly looked up. "We've seen you kick ass so we know you can take care of yourself."

"Wait a second…."

The women broke out in laughter before Megan could finish.

Kelly smiled. "Megan, you really should've joined us last night. I think I found Mr. Right."

Kelly's beauty stopped men in their tracks. They also enjoyed the tight, short dresses she wore. Today's dress was tangerine, complimenting her figure and complexion. Megan couldn't understand how her friend could walk on high heels in the snow and ice. And her legs had to be freezing. Megan wore thick stockings under her slacks and still felt the chill.

She swiveled her chair to face Kelly. "Sorry. I didn't feel like going out. You know how I am in this weather. I don't like to drive after dark unless it's for a story." Snow and darkness were a bad combination in Megan's mind. She stressed enough driving during the day in winter weather. Driving at night had her muscles so tight it would take a masseur several days to unravel them.

"Since you refuse to come out with us, we'll talk here," Kelly said.

Two serious looks focused on her. Uh-oh. They were ganging up on her. She silently groaned. Not again.

"Megan, we're worried about you. You haven't dated in months. We don't like seeing you alone. And don't say you aren't lonely because we won't believe you. It's worse in winter since you hibernate in your brownstone. It's time you move past Marcus and find a man." Kelly was her friend first and foremost and, dang it, she was usually right. Okay, always right.

Marcus Bryant had been Megan's fiancé until she'd found him in bed with her best friend, Merissa. He'd had the audacity to tell Megan he still loved her and wanted to work things out. How could he think she'd stay with him after she'd found him in bed with another woman? No matter what he'd said, he hadn't truly loved her. If he had, he'd have remained faithful.

"There's nothing wrong with my not dating. I haven't met the right man. And I'm not lonely." She wouldn't admit it, but she was lonely. Bob, the long-haired cat she'd adopted from the shelter, was great, but sometimes she wanted the conversation and closeness her cat couldn't provide.

Her belief in men had shattered her heart. She didn't trust herself not to choose another cheating, useless excuse for a man, or, apparently, a criminal. When she desired sex, one-night stands were the way to go. No strings. No heartbreak.

Victoria cast a withering look. "You don't even try. When we go out, men throw themselves at your feet, and you send every one of them packing."

"I know you don't need a man in your life, but having one can make life that much more fun," Kelly added.

Megan fought to keep from groaning out loud. They wouldn't relent. "First of all, men don't fall at my feet—they fall at Kelly's. The leftovers come to me. I don't want a man who speaks to me by default. Being second choice isn't fun," she insisted. "What do you expect me to do? Drag each man to bed until one sticks?" She'd never let that happen. Not any longer.

"Being a smartass isn't attractive on you, Megan. It's time you at least tried. There are plenty of men who come on to you and not Kelly. If you'd try, you might find you have something in common with one of them. You can do things with men without having sex," Victoria told her.

Megan couldn't share with her friends that she didn't want to do things outside the bed with men. They weren't worth it. She'd tried exposing her heart only to have it crushed, destroyed, left empty. It would not happen again.

They meant well, but she didn't want to have this conversation, particularly not after the elation for exposing Councilman Thomas. "Can we do this another time? I'm not in the mood to talk about my love life."

"You never are." Kelly frowned.

Before they could depart, Kristen Michaels, their boss and editor, approached her desk. "Megan. In my office. Now." She turned and walked away.

This can't be good.

Her friends leveled her sympathetic looks before they scattered.

Megan rubbed her lips with her pomegranate lip

balm before leaving her desk. She walked in slow, measured steps, attempting to overcome the sudden shakiness in her limbs and her racing heartbeat. Kristen wasn't happy. What had she done wrong? Had the councilman threatened to sue like he'd said? Surely they wouldn't hold her responsible.

Like her journalists, Kristen's desk stood in disarray, covered in paper and newspaper. She leaned back in her black executive chair. "I'm assuming you saw the police detectives leave my office earlier?"

Not sure if it was a question or a statement, Megan dropped into a burgundy armchair and nodded, looking into a pair of sharp, brown eyes. Her boss had a reputation for being tough, but Megan liked her anyway. Kristen played fair and supported her staff even when they came to her with far-fetched ideas for investigations.

"I kept them from dragging you out of here. They expect you at the station in the next two hours. They aren't happy that you captured a drug dealer in action, and we published it without informing them. Especially since it happened to be a high-profile citizen making the buy. Excuse me, *allegedly*." She stressed the last word with a tight grin on her face. "They threatened to charge you with obstruction of justice. I don't see how they can, and our lawyers agree." She cleared her throat. "You did an excellent job on the article. You didn't do anything wrong, or I wouldn't have accepted it. If you'd reported it to the police before you wrote the article, we wouldn't have had the exclusive on Councilman Thomas. They would've tried to keep it out of the news altogether."

Megan swallowed the lump in her throat. She'd

expected some fallout from the police for not contacting them first, but not a charge of obstruction of justice. She didn't care to go to jail.

"Until Kevin convinced me he had a good lead into Magic Shop and pestered me to let him dig further, I only allowed my journalists to report, not investigate them. I consider it too dangerous, and that's saying something. Now I've got you and Victoria, who pestered me also about digging into them. Don't get me wrong. I want to unmask the Magician but not at the expense of another journalist's life. I'm still not sure I'm doing the right thing, but I know you'd go behind my back, so would Victoria, since she was sweet on Kevin. If it gets too risky, I'm pulling the two of you back."

"Kristen, I won't pull back," Megan responded firmly, her muscles tensing, on alert. She'd do it on her own if necessary.

"I know you have a personal connection to this, Megan. I shouldn't have allowed you to take it." Her boss looked pointedly at her. "You can't cross that line. Keep it professional."

"No matter what happened to Kevin, our drug and prostitution problems are out of control. If one of us can find out who the crime boss is, our streets will be cleaner, safer." At least until someone else stepped into his shoes. Baltimore would never be drug-free.

"If either of you receives even one serious threat, you're both off this project."

She would find either her brother's killer or the Magician, preferably both, threats or not. She owed it to her family. Nodding, she said, "Don't worry. I'm sure I'll be fine."

"I don't like you walking around the west side of Pigtown at night, alone. I know Victoria is covered with her judo or whatever the hell kind of belt she has, but are you taking precautions for your safety? I want you to be safe."

Megan almost snorted aloud. Kristen wanted her journalists to get the story no matter what. The roughest part of Baltimore, a bit too close to the Orioles' stadium, had been dubbed Pigtown, but it didn't frighten Megan. Well, not all the time. Then she realized again that no one worried about Victoria. Did they really believe she wasn't capable of taking care of herself?

Clearing her throat, she responded, "I have a carry permit and a thirty-eight in my purse and pepper spray in my pocket."

She'd been on several dangerous streets and had yet to have a problem. She dressed to fit in and never identified herself as a journalist, but she'd convinced a few, here and there, to provide her with helpful information, but most people avoided her. Keyshawn had been the exception. He had to have known she followed him. That raised the question of why did he let her continue to do it? She'd ponder that later. The police came first.

"That's good. Hopefully, you won't have to use either."

She hoped so as well. Shooting a human being was not on her bucket list.

"What else do you have?" Kristen asked.

Megan showed her boss a photo, holding the one with her sexy criminal man back until she decided what to do with it. "I'm almost positive that's two Baltimore police officers. I'll find out their identities and see if there's a story there. Victoria is looking the photo over to see if she's seen any of them in the Dog Pound." She grimaced. Streetwalkers congregated in the area known as the Dog Pound, and she preferred to avoid it. Victoria could have that portion of the Magician's business.

"It'd be great if you could prove bribery." Kristen pushed the photo back across the desk to Megan. "We know many in the police department are corrupt."

True. It angered her just to think about it. "If we don't flush out the officers on the Magician's payroll before I expose him, it'll be my next project."

"Why aren't you playing the gang angle?"

"I don't care about the gang-bangers who pick fights and create their small bits of havoc. They aren't important in the scheme of things. I need the dealers who'll eventually lead me to a boss. From what I've learned, it's only problems that affect the drug or prostitution trade when the boss steps in."

"What about other crime?"

"There are definitely problems in the area. Crime rates are high, but with corrupt police officers and the problem solvers making people disappear, the murder rate is only slightly higher than average in Baltimore. That's mostly from gang fights. I'm keeping my eye on the police reports in case something happens that's noteworthy." Like disappearances.

People disappeared all the time and weren't reported missing. A few evenings ago, two dealers disappeared because they'd broken one of the organization's Cause of Death, or COD, rules. Apparently, some rules were never meant to be broken, even with criminals. Of course, no one would share them with her. They had yet to realize she didn't give up.

"Did Kevin's notes ever turn up to give you his leads? What he'd found?"

She shook her head. Immediately, tears formed, blurring her vision. If only he'd shared with her, they could've worked it together. She closed her eyes to clear them to remain in the here and now.

"Well then, keep your investigation on the drug trade, and let Victoria concentrate on the prostitution ring, and between the two of you, you'll find something worthwhile."

Megan nodded. "Any suggestions for dealing with the police?"

"Just be yourself. Yes, some officers're still pissed at you, but you can't let that stop you from standing strong. I trust these two detectives, so listen to them. While you're there, see if you can find the officers in the photo. Discreetly."

"I planned to scope out those on duty. I also intend to show the photo to my sources to see if they have names for me. I know I've seen these two men before. My bet is this is a boss with them." She tapped her finger on the largest man in the photo.

Kristen leaned forward, her arms on her desk, her hands clasped. "What makes you think that?"

"It's a feeling."

The intensity of her boss's stare startled her. "Hmm." She leaned back in her chair. "Trust your gut, but be careful."

Megan gave her a slight smile and nodded.

"Megan." Kristen paused. "I've hired someone to

32

replace Kevin."

She jumped from her chair, her heart pounding. "No, Kristen! What about when I find him?" *Alive or dead.*

The concern and pity in the other woman's eyes floored her.

"Megan, I have to fill that position," Kristen said softly.

Megan sniffed and looked down, losing the battle of preventing tears from sliding down her cheeks. "I know, but I have to keep up hope. He's my brother. I need…." She accepted the tissue handed across the desk to her, wiped her face, and blew her nose.

"I can't wait, Megan. I have a newspaper to run," Kristen said more firmly, but her voice filled with sympathy.

Megan walked back to her desk, understanding her boss's position, despite it being hard. She had to keep her mind on what needed to be done now. Kristen trusted the two detectives she needed to see. It didn't matter if they were happy that Megan had brutal police officers fired two years ago. She was proud of what she'd done. She raised her chin and smiled.

The police were the ones in the wrong. They let drug dealers stay on the streets. If they wouldn't uncover them, then she would. With that thought, the weight on her chest lifted and her confidence returned, at least concerning the police.

As for the other part of their conversation, the arrow piercing her heart started the flow of blood, emptying it. *Oh, Kevin.*

Her friends swarmed her desk as she returned. The three of them had no secrets. They were a formidable group, part of a larger investigative team at *Baltimore News First*.

"Well?" Victoria pushed aside some newspapers and sat on the edge of Megan's desk.

"The police are threatening to charge me with obstruction. I have to go to the station today."

Kelly gasped. "They can't do that. You were just doing your job."

Victoria chimed in, "What did they expect you to do? Turn the other way because it was a councilman? No good journalist would've passed up the opportunity you had."

That was the truth, at least not any journalist worth a grain of salt. Her mother used that phrase, and Megan still didn't understand it. Yet she often repeated it. "I guess I was supposed to avoid it all in the first place." She frowned. "I believe they're unhappy because I exposed crime they're allowing on the streets. Maybe by exposing Keyshawn in the press, they'll finally do something. She heaved a sigh. "There's something else. Kristen has replaced Kevin."

Kelly wrapped her arm around Megan's shoulders. "We know this is hard for you, but know we love you and are here for you."

"Thank you."

"Let's get out of here and get some food. I'm hungry." Victoria rubbed her belly.

Megan had two hours before she had to report to the police station and refused to arrive earlier than that.

"That sounds good as long as we don't return to the earlier conversation." She looked each one of her friends in the eyes.

They nodded.

"Okay, let's get out of here."

Megan rose and put on her blue scarf, white beanie hat, and heavy, white down jacket. She'd lived in Baltimore for four years and hadn't acclimated to the weather as people said she would. Her friends teased her about how heavily she bundled up to go outside on what they called "nice days." She couldn't believe the light coats they wore. When it came to the weather, she was still the girl from the South where it was rarely this cold.

****

After returning from lunch, Megan almost walked straight into her ex-friend, Merissa Attenborough. Her heart nearly exploded at the pain and anger that rolled inside her. "What are you doing here?" she asked tersely.

"I work here." She pointed to Kevin's old desk. "Right over there."

Bile rose in the back of Megan's throat and she fought to keep it down. Of all people to take her brother's place, it had to be one of the two people she couldn't trust. She wanted to rail at Kristen, but her boss wouldn't have known. Megan had always prided herself on workplace professionalism, but the big question was how was she to work with a woman she despised?

The home-wrecker had taken Kevin's spot. Nausea assailed her as she closed another door on accepting what had happened to her brother.

Avoiding her new colleague, she walked to her desk, settled in, and checked her voicemail. Of course, there was another call from Marcus. He wouldn't give up. She didn't know how many times she had to tell him it was over. And now Merissa would be near. Did he know?

"Hello, baby." She hated it when he called her baby, and she'd told him that while they'd been together. Yet he'd still called her that, and she'd never said a thing after the first time. That should've been a clue he didn't truly care for her.

"I had to call. Your article today reminded me about Kevin. I'm sorry, baby. I know how close you were. I liked him."

She tightened her grip on the telephone receiver. Her brother hadn't liked Marcus. Megan wished so hard she had listened to Kevin.

"I know you don't believe I still love you, but I do. I care about what happens to you. Please quit what you're doing. Even I know how dangerous this group is. I don't want to see you follow in Kevin's footsteps. I want a chance to make things up to you." He sighed. "I know how you are about a story, and that's why I worry." He paused. "Think about it. Bye, baby."

She held the receiver to her ear a moment longer, not listening to the recording of instructions to save or delete the message.

"Something wrong?" Kelly startled her. She stood beside Megan's desk with a look of concern covering her face.

Megan pressed the proper button to delete the message. "No."

"It was him again, wasn't it?" Kelly whispered.

Megan nodded and then turned to her computer to check her e-mail and press releases. He wasn't worth thinking about.

Midway through her search, she stopped. It had

happened again. Her investigative mind told her while these prison breaks happened infrequently and at different locations, they were all connected.

She turned to her friends. "Did you hear about the prison break in Chicago today?"

Before they could answer, Megan had decided what her next investigation would be. She'd get to the bottom of these escapes, no matter what it took.

Chapter Four

Megan pulled into the police station parking lot and restrained the strong urge to flee. All she had to do was put the car back in drive and go. She shook her head and released a weighty sigh. She could do this. She had to do this. Besides, she really needed to find the right policeman to help her investigation, someone not on the Magician's payroll. Maybe she'd get lucky today.

The noise hit her upon entering the station. The smell of unwashed, sweaty bodies followed. She didn't know whether to use her hands to cover her ears or to hold her nose closed.

Walking across the lobby, her throat constricted. Kristen actually trusted these two detectives, which should've relieved her, since her boss didn't care for policemen altogether. She worried a little about how they'd receive her. Her thoughts went to whether they'd try to ruin her career because she'd exposed a few brutal officers. Then again, her mind typically considered what was the worst that could happen.

The investigation two years earlier had destroyed her relationship with the police department. Reports of police brutality going unpunished had found its way to her desk. Appalled, she had immediately immersed herself into the investigation. The more she'd dug into the story, the greater her disgust with the department.

It hadn't surprised Megan that reports from the alleged victims had disappeared. The police hadn't realized that less paperwork never stopped a reporter. There was always a way to find the truth.

Early in her investigation, the officers involved found out about it. Driving home one day, she'd been pulled over for driving three miles over the speed limit. She'd driven away with a ticket stating she'd been twenty miles over the limit and a threat. They didn't get it. A good reporter didn't let go of their story because they received a threat. That meant someone was scared, there was something there. That made the hunt even better.

It'd been a front-page story. She'd named the six police officers who'd allegedly beaten their suspects into confessions. They had been immediately suspended. After a long police investigation, they were charged with numerous counts of police brutality and fired. Megan had considered it a job well done.

She'd worried about some type of retaliation, but nothing had happened. She later found out they'd been warned by the police chief that if anything did happen to her, the ex-officers would be relentlessly pursued. The day the final man left town had been a day of celebration for her. It had been the first day she'd let her guard down when she stepped outside. The first day she'd felt free again.

Now Megan had angered them again. Megan knew she should've reported to the police what she'd witnessed on the streets. She'd considered it but had immediately dismissed it. They'd have suppressed the story. No doubt she'd pay for it, possibly with jail time. She'd go to jail for a source, but not for this. She would fight with everything to avoid it.

Could they even put her in jail for not reporting a crime? She actually did report it to them, and the world, in print this morning. Shouldn't that count? Kristen said they'd said no, but she knew should've stopped by the newspaper's legal department before coming to the meeting.

When she reached the welcome desk, she squared her shoulders. "Hello."

"Yeah?" asked an overweight police officer with a nametag reading Officer Grimes. Her uniform stretched so tightly that Megan feared a button would pop off and hit her in the head. Her weight probably put her behind the desk, but her demeanor should've removed her from it. Obviously, customer service wasn't high on the academy's teaching list.

"I'm Megan Rogers, here to see Detective Cooper or Detective Phillips." She mentally crossed her fingers, ignoring the flutter in her belly. *Please let me get the nice one of the two.*

"Have a seat, and I'll check if they're here."

The thought of sitting on one of the filthy lobby chairs nauseated her.

A tall, African-American man with a highly starched white shirt and red tie walked into the lobby and called her name. Great. She had the poster boy for a police detective who she bet was by the book.

She pasted a smile on her face and extended her hand. "I'm Megan Rogers."

His large hand swallowed hers in a tight grip. "Detective Cooper. Detective Allan Cooper. Thanks for coming to the station." Releasing her hand, he said, "This way," before turning and walking away.

She hurried to keep up with him as he led her through a maze of desks taking in her surroundings. Plain-clothed and uniformed officers sat at them. Some were talking on the phone. Others talked to a person in the chair next to their workspace.

Detective Cooper stopped at an immaculate desk. Thankfully it sat far from the noise. He gestured to the chair beside his desk. "Have a seat, Ms. Rogers. Would you like something to drink? Coffee?"

Her gut clenched, her heart jerked, but she kept her features composed. "No, thank you."

"Listen," Detective Cooper started, "I could go on about how you failed your civic duty, and talk shit about how reporters are only out for themselves." Megan bit her tongue, holding back her need to challenge him. "But what's the point?" He snorted, looked pissed off as he ran a hand over his shiny, bald head. "Next time call the police first. Don't just stand there watching and taking pictures. Let us do our job. You'll still get a story out of it."

She nodded. "Yes, sir." Megan would have pretty much agreed to anything since she wanted the meeting over and done with, especially as she needed time to scope out the surrounding officers in the hope of finding the two cops from the previous night.

"I want a witness statement from you. Let's start with how you came to observe all you did. What were you doing on that side of town? It can be dangerous, especially in the evening."

She summarized her time on the street, skipping the fight she'd witnessed and the exchange with the possible police officers. They were hers to expose.

"How long were you there?"

"About two hours each day." Two hours of shivering and wishing for her fireplace and hot cocoa.

"Did you photograph every exchange?"

"Yes."

"We'll want a copy of all the pictures, and I don't want to hear about any confidentiality bullshit. I hope you'll save me the trouble of getting a warrant," he flatly stated.

She'd expected that request. "I brought you the photos on a thumb drive." She reached into her purse, removed the storage unit, and handed it to him.

He closed his hand around it. "I'm keeping this." He didn't ask.

She smiled sweetly, adding her Southern charm. "No problem. I made it specifically for you."

He snorted, and it almost made her laugh. She hadn't expected that sort of sound from this starchy detective. He hadn't mentioned any charges against her, and she didn't ask about them. Her tension eased, the tightness in her shoulders slowly relaxing.

It then hit her. They'd been bluffing to get her to the station. *Dang it all to hell and back.*

"You need to remember that we do the investigating. This is our case. We don't need reporters getting in the way of justice."

"I assure you that I fight for justice, too."

He waved her off. "Spare me the free speech lecture. I heard enough of it from your boss. Right now, I'm concerned for you."

Okay, he puzzled her. Were his hot and cold statements his version of good cop, bad cop? Or did he have a personality disorder?

"You put a picture of a drug dealer and a buyer, a

councilman at that, in your newspaper. Your name is on the article." He pointed at it. "You've interfered with a dealer's livelihood, and he's not going to be happy."

Wait until he heard what else she'd witnessed. No matter what he said, it would make the paper before she reported it to him.

"I'm glad if I stopped him from dealing. He should be arrested and not be on the streets."

"Do you realize how dangerous these people are? What you did was stupid. You just made an enemy, and you don't want Magic Shop as an enemy. You need to stop digging into their activities. People who anger them tend to disappear."

Kevin's face came to mind and how the police had blown her off, stating he'd probably just skipped town. She knew better.

Pretending a nonchalance she didn't feel, she shrugged and responded, "I make enemies all the time. I've received so many threats, I've lost count. I'm not stopping. It's my job." She believed the detective, heck, she knew it was dangerous, but for her brother's sake, she refused to quit. She'd keep her gun handy and always be aware of her surroundings.

"I wouldn't blow off a threat from Magic Shop if I were you. Leave exposing organized crime to us."

"Detective Cooper, I'm a journalist and my assignment is to find out who the Magician is. But, I thank you for your concern."

He shifted in his seat. "We're investigating them, and I'd rather you stopped. This is serious," he paused. "Just be careful."

He kept surprising her.

"Okay, settle in because we're here for a while.

We'll go through your night and each of these pictures." He reached down and plugged the thumb drive into his computer.

She inwardly groaned at the thought. She'd survive if that was what it took to catch the bad guys and, to a lesser extent, keep her from fighting a ridiculous obstruction charge.

****

Megan rubbed her gloved hands up and down her arms and stomped her feet to keep warm. She looked skyward and hoped the sun would win its battle of attempting to peek out of the fast-moving gray clouds before it set. Light flakes of snow landed on her face. She wished she could convince her sources to meet at a Starbucks instead of out in the bone-chilling cold on a street corner just outside Magic Shop territory.

Raven, a tall, thin, African-American man in his twenties, who continuously stroked his goatee when he spoke, was her best source. He didn't know the names of the men in the photos but told her he'd seen the two suspected officers around before, once in uniform. He also confirmed the other two were a couple of the organization's problem solvers.

After speaking with Tyrone, her heart beat a little faster. She had his name. AJ. No last name, just AJ. The man who'd scared her half to death and then invaded her dreams now had a name.

She returned to the newsroom to submit the article about AJ. She'd received a long lecture from Kristen about how she shouldn't have stuck around watching the fight. Not about the story itself, but the fact Megan had withheld the information earlier and had placed herself in significant danger for it. Thankfully her friends had left for the day because what she'd received from her boss was nothing compared to what she knew she'd receive from them.

Bob greeted her as she entered her brownstone door. She scratched behind his ears and relaxed at the responding purr. "Did you behave today? No parties? Are you to be a father again?" She chuckled as he meowed. "That had best be a no to the last question, or you will never go outside again."

She'd slipped out of her wet boots and into her comfy slippers when her cell phone rang. She checked the caller ID and smiled.

"Hi, Mom. Are you home?"

Megan's parents, Jeffrey and Tonya, vacationed in Palm Beach, Florida annually. The first time they'd visited had been to escape Hurricane Katrina. She wouldn't be surprised if when they retired from the casino they would move there.

"Megan Elizabeth Rogers, what have you been doing?" her mother asked in the voice that told Megan she was in trouble, especially since her full name had been spoken. "We just got home, and I've been reading your articles. You need to stop what you're doing, right now. Those druggies kill people."

She shook her head and silently sighed. Her parents had been overprotective of her and Kevin growing up and still were. Megan knew they wouldn't approve of what she was doing, but she wouldn't stop. Even for them.

She placed the phone between her shoulder and ear to feed Bob. You'd think she starved him with the way he acted when she opened a can of wet food. Heaven forbid he had to survive off the dry stuff in his bowl.

"You know I'm only doing my job."

"Your job doesn't require you to mix with the dregs of society, Megan Elizabeth."

She cringed. "Actually, it does. I'm an investigative reporter. I investigate, wherever it takes me." Why did she always have to remind her mother of that? "You know why I want to bring them down."

"Getting yourself killed won't bring justice for your brother. He wouldn't want you risking your life trying to avenge his disappearance."

"No matter what you say, Mom, I'm not stopping. This is my job. This is what I do," she stressed. "The Magician needs to be identified and removed from the streets, and I plan to do it."

"And you're very good at your job. We're proud of you, but we don't want to lose you, too."

How could she forget? She did worry about her safety at times, but her blood ran too hot to allow them to get away with Kevin's disappearance. "Mom, I am being safe." Now that she thought about it, it had been odd that no one bothered her on the streets.

"How close are you to ending this?" her mother whispered in a broken voice.

"Not as close as I'd like. Don't worry."

"I'm your mother. Of course, I worry like any good mother would."

She didn't want her mother more upset. "Have you talked to Leann since you've been home?"

"She's pregnant again." At twenty-eight, Leann, her sister, had two children, one six and one four. Megan loved her niece and nephew even though she saw them mostly via Skype.

Jealousy crept up Megan's spine. She'd wanted a

baby with Marcus, but it hadn't happened. "That's great."

"When are you going to settle down and get married?"

She groaned. She was asked this every time they spoke. And since her breakup, the answer had been the same. "When I find the right man."

"What about Marcus? Can't you two get back together?"

She slammed the refrigerator door after removing the milk.

Her mother loved him. Megan admitted that he was charming. But he wasn't faithful. She removed the cocoa from the cabinet and slammed that door. Dang the man!

"Listen, I need to go." She had to end the call before she received the lecture about still being single at her age. Heck, she was only twenty-five.

"Remember what I said. Stay out of the drug area."

"Goodbye, Mom. I love you."

She set the pot with milk on the stove to warm.

"You aren't going to listen to me, are you?"

"Mom."

"Goodbye, Megan. I love you, too. Take care of yourself."

Why was everyone on her about finding a man? Truthfully, she wanted a man, but she didn't want another cheating son of a biscuit eater, or a criminal. She lied. She wanted the criminal. She wanted to get hot and heavy with him, nothing more.

Megan blew on her cocoa to cool it and looked down at the photos and notes spread out on her dining table. She had to have missed something.

She felt a burning need to touch the photos of AJ.

The ringing telephone captured her attention. Only telemarketers called her on her home phone, so she answered, prepared to reply, "No thank you," to the person at the unlisted number.

She wasn't afforded an opportunity.

"You've messed with the wrong person, bitch. You will die," a low, male voice growled before ending the call.

Her adrenaline spiked and she collapsed back in her chair. Staring at the phone, she caught the tremble in her hand. Her first article had obviously made an impact, although not the one she'd hoped would happen. *What am I going to do now?*

Chapter Five

AJ almost spat out his coffee when he saw his face looking back at him from the newspaper. Dammit. His boss would be pissed. The enforcers were expected to stay under the radar when they fulfilled their orders.

Sure, people on the street knew what his job was and knew better than to interfere. But now, all of fucking Baltimore knew where he was and what he was doing. Not what he fucking needed. His boss would be nothing compared to what his brothers would have to say about his activities.

Megan Rogers. He sighed. The same reporter who exposed the councilman. She was very brave but very stupid. As expected, the ringing of his cell phone broke the silence.

"Yeah."

Too restless to sit, he paced the apartment. This call meant trouble. He was typically called last because every other method had failed.

"Did you see the fucking newspaper this morning?"

"Yeah, I'm looking at it now." He poured his coffee out in the sink, losing his taste for it.

"God fucking dammit! How'd she get that fucking picture?"

He wished he knew. He must be losing his edge, which could be deadly in his job.

"She's poking her fucking nose in where it doesn't fucking belong. She's been out snapping fucking pictures the past few nights, and she's got a fucking picture of me she keeps showing around, trying to find out who the fuck I am. We've had her fucking picture out so she can be avoided, but somehow she is still catching them in the fucking act. Thanks to her, the fucking police have pictures of more than a dozen of our dealers in action."

AJ dropped his head back and closed his eyes, the coffee swirling in his stomach. "I agree she's poking her nose where it doesn't belong." He knew where this call was headed, and he didn't like it.

He had one job. Make people disappear. Forever.

No matter what he'd become, he still held on to his morals regarding women. He didn't hurt them. And he couldn't imagine hurting Megan. If he hadn't been residing in hell, he'd have wanted to spend time with her and get to know her. But he'd just fuck that up also.

"I want you to put the fucking fear of the Magician in her. I'm sending you instead of one of the other fucking boys because they get a bit too fucking heavy-handed. I don't want her fucking hurt." Damian paused. "Yet. We can't fucking afford for another reporter to fucking disappear so soon. She needs to get the fuck out of our business."

Breathing a quiet sigh of relief, he thanked God that his boss had called him before one of the others. "I can give her the message."

"Do it." The call ended without an opportunity to respond.

Great, now he had to scare a woman he'd rather protect. Why the hell had he let himself sink this low?

50

****

Megan couldn't hold the newspaper in front of her face forever. The individuals in front of her weren't leaving until they had their say. The thought of telling them about the call put a cold shiver racing through her. Heck, the thought of the call itself did that. But, she had to face the music for what she'd done.

She sighed, calmly folding the newspaper, then placing it on her desk. Two frowning faces and one sour-looking one focused on her. Why Merissa had come over was beyond Megan. Did she think they'd be friends again? Like nothing happened?

"What's wrong with you? You stood there watching a fight. They could've turned on you, Megan." Kelly's hands flew through the air, anger punctuating each word.

"I was well hidden. Besides, you wouldn't have walked away." Megan had been lucky that AJ hadn't thoroughly searched the area. What would he have done with her had he found her? Beat her? Killed her? She shivered at the thought.

Looking unimpressed, Kelly rolled her eyes and walked away, pulling out her cell phone.

"Do you need me to go over the crime statistics in that area again? Especially crimes against women?" Victoria was a walking fountain of information. Megan freely admitted her jealousy of the reporter being able to read or hear something once and commit it to memory.

She gave her friend a slow smile. "I know it's not safe, but I protect myself, and I'll do what it takes."

"There are safer ways than trolling for trouble," Merissa said.

"Merissa's right. Use your sources to nail down something solid instead of walking down crack alley with trouble looking for you."

"Victoria, I'm tired of waiting. I needed to do something myself. Besides, it paid off yesterday." She'd identified criminals in Magic Shop. It disturbed her though that AJ happened to be one of them. Her attraction to him befuddled her mind.

Kelly returned and slapped a sheet of paper down on her desk. She tapped it with her long, ruby-red fingernail. "Call him and hire him," she demanded.

Megan picked up the paper and furrowed her eyebrows. "Who is Trent McKenzie?"

"I just spoke with him. He's into security and has agreed to discuss being your bodyguard."

She shook her head and held the paper out to Kelly. "I don't need a bodyguard."

Her friend crossed her arms over her chest. The stance pushed her breasts almost out of the short white dress with large red and blue flowers. "Yes, you do."

Victoria nodded and crossed her arms over her chest, matching Kelly's stance. Merissa just walked off.

"Call him, or we'll hire him ourselves."

Holding her hands out in surrender, Megan inwardly smiled at their caring. She hadn't told them about the call and knew she couldn't. Yet, she couldn't totally ignore it either. "Okay. Okay. I'll call him, but I'm not promising. Is that satisfactory?"

****

AJ's head ached. He didn't look forward to the job at hand. He should've followed his gut and taken her and run far away. His protective nature toward women was one of his biggest weaknesses, and wasn't that a fucking joke considering his next task.

Those beautiful dark blue eyes. He shook his head. He'd witnessed her fear, yet she'd still followed. Now he had to scare her away from his employer. Thank God, the man hadn't ordered him to kill her.

After running into her, he'd recovered quickly, remembering why he was there. Yeah, he'd rather have stayed and fucked her, but he'd had a job to do. He'd ensured the job won over his sizzling libido, but it had been a hard and bloody battle within him.

Once again, she confused his thoughts. Do his job and scare her off? Or protect her?

He had to remove his mind from the gutter. Leave it in his dreams and his hand.

Approaching her front door, he reminded himself again that his job was to scare her and nothing more.

He anticipated that she'd freak out when she saw him. She knew what he did for a living. Something would be wrong with her if she wasn't afraid. Of course, she had pulled that stunt of following him, so who knew with her?

She opened the door, and an alarm blazed across her pale face. He met her startled eyes with a sharp glare. When she opened her mouth to scream, he rushed forward and clamped his hand over her mouth, pushing her inside. He kicked the door shut and pulled her against him, her back against his front, and held her tightly while she struggled to fight him off, twisting and kicking.

Seeing what had been underneath the thick coat sent a ball of fire smacking him in the chest before rushing to his groin. Her tight, worn jeans and white, form-fitting sweater displayed a womanly body, not one of those emaciated model wannabees he used to date. That, coupled with her girl-next-door look, made her fucking beautiful in his eyes.

His cock throbbed to life.

He dipped his head to her long, blonde hair and inhaled. Pomegranates had just become his favorite fruit.

Shit. *Remember your purpose, AJ.* It was hard to push his lust away, but he had to. He snapped open his eyes and grunted when she landed a kick to his shin and pain radiated through his leg. Son of a bitch. He had a fighter on his hands. That made her even more desirable.

Shifting his weight to his good leg, he tightened his hold around her waist and arms. "I'm serious. I'm here to talk."

Her fruitless struggles continued.

He leaned close to her ear and lowered his voice, "If you want me to hurt you, I will. If you don't want me to hurt you, then cut this bullshit out, and let's have a conversation."

Now he just had to keep from kissing her.

Chapter Six

Megan froze at his statement. She'd opened the door expecting a package to be delivered.

Uneasiness overcame her. She'd expected Magic Shop to send her another message about the article, but not by sending someone to her home, especially an enforcer. This was bad, very, very bad.

"Okay. I'm going to remove my hand from your mouth. Scream and I'll just cover it back up. Then I'll rethink my position on hurting you. Do you understand me?"

She remained still, her chest tightening. Taking a deep breath, she closed her eyes, willing her racing pulse to slow while she figured out the best way to extricate herself from this situation. She slowly nodded.

"Good girl. Here goes."

"Let me go!" She almost fell to her knees when he released her. He had to stand a little over six foot, but he'd picked up her five feet six-inch frame and held her off the floor like she weighed nothing. She wasn't heavy, but she wasn't light either. She'd never overpower a man that strong.

He braced his legs apart and crossed his arms over his chest. He had the dark and dangerous look mastered. A look that, unfortunately, came complete with a pistol peeking out from under his jacket.

She swallowed the scream that burned the back of

her throat and turned away from him to run. She had to get to the rear door. No matter what he said, he could only be here for one reason. It was to kill her.

He grabbed her arm, halting her, and turned her toward him. She stood stiffly, her racing heart ready to explode. Their gazes locked, and he dropped her arm as if it had burned him.

Fear wrapped its frozen hands around her gut. She crossed her arms over her chest, not in an attempt to intimidate or stand strong—like that would matter to him—but to hide her trembling. She needed an escape option. And now!

"Tsk, tsk, Megan. Aren't you going to invite me to sit down or offer me a beverage?"

"No and no. Tell me what you want then leave, or I'll start screaming. My neighbors will call 911, and you'll be arrested." Her faltering voice brought out brightly gleaming eyes, and the corners of his mouth lifted into a sensual smile.

Her insides threatened to melt as lust launched through her, though not enough to abate her fear.

Her pistol. Hell. He stood between her and her purse. If she moved him closer to the fireplace, she had a statue on it that she could use to hit him over the head. Only she didn't want him that far into her home.

She sent a silent prayer that he'd told the truth about not hurting her.

AJ's expression snapped to a cold, menacing stare. "This is your warning to stop what you're doing. Stay out of Magic Shop business."

His gaze raked over her, and she couldn't miss the flash of hunger in his eyes. Chills crept across her flesh. His bold, lust-filled gaze set butterflies fluttering in her stomach from both fright and excitement.

"Tough." She planned to stand strong, but her quivering voice betrayed her.

"Not tough. You need to back off. These people can, and will, do terrible things to you should you continue with this witch-hunt of yours. I'd hate to see anything happen to you."

Megan knew the danger. She knew what could happen, but her brother deserved justice. People probably warned him off the story. In fact, this was more than likely how it started for him. She gritted her teeth. He'd never have given up and neither would she, no matter who showed up to threaten her. Although, hiring Trent McKenzie to protect her sounded better and better.

"You have to back off. I was sent to give you a message. I don't want to come back and deliver the punishment. You were lucky they only wanted to give you a verbal warning this time," he said gravely.

"I've already received one death threat this week. Unless you can top that, you're wasting your time." That wasn't the smartest thing to mention to a killer. "If that's all, then you can leave." On shaky legs, she attempted to move past him toward the door.

He reached out to her, her breath hitching. His gaze roamed her face, landing on her lips. Then, he lowered his mouth and kissed her. When she opened her mouth to protest, he took advantage, stroking his tongue inside, sending lightning bolts of desire directly to her core. Surrendering to the forceful domination of his lips, she no longer desired to withdraw from his passionate embrace.

Hearing a noise outside, she came to her senses and

pushed against his chest. She needed out of his embrace.

He broke away, as if he'd been burned. The shocked look in his eyes probably mirrored hers.

She had to get him out of her house. No matter how much he made her insides quiver and her pulse race, he had to leave. He'd said he wouldn't let her continue. What would he do when she did?

"Leave!"

He opened the door and spoke, his voice harsh. "Megan—"

"Just leave," she stated.

AJ narrowed his eyes at her. "Remember what I said." Then he turned and walked out of her life.

Or at least she hoped.

****

Lying in deep, hot water helped release the relentless chill from Megan's body. She soaked in a pomegranate-scented bath to help rid her of the tensions of the day. Tensions named AJ. Situations like this made her wish she cursed.

It was Kevin's thirtieth birthday, and he'd been due to marry the following week. Jenny Grant, her brother's fiancée, was three months pregnant when Kevin had disappeared. They'd vanished the same day as he had. Megan closed her eyes and said another silent prayer that they were safe.

The day Kevin had disappeared he'd told Megan he was developing a source. Raven said the talk was that her brother had witnessed something he shouldn't have, and Magic Shop took care of him.

The police hadn't acted like they cared, deciding that he and his girlfriend left town. She argued that

Magic Shop had murdered him. The police said that with no body, there was no murder.

After Kevin's disappearance, Megan had taken over his investigation before Kristen gave her the go-ahead. And that had been a hard-fought approval to work the story for the paper. She'd finish Kevin's work and make the criminals responsible for his death pay, no matter how long it took.

As much as it pained her, she believed Magic Shop had killed him. There was no other explanation. He wouldn't go without talking with someone in his family or leave Jenny and his baby. And Magic Shop wasn't holding him for ransom. The knife dug deeper into her chest. It was the only option, unless maybe he was in witness protection. She prayed that was the case, but she still would've expected him to fight for Jenny and the baby to go with him. She shook her head. He'd have fought or not gone.

Her investigation wasn't moving as fast as Megan liked, but she wouldn't give up. The theft of his notes shouldn't have surprised her. She wished she'd been able to decipher what leads he'd been following or who the new source had been. That individual might have known what happened. He or she might have even set her brother up.

Her head ached considering the possibilities.

An image of AJ's confused eyes after they'd kissed popped into her head. He might be her brother's killer. He'd admitted that he'd be the one to return if punishment was ordered.

She slid deeper into the water in an attempt to drown out the crawling sensation that ran over her skin. God, she was such a traitor to her brother for lusting after someone from Magic Shop.

Kevin would've insisted she stop investigating after she'd received that threat. Of course, if it had been him, he'd have kept working on the story. He'd be right to tell her that she should be worried. He'd never published a story on Magic Shop. He'd been waiting until he had it all. She'd, however, published two articles, and they'd sent someone to stop her. Not kill her.

She had a lightbulb moment. Maybe the two threats weren't connected even though the articles were about Magic Shop. One involved the councilman. Had the threats come from two fronts?

Chapter Seven

Megan grumbled as she emerged from her home. *It's Sunday, dang it.* Why Kristen had called the team in didn't matter. She'd learned to go with the flow with her boss a long time ago.

She couldn't control her racing heart when she noticed new faces on the street. Had Magic Shop decided to watch her? If they had, she couldn't put her sources at risk, which meant she couldn't ask them about the photos. The men were too valuable to her.

Dang it!

She took in a deep breath to calm her frayed nerves, but instead, the cold air sent a shiver traveling through her. She couldn't afford to be paranoid. It was a holiday, she rationalized. People had relatives over so that was probably who most of the people were. The erratic beating of her heart eased. The racing thoughts in her mind slowed but didn't completely disappear.

During the quiet drive, her mind wandered. Thoughts of her hunky bad boy and their meeting invaded. Dreaming about him last night brought thoughts of their heated kiss to the forefront of her awareness. She couldn't gain her balance with him. To find herself lusting after a man who'd threatened her confused the heck out of her.

The thought that he would prevent anyone from hurting her floated through her mind. Why would he disobey his boss for her? They'd just met. It was only a kiss between strangers that opened her mind to wonder what exactly his deal was. He stood there while Keyshawn took a beating and then acted like he didn't want to return to hurt her. Did he draw the line at hurting women? Oh, she hoped so.

Her curiosity to learn about him was even more startling than the lust she experienced, and her desire for his lips on hers again.

She didn't expect to see him again, or at least she hoped that she didn't, as she hated the thought of what another visit from him meant. A slight pressure rested on her chest. She had to remember he was an enforcer for a drug lord whom she planned to expose, possibly her brother's killer, not someone to enjoy kisses with.

She strolled into the newsroom to Kelly waiting at her desk, ready to ambush her.

Looking closer at her desk, she groaned in frustration, loudly. Not again. A beautiful bouquet of white orchids sat on her desk. Marcus. He wouldn't give up. Wait, how did he know she'd be at work today?

Kelly smiled. "Hi, Megan, let me guess. Marcus?"

Megan didn't find a card. Weird.

Kelly leaned in close. "Well, you know, I was near your house visiting my friend Christine. I saw a hot guy leave your place. Maybe the flowers are from that guy."

Hot guy? Who the heck? Oh. AJ. Hot? Definitely. Best, hot kiss she'd ever experienced. She hated to burst Kelly's hopeful look. "I'm afraid you won't like this."

Megan relayed the story, minus the heated kiss. Throughout the story, she heard gasps and, "Oh my

God," once or twice.

As soon as she finished, Kelly jumped up from her chair. "Megan, it's getting serious! They came to your home. Have you called Trent yet?" She looked around the newsroom. "What about Victoria? Did she get a visit too?"

Megan shrugged. She hadn't thought to call to warn her. No, she doubted her colleague received a visit. Their message had been for her alone. "Trent and I are meeting after work. Where is Victoria?"

"She'd already left town when Kristen called us in. She gave her a free pass for today," her friend said. "First, you need to drop this story. Second, you need more than a bodyguard. You need police protection, Southern belle."

She almost didn't tell her about the visit from AJ because she knew Kelly would react exactly like this. *Police protection my ass.* She'd hire Trent. Today. Then, he could hire more men if he felt it warranted.

"Now, Kelly, you know we get threats all the time. Why should this one be any different? Besides, it wasn't a death threat, and Trent will be better protection than the police."

She inwardly cringed. She hadn't told them about the death threat. There was still the puzzle of who was behind it, which worried her somewhat. Maybe it had been just a prank threat. The timing did coincide with the printing of her article about the councilman and Magic Shop dealers.

Before the need to hire a bodyguard, she'd been on the streets without personal protection many times and nothing had happened to her. She winced. Determined to find justice for Kevin, she'd neglected her own safety. No more. She had to be smart and smart meant hiring someone.

"Well, because we've heard they follow through with their threats, it may as well have been a death threat." Kelly flounced on the edge of the desk.

She realized what his next visit meant, but didn't want to believe it. AJ hadn't been specific on what punishment would follow should she continue. Since she refused to back down, she guessed she'd find out what he meant.

Thank God she'd decided to hire Trent. Hopefully, he could start right away. That eased her worry somewhat. It didn't stop her shuddering when she did think about it. Death. It was foolish to believe they wouldn't kill her.

"Truthfully, I am a little worried." Her paranoia this morning had been significantly higher than a little worry. "Kelly, there are so many what-ifs that my head's spinning."

"Megan, you have to tell the police. This has gone too far." Kelly's concern filled her voice.

"What do you think the police will do? They won't give me the one-on-one protection of a bodyguard." Telling her friends had been a mistake.

"Maybe not, but it's their job to protect citizens," Kelly insisted.

"Look, it was just a verbal threat." The thought of the police arresting AJ for the threat and his being in jail sent a cold shiver rushing through her body. Why could she not forget him?

Merissa strolled by the desk and smirked. More than likely she'd been eavesdropping.

"If he comes back, promise me you'll go to the

police," Kelly pleaded.

Megan let out a heavy sigh. Only one answer would halt this conversation, even if it was a lie because she seriously doubted she'd go to the police over AJ. "I promise. Now, let me call Trent."

****

"Megan, your cell's been ringing off the hook while you were in the break room." Kelly accepted the cup of coffee she handed her.

Someone needed to invent a way to infuse caffeine right into one's veins. She could definitely use it.

Please don't let it be Marcus. The flowers were more than enough for the day.

She scrolled through and saw the numerous missed calls from a blocked number.

She willed her phone to ring just one more time. If the phone rang as many times as Kelly said, it had to be important.

"Do you think it's a source on your drug investigation?" Kelly asked from her desk next to Megan's.

"I sure hope so."

Come on, ring.

Her friend chuckled and muttered something about her trying to use The Force to get her phone to ring.

Startled when it rang, she jumped and pressed the accept button before it had time to ring again.

She greeted her caller and listened. Her lips curved into a wide smile.

Jackpot!

****

AJ thought about his brothers. They would have his head if they knew what he'd been doing lately. They'd always tried to protect him, but they'd only made him feel like a child. That was why he'd never joined them at their firm, Hamilton Investigation & Security, or HIS as they called it.

Letting out a heavy sigh, he rose to refill his coffee cup. He hated lying to his older brother, Jesse, and his sister-in-law about what he'd been doing when they'd found him. By now, they'd probably heard about his blowup at the bureau. They'd never understand that this was his life now. That he didn't deserve anything better than this.

Pouring coffee into his mug, he shook his head. His brothers wouldn't leave things alone. They kept trying to drag him from the darkness that had engulfed his life, but their interference only plunged him deeper.

His life had begun spiraling after that fateful day. The day when he'd ruined his sister Emily's life. Flashes of his actions, his fists connecting with his foster brother's jaw pulled him deeper into his hell.

He'd been in a rage. After he'd kicked his foster brother out of the house, he'd immediately realized his mistake, but Jake had left. Once they'd found out about Emily's pregnancy, his life's mission had been to find Jake and bring him home. Because of AJ, the man didn't even know he had a daughter.

AJ and his brothers had used every resource available to them yet had been unable to locate him. They'd even checked John Does around the world. Jake had simply vanished.

AJ's continued failure of not being able to right his wrong had ruined his life. He'd faked being happy for so long, but he'd eventually hit rock bottom not long ago, never thinking he'd end up this way. Hell, he'd become a hitman for a crime lord.

Knocking at the door brought him out of his ruminations. Setting his cup down, he picked up his Beretta before checking the peephole. Hank. This couldn't be good.

He replaced his weapon and opened the door. "What's going on?" he asked without preamble.

Hank pushed his way past him and AJ allowed it. "Damian wants to meet at the warehouse this afternoon."

The beginning of a chill crawled down his spine. Damian usually contacted him directly for a meeting. Something wasn't right.

"Did Damian say *why* he wanted to see us all the way out there?" AJ asked the man before him. He walked to the kitchen counter and picked up his coffee cup, then took a sip of its contents and waited for Hank's answer.

"No. He just told me to pass word along to you. Since I was out, I stopped by." Hank scanned the room. "When are you gonna move out of this shithole?"

AJ wouldn't explain himself to anyone, let alone the man before him. Living in this rent-by-the-week, fleabag, one-room apartment provided him mobility for when he felt threatened. Being an enforcer sometimes meant attempted retaliation from relations of those he had made disappear. He needed to be able to move at a moment's notice, so week-to-week worked well for him.

"Have you heard when the next mission is, and if they'll use us?" AJ asked.

Unfortunately, not all escapes were as easy as the last one.

Hank shrugged. "Next couple of weeks. Why'd you wanna do that again? It was fucking boring."

AJ leaned against the wall so he could watch the door. "I was curious. It was easy money."

"Did you put fear in that reporter chick?" Hank asked, raising his eyebrows.

AJ didn't know her well but doubted anything could put fear into Megan. She was a strong-willed, stubborn woman and a dedicated journalist out for vengeance for her brother and one hell of a kisser.

Shit! She'd driven him to madness. He inwardly sighed, refocusing on his current problem. She'd have to wait.

Nonchalantly, he shrugged. "Sure."

"Is she a hot little piece under that jacket? Did you fuck her?" The other enforcer's sick grin proved that AJ had been the right choice to send.

He fought the urge to punch Hank in the face. "No, asshole, I didn't fuck her. I was there to send her a message, and that's all." The kiss had been a bonus. He wanted to do it again. He had to stop this line of thinking.

"I'd have taken the time to fuck her is all I'm sayin', no matter how she looked uncovered." He rose. "I'm outta here. See ya at the meet."

Once Hank left, AJ headed to the door, shut and locked it. AJ was confident there was no legitimate reason for a meeting at the warehouse. Something was up, and it had trouble written all over it.

For once, he wished he would swallow his pride and ask his brothers for help. He shook that thought away immediately. The hole he'd dug himself into was his to manage.

He rubbed his hand over the two-day stubble on his face, fighting the exhaustion attempting to overtake his body. Pouring himself another cup of coffee, his mind spun. Why did they need this meeting?

He walked into the living room, settled back on the worn, green sofa, and turned the TV to the news station. The news alert captured his attention. Denzel Wilkins had been captured. AJ jerked forward on the couch, spilling his coffee on the already stained rug. His heart pounded.

Fuck!

Chapter Eight

Anticipation curled through Megan. This was the major break she'd been hunting. If Raven's information was accurate, she'd have the opportunity to see one of the big bosses. He didn't know or wouldn't tell her which boss it would be or what the meeting was about. But his information had always been solid, so she trusted him.

She wished Victoria had been around to go with her. Then they could see if this boss crossed over to her part of the story.

Megan chewed her bottom lip. She wished she'd scheduled to meet with Trent sooner. Then maybe he'd have come along. She'd call him and see if he was available, but she was going. This was her lead and her chance. She'd publish the boss's photo and be one step closer to destroying the man who had ruined her family's lives.

Her stomach clenched, fighting to stop her pumped-up adrenaline. She needed to notify someone at work as to where she was going. She probably should notify Detectives Cooper and Phillips with the information. Of course, exposing a boss in a drug ring before informing the police would piss them off even more than they already were. They'd probably work to get a new law passed so they could toss her in jail.

Where are you, Kristen? She had to leave soon.

"I've watched you constantly looking at Kristen's office. Something's up, isn't it?" Kelly asked. "And don't say *nothing*. Something is going on. You're packed and ready to leave."

"Shh. I don't want Merissa to come over."

She wanted to tell Kristen first but couldn't hold back. "I have a lead on a meeting where a Magic Shop boss will be present." Megan's smile grew.

"This could be a big break in your story," Kelly said, her own excitement showing.

"I know. Isn't it great? I might expose one of their bosses. I hope it's the one I've been looking for. I need his name and what he does for the organization." Plus, it would put her one step closer to discovering the truth about her brother.

"Tell me about this meeting," Kelly urged. "How is it safe for you to watch?"

She relayed what she knew except for the location. She skirted around it in case Kelly decided to send the police.

Finding a place to hide where she could remain unseen, but hear the meeting would be the key. That might be difficult. At least the weather cooperated. Thankfully, it wasn't snowing. She wasn't sure if she'd have to hide outside, or if they could find a spot inside the scrap metal warehouse. It was so cliché for Magic Shop to meet at a warehouse. She almost rubbed her hands together in glee. Maybe there would be boxes or barrels to hide behind like in movies. She could only hope.

There would be somewhere for her to safely hide. She had to think positively. First, she had to call Trent and convince him to start right away.

****

She left a message on Trent's voice mail and was disappointed not to have him along. The thought of going alone had her insides a bit wobbly, but she was a journalist and wanted her story. If it didn't appear safe, then she'd leave and get the story another way. Somehow.

Checking her directions again, she spotted the exit off the highway. The roads had been salted, but her muscles tensed. Black ice terrified her.

She found a used car dealership within walking distance that happened to be closed today. It would be the perfect place to hide the car. The walk would be about a quarter of a mile through two inches of snow.

After parking, she noticed a potentially major problem. Snow covered the cars in the lot. She couldn't stop to do anything about it, or she wouldn't arrive in time to hide. Megan hoped no one noticed.

As she'd expected, the road to the warehouse hadn't been recently plowed. Like most businesses, they were closed.

She arrived an hour early, as her expected trek took her behind both warehouses, but appeared the safest way to arrive without announcing her presence by leaving obvious footprints in the main path.

Dressed in thick wool slacks, a pink Angora sweater, a white down coat, white beanie hat, and brown gloves, she wrapped her brown scarf tighter around her neck and stepped out into the cold. Her winter boots sank in the snow.

Shoving her hands in her jacket pockets, she dropped her head and walked swiftly across the lot then turned behind the lumber warehouse and followed the old railroad tracks. Then she found herself in front of the scrap metal warehouse. It was surprisingly well-maintained. Decay and graffiti didn't adorn the white stone building.

She tried the front door. Locked. She walked to the first bay on the clear sidewalk, but couldn't budge the blue garage-looking door. Megan stood with her hands on her hips and figured she'd have the same problem with the other five. The Employee Entrance door was also locked.

The meeting had to occur outside unless they had a key to the building, or broke in. That awarded her with numerous places to hide. Piles of metal beams and scrap metals stood in three large stacks.

She craved hiding behind the pile nearest to the middle of the warehouse but she'd have to leave tracks to get there and that, she didn't want. Instead, she settled on the pile closest to where she'd approached the building. Unless they checked behind the piles, she'd be safe. Cold, but safe.

When she heard the first vehicle approaching, she settled into a comfortable crouched position. It always sucked to be the first to arrive at a party. She peeked around the pile. A black SUV stopped at the other end of the warehouse. If they met near his SUV, she wouldn't be able to hear their conversation.

Dang it! She should've chanced the middle hiding place.

It was only a short wait before another black SUV arrived. Was this the company car of bad guys? She hoped the driver would park closer to her. He didn't.

A heater would be nice. Her fingers and toes were cold. She should've worn two pairs of gloves and two pairs of socks. Biloxi weather would be appreciated.

She wondered how many would attend the meeting. She might get lucky and catch more than one boss. Megan smiled, fighting the stiff, cold muscles in her face. This would be worth it.

She willed them to step out of their SUVs so she could get clear photos of them. Their tinted windows prevented her from seeing them. Typical.

Full of anxiety, her hands shook, and her heartbeat pounded so loudly she heard it in her ears, but in an exciting sort of way.

If she hadn't had to park so far away, she'd follow the boss when he departed. It wouldn't be wise, but in her career, she didn't always make sensible decisions for a story. No, this had to be enough. A third black SUV arrived and parked between the other two vehicles. In an almost synchronized manner, the men stepped out into the cold. They stopped too far away for her to hear.

Again she wished she'd moved to the middle. She couldn't risk it now. They'd see her. At least she'd get decent photos. Zoom was a wonderful invention.

She looked down to remove her right glove and unlocked the screen on her phone. She needed to buy gloves that allowed her to use the smartphone screen with them on her hands.

When she looked back up, she almost cried aloud. *No!* Two of the men had turned their backs to her before she could snap a photo of them.

They met in front of the middle vehicle. The guy facing her was the suspected boss she'd been looking for, the one in the photo. Finally.

She automatically snapped shots.

Long ago, she and Kevin created a game to help distinguish people they observed whose names were unknown. They made up funny nicknames instead of calling them man one, two, and three.

The boss was the largest of the men. His shoulders were the broadest she'd ever seen. He stood taller than the others, maybe six four with a blond buzz cut. From her photo, she had been able to tell his nose had been broken more than once. She easily dubbed him "Ape Man."

For the other two, she decided on "Sherlock" and "Watson." For no other reason than those names popped into her mind.

Something about the back of the men tugged at a memory, but she couldn't pull it forth.

****

AJ needed his best bullshitting skills working for him today. He wouldn't take the blame for Denzel's capture. He had nothing to do with it. The stupid fucker.

He and Hank nodded at each other and then turned to face Damian. They were forced to stand with their backs to where he'd seen footprints off in the distance. AJ ensured his Beretta would be easily accessible. He didn't need someone sneaking up behind him.

Fuck. He was an idiot for not asking for help. Even though his brothers didn't approve of the life he'd chosen, they still would've been there for him had he asked.

"Boys." Damian nodded at each of them.

"Damian," AJ replied.

"Hey, boss," Hank said.

"How're things with each of you?"

Not a good start. The man did not engage in mundane chit-chat.

"We haven't had anyone to beat up lately. Not since Keyshawn. My knuckles are getting soft." Hank cracked them.

The chief enforcer turned to AJ. "Did you take care of our little problem?"

AJ shrugged. "I gave her the message." He hoped she would give up on exposing the Magician.

He'd just met her but felt protective of her along with an unfamiliar emotion that confused him. This couldn't be happening now. The timing couldn't be shittier.

"She's a pain in our ass, just like her brother had been. If he hadn't overheard what he had, we wouldn't have had to kill him. Of course, if she gets too close, she might have an unfortunate accident."

His heartbeat skipped. When had this been decided? He had to convince her to quit digging. Had to push Trent to stop her. No matter what she thought of him, AJ didn't want to see her dead. He didn't want that job.

"I guess you heard that Denzel was caught."

"What? Denzel caught?" Hank asked, true surprise registered on his face. The man had no clue about current events.

Damian raised his eyebrows at the man.

"I heard it on the news. What happened?" Strung tight as a bow, AJ kept his voice calm and steady. His boss hadn't shown his hand yet.

"Marshals showed up at the safe house. You boys wouldn't know anything about that, would you?"

And there it was. They were blamed. Fuck.

"I know nothin' about it. I didn't know he got caught. I wouldn't talk to *no* marshal. Honest boss."

"Did he do something stupid?" AJ asked.

"No. We have another theory."

"What?" Hank stupidly asked.

He wanted to slap the enforcer on the back of his head to knock some sense into him. The idiot hadn't figured out how precarious their situation had become.

"You two boys are the only change we made when we busted him out. We've never had someone caught while under our protection."

"We drove in Chicago like we were told. We didn't drive him here, and we don't know where the safe house is." AJ knew, but he didn't think this would be the right moment to provide Damian with that information.

"Yeah, we just drove, boss." Hank visibly trembled. It must have finally occurred to him what was happening.

"It's just curious that we make this one small change and have a major problem. Having a client caught before being on his own is bad for business, especially when the client is Denzel Wilkins."

"Damian, I don't know what you want to hear from us, but we don't know anything about his being captured." AJ knew it no longer mattered what they said, Damian wouldn't believe them. The chances of getting out of here alive dwindled. If his boss didn't kill him, his brothers would for doing this alone.

"There's no other explanation. It's because of you two that our latest client was caught." Damian shouted loud enough to be heard in the next county.

"No, boss. We had nothin' to do with it. Honest."

Hank's voice faltered.

From behind his sunglasses, AJ closely observed the chief enforcer, sizing him up. He could take him even though the man was taller, had wider shoulders, larger muscles, and fifty pounds on him. It'd be like scrapping with his brothers. Only this would be to the death.

"Damian, Denzel had to have fucked up. We didn't do a thing to lead U.S. Marshals to his door. Again, we didn't know where he was so how could we do it?"

"I don't believe either of you! The question is whether it's one or *both* of you who are to blame."

"Boss, I had nothin' to do with it. Believe me," Hank pleaded.

"This is ludicrous. We're loyal to you. We wouldn't go behind your back and do something to hurt the organization." AJ tried reasoning but doubted it would help.

His boss looked at the man standing next to AJ. "Hank, I'd believe this type of fuck-up of you. You aren't always bright, and you run your mouth too much."

Damian turned to him. "You, I wouldn't believe it of. But one of you did it. Admit it, or both of you take the fall."

"I didn't do it, boss. I didn't do it," Hank swore fervently.

"You know I wouldn't do this. *We* wouldn't do this," AJ stated.

Their time was at an end. The Magician had been embarrassed, and someone would be held accountable. They would be the ones to disappear this time.

Damian drew so fast that he caught AJ off-guard

and squeezed off a shot before AJ could draw. AJ fired, not taking the time to bring his Beretta all of the way up Damian's body before his world went black.

****

Megan dropped her phone, a startled gasp escaping her lips. She reactively covered her mouth and stilled. A buzzing started in her ears while her heart raced faster than it ever had before. Had he heard her?

Holding his side, Ape Man raised his head in her direction.

She froze. *Oh God. Oh God. Oh God. Don't come after me. Don't come after me.*

He looked down at the blood on his hands, turned, and walked to his vehicle. His wound saved her. One of the men had shot him before he'd fallen to the ground.

Thank you, Sherlock.

She'd overheard bits of the conversation. She'd caught, the F-word, followed by, "…captured… I don't believe either of you." There had been no mistaking Ape Man's anger. But to kill them? She hadn't expected that in her wildest dreams.

She waited a few minutes after the boss left before she dared move. She fell over in the slushy snow, her legs no longer supporting her in the crouched position. She'd just witnessed two men being murdered. The unfamiliar state of panic rose within her. What should she do? She needed to call 911. She peeked at the bodies. Neither moved.

Her hands shook violently when she picked up her cell phone and wiped the snow from it. After three attempts, she finally typed her password correctly. Suddenly, the journalist burst from her. What a story this would be. Her investigation had taken a dangerous turn. A boss exposed. A boss caught in the act of murder.

When they arrived, the police officers would confiscate her cell phone. Once she explained what happened, they'd know she had photos or a video of the meeting.

She nibbled on her lower lip, darting worried glances around. She should take photos now and send them to her e-mail and then call the police.

She could do this. Maybe she couldn't. But she needed to if she wanted to get closer to her brother's killer. That had to trump her fear.

Her mind made up, she stood on wobbly legs and then walked toward the bodies. She had to take these photos, then call the police. She'd then return one of the dozen calls Trent had made to her. He'd be mighty upset when he learned what she'd witnessed, but he wasn't working for her yet.

Dead bodies made her skin crawl. Megan raised her phone and snapped two photos with both men in the shot. They may have been bad guys, but they didn't deserve to die like this, even though they'd probably done the same thing to other poor souls. Maybe even her brother. One killing didn't justify another.

Stepping closer, she stopped five feet from Watson and snapped a photo. She wanted a close-up of his face, so she swallowed hard and stepped closer. She'd never seen a dead body. She wasn't sure what to expect. She hoped his eyes weren't open. That blank stare was eerie on television, and she couldn't imagine how frightening it would be in real life. She shuddered thinking about it.

So much blood mixed in with the snow that she had to avoid stepping in it, or the police would know what she'd done. How would she explain her footsteps to them? Would they believe she came over to check their pulses? To help them?

Before moving forward, she took two deep breaths attempting to control her erratic breathing and racing pulse.

Stopping near Watson's shoulders, she snapped a photo of his face. She paused in recognition. She'd seen him before. He'd beaten up Keyshawn. He was…she knew his name. Hank.

Oh no. Did that mean? She spun around and took a hesitant step closer to Sherlock. She gasped when she saw his face. It was him. AJ. He was dead.

Tears pooled in her eyes and tremors shook her hands as she snapped photos of him. He couldn't be dead. Why did he have to be a bad guy? She couldn't forget what had happened between them or how quickly his hands had warmed her blood.

She wanted to drop to her knees and cradle his face. She knew they'd never had a relationship or a chance to find out where the heat between them would have gone, but it hadn't stopped her from dreaming. She had been connected with him on an elemental level. Her mouth pulled into a frown as an unexplained ache flooded her heart. What had he done to warrant his death?

Did it have to do with his visit to her? Was Hank supposed to be there with him? That thought soured her stomach. He'd have beaten her. Did AJ die because they'd been physical? Unfortunately, she doubted she'd ever find out. The boss spilling the beans was doubtful.

She looked around the area. It was desolate and deserted, the perfect place for a murder.

Something seized her ankle in a tight grip. She gasped, dropped her phone, looked down and her heart seized. AJ pointed a gun at her.

"What the hell are you doing here?" he ground out.

She screamed, wishing she was anywhere else but there.

Chapter Nine

The excruciating pain that seared through his chest woke him along with the awareness of not being alone. How long had he been out? His clothing was damp from lying in the snow, and the cold had seeped into him.

AJ struggled with his breathing, his lungs protesting his attempt at taking a deep one. *Son of a bitch!* He'd been shot in the chest at point-blank range. Thank God he'd worn his body armor. The one his brother called "the best money could buy and then some." *Thank you, Dev, for not being a frugal bastard.*

His brothers. Shit. They'd be beyond pissed at him. He'd really fucked up this time. Maybe they were right that he couldn't take care of himself, couldn't make the right decisions. They'd never said it aloud, but he knew they thought it.

He had to figure out what to do next because he couldn't hang around here. He was supposed to be dead. If he stayed, he would be.

AJ peered through tiny slits of his open eyes behind his dislodged sunglasses.

It would've been easy to vanish before anyone was the wiser. But now he had a complication. A journalist named Megan.

He didn't want to do it, but he had to. Could his life get any more complicated?

Wide, fear-filled eyes looked down at him. That was the second time he'd caused that look on her face. He didn't like it. He was a fucking asshole of the first degree. Right now, self-preservation was more important than her fear.

"What? Has the cat got your tongue? What the hell are you doing here? Are you alone?" He attempted to lift his head to look around. Huge mistake. It pulled at the painfully throbbing muscles in his chest.

It took several attempts for her to speak. "Y-you. You. I s-saw him shoo-shoot you. You're de-dead."

"What do you mean you saw him shoot me?" AJ groaned. "Dammit, Megan. Not again. When will you learn? This is a dangerous game you're playing." He waved his weapon. "Case in point."

She didn't get it. AJ could kill her right now. Was a headline so important to her that she didn't care if she ended up dead? How the hell was he going to get her to drop this pursuit? Was revenge for her brother worth her own life? Probably.

She made a frantic search of the area. "Let me go!"

Wasn't this what she'd said at their last meeting? Their last meeting. Fuck! Could his cock really be twitching right now thinking of kissing her again?

Enough about your small head. Use your big head to get out of this fucked-up situation.

She twisted her ankle, attempting to wrench it from his tight grip. Her arms flailed out to her sides as she lost her balance and fell.

"I'll let your ankle go, but I'm leaving my Beretta pointed at you. You just became my hostage." He allowed his lips to curve into what he hoped was a sinister smile.

The stricken look on her face tugged at his heart. She feared him. That should be a good thing.

What was it about her? He led a rough and tough life. He'd done things she couldn't even imagine. Things that still made him cringe. Yet, he wanted to protect her. To save her from herself and the foolish moves she kept making.

"No! You can't be serious."

"Oh yes. I'm deadly serious. Things have changed. You know I'm alive. I can't have you publicizing that fact. So, you have a choice. I can kill you now or take you with me." He raised an eyebrow at her shudder. "I thought you might prefer the nonlethal option. Now, sit there while I get up. Stand and run, and I'll have to shoot you. And don't try me, Megan. Not when my life is at stake."

"You have no reason to need me for a hostage. I won't tell anyone. I promise."

He laughed and stopped. Fire shot through his chest. Goddammit! Broken rib or just bruised? He didn't need this. He had to be 100 percent. At least he'd been lucky Damian had shot him in the chest instead of the head since he'd allowed the man to outdraw him. Damn lucky.

"Are you kidding me? You'll have it on the front page as soon as you can."

"But we... but we...."

"We kissed?" he asked in an acid tone. "One thing has nothing to do with the other."

She bristled, pulled her shoulders back, crossed her arms over her chest, and then raised her chin.

Damn, this woman stirred him.

"If I choose death, I don't believe you'll kill me."

Even in her defiance, the little minx shook so terribly he expected to feel the vibrations through the ground. Yet she tested him.

"You won't really kill me, will you?"

"Megan, that's what I do for a living. Why would you be any different? I warned you, didn't I? If you didn't mind your business, I told you what would happen. Now, you've pissed me off."

He struggled to stand. A sharp pain ripped through his chest and spots danced before his eyes, darkness rimming them, slowly closing in. He couldn't afford to pass out again. He halted on his hands and knees, his weapon no longer pointed at her, giving her a chance at escape and hoping she didn't run for it. Closing his eyes, he worked to control his rapid breathing and the nausea threatening to consume him.

AJ crawled on his hands and knees to Hank. No pulse. AJ patted him down taking his Sig Sauer P226 and the extra clip he carried, adding it to his arsenal. He'd best prepare for war.

He couldn't believe Denzel had been fucking captured. It was shitty luck he and Hank had been blamed. The boss had to make a point, and that meant AJ couldn't live. Even if he disappeared on his own, they'd search for him. He had to vanish permanently, for this to be settled. That was not how he planned to settle things though.

He finally made it to a standing position, surprised she hadn't taken the opportunity to run. He pointed the Beretta back at her. "Get up. Where's your car?" His gaze moved over the area, missing nothing.

She stood, wiped the snow from her luscious ass, and pointed.

"Let's go. We take your ride."

"You can take it. Just leave me." She stood rooted to the spot, reaching in her pocket for what he hoped were her keys.

"No can do. Let's have a look at what's in those pockets."

Her eyes widened, and he knew she had something she didn't want him to see. Instead of providing her the opportunity to pull anything from it, he reached into the pocket and grabbed her hand. Bingo. It was wrapped around something cylindrical.

He jerked it out of her hand and pocket. "Pepper spray. Were you really planning to use this on me?"

Her shoulders sagged in what he imagined was defeat. He checked her other pocket, and sure enough, keys were there. "Where's your purse?"

Her eyes widened again. What the hell was she hiding now?

"It's in the trunk of the car."

"Looks like we've a little bit of a walk so let's get a move on." They sloshed through the muddy snow toward the used car lot. "Where were you hidden? More importantly, did anyone see you?"

If they'd noticed her, she'd be lying dead beside Hank. Immense relief surged through AJ, flooring him.

She waved her hand over her shoulder. "I hid behind one of the stacks of metal."

"How'd you know about this meeting?"

She shrugged. "I have my sources." Her head snapped his way, and her eyes narrowed. "I'm not telling you who they are."

He enjoyed her display of defiance and bravery. She protected her sources even while facing possible death. He liked this woman more and more. Dammit. He had to quit thinking like that. He couldn't drag her into his miserable, dark world.

"I don't recall asking you," he drawled, wondering who within the organization would run their mouth off to a reporter.

"What happened? I couldn't hear a thing." Her voice cracked.

"Always the reporter, aren't you? Well, that conversation remains private."

She couldn't learn about the prison breaks. He followed her work. She was like a dog with a bone; she'd never let it go. She was already in over her head but didn't seem to realize it. Publicizing the escapes would change things dramatically. There'd be no more warnings for her, no accidents. It'd be downright, cold-blooded murder.

Trudging through the snow, about halfway to her car, he heard, "Would you slow down?"

"No. We don't know when a cleanup crew will arrive. The boss should've done it himself, but he left instead. I can't get caught here."

She darted him a quick look, one full of what looked like understanding, then nodded. "You wounded him. His side was bleeding."

Cold satisfaction slithered through AJ. "Good. He deserves to die for attempting to kill me." His anger hadn't subsided, nor had the pain in his chest. It had worsened with the exertion, the painful throbbing increasing with each accelerated heartbeat. This was not what he'd wanted when he'd woken up this morning.

"Where are we going?"

"You'll see when we get there."

She glanced at his pocket again, continuing to surprise him. He imagined her wheels were turning with ways to escape and the story she'd write. He had no idea which took precedence.

Sweat covered his body and rolled down his back. He had to get somewhere safe so he could take care of himself.

When they arrived at the car, he opened the trunk. Her gaze stuck on her purse. "Don't you dare touch it. My trigger finger won't hesitate." Pure lie.

He searched her handbag and found a gun. He'd been damn lucky she hadn't had it with her. Whether she'd have used it or not was irrelevant.

He added it to the pepper spray in his pocket. "Any weapons hidden in the car?"

She shook her head.

"Get in. Don't be foolish. You've done enough of that already today."

With a considerable amount of effort, he settled in the car, gasping for breath, each one more painful than the last. He closed his eyes, accepting the pain and turning his focus to remaining alive.

"Megan, you have to keep what you saw today quiet. No police and most of all, no newspaper."

"Are you kidding me?" She glanced over at him. "Two people, well, one person was murdered. I can't ignore that because you need to get away from these people. I have to tell the police, and there is no way I'd ignore this story."

He noticed a sparkle in her eye. That damn journalist in her. When would she finally get it? They'd come after her, and no amount of protection would be enough.

"Are you trying to get killed? That's what will happen if you print any of what you witnessed today. There are too many corrupt police officers. Going to the wrong one with this story will get you killed. Either way, you're dead. No story is worth it."

Her lips flattened, and he waited for her to snap and growl at his edict. Instead, she asked, "I know the right police officers to go to, and I'm hiring a bodyguard, so I'll be safe. Now, how do you know there are corrupt police officers?"

Of course, she zeroed in on a possible story instead of her life being at risk. Did she use digging into a story to overcome fear?

"I work for the bad guys, remember? I know lots of things," he stated flatly.

Her grip on the steering wheel tightened, her knuckles gradually turning white. "Let me interview you."

"No way. I've nothing to say to the press." Her fear of him seemed to lessen somewhat, yet, even with that small amount of fear, she wanted to get a story out of him. Good grief. This woman would drive anyone to drink with that stubborn determination.

Staring straight ahead, she quietly asked, "Why did you kiss me?"

Because you were a breath of fresh air when I needed it. You were more beautiful and appealing than anyone I have ever been with. Tasted the sweetest too. He allowed none of his thoughts to show on his face; instead, he raked his gaze over her slowly. "Are you kidding me? You're hot. Who wouldn't want to kiss you? I'd do a hell of a lot more if I didn't hurt."

Her mouth gaped open. "You disgusting pig," she

spat out.

"Now you're getting it, my little dove." What she thought of him shouldn't matter, but it did. It made his gut clench, but knew it was for the best.

"Quit calling me that!"

"Don't count on it, my little dove," he said to annoy her, realizing that although the endearment slipped out the first time, it fit her.

She visibly gritted her teeth. "Why do you call me that?"

He shrugged. "It just came to me when I saw you."

"Are you really an enforcer?"

She routed them back to the story. He had to hand it to her for tenacity. "I was."

"What's your last name?" she asked.

He looked at her and smiled. "Sands. AJ Sands." Before today, guilt had never taken hold of him when he'd lied to a woman. Sure, the "I'll call you," was a standard lie all men told, but this… this was bigger. She'd hate him if she ever found out the truth. But he couldn't suddenly become AJ Hamilton. Then his family could be used as bait.

"What will they do if they find you?"

"They'll kill me of course. I'm a walking dead man." He fought hard to keep his voice calm for her sake.

He looked around and scrunched his eyebrows. "Why the fuck are you driving so slowly?"

"I'm doing the speed limit, and I'm not going any faster," she said through clenched teeth.

He shook his head and smiled. Yep, a brave little dove.

"Why are you so determined to bring down Magic

Shop, Megan?" He knew. He just wanted to hear it from her.

"It's personal."

"I hope your life is worth it."

"Why did he try to kill you?"

He chuckled. *Fuck!* He'd be lucky if he didn't black out again with his stupidity increasing his own pain level. "You're good. I'm holding you hostage and all you're thinking about is a story. I'm not telling you what the meeting was about so that you can print it."

"You shouldn't have any loyalty to them. They don't want you around anymore. Get back at them by giving me the information, and I'll bring it to light. They will pay for trying to kill you."

And her brother, he knew she'd left off. "Sorry, Megan. It won't work."

Damian would pay for attempting to murder him. AJ would see to that before he vanished on his own terms, not theirs.

"You suck."

"How can such filthy ideas come out of a sweet, kissable mouth?" A mouth he wanted to taste again. A mouth he wanted wrapped around his dick. The taste of the lip balm she'd worn had him wanting more.

He mentally shook his head to clear it, needing to keep his mind on survival. And that included a pain pill. Hell, he probably needed the hospital. Yet all he could think about was Megan. He wanted to see her naked. Have his mouth on her plump breasts.

"I may be your hostage, but you're never going to kiss me again."

Damn his thoughts. "Never say never, Megan." He turned, met her gaze, and winked.

She scoffed, and he swallowed his chuckle.

"Get off at the next exit and then merge right."

With the holiday, the roads were nearly deserted. He wouldn't put it past her to attempt to gain someone's attention or stop the car and run, though.

"Take a left at the second light."

"Are you going to tell me where we're going?"

"You'll see when we get there."

She glanced around nervously. "This isn't a good part of town." The locks engaged and he smiled to himself. She'd rather stay with him, the man who'd threatened her with death, than have someone on these streets bother her. Funny how her mind worked.

"I know. Slow down. You can drop me at that corner." He pointed ahead.

"Dr-drop, drop you? You're letting me go?"

He'd never intended to hold her hostage longer than necessary. He hadn't wanted to do it in the first place but knew it had been the only way to get her out of there as quickly as possible. She would've called the police and waited. Bile formed in the back of his throat knowing they'd never have let her leave.

"On the condition that you keep quiet about what you witnessed today. If you don't, I'll be coming after you. I'm not joking, Megan. This is serious. Opening your mouth is a death sentence for you. Don't test me."

She pursed her lips but remained quiet.

"Megan," he all but growled, "I'm serious. You need to—"

"Thank you for letting me go," she interrupted.

"I won't do it until you agree."

It took her a moment, but she let out a heavy breath and finally answered, "Okay."

"You're free, Megan. I hate that you witnessed the shooting. It's something I wished you'd never have seen. I'm sorry if I shook you up more than you already were." Why the hell did he keep apologizing? He wouldn't have with anyone else.

He couldn't resist. He leaned over and kissed her on the cheek. It hurt to move toward her, but the pain had been worth the startled look on her face.

"Don't stop on your way out of the neighborhood. Stay safe, Megan. I won't forget you." And he knew he wouldn't. There was something about her that cried out for him to protect her and make her his.

He stepped out of the car and watched her drive away, the stabbing pain in his heart surprising him.

Goodbye, my little dove.

Chapter Ten

Megan locked the passenger door, pulled away from the curb, and with shaky hands, dug into her purse for her cell phone and turned on the speaker. She took the moment to pause, welcoming the easing of her taut shoulders as fear drained from her. AJ had let her go.

She swallowed, attempting to get her head around all that had happened. She knew she should call 911 about the murder and the kidnapping. But first…

"Kristen, I've got a great story for tomorrow's paper. I was an eyewitness to a murder." A shiver raced down her spine as she thought about what had transpired.

Megan professionally relayed what she'd witnessed up until the kidnapping. Her breath caught at her traitorous action, but he *had* held her at gunpoint. He could've killed her, but part of her wanted to hold back his story. The why of it fathomed her. He is a criminal.

Unfortunately, he happened to be a criminal she was attracted to.

"I'm on my way, and I'm already writing it in my head. I'll be able to make the deadline. I want it submitted before I meet with the police. I have to report this to them. I can't let this go."

AJ couldn't have truly believed she'd pass up this chance to expose a Magic Shop murderer. Death sentence or not, she'd print this. A cold shiver snaked down her spine, aware this could be the final nail in her coffin. They would retaliate. Trent had best be as good as his reputation. She hoped he'd start right away, and more importantly, wouldn't refuse the job considering the craphole she'd started digging for herself.

Dead air silenced the line. Had she been disconnected?

"Hello? Kristen?"

Her boss cleared her throat. "I'm here. I'm trying to decide which emotion is greater—how pissed I am for you doing this alone or how relieved I am that you are okay. How big of a newshole are you thinking?"

Skipping her boss's first statement, she answered, "I'm not sure yet. I'll know by the time I arrive." The why of keeping him secret kept her nerves in a jumble, and she didn't understand her worry for him. He said he killed for a living. Plus, he'd threatened her life. That alone was an important point she had to quit ignoring.

"I'll see what we can do. Let's get it to print quickly before the police try to force us to pull it. Have Kelly go through your photos and video and choose one for your article to save time."

"That works." She exited off the interstate.

"Are you all right, Megan?" The depth of concern in Kristen's voice surprised Megan. Of course, she'd never dealt with her boss in a situation like this.

"I'm still a bit shaken."

She'd never witnessed someone being murdered, nor been kidnapped at gunpoint either. The shock had worn off, and she didn't know how she felt about everything. Megan went back over whether AJ would've actually hurt or killed her. Would he follow through on his threat when she published the story?

"You'll feel better when we expose this killer. Now, you drive safe, and we'll see you shortly. And be prepared, there's a livid friend of Kelly's who says he's your bodyguard waiting for you." Her boss disconnected the call.

Trent wasn't even hired yet and he considered himself her bodyguard? She couldn't get upset over his pushing himself on her because she wanted him there. He would be livid when he heard her story. She cringed. Having him with her today would have been helpful.

She couldn't keep her mind clear of AJ. Her memories kept forcing themselves forward. He'd kissed her goodbye. She touched her cheek. She didn't know what to think of him. It shouldn't matter. She wouldn't see him again.

Parking at the building housing the newspaper, she hurried into the newsroom. She raced past a handsome blond-haired man who attempted to step in her path as she half ran to her desk. She tossed her cell phone to her coworker without breaking stride. "Thank you, Kelly. It's in video, so I trust you to make some still shots from it," she said over her shoulder.

"Where the fuck have you been?" the man she assumed was Trent asked in a sharp voice that bounced around the newsroom. Boy, he was handsome. Tall and lean, but with a beach-boy style that went with ocean blue eyes. "Don't call asking for my immediate help and then ignore my phone calls."

Still shaking, she stopped and willed herself to at least appear calm even though her insides were still jumping around. "I take it you're Trent." She held out her hand. "I'm Megan. Nice to meet you."

He narrowed his eyes and shook her hand. "Trent McKenzie."

"I'm sorry we weren't able to meet earlier. I'm glad you made it here to meet with me. I need a few minutes though—before we speak—to get my article written."

His nostrils flared, and he glared at her, obviously still angry at her for not answering the phone. She just couldn't have answered when he'd called. He'd see that when she explains. She didn't relish explaining it to him if he was that upset at her not picking up the phone. God knew how he'd be when he found out what she witnessed.

"No. We talk about this now," he snapped.

She stared at him wide-eyed, not knowing how best to handle the anger pulsing off Trent.

Trent sighed. "I don't mean to seem upset with you. I was worried. You called to have me go with you, after you'd said you wanted to hire me as a bodyguard, then I couldn't get in touch with you. I feared the worst."

Megan's mouth stood open when she didn't know how to respond. Flabbergasted was more like it. Without a doubt, she knew that he was the right man to have on her side.

Kelly interrupted the momentary quiet. "I'll choose a couple for different story angles. When you finish, you can make the final selection."

"You're good to me, Kelly." Looking away from Trent, she took off the rest of her outerwear, sat at her desk, pulled her hair back in a clip, and then her fingers magically flew over the keyboard. A first-hand experience was different from what she usually wrote, but she found the story easy to write, so she spilled it all.

Kelly approached her desk with a cup in her hand. "I thought you might need this. You haven't come up for air since you walked in."

The coffee smelled wonderful. "Thank you so much." Megan took a long drink, gasped as it burned her mouth, and then went back to her keyboard. Different emotions flowed through her. Her mental restraint kept these feelings on the page and not taking over her body.

She'd considered holding back that AJ had survived but decided he knew what he was doing. *He'd run and have a new life soon. He wouldn't even see the article. And if the bosses returned to clean up as he'd said, they would know he was indeed alive.* She repeatedly told herself so she could justify adding him to the story without feeling guilty… or like she was betraying him somehow.

She couldn't stop fretting about him. Where would he go? Would he run far away? She hoped he didn't stay for revenge. Men were stupid like that. Obviously, so were some women. But the Magician wanted him dead. He didn't stand a chance. *Please, run as far from here as you can, AJ.*

"Finished." She raised her arms over her head, linked her hands, and then leaned back in a much welcome stretch.

"You were there? You fucking witnessed this?" Trent bellowed. His face burned red, and his jaw tightened. He had to be a poor poker player. "What the fuck were you thinking, Megan?"

Obviously, he'd been reading over her shoulder,

and she'd been so wrapped up she hadn't noticed. At least it saved her from retelling him everything.

"Trent, I ask for your patience, please. I need a few more moments to finish this." Reliving it as part of her job was easier to focus on than the thought of reliving it while the two of them talked it through. If she started thinking of her own welfare and how close she'd come to being dead herself, she may just lose the hold she had on her carefully controlled emotions.

The first photo Kelly displayed was a still shot of the boss firing his weapon from the last of the video before she'd dropped her cell phone. It was perfect to go with the story.

She submitted her article and artwork and then expelled a breath in a long sigh of overburdened relief. Now, she would be required to relay the events to her friend and Trent. They wouldn't allow her to do anything else. Then she had to notify the police. She snorted. Her priorities might be a bit skewed.

Megan rubbed on her lip balm wondering if AJ had already left Baltimore. *Stop it! He's gone.*

"Where's Merissa?" Not that Megan should care. She was just glad the woman hadn't taken up space near her desk.

Kelly shrugged. "She left right after you. No one knows where she went."

"Based on those photos you had a very interesting afternoon," Trent said.

"We both saw the pictures, Megan. It must have been scary," Kelly added.

"We're all ears." Trent narrowed his eyes and crossed his arms over his broad chest. The gleam in his eyes told her she was in trouble, and he was going to make her retell the story even though he'd read what she'd written.

She relayed her story, from arriving at the warehouse to being released by AJ. They didn't interrupt her as she poured it all out, but heard a gasp from time to time. She choked up, tears stung her eyes, but she held them at bay. She could be strong and get through this. Breaking down at work, or even in front of Trent and Kelly, was not something she wanted to happen.

"Son of a bitch!" Trent walked away, removing his cell phone from his pocket.

"My God, Megan. I thought you'd be more careful. You were supposed to hire Trent."

"I went to observe a meeting. I told you that. It wasn't like I knew they'd start shooting at each other. Trent and I were to meet tonight for me to hire him. I did try to call to see if he was available earlier to go with me, but got his voicemail. Besides, I'm okay." If it had been Kelly's lead, she'd have done the same thing. It had sounded safe enough. Thinking on it now, she knew there were risks she probably shouldn't have taken, but she wouldn't allow herself to think about it now either. She took a deep breath and smiled as part of her brave front for Kelly.

Kelly furrowed her eyebrows. "This guy, the one who survived, sounds like a real bad guy. What if he comes back after you for publishing? Isn't that what he threatened?"

"Well, he did leave me alive. Besides, he's on the run, not after me. I have to tell the police the story." She didn't look forward to what the detectives would say. AJ had been overreacting. The police wouldn't have her killed. He'd seemed so sincere. A niggle of doubt crept into her mind.

"They'll be pissed at you for not telling them what you knew about the meeting." Kelly spoke the truth.

"They're always pissed at me, so I don't see how this will be any different."

Her friend stood. "You know you have a big problem, Megan."

She'd hoped to avoid this conversation. Hoped she'd just let it go and leave things to Trent.

"You witnessed a Magic Shop boss commit murder. I won't beat around the bush. They will attempt to kill you. You might not even make it to the police station from here."

Hearing it said so bluntly put the reality of her situation front and center. An internal tremor took over, but she pasted that smile back on to keep up that false front for the world. "I'm certain he didn't see me." The boss may have heard her, but he hadn't seen her. Not possible.

"Okay. You're probably safe driving to the station. Don't you think the Magician will find out? And very quickly?" Kelly asked.

The coffee tossed and turned in her stomach. She'd make the crime boss angry. The thought of witness protection popped into her head.

"Kelly, I'll talk with the police about protection this time."

"It needs to be protective custody but not from the local police. They'll lead the bad guys right to you." She paused as if a thought had suddenly occurred to her. "The FBI should be involved. Report this to them instead."

Megan hadn't thought about including the FBI. This conversation was way out of hand. If the two detectives she'd previously met with thought it serious enough, then she'd follow their advice. Well, follow most of it. Dang Kelly for making her worry.

"Surely the FBI won't care about one murder. They have a lot of major cases to handle," Megan suggested.

"This criminal enterprise involves major crimes. I believe they'd care. In fact, they'd probably jump on it."

"Look. I need to bring this to Detectives Cooper and Phillips. They're working the Magic Shop case."

"What can I do to change your mind?" Kelly asked.

"I'll tell you what. I'll go to the FBI also. If they both offer to protect me, I'll choose the FBI. Will that work?"

Her friend hugged her, a tear sliding down her face. "Don't go to the police, Megan. I beg you, don't go. Go straight to the FBI."

Her silent weeping took Megan by surprise. She didn't know what to say. This was too much to handle after the day she'd already endured.

She released Kelly.

Before Megan returned to her desk, Kelly hugged her again as if it would be the last time she'd see her. Surely her friend was overreacting. Megan would seek Trent's advice, but she had to report it, and she couldn't put it off any longer. Unfortunately, she'd have to discuss AJ. He was a victim, a witness. Though he'd also shot the boss and had held her hostage.

He had to be safe. She didn't want anything to happen to him.

Trent returned as she zipped her jacket. "Where do you think you're going now?"

"I need to report this to the police."

"Oh hell no, you're not!"

Chapter Eleven

Megan entered the police station with Trent grudgingly in tow. She'd hired him and then they'd had a long discussion about speaking with the detectives. He had a blatant mistrust of the police department, but after a few phone calls—presumably checking on the two detectives—he reluctantly agreed. He did make it a point to tell her he preferred she not go. That had given her pause for a moment, but her conscience wouldn't allow her to let the murder go unreported. His checking out the two detectives—even if only briefly—was enough for her.

A different officer greeted her. She wouldn't call it a pleasant greeting. It was more like a "why the hell are you bothering me" greeting. The woman did eye Trent appreciatively.

"I'm here to see Detective Cooper or Detective Phillips." One of them had to be here. She didn't want to return. Megan needed to tell them today before they saw it in print in the morning.

Detective Cooper walked toward her. "Hello, Ms. Rogers. I wasn't expecting you today. Witnessed more drug deals in progress that you failed to call in?" He chuckled.

His heavily starched blue shirt had to rub his skin. Either his wife was punishing him or he was a glutton for discomfort. She must be more nervous than she thought to veer off on something ridiculous. Yep. She shook a little.

"You told me if something happened to let you know. Well, something definitely happened today, and it wasn't a drug deal."

He quickly assessed her. "Come on back."

Trent grabbed her arm.

The detective raised a brow. "Who's this?"

"Detective Cooper, this is Trent McKenzie, my bodyguard."

The detective smiled. "So you listened after all. Good girl."

She bristled at his calling her a girl. "He'll accompany me." Another of Trent's requirements, although he did warn her that he would abandon her for a bit, but she'd always be in sight.

Following the detective through the maze to his desk, she didn't notice the noise like she had the first time. Her mind remained focused on her mission.

Stopping at the detective's desk, she looked across it and saw Detective Phillips. The man stood and reached out his hand. "Ms. Rogers, it's good to see you again. I hope."

He had a red stain on his green tie that had barely missed his white shirt. There she went again letting her mind wander to something trivial that wasn't a story or didn't concern her.

"Thank you."

She introduced Trent before he quickly excused himself. He stopped in the noisy area, and an officer stood and shook his hand. That must be who he said he'd be gathering information from.

"Have a seat, Ms. Rogers. May I get you

something to drink? Coffee?" Detective Cooper asked.

"I'll take a cup of coffee, black, please."

Detective Phillips walked away.

Detective Cooper gestured to the chair beside his desk.

"Have you stayed off the streets? I haven't seen any new drug deals in your newspaper."

So, he read her articles. That meant he was keeping tabs on her. As long as he wasn't hoping to put her in jail for something. However, she figured it more than likely had to do with her not showing them up again.

She nodded, unable to respond verbally. She needed that coffee. Something to still the hands she kept clasping and unclasping in her lap. This nervous fidgeting wasn't her. She didn't want to have this meeting, listen to their censure, and relive the day.

He leaned toward her and lowered his voice. "I wanted to tell you that I'm glad you flushed out the officers abusing suspects. I'd have rather we'd found out ourselves, and it hadn't been front-page news, but I'm glad they're off the streets. If anyone asks, I'll deny saying this to you." He straightened, returning to the poster boy detective.

Wow. "Thank you," she said with a slight smile of appreciation.

Would he still feel the same when she exposed corrupt police officers? It would be public again. She couldn't trust them to investigate their own, or those officers would've already been off the force. The Magician probably had internal affairs on his payroll.

"What're you involved in now? Why did you need to see me?" He pulled out a legal pad and pencil and began tapping it on the paper. He eyed her curiously.

"You're very serious."

She nervously cleared her lump-filled throat. "I witnessed a murder." She closed her eyes. A dead man in a pool of blood flooded her vision, the image finally sinking in. Her bravado failing, she struggled to control the almost overwhelming feeling of despair.

His pencil stilled. "Excuse me. Did you say murder?"

A slow nod. "Yes."

"Let me get a homicide detective over here."

She put her hand on his arm. "No. Please. I only want to work with you two." She'd walk out of here if he handed her over to someone she didn't know or trust. She wouldn't need to walk. Trent would drag her out if that happened.

"It doesn't work like that."

"But it involves Magic Shop."

He raised his eyebrows. "Let's wait for Joe, so you won't have to start over midway through your story. Then we'll decide what to do. I'm guessing you have pictures, too."

"Yes." She reached into her purse for the thumb drive Kelly had prepared. More of this and she'd need to start charging the police department for them.

"I'd like to tell you my story before you look at the photos and video."

He accepted the thumb drive and flattened his lips. "Video?"

"Please." She didn't want him to see everything just yet. He might put out an APB or something on AJ before he could escape the city.

Detective Cooper's reluctance to agree with her was noticeable. He looked at the thumb drive and sighed. "We'll wait. This time."

His partner returned with her coffee.

"Thank you." Her hands absorbed the warmth, heating her chilled fingers. It worked, but she found herself stuck with a terrible tasting coffee. How could they actually call this coffee?

"Joe, you need to hear her story. It involves murder." A knowing look passed between the detectives.

She hated when they did that. She wanted to know what they were thinking.

"We're all ears."

She took a deep breath and slowly released it. Just the facts, Trent had instructed her. *Get it over with so it's out of my mind.* Surely telling it the third time would ease the turmoil within her.

"I received a tip about a meeting with a boss in Magic Shop. I arrived early and found a good hiding place. There were three of them, but they met too far away for me to hear what was being discussed. Not long into the meeting, the one I suspect was the boss, shot the other two men in the chest. One of the guys shot him. I think he'll need an emergency room. He was bleeding pretty badly."

"You went to this meeting and didn't call us first. Didn't take your bodyguard? Did you not listen to what we told you before? You could've been killed." The harsh tone in Detective Phillips's voice surprised her. He'd always been polite with her.

He was right though. She could've been killed. If the boss hadn't been shot, he might've come for her. No, he hadn't known she'd been there.

"And their pictures are on here? Video of this

occurring?" Detective Cooper held up the storage device.

"Yes, but I'm not done with my story." Surely they heard her thundering heart battering her ribcage. If the loudness of it in her ears was any indication, officers on the next desks over had to hear it.

She relayed her experience with AJ. They appeared very interested in him. Of course they'd be interested. They had another witness. Their frowns deepened when she informed them that he'd held her hostage. She wished they'd ignore that part of her interaction with him. He hadn't hurt her. That didn't diminish their interest.

They made her walk through the story again, this time more thoroughly and with the video. They froze frames from time to time. One of them let a name slip. Damian Powell was Magic Shop's chief enforcer.

Detective Cooper gestured to the photo of AJ. "He just let you go?" Disbelief was written all over his face.

She slowly nodded. "He had me drop him off at a corner." A sudden stab of guilt pressed in her chest.

"Did he say why he let you go?"

She shook her head. "No. He told me to keep quiet about what I saw though."

The detectives looked at each other again. She and Kevin had that same type of silent communication. Her eyes misted thinking about it.

If Damian wasn't her brother's killer, he'd probably ordered it since he was more senior than the enforcers. It was a good start to finishing this.

"What else do you need me to do to bring this killer to justice?"

"First, we'll locate the shooter," Detective Cooper

said.

"Once you have, what will I need to do?" She forced down the remainder of the terrible coffee and looked around for a garbage can.

Allan held out his hand and took her cup, tossing it into a gray plastic garbage can under his desk. "We'll go through your statement again so the DA can build the case and bring charges. We have to make sure we have all of our ducks in a row. We wouldn't want to screw this one up. We need the man who survived—AJ you said his name was—to make this case stronger. Two witnesses are better than one, and he obviously knew what had been discussed at the meeting."

"Okay, that sounds easy enough. You have my statement and the photos. What about for trial? Will I need to testify?"

Detective Phillips cleared his throat. "We need you to testify, but that worries us."

"I know they're dangerous, but it needs to be done. These murders have to stop."

A hand soothingly touched her shoulder, and she looked back. Trent had returned with a pinched look on his face.

"It's your safety we're worried about. The last people scheduled to testify against someone in Magic Shop disappeared."

"I'd hate for him to get away with it. I'll testify, even if it's risky."

He gave a tight nod. "Ms. Rogers, are you planning to publish this?"

"Yes. I've already submitted my article. It'll be in the morning edition. It's too late to pull back."

Detective Cooper looked at her. "Ms. Rogers, we

need to hide you. When you print that article announcing to the world that you're a witness to this crime, your life will be in serious danger, especially if you print the killer's photo. By the look on your face, I'm guessing that you did just that." He sighed heavily. "Ms. Rogers, you know this group isn't shy about eliminating threats to them. And now, you're a threat."

Trent's hand tightened on her shoulder, but he remained silent, allowing her to decide.

"I already have a bodyguard. Isn't that enough?" Her stomach clenched and her voice shook. She could no longer believe things would work out. They might, but not to her advantage.

"They would get around bodyguards. They wouldn't care if they took them out to get to you."

Trent cleared his throat. "We can protect her. She'll leave for a safe house today."

She looked up at him, wondering when he'd got this new plan of his figured out.

"While we set things in motion, you're at risk on the street." Detective Phillips looked up from his notes, motioning to someone.

"I'll be safe. I'll report it to the FBI after I leave here." She watched them exchange another glance. According to what she'd learned, they'd worked this case for years. The FBI taking over wouldn't sit well. It wouldn't with her if another reporter was suddenly assigned to a story she'd worked on that long.

"Ms. Rogers, we'll take care of that for you. They're better equipped to protect you for the long term, but since you're already working with us, we'll get you set up first. A couple of days in a hotel, then a safe house once we have everything ready."

Her thoughts raced. They truly thought that Trent wouldn't be enough. In the back of her mind, she'd known the truth. She just hadn't wanted to see it. She hadn't wanted it to be true.

"Megan, we can hide you just as well as they can, if not better," Trent said. "In fact, I'd prefer it."

"Look here. This is now a police matter, and she needs to go into protective custody," Detective Cooper countered.

She didn't need them fighting it out, nor did she want Trent in the line of fire. She liked him and didn't want him killed trying to protect her. The police did this for a living. Besides, her bank account wasn't deep enough to pay him until there was a trial.

She sagged in defeat. Once she finished with this boss, she'd return and tie things up. She wanted Kevin's killer, not just the man who'd ordered it.

"What does protective custody entail?"

Detective Phillips explained it to her while his partner excused himself.

"How long will I stay there?"

"At least until after the trial."

While not what she preferred, her choice was made. She couldn't risk it. Protective custody it was. She couldn't seek her vengeance if she wound up dead. They needed to bring Damian to trial fast before his boss hid his tracks deeper than they already were.

"Thank you for helping me. I'll go home and get everything squared away."

Detective Cooper returned. "No. You stay here until we put things in motion with your protection detail to take you to the hotel."

She shook her head. "My article hasn't been

published yet. They don't know I witnessed it. I'm safe until tomorrow morning."

After arguing with her for ten minutes, they compromised and agreed to give her a few hours to pack and do whatever else she needed before she was whisked away to a safe house as long as Trent's team and policemen accompanied her until then.

"We'll pick you up in two hours. We won't push it back any later than that, Ms. Rogers. That's already longer than we think is safe," Detective Phillips stated.

"It's the only way I'll do it." No one knew she'd been at the meeting except her coworkers and AJ. She had some time to prepare.

After they'd reviewed with her what to expect, she trudged home, listening to Trent attempt to talk her out of it.

He disapproved of her trusting the police to protect her. Like AJ, Trent stated there were many dirty cops. It only took one to find out her location, and she'd be dead. He pushed for her to come with him. He'd protect her. He mentioned reaching out to a group called HIS for help.

She explained the finances, and he offered to do it for free. She wouldn't allow him to do that. This could take a long time, and he needed to eat.

He stated he wouldn't give up trying to convince her to stay with him.

Her life was about to change, but it was not the way it was supposed to happen. She'd planned to shut down their business and expose the leaders. Instead, they had her hiding from them. Her pulse sped up. She couldn't let them get away with this.

****

AJ ensured Megan was out of sight before he walked to the apartment he rented. Entering, he yanked off his jacket, turtleneck, and body armor. Red-hot pain radiated through his chest as he lifted his arms above his head. His chest had already colored black and blue. He didn't believe any ribs were fractured. Even if they were, he couldn't walk up to the ER. Magic Shop would be waiting for him.

He'd never experienced this level of pain. With the pressure on his chest and the inability to breathe deeply, his energy and wherewithal were sliding away. He couldn't imagine the pain of actually being shot. A thought struck him. His brother Matt knew the pain that accompanied taking a bullet so AJ gritted his teeth through this pittance of pain compared to what his brother had endured.

It wasn't the time to think of his brothers, or—as his mind tended to do lately—slip to HIS. That was how his oldest brother Jesse met his wife, Kate, AJ's old FBI partner. Some maniac had attempted to kill her to get back at his brother. Little did the idiot know they hadn't mattered to each other. Well, at that time. They did later.

AJ had never seen a couple so much in love with each other. And Jesse's daughter, Reagan, proudly showed off her new momma.

His brother and sister-in-law had sought him out about a month ago. They'd been worried about him being out of contact for too long on his undercover assignment. The FBI was funny about using all resources it could get its hands on to find you when they needed. And two former FBI agents who were family were about as easy as it got to extra assets.

He'd had to lie by giving them some bullshit excuse about being unable to make his meets with his contact. He imagined they were frustrated since he'd had the big blowout at the FBI office, tending his resignation and burying himself deeper in this underworld.

Not locating Jake was destroying him. He'd lost sight of himself, which nudged him into a world that ate and sucked at his soul. He was no longer the same man. The happy-go-lucky AJ, as Kate used to call him, had vanished, and he didn't know if that man would return.

No matter what the family thought of him, he knew they'd aid him. But there was no way he would let them get involved in the mess he'd made of his life.

He needed to get moving in order to stay alive. And he definitely wanted to stay alive.

AJ would leave town until things cooled down. He still had some contacts who would assist him. The ones who knew appearances weren't everything. Then he'd return for those fuckers. The Magician was toast. He'd find that bastard if it was the last thing he did. It could be. They'd tried to kill him once already.

Shit. Pain spread across his chest and his breathing became constricted as he tensed his muscles in anger.

Fucking Denzel. All that work to break him out, and Denzel had fucked it up.

AJ pulled a bullet from his Kevlar vest, looked at it, and then dropped it in his pocket while his stomach grumbled. He hadn't eaten since breakfast and needed fuel until he could settle down tonight. He reached for the smoked turkey breast from his refrigerator and ate it straight from the package as he grabbed his "go bag." A bag already packed to depart quickly such as in cases like this. He wouldn't be stupid enough to be caught at a drive-through. Magic Shop worked many of them. They sold a "heroin in a Kids' Meal" special, and that made his fucking anger spike.

He added the remainder of the turkey breast to his bag. It would keep for a while. He fit a few pieces of fruit in it, picked up a banana, peeled it and took a bite.

No matter what he wanted, he'd have to ask for help, but not from his brothers. He didn't have a choice. Magic Shop was too large. They'd turn over every stone to find him.

Before closing up the bag, he added extra clips and boxes of ammo to the bulging black duffel bag. He checked the clip on both his primary and backup weapons. Two handy weapons, well, three counting Hank's. He might need them all.

At the nightstand, he picked up the forest-green lamp and thrust it against the side table. Shards of ceramic covered the carpet. Mixed in with the mess was the cash he'd stashed away. Five thousand dollars should hold him for a while.

Two phones had already been removed from under a floorboard in the back of the room and were in his pockets. He placed his current cell phone on the kitchen table. *Let them track it all they want.*

Damn Megan. What should he do about her?

No matter what she'd said, she wouldn't pass up the story. There was no doubt in his mind that she would run with it or that they would try to kill her. The crime boss wouldn't sit there while one of his lieutenants was accused of murder.

He lowered his head, pissed off that he had no alternative but to reach out to her again. His conscience couldn't take skipping out while she was in such danger. He had to go by her house and at least let her know what to expect from Magic Shop.

AJ pulled an encrypted cell phone from his pocket and dialed the familiar number. When it was answered, he said, "I may need your help. They tried to kill me."

Chapter Twelve

Jeremy, Trent's Security partner, met Megan and Trent at the door to her home. After being cleared, she stepped inside and strode into the living room. She had quite a bit to do. No time to screw around.

Kelly had to forgive her for not contacting the FBI personally. The detectives would take care of it. Megan hoped they didn't take the case away, but she expected it to happen.

Detective Cooper had assured her that as few people as possible would know where she'd be located. Knowing he led her protection, she didn't worry.

She checked her watch and thought of Kevin. *I'm doing this for you, big brother. Damian will be the first to pay.*

"Let's talk for a moment," Trent said, following her to the living room.

She assumed it was another attempt to talk her into retaining him longer. She wasn't up for it.

"It's not what you think." He gestured to the couch. "Have a seat."

She did so begrudgingly, wanting to spend her time back and getting things in order, but she felt she owed him her focus.

"It's about this AJ Sands."

Her eyebrows rose and her heart thudded heavily. "What about him?"

"First, are you sure you're okay?" He flashed a smile that lit up his face.

She nodded. "I'm fine. What do you want to talk about with AJ?"

A noise from the rear of the house alerted her that Bob entered through the cat door. It also had Trent springing to his feet, his hand on his weapon. Bob strutted into the room and wound around Megan's legs with several loud meows before she lifted him. "This is Bob."

"Crap." Trent took a step back, and Megan tilted her head to the side and looked at him.

"Is something wrong? You don't like cats?"

He put up his hands in surrender. "I thought animals loved me until one little spotted dog growled at me and wouldn't let me near her master."

She lightly chuckled. "Bob's not running away or hissing. I think you're okay. Come closer."

Trent dropped his head and shook it, muttering something under his breath.

"What?" His comical behavior brought a smile to her lips. What could've happened with this dog to make this rather large man afraid of her cat?

"Okay, but if it bites me, you're taking me to the hospital. Without the damn cat."

"Aww. Come on, big baby." She enjoyed teasing him, loved the ease of their conversation, especially considering the madness going on. The thirty seconds of reprieve was welcome.

"Big baby, huh? Let's see then, shall we?"

If she wasn't focused on going into protective custody, she could allow that sinful grin and twinkle in his eye into her heart.

Trent stepped forward and slowly stretched his hand to Bob, who immediately nudged his head under it, purring loudly.

"He likes you. No problem. Here, now hold him." She dumped the cat into his arms.

"What the hell do you feed this thing? It weighs a ton."

"He's big-boned," she defended her cat. He had no fat on him. He was actually a large-sized cat. "And for the record, Bob is a he, not an it. Now, what'd you want to talk about with AJ?"

Trent, holding the cat, sat down on the couch and methodically began petting Bob. His silence unnerved her. He finally cleared his throat. "How well do you know AJ? What does he look like? Did you meet him before this?"

Wringing her hands in her lap, she sat straight. "I don't know him except for seeing him the time he threatened me and the time he kidnapped me." That sounded horrible when she put it all together. "He's a little over six feet tall with dark hair. He's built like you, broad but not too broad. Why?"

"If it's who I think it is, I know him." Trent let out an exasperated sigh and looked up, blatant pain in his eyes. "AJ and I were in the FBI together. Not too long ago in fact."

"What?" she croaked. AJ, FBI? Was he undercover? A secret part of her wished for it to be so, the thought of her being attracted to a "normal" man for a change, spurring her on.

"We were. Right after we'd closed a case where his old partner, Kate, who is now his sister-in-law almost died, he disappeared for a month or so, presumably undercover. He showed up at the office and had a big blowout with his boss, and said he'd had enough of the bullshit. He resigned.

She shook her head in disbelief. "Could he...?" She stopped and cleared her throat. "Could he have been dirty?"

"That's what I've been thinking about. I wouldn't have thought so, but to go straight from the bureau to this? It's possible. Maybe that's where he was when he disappeared for that time before he quit. Maybe he had been setting this life up for himself."

She cleared her throat. "Why did you leave the FBI?"

Trent's face turned to a mask of stone. "A woman." He dumped Bob out of his lap and stood, ending the line of conversation. "I'll cook up something to eat while you make your phone calls."

In a state of bewilderment, she didn't have the energy to tell him not to bother or that she didn't have time. Instead, she hit speed dial with a heavy heart, not sure if she could make this phone call. But Megan wouldn't disappear on her mother. Not after Kevin.

"Hi, Mom." She mustered as much happiness in her voice as she could.

"Hi, honey. What's going on?"

She wasn't ready to answer that question. They'd get to it soon enough. "What've you been doing?"

"I'm crocheting your sister a scarf. The one she wears is getting ratty."

That ratty scarf meant something special to her sister. It was the first gift from her husband. She doubted Leann would change it out, even if the new one was from their mother.

"How's Dad? What's he been involved in lately?" Megan placed the phone between her ear and shoulder and applied lip balm. It had become a habit with the harsh winds. It had also been something she found calmed her somewhat.

"Oh, your father worked with the police department fingerprinting kids last weekend." Her dad was active in every organization possible. He was the Director of Security at a casino. Most of his buddies were police officers. She'd always wondered why he'd ended up in security instead of becoming a police officer but had never asked.

"That's a valuable thing for parents. I'm glad he was able to help. I'm sure it meant a lot to him."

Quit beating around the bush. Just tell her.

"You know him. If he has time off, he has time to do something useful." Tonya chuckled.

A true smile emerged across Megan's face. She remembered her mother shooing her father out the door with a broom, telling him to go find something to do when he would aggravate her while she cleaned. He'd laugh, kiss her, and quickly escape through the front door.

Megan took a deep breath. Her heart pained at how her mother would react. "Mom, there's a reason I'm calling."

Her mother hesitated. "What is it, honey?"

"I witnessed a murder today."

Her mother gasped.

"I'm being put into protective custody until the trial. While I'm there, I can't have any contact with you or Dad."

"Oh, honey. It must've been horrible to see that.

How are you holding up?"

"I'm doing okay."

"Don't lie to me, Megan Elizabeth." If the situation hadn't been so serious, she'd have smiled at her mother's use of her middle name in her stern voice.

"Truly, Mom, I'm okay. I keep seeing it happen, but I'll be all right. Honest."

"Where will they take you? And who's taking you? The police? The FBI? Federal marshals?"

Megan leaned back against the kitchen counter, wanting to rush around the house and pack, but her mother deserved her full focus so she crossed her ankles to ground herself. "It's the local police to start and then probably the FBI. I don't know where they're taking me yet, and if I did, I couldn't tell you. I have to be cut off from everyone. They say it's the only way to remain safe."

Crying on the line began.

"Oh, Mom, don't cry." She'd never wanted to hurt her family in the process of seeking the truth about her brother. And the fact that she'd be separated from them definitely hurt her mother.

Tonya sniffed. "I'm okay. I'm just scared for you. You have to go away. I don't want to lose you like I did your brother."

Megan closed her eyes and inhaled a deep breath, holding it a moment before slowly releasing it. "Since I'll be in protective custody, the bad guys won't be able to find me. I'll have the police protecting me. I'll be safe. You don't have to worry about losing me. I'll be back after the trial. We can take a vacation together. You've always wanted to see the Grand Canyon, so let's plan on that." How else could she smooth this over?

"Why can't you use the telephone or your cell phone to call us? Can you Skype?"

"No phone calls, and I doubt I can Skype."

"Can you at least e-mail? Then I'll know you're safe."

"I can't promise, but I'll try."

"Okay, I'll wait to see. E-mail is at least something."

Relief relaxed her tense shoulders. Her mother had been somewhat mollified. "Mom, this is the right thing for me to do. I need to testify against this guy, or he'll get away with murder." She couldn't bring herself to disclose to her mother the possible link between Damian and her brother. Needless to say, Damian deserved to be in prison, forever, and she had the potential to help the prosecution in that cause.

"I know, but it doesn't make it any easier to take. I'm proud of you, and I know that your father will be too."

"Thank you." Tears silently slid down her face. This would only be a temporary goodbye to her parents, but it didn't make it any easier.

"You had best e-mail me often so I know you're okay."

"I'll try. I have to go, Mom, sorry. I need to pack and prepare the house to be empty."

She did have plenty to do, but she was eager to end the call, not wanting her mother to hear her cry.

"I understand. We love you, Megan. E-mail me as soon as you can. Listen to the FBI and stay safe. I want to see you again soon."

"I love you, Mom. Tell Dad I love him too."

She'd miss her mother's voice. Although this was for a short term, it felt like it would be for eternity.

She turned to find Trent watching her. Her lower lip trembled as her eyes overflowed with tears. Megan suddenly found herself in his arms. She wrapped her arms around him and cried into his chest as her heart felt like it was being smashed to pieces. Her family was important to her and knowing she wouldn't be able to speak with them when she wanted crushed her spirit and left her bereft.

He placed his chin on the top of her head. "Oh, doll."

She sniffled and pulled back, looking into a pair of blazing eyes.

Trent placed his hand on her cheek. "I wish you'd come with me. We can protect you."

Megan blinked back the remaining tears attempting to trickle over.

He ran his fingers through her hair. "It'll be all right. Even though you won't stay with me, I'll be watching over you."

She nodded and broke free of their embrace, wiping at the tears staining her cheeks.

He cleared his throat. "Go pack. I'll fix something to eat and then clean out the fridge for you."

She nodded and did something unexpected, even to herself. She kissed his cheek.

Bob refused to be ignored any longer and meowed loudly. She'd failed to mention to the detectives he would be part of the deal. She hadn't wanted them to say no. When they arrived, it'd be too late for her to find other accommodations so she'd be forced to take him.

Since she'd be holed up, packing took less than ten minutes. She threw in jeans, sweatshirts, sweaters, and one nice outfit for court. Finally, she tossed in the toiletries. They'd have a washing machine, so she didn't need to carry too much. One bag for later and a smaller one for the few days at the hotel. After collecting her laptop, notes, and Bob's items, she placed everything just inside her bedroom door.

Glancing at the time, she ascertained she had more than enough for what she needed, which was a good bubble bath, another good cry and to forget her kidnapper and this crazy day.

****

The bath relaxed Megan. She closed her eyes, sank deep in the water, inhaled the soft scent of pomegranate, and allowed her mind to drift. The myriad of emotions she'd experienced throughout the day returned, almost suffocating her. She broke down with a good cry.

A noise jerked her from a doze. She stiffened at the sound of shattering glass. Her eyes widened as bullets tore through the drywall. She screamed, covered her ears with her hands and ducked down further into the bathtub. Her heart thudded, attempting to break free of her chest. Her shaking created ripples in the water.

This couldn't be happening. Her article hadn't been published yet. Only her coworkers and the police knew. People she trusted. How could Magic Shop know?

It'd been less than two hours.

A leak at the paper? It was always possible. There were others who'd seen the article before it was printed. Then it hit her. Corrupt police officers. Detective Cooper would've had to share his plans for her with the police officers who'd be charged with keeping her safe. One of them must be on the take.

Stupid. Stupid. Stupid. She should've gone to the FBI first. She should've listened to Kelly and AJ. Or let Trent steal her away from it all.

As suddenly as it started, it stopped. What was she to do now?

"Trent," she whispered, wanting to call out to him, but afraid to let anyone know where she was located.

Don't let him be hurt because of her.

The police safe house was obviously no longer safe. She wondered if the FBI was involved yet. Could it have been an FBI agent who leaked the information about her? She rubbed her brow. Enough worrying about who it was—she had to move.

Her cell phone was on the basin, just out of her reach. She didn't want to leave the safety of her bathtub.

She didn't know if they were reloading, leaving, or coming in to make sure she was dead. She took several deep, calming breaths, trying not to get hysterical. She couldn't let fear paralyze her.

Megan scrambled from the bathtub, stepped in front of the sink and reached for her phone. As she picked it up, she caught movement in the mirror. Her heart lurched. She forced breath into constricted lungs, whirled around toward him, and screamed.

She grabbed anything close to her and threw it at her attacker. "Stay away from me!"

****

AJ scanned the area before he unlocked the car he'd had hidden and pulled onto the road.

AJ parallel parked a couple of blocks from her

128

house. He stepped out of the car and cautiously walked forward when he heard rapid gunfire. His mouth went dry. They knew.

Oh, fuck no! They would *not* kill her. He wouldn't allow it to happen.

He sprinted around the corner, pulling his Beretta from his side holster, all senses honed in on finding the shooter. *Gotcha, bastard.* He fired on the run, and the man crumpled to the ground. Rushing to him, AJ kicked the AK-47 away and recognized the man. Joe King. Another enforcer. Son of a bitch!

Fear flooded his senses, and his pulse accelerated. Had the man killed her? He needed to know. She had to be safe.

He reached down and checked the man's pulse. Dead. Working this case, he'd become jaded, a shell of I-couldn't-give-a-shit-about-anything. Nothing fazed his closed-off emotions until he'd met Megan. Since then, he'd become a tangle of unwanted emotions, like the rage that burned inside him at the situation.

AJ had less time than he'd thought. He had to get her out of here, now, if she was alive. He turned toward her house, tension tightening the knot in his gut. The thought of her dead or wounded had him pushing beside the pulsing pain in his chest and hustling across the street where he found two police officers and another man unconscious with multiple gunshot wounds, weapons still holstered. Hell of a lot of good they did protecting her. AJ couldn't deal with them right now. Megan was his priority.

With little effort, he opened the bullet-riddled front door, conducting a room-to-room sweep.

"Stop the fuck right there!"

He froze, eyes scanning the room for the body that accompanied the voice. A voice he knew well. *Well, I'll be damned. Megan got smart and hired some help.* Then those crazy emotions she stirred within him spun up and out of control, all bursting forth at once—pride at her hopefully hiring Trent—anger at himself for wasting the time to come here—and then jealously that Trent had been there for another reason. He slammed down the lid on all of that and focused on ensuring she was safe. "Trent? Is that you, man?"

His senses honed in on where he'd heard his friend speak. Heavy breathing reached his ears as a prick of unease slid back up his spine.

"AJ? Did you come to finish the job? I have no problem killing you if that's the case."

What the fuck? Finish the job? Trent couldn't really believe that. Then, it struck him—she was alive. He'd arrived in time. A rush of relief flowed through him before he tensed again at the threat still over their heads. He just had to get them out of here. "No. I'm here to help you get her out of here."

Silence.

He didn't have time to fuck around with this. The men could be regrouping as he tried to make Trent see reason. "I promise." A thought occurred to him, and he added, "Spit in my palm and shake your hand promise." They'd started that method of promising each other at five years old after watching it on a TV show.

He heard a chuckle. "In the kitchen."

AJ glanced at the bloody handprints on the wall and watched Trent lower himself to a sitting position with his back to the cabinets, his left leg bleeding profusely. AJ grabbed a towel off the counter and put it on his friend's wound to staunch the bleeding.

"Goddamn fuckers hit me with one of the first shots." Trent applied pressure to the wound and grimaced. "Get upstairs and check on Megan. She's in the bathroom."

"You going to be okay?"

"Fuck worrying about me. Get her the hell out of here!"

AJ didn't need to be told twice.

Racing up the staircase, he cautiously approached the bathroom. He opened the door and couldn't believe his eyes. She stood with her back to him, nude.

Warmth radiated through him pulsing with pleasure and relief.

She caught sight of him in the mirror, turned and screamed.

He really had to stop making her do that.

AJ couldn't help himself. His gaze swept up and down her body, his mouth curved into a smile.

She stammered, shouting at him.

"Good to see you, my little dove. All of you. Get dressed. It's time to go."

Chapter Thirteen

AJ ducked as a hot pink hair dryer flew past his head. "Megan, calm down. I'm here to save you."

Her eyes narrowed to menacing slits. "Save me, my ass. You're one of the bad guys. You promised to come back if I told anyone." She hefted a bottle of some hair care product he caught but not before it bounced off his chest.

"Fuck!" His breath left him in a whoosh. Of all the places for her to hit him. If his eyes hadn't been on her plump, pale, bare breasts, he'd have deflected it sooner.

She continued to throw items at him. "What've you done with Trent?"

With the counter bare, she looked down, released a squeak, and reached for a towel but not before a blush crept up her face.

Damn, AJ craved her.

"Megan, I'm no longer one of the bad guys, remember? Think about it. I wouldn't have been sent to kill you. I'm here to protect you." A small pang in his heart developed at the sight of her bloodless face and puffy red eyes.

"Trent's okay, but he's injured. He wants me to get you out of here."

Her grip tightened on the towel. "I don't believe you."

She shouldn't. But if he'd been the shooter, she'd

be dead instead of having this conversation. "Get dressed and let's get downstairs and see him. But be fucking quick about it."

Damian had said if warranted, they'd make her death look like an accident. How the fuck did he think spraying her house with bullets would look like an accident? It made AJ despise the man more.

He decided not to sugarcoat it. "I killed your shooter. When he doesn't return with a confirmation of your kill, they'll send someone else to finish the job. They won't stop until you're dead. They won't tolerate witnesses, Megan. I thought I'd made that clear."

He refused to let them kill her. The need to protect her kept leaping forward. Since Trent couldn't take her, she'd leave with him. Not what he'd wanted or needed her okay, but if she refused, he'd tie her up and throw her over his shoulder. No was an unacceptable answer at this point.

"You're safest if you come with me. I won't let anyone harm you. You have my promise on that."

"If I don't go, are you going to kidnap me again?"

"Yes," he said in a harsher voice than intended.

She huffed out a breath. "Why would you take me? I'm nothing to you. We only kissed."

He closed his eyes. It may have only been a kiss, but she meant something or he wouldn't be here instead of saving his own sorry ass. He'd do the same for any woman but protecting Megan was more important than his own life. He captured her gaze. "Megan, I won't leave you to your death."

She made a sound of abject despair. "I want to talk to Trent first."

"Fair enough, but we have to hurry."

"Where will we go? What will we do? Can I keep in touch with my family? Will it be like protective custody where I'm cut off from everything?" she asked in a rush of breath.

A chuckle painfully escaped him. "That's a load of questions. We're heading somewhere they won't find us." His immediate answer to all of her questions was "no," but that would've halted their departure. He hoped she wouldn't fight him on rules necessary to stay alive. Of course she would. This could get very interesting.

"We can't stand here playing twenty questions. Are you coming?"

She took a deep breath, stayed quiet for a long minute and then nodded. "If Trent tells me to, I'll go with you. Turn around."

A smile played on his lips. "What's the difference? I've already seen your hot body."

By the immediate reddening of her face and the narrowing of her eyes, he realized that he'd said the wrong thing. If she'd had anything left to throw, he imagined her target would be his groin. His thickened groin.

She pointed her finger toward the door, stomped her bare foot, and yelled, "Get out!"

He turned and walked out of the bathroom smiling. That little spitfire heated his blood. It would be hard to keep his hands off her while they are locked up together. If they became involved, she'd expect something he couldn't give. He wouldn't let things get that far.

While she dressed, he pulled out his secure cell phone and dialed. "Change of plan. I've added baggage, female baggage."

****

Megan reappeared in loose-fitting jeans, an oversized Baltimore Ravens sweatshirt, and brown boots.

She rushed downstairs to Trent and knelt beside him. "Oh my God! Trent, are you okay?" Her fingers tenderly brushed hair from his face. "Of course you're not, you've been shot. Should I call an ambulance? What can I do?"

AJ shifted against the wall.

"Doll, listen to me, there isn't much time. Go with, AJ. No matter who he is now, he'll keep you safe. I trust that."

"What about you? I can't leave you for them to return and murder you."

Trent placed a slightly bloodied hand on her cheek, boiling AJ's blood. What intimacies had they shared? Had they been to bed together already? There had been the light scent of her lip stuff he'd smelled on Trent when he'd leaned over the injured man. *Fuck!*

"Come on, Megan. Let's go," AJ ordered.

"Go. I've already called someone. I'll be fine." Trent smiled sadly. "I'll miss you, doll. Listen to him. I'll talk with you soon." He leaned forward and kissed her forehead.

AJ saw red. What the fuck? He'd had enough. "Let's go." He didn't care how dangerous his voice sounded.

"Let me grab my bags and Bob."

He snapped his eyes to Trent for help.

"She had bags packed for protective custody." He turned to her. "I'll take care of Bob. Grab only your hotel bag and go."

She bit her bottom lip. "Are you sure?"

"Yes. Now go, Megan," he demanded.

"Where's the bag?" They had to leave. AJ's patience had stretched to its limit. He couldn't watch her and Trent any longer, and he sure as hell didn't plan to wait for more of Magic Shop.

She turned to AJ, sadness in her eyes. Son of a bitch! She'd already fallen for Trent. He shouldn't care. Shouldn't.

"I'll get it," she told him before racing from the room.

"Keep her safe, AJ, or I'll hunt you down."

Megan returned with a small, wheeled suitcase, a laptop bag, and a purse. He snatched the overnight bag from her, grabbed her arm, and ushered her, none too gently, toward the door. "Come on. Loverboy will be fine." AJ gritted his teeth.

He opened the car door for her and then put her bag in the back seat of the baby-blue Honda Civic.

Damn Trent. Jesse had been right to call him, "God's gift to women." Trent had only been around her a short time, and he'd already snatched her heart. He'd break it like all of the other women he'd dated.

AJ almost laughed out loud. Who was he to talk? That used to be his life also.

"Where'd you get this car? Please don't tell me you stole it." She licked her lower lip.

His hand itched to touch her cheek and kiss her forehead like Trent had. AJ didn't have the right. She'd probably slap him, and he didn't need her anger.

"The less you know the better."

He had to put as much distance as possible between

her house and Magic Shop turf before they found out she'd survived. They had an advantage. Her pursuers wouldn't be looking for a couple.

She turned to him. "Where are we going?"

Her vulnerable gaze shattered his determination to remain cold and distant into a million pieces. "You'll see when we get there."

"I've heard that before," she mumbled.

He laughed. *Damn it. That fucking hurt.* He'd been oblivious to the pain when he'd been rescuing her as adrenaline had pumped through his body at record speed. Now that he'd found her alive, the pain hit his body with a vengeance.

"Get used to it with me, my little dove. I'm glad this time you're with me on your own. I didn't want to hold a weapon on you again or throw you over my shoulder."

"Yeah, why did you hold me hostage? You didn't need me." Her hands fidgeted in her lap.

"I needed a way out of there, and I needed to get you to leave before anyone showed up, or you talked to the police. I didn't expect you to take me where I needed to go so I took the situation in hand." When would she understand that even though he was an asshole, everything he'd done had been to protect her? No way would he have left her at the scene knowing what would happen to her.

"If you'd have asked, I might've taken you."

He merged onto the interstate. "It doesn't matter. It's over." A phone rang in his pocket and he pulled it out, looked at the number, and answered.

"Yeah?" he asked harshly.

"It's Todd."

"How'd you get this number?" AJ growled.

"Our mutual friend thought you might need some help since someone's trying to kill you and that reporter."

Fuck. AJ trusted him, but the more people who knew, the greater the risk to him and Megan.

"Anything I can do to help?"

"Not unless you can remove the hit on me."

Todd laughed. "I wish that I could. So, now you're on the run and have a woman with you. I know you, AJ. You aren't going far. You aren't going to let this go. Why not move on and stay alive?"

"I'm not moving on. The Magician tried to have me killed. I'll find out who that fucker is."

"If they find you, they'll kill you and the girl too."

AJ checked the rearview mirror. "Then I'd best make sure they can't find us."

The man sighed. "Do you know where you're headed?"

"I have an idea. When I get there, I'll let our big-mouth friend know."

Todd chuckled. "Okay. Let me know when you need me. I'll be there."

He returned the phone to his pocket. He'd have to give Arthur a piece of his mind. If AJ had wanted other people to know his situation, he'd have told them. He'd wanted help from Arthur and Arthur alone. Otherwise why the hell would he call him and not Jesse?

"Where are we going?" she asked again.

Did she ever stop asking fucking questions?

AJ glanced at her tense body. "We need to stay out of sight, so we'll find a hotel and park in it for the night. But don't get too comfortable, we'll be changing hotels often."

She gasped. "We're stopping soon. Why aren't we heading out of state or something? I thought you said we had to leave."

"Because I have some unfinished business."

His direct statement ended the conversation.

****

Their hotel surprised Megan. She'd expected a seedy motel that rented by the hour. Some place that kept your privacy for a price. Not a chain hotel. She definitely watched too much television.

AJ swiped the card key and opened the door. "If all goes well, this is home sweet home for a couple of days."

"Why can't we have separate rooms?" she asked nervously. Sex between them couldn't happen. Dang if she still didn't desire him though.

"Because I can't protect you if you aren't near me. Now that we're here, you and I need to have a little chat."

She removed her shoes and sat on the bed he'd dropped her bag on. The weight of everything that had happened to her—and all that she'd seen—pressed on her and she wanted to curl up into a ball and wish it all away. Pretend none of it had occurred. It couldn't happen. There were possibly dead police officers at her home—professionals who'd been there to protect her. *Her!*

She dropped her head in her hands and fought back a sob. Things weren't supposed to have happened like it had. No one should've been hurt because she wrote a story.

"Dammit, Megan. Look at me," AJ growled.

Taking a fortifying breath, she did and wasn't prepared for the level of rage stewing in his eyes.

"What in the hell were you thinking? I told you not to go to the police," he yelled, pointing his index finger at her.

Her anger sparked, blood pumping fast through her veins. She jumped off the bed and raised her voice to match his. "Why would I listen to you? You're one of them. And I witnessed a murder. Reporting it is what a law-abiding citizen does."

"Have I hurt you, Megan? I've tried to do nothing but keep you safe, but you just won't listen. You had to do things your way. Now look at what happened. They tried to kill you."

"You have a death warrant too, so what's the difference?" she asked defiantly, her arms across her chest.

He prowled closer. "The difference is that I expect to probably die, and you expect to live. One of us is wrong, and I've been playing this game far longer than you. I think I know what I'm talking about."

"Not this time." He had to be wrong. He was supposed to keep her safe. Trent assured her that he would.

"Why can't you trust me?"

"I don't know anything about you except you kill for a living."

"You're right."

Bile burned the back of her throat. He said it so casually. He definitely was a killer. She'd hoped he'd only been trying to scare her before.

She sighed in defeat. AJ was right. She was playing a game in his world now. She thought about what Trent

His Choice

told her. "Okay, I'll try to trust you."

"That's all I ask. It'll be tough these next few days. I need you with me. I need you to remain calm and follow directions, no matter what they are." He sat on the bed closest to the door and slowly wiped his hand down his face.

"I'll do whatever you tell me." She took a seat, pulled her knees to her chest, wrapped her arms around them and rested the right side of her face on top of them. "I don't want to die," she whispered.

"You won't if you listen to me. The first thing is no phone calls. Give me your cell phone." He held out his hand.

She jerked her head up. "How come you get to keep your phone?"

"I'm actually keeping two phones. Trust me, we'll need them."

She snatched her purse off the bed and found her phone, wanting to throw it at him. He asked too much. "Is this really necessary? I promise not to make any phone calls." She waved it in front of her. "Doesn't trust work both ways?"

"I trust you. But they could track us through your phone."

"May I call my boss first? I won't tell her where we are, I promise. You can monitor the call to make sure I don't say anything wrong."

"Why is it so important that you call her?"

"She expects me to be in police custody. She's probably already heard about the shooting. I want to let her know I'm okay. She'll tell my mom I'm okay, but she won't say anything to anyone." Well, except for Kelly and Victoria, and probably Merissa since she was

141

now part of the team, but he didn't need to know that.

He rubbed a palm over the lower half of his face. His end-of-the-day stubble scratching it broke the silence. "That is the only call you may make, and be quick. Let's go over what you'll say."

She sighed. "I guess I don't have a choice, do I?" As she reached over to hand him her cell phone, it rang. She pulled it back and answered.

Would he snatch it from her? He certainly looked as if he would.

"Hello."

"Thank God, baby."

She should've checked the caller ID. "Hello, Marcus."

AJ's jaw tightened. His gaze bored into hers. That was not the look of a happy man.

"Thank God, you're okay. I just heard. Where are you? I'll come get you and protect you."

"No," she quickly replied.

"Come on, baby. You don't have to forgive me or even like me, but you need someone to keep you safe. We'll catch a flight and get away from here until it all blows over."

"I'm safe. You don't need to worry about me." Oddly, she felt safe with AJ. Maybe because Trent told her she'd be safe. Maybe because her body craved his.

AJ ran his finger across his throat. His "get off the dang phone" message was loud and clear. Except dang wasn't the word that seemed to vibrate from his tense body.

Wow. The tightness in his muscles displayed the well-defined sculpted body. She almost drooled. She had to get hold of herself. This would not happen.

"I do worry. I still love you. Where are you, baby? I'll come get you. Please let me keep you safe."

He didn't listen or give up. "I'm fine where I am. Goodbye, Marcus." She ended the call before he could beg again.

AJ crossed his arms across his broad chest and narrowed his eyes. "Who was that?"

She shrugged. "No one important."

"I'll decide who's important. Now, who is Marcus?" A muscle in his jaw twitched.

"He's my ex-fiancé." She almost added cheating son of a gun.

"How long?"

She looked at him, confused. "How long what?"

"How long since you split?"

"Six months."

He reached for her cell phone.

"I still get to call Kristen before I give it to you." She held it protectively against her chest.

"Here use this one." He pulled one from his pocket. Not the one he'd used earlier. "Make it quick."

****

AJ lounged in the other chair in the room, legs outstretched, munching on turkey and fruit. His appetite waned when Megan's disappearance headlined the local news report.

He switched it off and discussed his rules with her. He wondered if her being online could create an electronic trail that would make it easy for Magic Shop to find them. He'd have to ask Devon, his computer genius brother. AJ wasn't up-to-date on what type of electronic surveillance equipment was available, and that concerned him.

She refused to give up her work. She had an article to write, and she assured him she'd complete it before she turned in for the night. They negotiated that she'd be online only long enough to send the article and give her mother a one-line e-mail stating she was okay. He'd play her using the laptop by ear.

He watched her work. With her hair pulled up in a clip, he fought the urge to walk over and kiss the exposed length of her silky neck. She was the sexiest woman he'd ever met.

She'd kissed him back at her house, but he doubted she'd allow anything now. She tried to distance herself from him, letting him know she wasn't interested. But her eyes said something different. The blue in her eyes would darken to a midnight blue, desire hidden in them.

Dammit. She's possibly Trent's, and definitely not a plaything. Get it together. Protect her. And only protect her.

She typed fast and furiously. AJ knew she wouldn't pass up an article on the attempt on her life. It would be big news. A reporter had been targeted and disappeared. She didn't seem to realize that she was taunting the Magician. AJ didn't like it.

He knew she did this for her brother, and she wouldn't stop until she'd found the boss. The fucker tried to have him killed which gave them the same mission, but the attempts on their lives put a crimp in both of their plans.

She reached up and stretched her arms, leaning back, unintentionally pushing her breasts up and out. He couldn't get involved with her. He'd watched his brother get involved with his old partner when protecting her. It had almost cost her life.

AJ wanted her though. The depth of this need surprised him. Around her, his pulse raced, and blood rushed south. He had to be strong enough to hold back.

"Finished." She closed her laptop and stood. A joyous smile brightened her face. It tugged at something deep within him.

"Please, tell me you did as we'd agreed and didn't say anything about us."

She shook her head. "No. They don't know where I went or who I left with."

"I still think you shouldn't have written the story. You're taunting the Magician by publicizing you're alive and still attacking Magic Shop through your writing."

Megan was on the run for her life, and she wasn't afraid like she should be. She'd almost been killed but seemed excited because she had a story out of it. He didn't know what to do with her. He shook his head. He'd tackle it tomorrow.

"It's been a long day. It's time we turned in." He placed one weapon on the nightstand and another under his pillow.

She crawled into the bed and pulled the covers up to her chin, her eyes following him.

As he pulled his shirt over his head, she gasped.

"Does it hurt?"

"Of course it fucking hurts. Fielding bullets with your chest is painful." He automatically touched it and winced.

"What's the tattoo?"

He looked down as if he'd just discovered the tattoo partially hidden behind the discoloration. Looking up he shrugged and dropped his pants. "Not

145

important."

He caught her gaze following the line of hair on his chest to his boxers. Her gaze riveted on his groin. When she saw movement, her eyes snapped to his face.

"My little dove, what do you expect when you're staring as if you plan to devour me? It's no secret I want you but now is not the time. You can relax and sleep. I'm not coming to your bed tonight," he lowered his voice, "unless you invite me."

He couldn't decipher her expression before she rolled away from him. He chuckled, painfully, and climbed into bed, alert and with a semi-erection.

Eyes and ears open, he had to find a way to handle his lust and protect her. He dozed with images of her creamy skin, her shapely legs that had wrapped around his waist, the deep thrusts inside her tight pussy having the orgasm of all orgasms.

He jerked awake. Holy shit! He'd almost come dreaming of being inside her. He was beyond fucked on this one.

Chapter Fourteen

Megan slowly awoke to light entering through the open door. The sun broke the horizon with beautiful orange and yellow hues. It took her a moment to remember where she was. Panic clawed at her, and she bolted upright in the bed, her heart rate accelerating. Had she been found?

AJ's large body shifted, blocking the light, and she relaxed. He'd kept her safe as promised.

He looked around outside and then bent to pick up the newspaper from the floor. A fine ass came into view and her mouth watered. *Stop it! Stop it! You don't want this. He's a criminal and nothing can come of the two of us together.* With that settled, at least for the moment, she looked away. The delicious smell of coffee floated toward her. She spied two steaming cups by the small coffeemaker in the room. If he'd been trying to worm his way into her heart, this was a great start.

When the door closed, she forgot the coffee and jumped up from the bed, pointing at the newspaper. "Is that it?"

He chuckled and cursed. "Yeah. The murder is the main story. I don't know about your article on them trying to kill you."

She smiled, grabbed the newspaper from him, and sat at the desk. Yes! Her article made the front page, above the fold. She tingled with excitement.

"The paper had already started printing when I submitted the second article. Remember how late it was?" She shrugged. "It'll be in tomorrow's newspaper. Look at this photo."

AJ peered over her shoulder and grunted. "You're good with your camera." He straightened and handed her a cup of coffee. "I didn't know how you took your coffee, so here's both sugar and cream from those little packets."

"Thank you. Thank you," she said without looking up from the newspaper. "I take it black, unless it's too strong. Then I have to add some sugar to make it tolerable." She remembered the coffee at the police station she'd suffered through. She wondered what Detectives Cooper and Phillips would think about her disappearance. They'd probably think Magic Shop had done away with her. No body, no murder. Maybe she should call them and let them know she was alive and safe.

"I thought after you read the newspaper, we'd grab some breakfast."

"I thought we had to stay here." It would be nice to enjoy a good meal. Their dinner last night left a lot to be desired.

"We can get out within limits. I don't expect us to run into anyone this far away from Baltimore, but we won't live in the open. Besides, we'll be wearing ball caps and sunglasses, and everyone knows that makes anyone unrecognizable." A silly grin formed on his face, and he winked at her.

"Do I need to cut and dye my hair too?"

"You'll do no such thing with your beautiful hair,"

he said sternly. An intense look flooded his face, catching her off-guard for a moment. "I have to ask you, Megan. Was it worth it?"

She scrutinized his handsome features. Good grief, he was serious and appeared to genuinely want to know her answer, and it had nothing to do with her hair. He may not appreciate her response, but it was the truth. "Yes. He's a killer and needed to be exposed and brought to justice," she stated proudly.

"You've got your priorities all wrong. Staying alive should've come first."

****

"Cold?" AJ asked with a flicker of amusement in his eyes.

"Freezing." Megan pulled her blue scarf over the lower half of her face. "How can you stay warm in only that leather jacket?"

He smiled. "I'm tough." His expression turned serious. "Let me leave the room first."

She shrugged. It didn't matter to her. She was used to the poor manners of Baltimore men. She'd never expected him to hold the door open for her, and she'd promised to do as he said.

Wait. He was making himself a target. She didn't like it since he'd put his body armor on her. She'd complained about it being too large and uncomfortable, but he'd told her to suck it up. It beat the alternative. She'd asked about his not wearing any and he assured her that he'd have some later. That wouldn't help him now.

"How long can we keep this car?" she asked as they approached the Honda.

He scanned the parking lot. "We'll ditch it soon.

Don't worry. I'll have us some wheels. I might even get some legit ones." He looked at her with that killer smile and winked.

She couldn't get a grasp on this man. One minute he was the bad criminal, surly and harsh, and then he was this lovable, sexy man who flirted with her. Did bad boys have both sides? As long as he kept her safe, she'd deal with both of them.

"That'd be nice. I don't agree with you about not taking my car. It's perfectly fine." She slid into the passenger seat.

"We've been over this. Corrupt police officers would've put out an APB on your car. We're actually safer in something stolen."

A shiver crawled up her spine. "I'm glad you took me along with you. I'd have done so many things wrong." She would never have lived this long if it hadn't been for him. Heck, she already owed him her life.

He reached over, took her hand and squeezed it. "Don't worry. I'll take care of you." He squeezed her hand again and then released it.

Why had he done that? It was a reassuring but intimate gesture. The thought of his hands on her made her shift in her seat. A spark started in her middle. *No. No. No.*

A short drive later, he turned into the parking lot of a building resembling a shack.

"Have you eaten here before?" she asked. The place didn't look promising, but she did say she'd trust him. Try to trust him anyway.

"Yeah, I've eaten here. It's not bad. It's not gourmet, but you'll enjoy it. Besides, it's out of the way and isn't busy."

The inside of the building also looked like a shack. On purpose. No other diners were about, so they had the restaurant to themselves. AJ sat them in the back corner where he faced the entire room. She didn't like having her back to the door, but she didn't wish to sit beside AJ either. It'd be too close. Way too close.

They looked at paper menus with four breakfast choices. He ordered the house special, three eggs, bacon, sausage, hash browns, and pancakes. She ordered a bacon and egg sandwich. Megan hoped their waitress, Kimberly, would bring a carafe of coffee, or Megan would run her ragged. She needed to feed her caffeine addiction.

His constantly glancing over her shoulder to the doorway set her nerves on edge. Maybe they should've remained hidden. He nodded, and she followed his gaze. Whew, just another couple. He didn't appear worried.

The couple approached their table, and she resisted the compelling urge to run. Fear robbed her heart of oxygen. The tall man could've been AJ's brother they looked so similar. He had a broader chest, but he…. Oh God. He has a gun.

Her eyes flew to AJ's. He had a warm smile for the woman who also wore a gun under her open jacket.

"Megan, I'd like to introduce you to my big brother Jesse and his wife, Kate. Kate, Jesse, this is Megan Rogers."

They greeted her with a curious glint in their eyes.

"My little dove, I need to speak with my brother privately. Are you okay sitting with Kate for a few minutes?"

In her peripheral vision, she caught two sets of eyebrows raised at his endearment for her. What would they think? Would they think they were a couple?

"She'll be fine, AJ. Now, get your ass up. You have one pissed-off family. You've some serious explaining to do, and I've restrained your brother long enough." Kate slid into the vacant chair.

Megan slowly nodded, and AJ rose from the table. The men moved across the restaurant.

Kate offered a warm smile. "I love this place. The food is amazing. Oh, Trent wanted me to tell you he's well on his way to recovery."

What kind of horrible person was she? She'd forgotten about Trent. Her thoughts had been on AJ, their safety, and her desire for him.

Her shoulders sagged in relief. "I'm so glad to hear it. I'm sorry he was hurt trying to protect me."

Kate waved her hand in a dismissive gesture. "Don't worry about it. These men seem to see it as some sort of proud battle scar." She rolled her eyes.

Megan laughed, cheerfulness lifting her mood. She liked this woman. "Trent told me you were once AJ's FBI partner."

Her smile faded. "Yes. That was before." Her eyes took on a faraway gaze. She shook her head, wiping away the cloud from her blue-green eyes. "I read your article today. Brilliant work."

Megan wanted to scream, "Before what?" Instead, she moved along with the conversation change. "Thank you."

AJ's sister-in-law leaned forward. "That was foolish, Megan. Even as a trained FBI agent, I wouldn't have been there alone."

She bristled. "It was only supposed to be a meeting."

"Hmm. No matter what it was, I'm glad you're safe and happened to be there to get him out alive."

Had he told them how he'd acquired her assistance? Doubtful. Today, she was glad he'd done it. Well, not held her at gunpoint, but that she'd helped him. Otherwise, she'd be dead. Trent couldn't have defended her for long without being able to stand.

"Bob is doing well and getting along with Dottie, my Dalmatian. He put her in her place, and they've been best friends ever since. They tend to cuddle in front of the fireplace." Kate chuckled.

Trent had taken care of him as promised. It was one less thing to be concerned about.

"I'm not sure if AJ told you, but his brothers own a security firm called HIS."

"Trent mentioned the name." Megan hadn't learned anything personal about AJ. Maybe it was time. If his brothers had an honest business, why didn't he work with them? Was he just the rebel of the family? No matter. At least he'd asked for their help when they'd needed it.

"Good." Kate looked at her husband and smiled. So much warmth and love passed between them. Megan hoped she'd have that smile on her face one day.

"The brothers are out of town, so there's no one here to guard the safe house. But Jesse and I would like you to stay with us. There's plenty of room. The best security money can buy surrounds our home."

Should she trust a woman she'd just met or AJ? Both wanted to protect her, but one was hell-bent on bringing down Magic Shop. It was a no-brainer for her. She wanted them destroyed too, even if it meant staying with AJ to accomplish it.

"Thank you, but I'll stay where I am."

Kate raised her eyebrows. A slow smile crawled along her face. "The offer is always there. He has our secure number. Now, do you know how to use a weapon?"

"Of course. I have a—" Megan broke off. "Dang it! He took mine away from me and hasn't returned it."

A soft laugh floated across the table. "Typical. He and his brothers think they're the only ones who can protect women."

She had so many questions she wanted to ask about AJ, but the men returned to the table.

Kate stood and smiled back at her. "It was nice meeting you, Megan. Remember, we're here for you."

"I told you she wouldn't go," AJ stated.

"I had to try. Make sure to return her weapon."

The two hugged, and the couple left.

"I like her."

AJ smiled. "She is great. I do miss chatting with her every day."

She burned to ask why he'd left the FBI, but knew it was a taboo subject. Maybe after they were around each other a while and he began to trust her…. "What did you discuss with your brother?"

The food arrived rescuing him from answering right away.

"Dig in, Megan. We need to get a move on."

She could be patient. She'd find out soon enough.

****

After taking a quick detour to pick up a few

groceries, they entered their hotel room and set the bags on the small desk. Thank goodness she'd made a quick list on the drive there because AJ had rushed her through the store in record time.

Megan couldn't help herself. She had to get to know him better. "Where did you grow up?" She put away the cups of yogurt. She loved the strawberry cheesecake flavor and wanted to hug whoever had created it.

He hesitated. "Silver Spring."

Interesting. Nice area. "What made you move to Baltimore?"

"A job."

When he didn't expound, she asked, "Was it this job?"

He shook his head and chuckled. "No."

"How long have you lived here?"

"Long enough."

Hmm. Still evasive. "I've lived here four years and still haven't become accustomed to the winters."

He smiled. "I noticed."

Megan removed bananas from a bag. "Growing up in Maryland must be what toughened you up so you can wear only a light jacket." He looked sexy in that jacket. Of course, he flat-out looked sexy. Muscled, but not like a body builder, and thankfully he didn't have that chest where his breasts were larger than hers. Not sexy to her.

He grunted, moved the desk chair in front of the television and turned on the news.

"Do you have a girlfriend or a wife?" *Please, say no. Please, say no.*

He turned, and looked at her with a half smile.

"Why? Are you interested in filling in?"

"That's not why I asked," she stammered. "I'm just trying to get to know you. We'll be stuck with each other for a while, so it seemed like the right thing to do." She shouldn't have asked that question. It was none of her business. She wouldn't be either to him. Wait. He didn't answer the question.

His gaze drifted down her body. "Oh, I think we know each other pretty well."

Her body tingled as he stopped on her breasts and continued scanning the rest of her. Had he noticed her nipples hardening? She didn't dare look down to see if they showed through her bra and sweater.

He captured her gaze, his eyes hooded with desire. "But I'm willing to learn more about you."

She opened her mouth to speak, but nothing came out. She hadn't been talking about learning more about each other in that sense. But it did sound good.

He chuckled and winked at her.

Dang him. He toyed with her and enjoyed it. Did that mean he wanted sex with her?

The problem was that her body hummed remembering how excited it'd become with just a kiss.

"You may ask questions, as long as when we talk about me, it's off the record. I don't want to find my profile in the newspaper."

She barely caught what he'd said. She had to get hold of her libido.

"What's in your head now?"

Did he know what she'd been thinking? She cleared her throat. "The police planned to call the FBI, but my friend didn't trust them. She's calling them herself. She was worried about my safety with the police. She was right. I should've listened to her when she, well both of you, told me to avoid them."

He looked at her and something dangerous flashed in his eyes. "FBI? Great. Now we'll have them on our trail, too. They want you since you have the ability to put Damian away," he paused. "I can take you to them if you want. You'd be safe."

Megan shook her head. "No. I don't trust any of them. I doubt anyone in the FBI is on Magic Shop's payroll, but I'm not chancing it."

She'd again forgotten he was a criminal. He was probably wanted. Would protecting her put him in prison? "Are you running from the FBI?" Her heartbeat skipped, afraid of his answer. Picturing him behind bars forced a sick feeling in her stomach.

She tossed the plastic bags in the garbage can and moved to her bed, sat and waited.

He captured her gaze. "No. Don't worry about me. I'm not running from anyone except the Magician." He turned away and added, "At least not yet."

A rush of relief pulsed through her. She couldn't hold back her smile.

****

"Shit. You made the national news. Now your picture is everywhere."

Megan rose, moved closer to the television, and cringed at her photo. "What do we do now?"

AJ looked at her and absorbed the fear in her eyes. Maybe he should hand her off. She'd be safer. His plan would take him into the devil's lair at some point. He couldn't take her there. He rubbed his temples to ward off the growing headache. She fucked up his mind too much just by being near.

157

"This means if you're staying with me, you'll have to change that lovely hair, and going out to breakfast is no longer an option. We'll also be moving soon."

He should've expected her to make the national news. She was a journalist, after all.

"Are you sure you don't want to go with the FBI or my brother instead?"

Jesse had suggested putting something in her drink to knock her out so they could move her to HIS headquarters, but AJ couldn't let her go even though he knew it would be better for her.

"No, I'll stay with you, if you'll let me."

He nodded, wanting to hold her and reassure her that it would be all right. Hugging her wasn't an option. Touching her wasn't an option either. She might be Trent's girl. He wouldn't do that to his old friend.

She climbed back on her bed with her knees pulled up, her arms wrapped around her legs, resting her head on her knees. Her vulnerability flashed brightly.

He stood, walked toward her bed and sat beside her. "Don't worry about it, my little dove. I should've expected it. You've been working a high-profile investigation, you witnessed a murder, your house was shot up, and you disappeared. There's no way the media would overlook all of that."

"Maybe something else will happen that will knock me off the national news," she said hopefully.

"It would only bump you down, but they won't drop your story." He had to rethink his plan. No matter what he told her, this was bad news. She stood out and would easily be recognized. His only regret was that they would need to change her silky, pomegranate-smelling hair.

She looked up. "What color should I go?"

He studied her. "How about auburn?" He'd always had a thing for auburn hair. He should've said a dark raven because he'd already been irresistibly drawn to her since they'd met. He didn't need to add more fuel to the fire that burned within him for her.

Megan smiled. "That'll work."

He didn't like what he would have to do. "When we go to buy the hair dye, I'll have to leave you alone in the car. You'll need to keep your hat on and your head down."

The panicked look in her eyes shoved a knife in his heart. "I'll only be gone for a few minutes, Megan. I'll return your weapon and make sure it's safe before I go into the store." There was no other way. If she walked in, even with the ball cap, she could be recognized.

Someone would call in and then their car would be on camera, their pictures all over the news again with him as a kidnapper. He had to take the better of the two bad situations, and that meant trusting her to take care of herself.

"Okay," she said with a determined smile.

He tucked a strand of her hair behind her ear, his hand lightly touching her cheek. "Let's wait to do it late tonight."

He wanted to run his fingers through her hair before they changed it. He wanted to wrap it around his hands while he devoured her lips and made her his, body and soul. And then what? Break her heart because they didn't belong in the same world?

"What do we do now?" she asked.

He rose from the bed. "We can watch television. It's our only option." Sex couldn't be an option no matter how much he craved it. To cool his blood and slow the rush of it to his groin, he kept repeating the mantra, *Not mine.*

"The TV will be your best friend for a little while."

She stood and picked up the TV remote. "I have cards in my bag, but I'd rather watch TV. Can we order a movie?"

"That's a good idea." Anything to keep him from dragging her to bed.

"I forgot to ask. How are we paying? I don't have much cash. I'm guessing you don't want me to use my credit cards."

He smiled. "Don't worry about it. I've got it covered."

****

Megan stared out into darkness only broken by the headlights of the car as they made the long drive to a drugstore. AJ shifted the car into Park, and turned in his seat, one arm rested on the steering wheel, the other on the back of her seat.

"I'll be quick. I'll leave the car running, so you'll have heat. Here's your weapon. Do you know how to use it?"

She'd shot a twelve-gauge shotgun growing up. What true southern girl hadn't? "I've had this for a while but haven't fired it." She stared at the pistol she'd carried around all those weeks on the streets. Things had changed, her life now surreal. She might actually have to shoot someone.

She released a deep breath, reached out and reluctantly accepted it, expecting it to burn her hand.

"This is serious, Megan. You have to shoot. You can't hesitate, or you will be dead."

"Okay." She hoped she could pull the trigger. The thought of this added pressure to her rapidly beating heart.

"If someone recognizes you, jump in the driver's seat and get the hell out of here."

Her eyes widened. "What about you?" She couldn't leave him. They were in this together.

"I'll find you." He looked at her for a minute longer. "Ready?"

She took a deep breath and let it out in a ragged sigh. "Yes."

He turned off the dome light, opened the car door and stepped out into the night.

She watched him walk into the store and then she nervously looked around. Snow had built on the lone car in the parking lot. Probably the employee's car. A siren screamed somewhere. A jet flew low, coming in for a landing. Dogs barked back and forth.

Nothing out of the ordinary so far as she could tell.

The seriousness of their situation didn't elude her. Her curiosity and determination were the reason for her need to run. She jumped when another car drove into the parking lot. Could they have found them already? She tightened her hold on the pistol and watched the car closely.

An elderly man stepped out of a Cadillac. He briefly glanced her way before walking into the store.

She relaxed a little and loosened her grip on the pistol. She looked toward the door of the store. *Hurry up, AJ.* She expelled a sigh of relief when she saw him walking toward the car.

****

Megan stepped out of the bathroom with her damp

hair framing her face. "Well?"

He stared. No, gawked would be a better word. Was there any way she wasn't sexy?

"It'll lighten a little when it's dry." She ran her fingers through the long strands.

"It'll work. It'll fool most people," he croaked.

"Okay. I'll dry it then." She turned and disappeared into the bathroom.

I am so fucked. When I look at her, I have to think about saving her not exploring her body.

He paced the small hotel room. He needed a new plan to draw out the Magician, but all he could think about was Megan. Remembering her naked stirred him. He wanted to touch her and taste her all over.

Having sex with her would be a mistake, but damn if he wasn't weakening. All he could do was remember her taste. His resistance was fast crumbling where his little dove was concerned.

****

Megan exited the bathroom wearing pink fleece pajama pants and a white long-sleeved T-shirt.

AJ's eyes moved from her breasts to her hair. "Uh. You were right; it's lighter. I like it."

She swooshed her hair and smiled. "I feel like a different person."

Moving past him to her bed, he surprised her when he reached out and caught her in his arms, jerking her to her chest. Before she could think straight, his lips melted over hers in a hot, searing kiss that left her limp with desire.

Heart pounding in excitement, she slid her hands up his arms, resting on his shoulders before wrapping them around his neck. She pulled him closer, boldly rubbing herself against his hardness, heating her blood and her core.

He quickly jerked back, set her away, and dropped his hands. After several gulps of air, he spoke, "I'm sorry. I shouldn't have done that."

Bewilderment shocked her, then a flush of anger surfaced and all the heated desire she'd been feeling vanished. Her hands flew to her hips. "Shouldn't have done what? Kiss me? Make me want you? Why exactly are you sorry, AJ?"

He ran his fingers through his hair. "You know why." He turned and escaped into the bathroom.

What the hell just happened?

Chapter Fifteen

AJ scanned the area outside the hotel room. They needed to move soon. They'd already been here longer than he liked.

He scooped up the newspaper from the doorstep. A smile escaped him as he noted the front page. Standing, he scanned the area once more. Satisfied, he closed and locked the door.

After placing the newspaper on the desk and watched Megan sleep. What he wouldn't give to wake up to her each morning. *What the fuck am I thinking? She's possibly Trent's woman, and only with me because he's injured.* Reality slipped in and he knew he was using that logic as an excuse to cover his real reason to leave her alone. Truly, she was too good for someone like him who lived the life he did. She deserved so much more than he could give her. He could only drag her down and he wouldn't do that.

Last night he'd overstepped boundaries. Killers breathed down their necks and distractions could be deadly. And hell, she distracted him. Whenever she approached, blood rushed to his groin, and his damned dick stood at attention. No matter what he told himself, he wanted her with an urgency he didn't understand. Didn't want to understand.

Megan woke, stretched and yawned. She had that mussed-up morning look. It was damn sexy. Fuck. He should hand her off to someone else. Jesse and Kate offered to take her. He wasn't sure he could handle this attraction to her.

She jumped from the bed, picked up the newspaper and gasped. "It's on the front page, above the fold!"

Oh, how adorable she looked when she saw her articles in print.

He set a cup of coffee on the desk and smiled at her. He allowed himself to savor being near her, drinking in the sight of her, warmth slowly spreading through him. His heart turned over. She should be his. If only….

"Front page, two days in a row," she whispered in awe.

"Megan, you're an exceptional journalist."

Her excitement burst forth, and she stood and hugged him. "Thank you." When she realized what she had done, she jumped back. "I'm sorry."

He grunted. "Don't worry about it. You're happy. A hug isn't out of line." Her breasts had brushed against his chest. He couldn't handle another embrace without throwing her to the floor.

Returning to her seat, she drank coffee and read the newspaper. Read about her narrow escape from death.

He needed time to find out about the next prison break. Another convict apprehended would bring their boss out faster than losing drug money from the streets. First, he needed to see to their safety. They'd move tomorrow. He'd forgotten to ask his brother to provide him with new wheels. He needed to rectify that.

AJ pulled the secure phone from his pocket and dialed. "Jesse said you'd help. We need wheels that won't attract police attention. Will you do that?"

"Good morning to you too, my lost little brother."

He didn't need the lecture Devon, another of his older brothers, would give him. Jesse had already burned his ears with their disappointment of how he'd chosen to live. His brother hadn't actually said disappointed, but AJ knew what he'd meant. Impatiently, he asked, "Can you do it?"

"How could you even doubt my ability to do something so simple?" Devon responded indignantly.

"Good. I need it filled with toys so I can work, and I'm not sure exactly what I'll need."

"I can do that, too." As a former CIA agent, his brother provided anything and everything the HIS team needed. AJ had never asked how they acquired their supplies, because he wasn't sure he wanted to know the answer.

The crinkling of a folding newspaper reached his ears. "This journalist is trouble, AJ. She's making it worse. Can't you stop her?"

He chuckled. "Are you kidding me? She's just as eager as I am to get the fucker. If I tried to stop her, she'd just take off on her own to get things done. At least now I can watch over her." He glanced her way, catching her absorbed in reading.

"Have you talked her into coming here yet?"

"She refused."

"Why won't you walk away? At least until everyone returns? You know we'll help you with this."

"He tried to have me killed, Dev. I won't walk away, and I'm not waiting."

His brother inhaled and exhaled loudly. "Okay. Where and when?"

AJ provided an address, and they agreed on a time

when transportation would be available. A small weight lifted from his shoulders. One thing down.

"We need to get on the Internet without being located."

"Ha, little brother, you know I can do that quicker than you can pick up a woman."

He smiled. "You take good care of me, Dev."

"Just remember that when I need something from you." His brother chuckled.

Megan stood and walked to her suitcase with a sly smile on her face. Ah, she'd been listening.

She lugged her bag to the bathroom with her. "I have the shower first."

She'd paid attention to him about not unpacking in the event they had to depart quickly. He hated she had to live this way, but he was damn proud of her for taking it in stride. He'd keep her safe until he could return her back to her world.

****

AJ couldn't wait any longer to make his calls even if Megan listened. He pulled out the burner phone.

"Blade, I need information."

"Whatcha' want, AJ?"

"I need the Magician."

The man chuckled. "Come on. We've been through that before. I don't know who he is or where he hides."

He'd met Blade when he'd been sent with another enforcer to give him a message. It had been eye-opening. Jimmy Baldwin liked to have Blade regularly beaten up to show the other dealers he could and would hurt them if he wanted. AJ couldn't figure out why Jimmy chose this particular dealer as his victim, and Blade wouldn't share why.

His informant wanted Jimmy to have payback, but he wasn't capable of doing it himself. AJ promised to take care of the man if he helped him find the organization's boss. Blade knew he'd be out of a job if that happened, but didn't care, as someone else would take over almost immediately. Someone he hoped to whom he wouldn't be the example.

"I know you don't know who he is, but someone else might. I'm also looking for anything you hear about an upcoming secret mission."

"All right, man. Let me see what I can find out."

"That's all I ask. Call me on this phone when you have something. Don't let anyone know we spoke."

"I never do. I heard they're going fucking nuts looking for you. You'd best keep your head down," Blade advised.

"I'll do that."

He didn't expect the dealer to have anything new when he'd called, but he was AJ's best informant. Blade could ferret out information like no one else. He had no doubt the man would find something useful.

Megan held his gaze with a raised eyebrow. "Blade?"

Of course, she'd listened.

"He wants to sound dangerous," he answered with a mischievous smile.

"I have some contacts too, but I need the phone."

They'd been useful to her before. She'd exposed several dealers on the streets plus the councilman. Hell, she'd been at his meeting with Damian. A meeting only three people, well four if they counted the Magician, knew about. They were damn good sources. They could use all the help they could get right now.

"Come on. I won't say where we are or that I'm with you." She tilted her head and added a smile.

"Make it quick."

"May I give them this number so they can call me when they find out something?"

He sighed. "Go ahead."

She jumped up and took the phone from him. "Oh, and I'm calling Kristen."

He shrugged. Devon had cleared her boss. "Be careful what you say. Talk where I can hear you."

****

Megan watched AJ stretch out his glorious body on his bed, his back propped against the headboard, and his feet crossed with a bored look on his face. She wanted to kiss it away, watch his eyes darken with desire. She wanted him and wouldn't fight it any longer.

Even now looking at him had her heartbeat accelerating. She had no idea what she was supposed to know when he'd stopped kissing her, but she'd find out so it didn't prevent him from stopping next time. And, there would be a next time.

"Yo."

"Raven, what's the word on the street?"

"Lady, word is that everyone is looking for you. The good guys and the bad. I heard the Feds got involved."

"Yeah. I'm kind of in a bind. I need information. I'm looking for the Magician or where I can find him."

"Since when did you jump back to the top? I thought you wanted to take down every level of Magic Shop before you got to him?"

"You know my plan was for him all along. I just

had to start at the bottom because it was all I had."

"Well, if this helps, I heard a rumor he's pissed with Damian. The one you got a picture of offing those guys. That was bitchin'."

"Thanks. Would you try to find out where I can find the man? This is important."

"He's got a hit out on you. Why you trying to find him? Do you have a death wish or something?"

Why did everyone keep asking her that? "It's because he has a hit on me that I want to find him. Besides, you know he had my brother killed."

He sighed. "Okay. I'll see what I can do."

"I'll take anything you can find out."

"Will do."

"Thanks, Raven."

She disconnected the call and looked at AJ. "The boss is pissed at Damian."

AJ's eyes remained focused on the television. "Of course he is, but Damian can't help us find what we need because he's probably in hiding. You did plaster his photo across the front page of your newspaper."

"Don't you think it's time we share information? It might help us get closer to finding him." She crossed her fingers behind her back. *Please. Please.*

"Not yet. I'm sure you don't have anything I can use."

Dang him for being right. He knew all about them. She didn't have a story if she couldn't get more information. "Why won't you share with me?"

"Because you'll use the information to write an article that broadens the bull's-eye on your back. And, we'd probably lose our chance."

Megan would write about it. It was what she did.

170

"I'm not worried about me. People have a right to know what's happening on the streets of Baltimore." She sighed. "But, for the sake of our investigation, I might not write it. Yet."

He'd tried to put his foot down on her writing articles. No way would she listen to him on her work. She knew her articles would help them. He just didn't see it.

"Finished with your calls? I have more to make."

"No. I have another call to make. Can't you use your other phone?"

He gave her a look that had her rolling her eyes. "Okay, I'll be quick."

She called Tyrone and learned that since things got screwed up, the big boss might personally get involved.

Maybe her witnessing Damian killing Hank would bring out the boss. That was the best news she'd heard.

She needed to call Kristen before AJ changed his mind. She dialed the newsroom.

"Michaels."

"Hello, Kristen."

"Megan! Where are you? Are you safe?"

"I'm safe."

"Good. Good. Your article is a hit. Our sales are through the roof."

Elation filled Megan. The more people knew what happens in Magic Shop, the better. "Thanks for the front page exposure."

"The story deserved it. What's next? What do you have on the Magician?"

"Nothing. But I'm not giving up. I have my sources on it."

"Well, being on the run could negatively impact

writing stories. I don't expect anything out of you. I considered yesterday a bonus."

"I'll find something. Just give me time."

"Megan, come in and let's get you to the FBI. They've been driving me nuts."

Megan's hands shook at the thought of the Feds tracking her down. "If you tell them we talked, we won't be able to anymore."

"I understand. Oh, that bastard Marcus came by to see if I'd heard from you. He sounded truly worried."

Megan tightened her grip on the phone. "Ignore him."

"I told him to leave, like the dozens of times he's come for you over the past few weeks I don't like you on the run by yourself."

She wished she could tell her not to worry, that she was with AJ. "How's the team?"

"Worried about you. Tell me where you are, and I'll drive you personally to the FBI office."

"Sorry, Kristen. I don't trust them."

She had to end the call before she slipped and told Kristen everything. "I have to go. You can reach me at this number for a day or two." She rattled off the number, not knowing when AJ would change out the phones.

"Wait! Victoria wants to speak with you."

"Hey, Megan, I can tell you're in a hurry, so I'll be quick. I've tracked the ownership of the building the brothel is located to a dummy corporation owned by another dummy corporation. I still haven't seen anyone important or one that matches the men in your photos. I've heard a rumor of another brothel that I'm checking out tonight. Maybe I'll have more luck there.

"Call me when you have more time, and we can compare notes."

Maybe Victoria could find something at the other location. Anything that could help them finish this. "Thanks, Victoria. I'll call when I can."

She ended her call and handed AJ the cell phone. "It's all yours."

****

"What? You look like you're a kid waiting to sit on Santa's lap," AJ said.

A chuckle burst from her. "We might be drawing him out."

"That's what we want. If we disrupt things enough, he'll have to come out and fix it himself." That thought gave him an idea for part of his new plan.

"Rumor is he's pissed."

"I don't doubt it. You made one of his advisors' crimes public. Plus, we're both still alive."

She smiled at him. "You probably sent Damian to the hospital."

"I'm sure he's long gone. Now, let me finish up with my informants."

He called Javier and received the same answers.

When he finished his last call, he walked over to Megan. She had papers and photographs spread out on the desk with a determined look on her face. "Looking for another story?" he asked jokingly.

"No. I'm just looking at these photos. I snapped a lot while I walked the streets. Especially when someone didn't look like they fit in. I'm sure there's something in them. Someone important. My sources haven't seen any of my recent photos to help me identify anyone."

He peered over her shoulder and almost choked on

his water. She had a photo of Jimmy, Carl, and Paul, a street boss and two advisors. He picked up the photo, curious as to where she'd captured them together.

Having a photo of Jimmy and Carl was bad enough. Prison escapees didn't like their photo taken. But Paul was the Magician's most secret advisor. Only a handful of people knew about him.

If they knew she had a photo of the bosses, they'd double their efforts to find her before she realized it and published it.

"Do you know those men?" she asked softly.

"Yes."

"I had to get their photo. They didn't belong. Who are they?"

He set the photo down and moved to his bed. "Don't you think it's time you told me why you're so ferocious with this?"

Her shoulders stiffened. She slid the photos back into her laptop bag. "I'm an investigative reporter. I investigate. This needed investigating."

"Are you sure it had nothing to do with your brother's disappearance last month?"

Her head whipped around so fast he wouldn't be surprised if she had whiplash. "What do you know about that?"

"Just what I've heard. He worked at the same newspaper as you. I'm guessing since you're so far from home, you moved here to be close to him." He paused and assessed her. "He was investigating Magic Shop when he disappeared, and they secretly took credit."

Slowly, she asked, "Were you involved in his disappearance?"

"No." He wished he could give her an answer to soothe her pain.

"Were you there when he disappeared or did you hear about it?" she asked hopefully.

"I heard he found out something he shouldn't have." Kevin overheard Tim, Ted, and Paul discussing past prison breaks and where the latest escapees had been relocated.

Why they left the other reporter alone, the one digging into the prostitution ring baffled him. It might be because she hadn't reported anything like Megan. But she had recently stumbled across one of the brothels, one filled with trafficked women. He'd have Jesse take care of that also.

Sadness overshadowed her expression. "But he never shared anything with me."

He sighed. Pain radiated from her eyes. He didn't like seeing her this way. "Maybe he was trying to protect you. Maybe he didn't have time to share."

They didn't give Kevin enough time to go to the police or FBI with what he'd found out. He was taken care of immediately before he had an opportunity to speak with anyone.

He watched the tears slip down her face and couldn't stand it. He rose and walked to her, offering his hand. She accepted it and stood. He wrapped his arms around her waist, pulling her tightly against him. He pressed kisses against her silky hair, his hands rubbing up and down her back. He inhaled the scent of her hair and smiled.

Tightening her hold, she tucked her face in closer to him. "I'm sorry."

"It's okay. You can use my shoulder anytime, my

little dove."

She pulled her head back and looked up at him. All he could do was fixate on those beautiful, wet, dark blue eyes holding him captive. He witnessed sadness and pain in them and wanted to take it away.

The need to touch her overrode his sense of detachment. He brushed a strand of her hair behind her ear, then slowly lowered his head, while cursing himself. That single moment wasn't enough. Somehow he knew it would never be enough and he was powerless to stop it. Hell, he didn't want to stop it. He wanted to be with her.

No longer able to listen to his reasons for leaving her alone, he leaned his head down and gently covered her mouth with his. She tasted so goddamn sweet.

Raising his head, he looked into her eyes again and saw the blue darken even deeper as desire flickered and finally held on.

His jeans tightened as his cock swelled. "What about Trent?" he asked in a raspy voice. He'd surmised there'd been little chance she was with his friend since she hadn't pushed to see the injured Trent, but he had to check. He did have some morals.

"What about him?" Confusion marred her features.

"I won't take a friend's girlfriend, but you tempt me something fierce, Megan."

"Trent and I aren't together."

Relief thundered in his heart, and he smiled. "Good."

AJ raised his hands to either side of her face, and his lips descended to meet hers. His mouth covered hers hungrily, their tongues tangling, exploring. With only a kiss, sparks of pleasure wound their way to his cock.

She slid her hands up his chest and wound her arms around his neck, pulled herself closer and sighed against his mouth. Her breasts rubbed against his chest, the feel of them elicited a low growl from deep in his throat. This woman had no idea what she did to him, how much he craved her.

His hands left her face, slowly traveling up and down her sides, reaching the hem of her sweater and tugging it up. She didn't protest. Instead, she stepped back and raised her arms. After removing her sweater, he quickly divested her of her bra.

His heart pounded. "Beautiful," he murmured.

AJ reached for her breast, his thumb lightly circling her rosy, puckered nipple. He watched goosebumps form on her body. She closed her eyes and a soft whimper escaped, making a naked craving flood his veins.

"Megan, I won't stop unless you tell me now."

Holding his heated gaze, she whispered, "Don't stop."

They stepped to his bed, and he gently eased her down onto the mattress.

His body sizzled as she watched him remove his weapons and pull his sweatshirt over his head. He lay down beside her and stretched out on his side, turning to her.

She reached a hand up to touch his chest with featherlight strokes around his bruising. He closed his eyes and sighed. The cool brush of her fingers set his chest to tingling instead of the pain her touch should've caused his injury.

She gasped. "It's a dove. What does it say?"

Damn. She'd made out his tattoo from beneath the

mess covering his chest. He didn't wish to discuss it now.

His mouth landed on hers for a deep, scorching kiss where the heat level increased as she met his fire with her own. He burned deep for her, wanted to engulf himself in her essence, fan the flames, let it reach its hottest, and then help it explode.

His lips left hers and kissed a trail down her ivory, silky body, stopping to play at her neck, nipping it playfully. She leaned her head to the side, giving him full access to his playground.

He spent another minute playing before his mouth made a path to her breast. His tongue slowly circled her areola, the rosy peaks instantly firmed. He flicked her nipple with his tongue, teased the taut bud and then tugged on it with his teeth.

Her hands stilled in his hair and her breath released in long surrendering moans. His cock almost burst through his jeans at the sensual sound. An urgent need to fuck her hard and fast battled a need to bask in a slow, sensual bout of sex.

Right then he decided she'd stay with him. That'd give him plenty of time to fulfill his fantasies with her. But he needed to get inside her velvety heat now.

His mouth left her breast and recaptured her lips. His hands slid across her soft belly over the new goose bumps forming under his touch. He tugged at the waistband of her jeans. "I want to taste you."

Blood pumped faster through his veins when her eager hands left his hair and moved down his stomach. Unbuttoning his jeans, she smiled and then reached in and released him. His breath rushed out at the blessed relief from confinement, and finally being held tight in

Megan's hand, slowly moving up and down. A groan escaped him. If she kept up the movement, he'd embarrass himself.

"I don't want to wait that long. I want you now." She moved provocatively against him. His little dove wasn't a timid lover. He thanked his lucky stars for that. He liked her fire.

"I want you too, but I want to take my time with you."

His mouth left hers, trailing damp heated kisses down her body, taking his time with each one, listening to her soft whimpers. He looked up from her stomach and smiled at her watching him. He moved lower, the scent of her arousal calling to him.

Arriving at the top of her jeans, he reached for the zipper, slowly releasing it, teasing her, drawing things out, ensuring they both enjoyed it, that they both exploded from the fireball building inside them. He smiled, his arousal increasing when she lifted her hips to aid him in removing her jeans. It appeared she felt the same madness that drove him into this sexual stupor.

He kissed her mound through her panties, eager to taste her, to feel her come on his tongue.

She exhaled a ragged breath.

A cell phone rang.

Fuck! He couldn't ignore it, but the caller had best have a damn good reason for calling him now.

Regretfully, he jumped from the bed and answered the call.

"Get out now!"

Chapter Sixteen

"Get dressed! We're leaving," AJ ordered, pushing his cock back into his jeans and then reaching for his sweatshirt.

With the urgency in his voice, Megan knew they'd been found. She jumped up and scrambled into her jeans and sweater, bypassing her bra. There was no time to get back into that contraption. Plus her hands shook too much to even attempt the clasps.

"Grab your bags." He checked his weapons, tossing his empty holsters in his bag.

It must be worse than she thought if he didn't take the time to put them on. Fear returned, carrying the trembling and the racing heartbeat with it. She hated it. Hated she couldn't remain fearless like AJ.

He quickly tossed the Kevlar vest over her. "You ready? We have to move." He turned and peeked out the curtain.

She picked up her bags, thankful she'd followed his direction to keep everything ready to go. She'd have unpacked and would now be leaving with only the clothes on her back. It showed her how much she needed him to stay alive. She held her gun. "I'm ready."

"Let's go. You stick with me no matter what."

She watched his eyes roam over the areas outside the door with his weapon in front of him before he opened it fully.

He led her at a hurried pace, constantly scanning the vicinity. She barely kept up with him. She'd drop her bags and run if she had to. He was the only one who knew what they were doing.

The trunk popped open as they approached. *Thank you, fancy car remotes.* They dumped their bags and hurriedly jumped in the car. AJ had the car moving almost before they closed the doors.

"How did they find us?" she asked in a shaky voice, her heart attempting to break out of her chest, with the intensely hard, fast hammering. She kept glancing around, expecting to find gunmen standing behind them pointing a weapon at her and AJ.

"I'm not sure. We'll think about that later. Keep your head down."

She didn't question and did as he commanded. Magic Shop had found them. How could they have tracked them? Had someone seen them when they went out? What about using the phones? Couldn't they triangulate their location or something like that? Oh no. She'd used the Internet. Wasn't that how criminals were captured on crime shows?

How long before they stopped the manhunt for them? Would it ever stop? Would they ever be safe? She knew the answer but didn't like it. A ragged, nervous breath escaped her.

He turned right out of the parking lot and swore. "Buckle up."

It took her trembling hands several tries before she locked the mechanism into place.

"Get back down."

She held on as AJ turned a corner and his tires

squealed from their increasing rate of speed. He pulled out a phone.

"I need help now!"

She swallowed the bile rising in her throat. They were being chased.

Oh God. Oh God. Oh God.

Would these men shoot at them out in the open on the street? What kind of help did AJ ask for? Would it be in time? She hated having nothing but questions and no one to answer them.

She squeezed her eyes closed tightly and fisted her hands. They would survive this. He would save them, and she'd do whatever it took to aid him.

Several metallic tings sounded and fright seized her, freezing her limbs as her pulse raced beyond reason. Oh. My. God! She squeezed her eyes closed, hoping to block out the deadly truth. This couldn't be happening, but it sounded like they'd been shot at— right out in the open. She took several deep breaths, hoping to remain calm, but panic jetted uncontrollably through her body.

"Shit! Goddamn fuckers!"

She turned her head and peeked up at him. "Did they… did they just shoot at us?"

He checked the rearview mirror. "Don't worry about it. Just keep your head down."

Several unexpected turns tossed her back and forth until her seatbelt snapped her back each time. It had been several minutes, and he hadn't shaken them. The one bit of enlightening news was that they hadn't been shot at again.

Police sirens burst into her thoughts. *No! No! No!*

"AJ, slow down! The police will catch us." What

was wrong with him? Did he plan to go on a high-speed chase like some crazy wanting publicity?

He reached over and rubbed her back. She wanted to lift her head and rush into his arms while he told her everything would be okay.

"Trust me."

The sound of the sirens slowly faded, and AJ slowed.

"Okay, you can sit up now."

She jerked up and craned her neck to look out the back window. "Where are they? Did you outrun them?"

He laughed. "No. I'd say they're explaining the weapons they're carrying to two police officers."

"Was that the help you asked for?"

He turned and smiled at her, warming her heart. That half smile and wink melted her insides. She basically fell into a puddle around him.

"Never underestimate the power of the Hamilton brothers."

****

Thank you, Blade, for saving our asses!

AJ released a long, heavy sigh. The adrenaline spike had ended, but his muscles remained tight, ready for action. He owed his informant. Big time.

"Do you…?" Megan asked in a shaky breath, "Do you think they tracked us because I used my laptop?"

"I don't know. Did you use your e-mail? Open any of them?"

She nodded. "I opened a message from Kristen and one from my mom. I was quick in my responses then I went off-line."

He clenched his jaw until the muscles ached. He couldn't catch a fucking break. He didn't know if that led the enforcers to them or not. They'd left the room a couple of times and may have been spotted. Too many things could've been the cause of them being found. He knew they'd been there too long. He had to get on the ball. It wasn't just his life at stake anymore.

Why she trusted him with her life was beyond him. Their first meeting hadn't been pleasant. Hold that. There'd been part of it that had been real pleasant. Shit. She drove him to madness.

Who the fuck was he kidding? There could be no happy ending for the two of them. She had no idea what would happen when this ended. But dammit, he liked her. He liked being around her. He wanted to fuck her from here to Sunday and back.

He looked over at his passenger. She stared straight ahead, the fear in her eyes subsiding a little. She couldn't fool him though. She tried to put on a brave front but failed miserably. She still trembled slightly, and she kept wringing her hands in her lap.

He didn't know what to do to ease her fear. She should be afraid. That had been too close a call. They'd been caught with their pants down, literally.

He had to be ready for anything. He couldn't do that if he had his cock buried deep inside of her. Fuck! That image launched a rush of blood to his twitching cock. What was it about this woman that had him losing control?

No matter how much he wanted her, he had to remain alert, which meant no sex. Hell. Who was he kidding? He'd be buried balls deep inside her as soon as she allowed him. With that fucking image burned in his mind, he inwardly sighed and forced himself to focus on their next move.

Once he was certain they weren't being followed, he turned toward I-695.

"Where are we going?" she asked.

He chuckled and wished he hadn't. He needed her magic hands softly touching his chest, taking away the remnants of pain. He mentally shook his head and cleared his throat. "Are you always planning to ask me that?"

She looked at him and crossed her arms under her breasts. It emphasized her braless state and made his mouth water. Damn. She tempted him even when she wasn't trying.

"Why wouldn't I? Why would you keep it a secret? It's not like I'm going to tell anyone."

He merged onto the interstate and sighed. She had a valid point. "We're moving to Elliott City. There's a Residence Inn we'll stay at. It has a kitchenette, so our only risk is purchasing groceries.

"We need to lay low a few more days. It's too risky for either of us on the streets, and that's where we'll get what we need."

He knew the risks of heading back out, but he needed to pay the bastard back for shooting at him and Megan. Someone had to know about the next prison break or more about the Magician. He would find the right person.

"I guess we could use my sources during that time, but they haven't found him before."

"I doubt they'll find him now. It's like you said. We've disrupted things, and we're going to find a way to disrupt things even more. He'll come out to fix the problems. When he does, we'll be there."

She unfolded her arms. "You mean we are going

out on the streets? I thought you just said it wasn't safe."

For thinking it wasn't safe, she sure had a lot of excitement at the prospect of being out. Her determination to unmask the crime boss appeared to have once again overridden her fear. Not what he needed right now. She tended to act foolishly in her pursuit. He'd spend as much time keeping her out of trouble as he would tracking his prey.

"We're not going just yet. Be patient. I have a plan."

"Do you plan to share it with me?"

"Not yet."

She narrowed her eyes at him and jerked back facing front, her back stiff as a board.

He'd made her angry, but he couldn't share. She had no patience. Nor could she keep things out of print. If anger kept her safe, then so be it.

Having her with him had changed everything. He'd had a direct attack planned that would no longer work now that she'd become involved. He'd devised a new one where she'd play an important role. A part she would love.

She turned to him and broke the silence. "I'm writing an article about being on the run and our experiences so far."

Dammit! Fucking journalists and their need to write about every-fucking-thing. This article wouldn't be a direct attack on Magic Shop's business, but it would be a slap in the face. It could get things slowly rolling in the direction he needed. She had a good idea.

"As long as you don't give away our location or mention me."

"But it won't be a story without you. I can be general and not describe you. It could be as if you were one of my bodyguards who survived. I promise."

He sighed. There'd be no use arguing with her. She had determination written all over her face. "Okay. As long as I read and approve your article first." He'd make sure she didn't accidentally give anything away. Didn't help them realize he was the one protecting her. They needed to think him long gone so he could sneak up on them.

She smiled. "Thank you. Oh, is it safe for me to get online to send the article?"

He grunted. "You won't be using your laptop anymore. I'll set you up safely later today on a different one. We're making a few changes. You're not using your e-mail. You can't even check it. We'll set you up with a new e-mail address each time you send an article. You won't use the same one twice."

He reached over, opened his hand, palm up, fingers spread, waiting. His heart did a little flip-flop when she quickly laced her fingers through his.

He merged onto I-70 West and knew their relationship had changed.

****

Megan's excitement over their new hotel room with the yellow sofa they lounged on, gave him a deep-down joy that had been buried too long. The room resembled a small one-bedroom apartment with a closet-sized kitchen, a dining table with four chairs, a desk, and most importantly, a queen bed behind a closed door. The heavy, white down comforter on the bed called to him to dive deep under it with her.

He needed to put things in motion, and he needed

to keep his hands off Megan. He pulled the encrypted phone from his pocket, dialed, stood, and then paced.

"Hey, AJ."

"They fucking found us."

Silence greeted him from the other end of the line.

"If it hadn't been for one of my informants, we'd be dead."

Devon sighed. "This has gone too far. Wait until Brad, Matt, and the team return."

"Is the ride ready?"

"It's there with the toys."

The toys he expected included several burner phones, a laptop with a secure connection, binoculars, night-vision goggles, slap-on GPS trackers, bugs, weapons, and more, some of which would be illegal to use. Desperate times call for desperate measures.

"Thanks."

"No problem. Anything else I can do to help?"

"Finding me the Magician would be helpful."

His brother laughed. "Wouldn't this be much easier if I knew? I wouldn't have to worry about whether you'll stay alive. I would like to have a beer with you again at some point. And, I'm sure Dad would too."

Their father, Alexander Blake Hamilton, was a U.S. Senator. Their mother had died eighteen years ago, but their father had still made time for each child, building strong bonds between them. He would chew AJ out if he knew what his son had involved himself in.

"First of all, you don't drink anymore. Second, I'll stay alive."

A deep chuckle floated from the receiver. "I'm glad to hear it. I like having you around."

"How's it been, finding the money?"

He had allowed himself to ask for Devon's help in searching for the money. Devon had always found any assets he sought. AJ didn't consider it really asking his brothers for help. It was different asking for help from Dev instead of Jesse though. Devon stayed behind a computer. No one admitted it, but he was the backbone of HIS.

"Slow. I'm putting in time when the boys don't need me. I'll say that Lawrence is good. But, I'm better. I just need a little time."

Lawrence Mann laundered the organization's money. They thought he was their deepest secret. Ha. That'd been the easiest information to come by. The man may be good at hiding money, but he sucked at keeping it a secret.

"Keep at it. I want him and his money." Once they bled the crime boss's accounts dry, there would be no money for his criminal defense. No money for bribes. People would turn their backs on him.

AJ grinned. That was only the beginning of what he had planned for that fucker. He'd had a long time to figure out what would work to bring the Magician down. With Megan and HIS as his secret weapons, he would finally win.

Chapter Seventeen

"Do you think the FBI believes I'm dead?" The only people who knew for certain Megan was alive were the ones attempting to kill them, their sources, and a few close friends. Her friends wanted her safe, and Magic Shop wouldn't publicize their screw-up.

The police might have assumed Magic Shop had killed her; the body disposed of where they'd never find it. Unless Trent had spoken with them. She doubted that though. Would she and AJ run from the FBI if they located them?

"I think they're still looking for you," AJ answered confidently.

The burner cell phone rang. Megan looked over AJ's shoulder as he pulled it from his pocket.

"That's for me." She held out her hand for the phone and he complied, but he didn't appear happy about it.

"Hi, Kristen," she said happily.

"I called to check on you."

She craved to tell her everything but heeded AJ's advice. Magic Shop might know they were together, but no one else needed to know for sure. Except for his family. "I'm fine. I'm glad you called. I want to write an article on my experiences on the run."

"Kelly is already covering your story."

"No. This is different. I think you'll like it. But it

needs to come from me, not through Kelly." She swallowed and continued, "Kristen, I've had help, so it's two people on the run, and we were almost caught today."

AJ observed her closely. His scrutiny almost unraveled her. The hard jaw and even harder eyes reminded her of when they'd first run into each other. She turned her back to him to avoid another shiver inch down her spine.

"You've got someone with you? Who?"

"That's not important. Trust me on the article."

"Get it to me, and I'll consider it."

She smiled. This would be the article of articles. "You won't regret it."

"Think about letting me come get you."

She had to lie. "I'll think about it."

"Victoria said she'd get in touch with you soon. I gave her this number since I knew you'd want her information as quickly as possible."

Megan ended the call.

Oh, AJ will be pissed when he found out another person had their number. Victoria was the only one of the two of them on the street right now investigating. There had to be some way to tie the prostitution ring and the Magician together. She wondered how he had been able to keep this entire secret for so long.

Maybe he wouldn't have kept it all so secret if he didn't have people disappear so quickly. Kevin might have overheard the boss's name and that was why they'd ended his life. She couldn't let it end hers. She promised Kevin she'd do this.

"Are you sure it was smart to tell her about me?"

She nodded. "Yeah. She doesn't know it's you."

He stood. "Let's get the grocery shopping out of the way."

Again, they stocked up for a few days. She didn't say anything when he added a box of condoms to their cart. He wanted to finish what they started and so did she.

They approached an SUV instead of the Honda. She shook her head. Of course it was black.

"Is this your SUV?" she asked.

He nodded. "It is now."

"Won't they know it's yours?"

"Don't worry, Megan."

The vehicle waiting meant he really had planned their next move. She knew his friend, Devon, had provided this for them, and she was thankful.

The pressure on her chest lightened. They no longer had to worry about the police stopping them for a stolen vehicle.

AJ opened the back of the SUV and grabbed a laptop bag and another cell phone. Ample weapons and black bags holding who-knew-what filled the back of the vehicle. Did they really need all that?

If there was any chance of AJ living a normal life, people like Devon—who provided weapons—couldn't be a part of it.

****

Back in the hotel room, AJ opened the new phone and dialed.

"Thanks, man. How'd you find out they were coming after me?" He paced the room. He couldn't sit still, as if nervous energy consumed him.

"I was trying to get your info, and I ended up near your enforcer buds. I figured if you were found, they'd be the ones to go after you. So I stayed a bit."

Blade had good instincts. "What happened?"

"I saw Trey gettin' in the SUV, yelling at Alex that they had you. I called you as soon as I could. I couldn't just run off. Someone would remember that when you got away."

Trey Holt and Alex Childs were the only two enforcers Damian had left in his employ. He'd killed Hank. AJ had killed Joe. And of course, a bullet in the chest had terminated AJ's employment.

"You're right. It was tight, but we made it. Have you heard anything else?"

"Damian is just getting up and around. He looks like shit. He didn't even jump in the truck with them. You'd think he'd want to be the one to take you down since you shot him."

AJ smiled. He wished he had killed the bastard. But, making him look foolish would also work in his favor. "Anything else?"

"They're focused on the girl, that reporter. They've got a hard-on for her. She's a priority target."

Shit! He'd hoped they'd think she was out of state and concentrate on him. "Thanks again."

"You owe me."

Megan looked at him after he ended the call. "Did you learn anything?"

He walked to the refrigerator and picked up a bottle of water to give him a minute to think. He couldn't tell her she was their priority. He needed her fearful of their situation not frightened shitless.

"He told me how he found out they were coming." He took a drink of water considering what else he should share. "Damian's back on the street."

"I'm surprised he isn't dead for letting you get away."

AJ shook his head. "He's too important. He's also alive because he needs to clean up his mess." He gestured with his finger between the two of them. "Us. After that, who knows what will happen to him."

"I don't approve of murder. Although, I so wish you'd killed him."

The encrypted cell phone rang. Damn. They were in contact with too many people. He had to put a stop to some of it.

"Yeah?"

"I heard you had a close call," Todd said.

He took a long drink of water. How the fuck had it spread around so quickly? He glanced at his watch. Yeah, it'd be about time others found out. "We did."

"I still can't believe you're staying to track down that bastard. I don't want to go to your funeral."

"Don't worry about me." Did he really need Todd? Even though he wanted to do this by himself, he might. Arthur had been right on that point.

"Is the girl okay?"

"Yeah." AJ didn't appreciate Todd's interest in Megan, even knowing it was straight-up curiosity. He had no right to allow jealousy to grab him. Shit! He pinched the bridge of his nose with his thumb and forefinger. He didn't need this right now.

"Did you find a good place to hide?"

"Yeah." No one except his brothers would know where they were this time. He doubted Arthur told anyone, but one could never be too careful that someone hadn't overheard him.

"Are you going to tell me? It'd be good if someone

knew where you were in case something happens and the girl needs protecting."

"No," AJ said flatly.

"All right. You know I'm here if you need me. Megan's fiancé, Marcus, is making a ruckus about the FBI finding her. He does have some pull with them. He's a golfing buddy with a couple of high-ranking people. He wants her found and brought in."

"Ex-fiancé," AJ said through clenched teeth.

Todd laughed. "That's not what he's supposedly saying."

"I'm getting off the phone."

"Okay. Keep yourself alive."

"Yeah," he said ending the call.

Before he put the secure phone in his pocket, the old burner phone rang. What the fuck? He had to get rid of it. He'd held onto it for long enough.

He hesitated at the blocked number. It went against his rules to answer a call when he didn't know the caller, but Megan had provided her sources with this number.

"Hello," he snarled.

"Can I talk to Megan?" the male caller asked nervously.

He walked over to the couch and handed her the cell phone. She sat with her legs folded underneath her. She looked calm and relaxed. His little dove. His heart warmed. He wanted to keep her this way. Keep the enthusiasm he'd witnessed in her alive.

He'd always been protective of women, but something about Megan made him dig deeper into that role. Deeper than when his partner's life had been threatened, and he hadn't thought that possible.

Keeping her with him could be the most colossal mistake of his life. He needed her for his new plan, but if she wasn't with him, he wouldn't need one. He'd have already pushed things to the limit.

Letting his dick lead him could only cause problems. Put their lives at a greater risk. Yet he couldn't ignore the sexual awareness between them. He needed to feel alive before he slinked back to his world. Remembering their time together would keep him warm in his lonely bed for a long time.

He continued to question himself. Was he doing the right thing? He purposely put them far enough away so they wouldn't have to worry about another close call.

She wanted him as much as he wanted her. He'd heard her breath hitch when they accidentally touched hands. He'd seen the change in her eyes when they neared each other. Would she get the wrong idea? Think it meant more than it did? He couldn't give her more than the here and now. Would it be enough for her?

****

Megan gave him a questioning look before accepting the phone. "Hello."

"It's Raven."

Her pulse spiked in excitement. He had information. "What's up?" She straightened out her legs and leaped from the couch.

"They know that you're with that enforcer dude, the one who's supposed to be dead. They also know you colored your hair and have passed the word around to everyone to keep an eye out for you."

She closed her eyes. They'd left the box of color in the trash. This was bad. AJ said not to worry, but how could she not?

She cleared her throat in an attempt to strengthen her voice. "Thanks. Anything else?"

"Nothing that would help you. The streets are quiet. Everyone is scared of what's gonna happen since there've been so many fuck-ups."

"That's good to know."

"That's all I got."

"I appreciate it, Raven. Thanks for calling."

"Anything for you, sweetheart."

She smiled and gave him the new burner phone number. "Bye."

He ended the call without responding.

She took a deep breath and then walked to AJ. She returned the phone and sat beside him on the couch she'd earlier vacated.

From his usual position of a remote in hand and his focus on the TV, he asked, "What's good to know?"

"They know I'm with you and that I colored my hair."

He shrugged. "We kind of figured that."

Dang his nonchalance. Didn't they have the advantage when they thought the two were traveling separately? Wouldn't it be harder to hide now? She swallowed. She had to trust him. She had no other choice.

"Raven says everyone is scared of what's expected to happen since they didn't kill us."

AJ finally looked at her. "It'll pass after a few days."

"Good. I hate that my sources have to worry. I don't want them found out."

"Care to share your sources?" he asked as one

eyebrow rose.

Maybe now was the time. Her spirits lifted. "Not unless you share yours." Her lips curved into a smile.

"Not a chance." A sexy grin spread across his face.

She shrugged, rose, and walked toward the kitchen. She cooked chicken, broccoli, and wild rice for dinner. Cooking helped keep her mind off what would happen later. She had no doubts that she wanted AJ. Wanted how his touch sent goosebumps over her flesh. Wanted how his touch set her core on fire. Wanted how his kiss made the rest of the world fade away to only the two of them.

No, she wouldn't pass up the opportunity.

She ignored the little pull at her brain reminding her of the two main reasons for not sleeping with him. They'd be together for a while, and they'd inevitably get close. Could she keep her heart from getting involved? Well, she had to. He lived in a different world than she did. He was someone who might be arrested at the end of this or worse yet, die. A chill gripped her spine in its frozen descent.

No matter what happened, he'd leave her. They didn't fit together, except in each other's arms. Her cheeks warmed thinking about it. She wasn't embarrassed about any of their sexual activity. She did regret they had been interrupted. She'd been ready for him to slide inside her. Ready for him to give her the pleasure his touch promised.

Sex. She had no problem with just sex. Have fun and then return home. Easy. It would be a welcome escape and distraction.

He studied her. "Let's sit down and play cards or watch a movie."

She relaxed at the suggestion. No matter how much bravado she had about rolling around in bed with him, no matter how much her body ached for him, for some reason, she was nervous. "I'll pop the popcorn for a movie."

She leaned against the kitchen counter while the popcorn popped, her thoughts returning to their lovemaking. Not lovemaking, almost sex. She wanted to fan herself from the heat rising within her by thinking of it.

In the hotel room, he'd been gentle, taking his time. How many other sides existed in this sexual being? She looked forward to finding out. She doubted her experiences would keep up with his, but she was willing to try.

He broke into her thoughts. "Are you planning to sit down and watch the movie?"

She jumped. Did he realize what she'd been thinking? *Calm down. Slow the breathing and he'll never know.* "I'm coming." She pulled the popcorn from the microwave and hesitated.

****

AJ wanted to laugh as she stood, staring at the couch. He smiled and touched the space beside him. "Here you go."

His pulse spiked when she sat close. He risked it and put an arm behind her. Tension eased in his shoulders when she didn't push away or sit forward. She hadn't snuggled into him, but he'd take one thing at a time.

Sexual tension crackled between them. If she hadn't appeared skittish, they'd be testing out the bed right now. But he noticed the slight tremble in her hands. It could be from desire, but more than likely it was nerves.

Anticipation rolled through him, driving his lust and determination. She'd have to get ready because he would fuck her tonight.

Chapter Eighteen

AJ's choice of a scary movie for them to watch had been wise. Megan had jumped closer to him and finally relaxed and then snuggled close.

After clicking the TV off, he rose and offered her his hand with the obvious question in his eyes. She looked up at him, took his hand, and stood.

He pulled her to him. "Megan, we're finishing what we started earlier. Are you okay with that?"

Her eyes slowly darkened, and her body quivered before she whispered, "Yes."

Slipping his hand behind her head, wrapping it in her silky strands, he leaned over and took her lips with his in a deep, slow kiss, his tongue claiming her mouth. Her heavenly sweetness rocketed heat through his gut straight to his groin.

AJ tightened his hold on her, pulling her closer, needing to feel every inch of her against him. The resulting whimper encouraged him. He deepened the kiss, hungry for her, and her body melted against his.

Pulling back, he looked at her lips, swollen and wet. God, she was sexy.

He shot her a reassuring smile and led the way to the bedroom, hoping she didn't change her mind. They stopped beside the bed, locked in a smoldering gaze that could've set the room ablaze.

AJ reached forward and slowly slid her sweater

over her head. He swallowed a burning lump in his throat. She hadn't put her bra back on.

His trembling hands reached up to grasp her breasts, lightly massaging them, his thumbs circling her puckered nipples, ready for him to suckle. She tossed her head back and released a soft, feminine sigh when he pinched them between his thumbs and forefingers.

Sliding his hands down her soft belly to the tops of her jeans, he hadn't expected to find resistance.

Megan stayed his hand. "No. You're hurt. I saw the pain in your eyes the last time you were over me. Let me do this."

He'd never sat back and let the woman lead. Her pleading eyes couldn't be denied. AJ dropped his arms to his sides as a tremor slid through his body.

She smiled. "You need to get rid of your weapons first."

After removing them, he ripped his sweatshirt over his head.

Her featherlight, lust-arousing exploration of his naked chest sent ripples of excitement through his tense body. She set him on fire with just her touch. No woman had ever sent that level of heat through his body.

"Am I hurting you?"

He looked down, watching her hand make circles around his nipple. "Not a chance."

"Good."

She glided her hand down his abdomen, smirking slightly at his indrawn breath when she reached the bulge in his jeans. Megan slid his zipper down slowly, drawing out the anticipated pleasure, and driving him close to insane. The same thing he'd done to her earlier.

The minx.

Snagging her hand, he growled, "I'll take off mine, and you take off yours."

Quickly unzipping his pants, he eased his cock from the tight grasp of his jeans, then wrapped his hand around it, moving his hand slowly up and down the shaft as he watched her undress.

Raking his gaze over her body, his breath quickened. He had to take some control back from this tease. Stilling his hand, he nodded to the bed. "On the bed."

Megan shook her head. "After you."

He ached too much for an argument. As long as they were flesh to flesh, he didn't care how it happened. He moved to the bed, stretched out, and waited for whatever she had planned for him.

She crawled and leveled herself over him, remaining on her hands and knees. His cock throbbed at the thought of taking her from behind in that position.

Unable to resist the temptation, his hands reached up and covered her silky breasts. She murmured his name as she leaned down and covered his mouth with hers in a smoldering kiss that heated with each passing second, threatening to rip his self-control to shreds.

Slowly lifting her head, she whispered, "Lie still," before she pressed butterfly kisses searing down his neck, past his chest, and to his stomach.

He pushed her hair from her face so he could watch her lips descend to his swollen cock. A sight he refused to miss.

Her eyes sparkled mischievously before she wrapped her hand around his engorged length, slowly sliding her hand up and down. Leaning in, she took the head of his cock into her mouth. The wet warmth pulled his remaining blood causing it to rush to his groin, leaving him lightheaded, but wanting to flip her over and pound into her.

"Turn around," he said in a raspy voice.

She lifted her head, cocked it and nodded. Watching her swing her tight ass around, placing her wet pussy in his face almost set him off. He took a deep breath, fighting to keep from spilling himself. The smell of her arousal didn't help him want to take things slowly.

She didn't speak, just slid his length to the back of her throat and then back again, her mouth and hand working in tandem. She added her tongue stroking up and down. A primal groan tore from his chest, spinning him in a jumble of heat and pleasure.

AJ took a deep breath to slow the pulsing of his cock as naked desire rushed through his veins.

He took in the glorious sight before him. Pink, wet, addicting.

With his tongue, he stroked over her nub and felt her tense, her whimper vibrating over his cock.

He parted her soft, naked lips and licked her hot center, finally tasting her. Ambrosia. "Your scent and taste are intoxicating," he said hoarsely.

She hummed something in return while still sucking his cock. He threw his head back and sucked in deep breath after deep breath. Not yet. Not fucking yet.

No longer teasing, his tongue returned to work, thrusting in and out of her core while his thumb stroked her clit. He inserted a finger in her slick entrance and then another. He licked her swollen nub and tugged on it with his teeth, sucked on it with his lips.

She tensed, her mouth and hand stilled on him. She pushed her core closer to his mouth, and then let out a cry with spasms rocking her body as an orgasm overtook her.

The vibrations of her sounds on his cock drew his balls tight.

"Megan, I don't want to come in your mouth, and I'm that close.

She took a deep breath, released him and then climbed off. She reached for a condom, ripped the package and sheathed him.

Before he could take his next breath, Megan had straddled him and inched herself down his cock, taking him deeper and deeper until she took him to the hilt and sat flush with him. She leaned down on her forearms and gazed at him. "That was amazing. No one has ever made me come that quickly."

He grinned, happy he was her first for something. "Kiss me and taste yourself," he challenged.

She smiled and leaned down for a deep, slow kiss.

His blood heated.

She lifted her head. "Ready?"

"I was born ready." He held her hips tight and guided them up and down his shaft.

She leaned forward enticing his mouth with her breast.

The little hitch in her breath when his teeth grazed her nipple pushed another jolt of lust spearing through him.

"Find it. Find what you need, Megan."

She adjusted their rhythm, arched her back, and released a sensual moan.

Watching her ride him with a flushed face wearing

a smile that spoke of pleasure nearly cast him over the edge.

He reached down and rubbed his finger over her swollen nub, helping drive her closer to her climb. She'd come again before he would.

She squeezed her nipple with one hand, and he thought he might lose it right there.

Holy fucking shit! Normally a woman taking her own pleasure with him didn't cause such a reaction, but watching Megan touch herself, his cock throbbed harder, his need burned stronger.

Megan's eyes closed, her cheeks flushed, and her head rolled back. His balls decided he'd held on long enough after she clenched around him and cried out as a second orgasm rocked her.

He didn't wish for this to end. Gritting his teeth, he controlled his much-desired release, keeping it at bay.

Before she could move from her position atop him, he sat up; his arms placed behind holding him up, and began making small, circular rotations of his pelvis. Leaning forward, he pressed teasing kisses to her neck.

Megan tightened around him, tormenting him, destroying his ability to hold on any longer. A mixture of a grunt and groan ripped from him as an orgasm burst forth, sending his senses reeling out of control.

So lost in ecstasy, it took him a moment to realize that she'd climbed off and dropped beside him, cuddling in the arm he'd stretched out to his side. He pulled her closer and breathed in her scent. He gave her a quick kiss on the forehead before he went to the bathroom to clean up.

AJ braced his hands on the vanity counter and hung his head. A cold hand held his heart, crushing it in its grasp. That orgasm had shaken him to the core, reaching uncharted territory. He feared he wouldn't get enough of Megan; especially knowing their time together was limited. And nothing could change that.

Chapter Nineteen

Megan woke languid and content and found AJ watching her from the doorway to the bedroom. Leaning against the doorframe, one foot crossed over the other, he held a newspaper and a coffee cup. Pure lust rippled through her.

She sat up in bed, holding the sheet over her breasts to hide her stiffening nipples. Memories of what had happened the night before made them ache for his touch.

She cleared her throat. "Is that newspaper for me?"

He sauntered toward her in tight jeans and a forest-green sweater that uniquely displayed his firm and muscular body.

He handed her the coffee and set the newspaper on the nightstand.

Megan took a quick sip. "Hmm." The day could now begin.

"We have a large snowstorm coming through." He sat on the edge of the bed.

"That will slow down our information from informants if they can't get out on the streets."

"We'll make do. It also keeps them from chasing us. So, you can relax."

Relax? How could she relax when they wouldn't even leave the room? They'd be shut up together possibly for days. She wanted him, but what happened last night couldn't happen every day. Raw panic crept its way into her bloodstream, raising her pulse rate.

"I didn't think about that." The sheet slipped down when she set the coffee back on the nightstand. She grabbed it and picked up the newspaper.

AJ leaned forward and kissed her lightly on the lips and then surged up from the bed. "I'll cook breakfast. How do omelets sound?"

"That sounds great." She observed him as he walked stiffly to the kitchen. That'd been odd. She shrugged. Who knew the minds of men?

She opened the newspaper and flipped through the pages, wishing she had an article in print. Today she'd write the article she'd promised Kristen. She should've been writing it last night instead of snuggling and then making love with AJ.

While AJ cooked, she slipped from the bed and hauled her suitcase into the bathroom. She started the shower and waited for the water to warm. Looking in the mirror, she noticed the whisker burns and a love mark on her neck. She didn't regret a thing.

****

Writing the article of her life on the run made Megan truly grasp the seriousness of the fact that people were trying to kill her. The sick feeling in her stomach worsened with each word she typed. She remembered the terror that had wrapped itself around her body when they'd shot up her home. Then, sorrow at the thought of the police who'd been downed, plus Trent and his partner. Hoping everyone was okay was the best she could do while in hiding.

She had no idea how AJ would react being the major focus of her article. She couldn't ignore how he'd been protecting her, keeping her alive even when it wasn't his responsibility. He could've left her at the restaurant, so she had no choice but to go with his brother and Kate. But he'd allowed her to choose. She hadn't thought to ask him why. One would think he'd prefer to do this on his own.

If she asked, she'd probably get his usual evasiveness for an answer.

He'd drawn the line at several things in her article, and one had been describing him. Even though Magic Shop suspected they were together, she didn't need to confirm it. His physical description would have the ladies falling in love. He was gorgeous... a criminal... and a hero. No woman would pass up the article or the man even though he lived a dangerous life. Heck, that'd make him more appealing to some. Jealousy clawed at her with thoughts of another woman wanting him. *Good grief, he doesn't belong to me.*

She had to admit that she'd become attached to him even though she continued to fight it. It wasn't just the attraction or the way her breath quickened when he neared. When what she now called the "fun AJ" appeared, he was enjoyable to be around. That AJ never stuck around for long though. It seemed that whenever he realized he was having fun, the "brooding AJ" returned as if he wasn't allowed to be happy.

She stretched and leaned back in her chair. After covering a yawn, she turned to him and caught him staring at her. Butterflies fluttered in her stomach. His face may have been impassive, but the desire in his eyes flamed hot.

"I'm done. Would you like to read it?"

"Of course." He gestured for her to move.

She paced, nervous about what he'd think. Those butterflies now bounced off the walls in her stomach waiting for some response from him. She'd poured a lot of herself into this article. Her experiences only continued to escalate in terms of danger. While that made great copy, it wasn't so great for Megan's nerves.

He turned back to her. "You did a great job. Your boss will love it."

She beamed at him. It meant so much to her to have his approval. Her butterflies now had it together and fluttered only for him, for the praise he'd bestowed.

"There's only one problem. You made me out to be some kind of hero."

Then he chose to yank her down from her floating cloud of joy. Her smile vanished. "But you have been my hero. You've done everything to save me. I'd be dead if not for you."

He looked away and cleared his throat. "Megan, I'm no hero. I don't like being characterized as one."

She put her hands on her hips. "Tough. What I wrote is accurate. You may not think you've been my hero, but that article is my viewpoint."

What was wrong with him? He'd been nothing but a hero. Was it the term? Did "brooding AJ" think he didn't deserve such a righteous name? She had to break into that mind of his and learn what made him tick. Most men would be over the moon to be called that.

He leaned forward, elbows on his thighs. "Megan—"

"No." She broke in, waving her arm to stop his words. "The article doesn't break any of your rules. You dictated what I couldn't write, but not what I could write. I'm submitting it as it is."

Dropping his head in his hands, he let out a long, exasperated sigh. "Okay. Submit it."

Yes! "You need to show me how to send it securely."

"I'll do that for you."

She set her hand on his shoulder sending tingling warmth traveling up her arm and spreading throughout her body.

A crooked smile curved his lips. "Okay, let's send in your Pulitzer article."

****

"Kristen, I'm sorry."

"I was disappointed when I didn't receive the article yesterday, but what I just received makes up for it. It's excellent. The readers will love it."

Megan released a relieved breath. Worrying that her boss might not like it had left her sitting on pins and needles waiting for a response. AJ had attempted to help her relax with a card game and a movie. She sat only for a minute or two before she jumped back up to pace, every muscle tense, and every nerve on edge. "Thanks."

"Now, who is this mysterious man you're with? How do you know that you can trust him? In fact, how do you know him?"

Her smile collapsed. She wanted to tell her boss, but she'd promised not to divulge anything specific about him. "I can't tell you, Kristen."

A heavy sigh floated through the phone. "I still think you need to come in and go to the FBI. You're living too dangerously. Let me pick you up and bring you to safety. He can come too."

"Thanks for the offer, but I'm staying with him,

and we're not coming in."

"Why?"

Why was a really good question. She didn't trust law enforcement after the protection fiasco. The FBI hadn't done anything to her. She should trust them. But the more she learned about the Magician, the longer she saw how far his arms reached. "I know he'll keep me alive."

A rustling noise sounded in the background and then another voice came through the phone.

"Megan, it's Victoria. Remember the photos you showed me of people you thought might be important?"

She gripped the phone tighter. Holding her breath, she responded, "Yes." Could it be? Did she find something?

"I saw two of them come around one of the brothels. One was that guy you saw murder someone."

Great. Damian was more active than she'd hoped.

"I also have some names." Victoria's excitement burst through in her voice.

Megan moved the phone to her left ear and grabbed a pen. Her blood pumping fast, she couldn't believe their luck. And now was the right time.

"I kept hearing the Richards brothers' name mentioned, but couldn't find out who they were. Well, they run the two brothels and the streets. I took some photos that I'd like you to look at in case you see someone you know. Where do I send them?"

Dang it all to hell and back! This could help them, but she knew AJ wouldn't allow her to accept another e-mail. She cleared her dry throat. "There's no way to send them to me. I'll have to look at them another time."

"Oh. Well, I'll figure it out. If you find something new, please let me know. It's time for us to finish this."

She couldn't help but smile. "Okay."

"Bye, Megan."

"Keep in touch with me, so I know you're okay," her boss said in closing.

*****

AJ had finally settled Megan into a bath. If that much worry and anxiety went into getting an article printed, he could live without it. It had taken most of the day for her to connect with her boss. He thought he'd have to give her a sedative.

After they'd cooked dinner, they'd talked. Well, she'd talked. He'd grunted and turned conversations around, off him as the subject. The woman could ask questions.

He'd finally convinced her to take a long soak in the tub to relax her tense muscles. And to give him time to think about what to do next.

Sharing information on the drug operation with her tomorrow would help begin the disruption of Magic Shop's business. They'd hit him on all fronts. But they'd start slow.

She'd talked about the woman who worked the prostitution angle. He hadn't decided what to do with that. His knowledge of that area of business was limited.

He wanted to trust her with the prison break information but didn't want to argue over her publishing it or her doing it behind his back. He'd figure it out. He always did.

Dropping the curtain in the main room, he sighed. It'd been a good thing he hadn't planned to move yet.

The snow hadn't stopped all day. According to the news, the salt trucks couldn't move fast enough to keep the roads from freezing before they made another run.

He looked at his watch. He wanted to go to bed, but someone was still absent.

AJ knocked on the bathroom door, calling her name. When Megan didn't answer, fear gripped him and he rushed into the room.

He dropped his head and released a heavy breath. She'd only fallen asleep.

What the hell was he doing keeping her with him? It was about to get very dangerous, and he planned to take her into it. She may not have always acted brave, but she'd followed his instructions. What he'd seen of her on a story, bravery flew out the window for foolishness and stupidity. And he'd have her on a story to help him bring the Magician in the open.

Self-disgust rolled through his stomach. He'd allowed himself to become who he was. Someone as good and bright as Megan shouldn't even associate with him. And she shouldn't be having sex with him.

He should discourage her. Nothing could ever come of the two of them. Yet, inside her, the darkness and guilt disappeared. He felt whole again.

Deciding it best that he sleep on the pullout couch, AJ softly called her name to wake her.

She sighed in her sleep.

"Megan," he called louder.

"Go away, Kevin. It's my turn," she mumbled.

His heart seized. She'd hate him if she ever found out that he'd lied to her. He knew all about what had happened to her brother. Hell, he'd been the enforcer called to take care of Kevin. But he'd been running late and another enforcer had stepped into his job.

Reaching down, he shook her. "Come on, my little dove. It's time to go to bed."

She reached up and wound her arms around his neck but made no move to stand.

Hell. It was hard enough seeing her lying there in the water, now he had to dry her off too. Glancing down at her pile of clothing, his eyes took in the lacy matching blue bra and panties. He really had fucked up his life to be punished so badly.

He lifted her. "Come on. Stand up for me."

After somehow drying her and leading her to the bed, he covered her and looked down as her eyes fluttered closed.

"I'm sorry I didn't wear that lip stuff you like," she whispered.

There was no help for it. He moved to the other side of the bed, took off his clothes, and slid in beside her. He pulled her snug against him, against his painful erection. And there was definitely no hope for it. She was his, for as long as he could have her.

Chapter Twenty

The winds howled, and the snow blew in all directions. The quiet, cozy hotel room provided AJ and Megan with a short reprieve from reality. Looking out the window, he took note of every vehicle that departed and arrived during the night. He didn't see them, but he knew his brother and sister-in-law took turns watching the hotel, providing them with an extra level of security.

That had been the only reason he'd allowed himself and Megan the sexual diversion. He wouldn't put her life at risk just to get some. Even if that some came from her.

He needed to be out there. On the streets. Not holed up here with a woman who had a girl-next-door look during the day but was a tigress at night. The perfect combination in his book.

The air crackled the moment she stepped into the room. That damn euphoric scented perfume drifted his way, and he felt himself stir. Fuck. Normally he would've tired of a woman already. This had to be the shittiest time in his life to be attracted to a good woman, one he could see a life with.

More weight added itself to his already heavy heart.

"I really like this hair color. It's fun."

He didn't turn. "It looks good on you. But so did

your natural color." Hell, with her, blonde or auburn worked for him. He imagined anything would work on her.

"Is it okay to use the laundry room? Everything I have is dirty. I'm already out of a few personal items."

The thought of her with no underwear shot more desire into his already aching groin. "As long as I'm with you." A snapshot of taking her on top of the washing machine flashed in his mind. He dropped his head and rubbed his forehead. They had to leave soon.

"Okay. Where's the newspaper?"

He turned and pointed to the desk, waiting to see her face. Her joy when she saw her article on the front page brought short bursts of lightness to his world.

The public loved her. Her story would excite them and then have them fearing for her life.

Reading the article, she absently picked up the cup he'd placed before her and took a drink, her eyes never leaving the newspaper.

He chuckled.

"I can't believe it. Front page again, above the fold." She turned that bright smile his way. Something shifted inside him. If only things could have been different. If only.

"You're big news, Megan. Of course, they'd put your message on the front page. They love you and are happy you're alive."

She frowned. "I don't know what I'll do next. My sources haven't found anything new."

"How about some breakfast? Scrambled eggs and bacon?"

"You don't have to cook. I can do it."

He removed the items from the refrigerator and set

them on the counter. "You cook lunch and dinner. It's the least I can do."

He didn't understand why he hadn't told her that he could help with her next article. He couldn't wrap his mind around why he worried what Magic Shop would do to her if she wrote any more. They were already trying to kill her. And with her tenacity, keeping her alive would be harder than he ever imagined.

Setting plates of their cooked food on the table, he called out, "Breakfast is ready."

She sauntered to the table and they sat. "Mm, this looks good. Thank you," she said.

He cleared his throat. "It's time for me to help you with Magic Shop."

Megan gasped and looked at him. "Really?"

AJ stopped, his fork midway to his mouth. "Yeah. Really."

"Oh my God! You probably know so much." She almost bounced out of the chair with excitement.

Making her happy drove a rush of warmth unlike any he'd ever known through his veins creating a lightheadedness that relaxed his muscles, beginning with his head and sliding down to his toes. This woman caused more emotions in him then he thought possible.

"I can't wait to hear what information you have." She pushed her plate away. "Do you know the bosses?" She started to rise from the table.

"Sit and eat," he commanded. "We'll talk when we're finished."

She pulled her plate back to her and pushed her eggs around.

He held back a smile. Patience was not one of her virtues.

"What made you change your mind?"

He swallowed and thought for a moment about how to explain it to her without her overzealousness taking flight. "It's time to begin disrupting his business."

"You know the police won't do anything about them."

"You of all people should know the power of the press. With enough coverage and pressure, they'll have to do something. They won't take the Magician down. But that's okay." He paused. "We will."

"Yes, we will." She nodded.

He pushed the lump blocking his throat down. He had to try. "Megan, I'm not sure the payment for doing this is worth avenging your brother. If you're on the street, there's a chance they'll kill you. Being dead won't help you find your brother's killer. I can do this alone. I can still take you to my brother's home where it's safe."

"Are you kidding me? I may have started this for my brother, but I'm doing this for me now. They tried to kill me, AJ! They are still trying to kill me. There's no way I'm walking away. If you don't want me with you, then let me know now."

Oh, he wanted her with him. He studied her. He had to take her with him to keep her safe. She'd never make it on her own. She'd already proven that when she hadn't listened to him about reporting what she'd witnessed to the police. "Okay then. Let's get started."

After clearing the table, Megan spread her photos and notes.

"Tell me what you know," he urged.

"I spent most of the last month getting information

from my sources. They're not part of Magic Shop, so information was limited. They gave me names and helped me understand how things on the drug side were run. I thought I could expose the head of the organization straight away. I just can't fathom that no one knows who he is. I wonder if even his bosses know who he is."

She glanced at him as if gauging his reaction. "Anyway, it wasn't until recently that I realized I had to start one layer at a time, beginning with the street dealers while Victoria tackled the prostitution side. We've yet to find an overlap."

The thought of her in that neighborhood, especially at night, without protection, shot a ball of anger surging forward. "Do you know how dangerous that was? Walking around was one thing, but they wouldn't have hesitated to kill you had they caught you taking pictures."

Megan huffed. "I can take a photo without someone knowing it. No one bothered me."

"That's because they were told to avoid you. They wanted to stay out of the newspaper. It's the same with the other reporter, except she's not running around snapping pictures and printing articles. She's just being nosy."

"Humph. Well, I know they layer things. I received a tip from a source and found Keyshawn dealing in the open. By the way, he's not very happy with me. He called me with a death threat."

AJ's back snapped straight. "What do you mean death threat? Why didn't you tell me about it?"

"I did tell you when you came to my house that I'd already been threatened. I just never said whom it was from. And it could've been the councilman's office. It doesn't matter now since we're on the run for our lives anyway."

Valid point. What the hell kind of profession did she have? Did all reporters live with death threats?

"I'm sorry. I didn't pay attention. My mind had been diverted to other things." He flashed a half smile and a wink.

Pink crept up her neck to her cheeks. So damn adorable.

Shifting in the chair, she took a minute before responding. "Well, good riddance to him. I know his boss is Jimmy, but I haven't been able to locate him. I thought following the dealer might lead me to him, but then you got to Keyshawn and, well, you know."

He'd stood there while Hank delivered Magic Shop punishment. Things began sliding downhill for her from there. His visit, her observing a murder, his kidnapping her, her being shot at. She couldn't say she hadn't had a few interesting days.

Megan frowned. "My sources couldn't help me find Jimmy."

"Unless they're a dealer, they probably wouldn't know where to find him. He's good at keeping a low profile." He cleared his throat. "Jimmy is an escaped convict. His real name is Hugh Brown. He paid to be broken out of a New Mexico prison a few years ago."

Her hand covered her mouth on a gasp. "What? An escaped convict. Why hasn't anyone arrested him?"

It always sounded so easy. Just arrest him. Little did she know.

"After the initial prison break, the convict's photo is plastered on the news, but the story eventually fades, and people forget. Plus, Jimmy is far away from home and under the Magician's protection so even if anyone suspected he was Hugh, they wouldn't open their mouths about it."

"How do you know all of this?"

He shrugged off the importance of how he'd acquired his information.

"This would bring him off the street and get him arrested. We should call the FBI or the U.S. Marshals and let them know that he's here."

"That's the plan. We need him for the plan so that means you can't print this story, yet. Otherwise, we'll never find him when we need him. We're not ready for him to get picked up."

"What is the plan?"

"Later." He hated to flatten the hope floating in her eyes, but it had to be done.

"Dang it, AJ! You said you'd share with me."

Angry yet not cursing made her the most precious woman in his eyes. "I am. Just not the plan yet. We'll go through that soon enough."

Wheels turned, but he couldn't figure out where her thoughts were headed. Too many expressions flashed across her face.

Surprising him, she nodded. "May I at least expose him as part of the drug ring? I won't use his photo."

He sighed. He knew she'd have a tough time handling this. "Not yet. He could go underground. I want him arrested when the right time comes. Now, what else do you know?"

She narrowed her eyes at him before she turned back to the table. "At first I thought the Magician might be a policeman, but now I'm not sure."

AJ raised an eyebrow. "What makes you say that?"

"Well, why stay in a dangerous job if you're wealthy and powerful?"

"The rush? The power? Remember firemen who become arsonists? There are many reasons he might stay."

"Yeah. Well, I think he's a businessman."

"Interesting. What else do you know?"

"That's about it. I told you I hadn't been working it long."

He held his hands up. "That's okay."

"I have these photos." She gestured to the ones scattered on the table.

"You have many dealers here." He picked up a photo and whistled. "You did well, Megan. This is a top man. Carl Smith runs the entire drug ring. He's an escaped convict also. His real name is George Savage, escaped from Nevada. The crime boss has a soft spot for escaped convicts."

"Is that a photo of him?" She attempted to snatch the photo from him.

"He's right here with Jimmy." AJ set the photo on the table and turned it to face her. It was the same photo he'd seen earlier with three bosses. He pointed out Carl.

She bit her bottom lip.

That made him want to take it in his mouth and…. He cleared his throat to halt his wayward thoughts.

"Do you know who the third man is?"

He shrugged. "I have a hunch." Of course he knew, but he refused to tell her at this point. Paul White was the boss of the prison break team. If AJ told her, she'd connect the dots.

"How will we find out who he is?" She picked up

the photo and studied it intently. "This is one of the pictures my contacts haven't seen. They might be able to help. Oh, do you think he's the one who runs prostitution? I showed it to Victoria, but she hadn't seen any of them. She took copies to her sources though. Just in case."

Shit. This Victoria had best watch her back if she showed that photo around. "First, you need to tell your friend to keep that photo secret. If she shows it around, she'll be in the same situation as you are."

Megan's eyes widened, and she nodded.

"I think my informants should see the photos first." Only a handful of people knew Paul and his standing in the organization. They weren't people on the street, but one of her damned sources already knew too much. Who was to say he might by chance know about this boss? No. He couldn't know about the prison escapes, or he'd have already informed Megan.

"But we have to see them in order to show these to them."

"Remember I said at some point we would hit the street. That time is almost here."

Her eyes glittered with apprehension. It speared his busted heart.

"Do you think we can do it and stay alive?"

God, he sure hoped so. "I'll keep you safe."

Safe or not, he had to get on the streets if he wanted to end this and bust up the next prison break. It was an important part of his plan. He needed the Magician angry with all his advisors at once, and AJ only had one shot at getting to Paul.

Based on what he'd learned, the organization's boss handled problems with his advisors face-to-face.

Damian thought he'd been impressing AJ by telling him that he knew the boss and various little things that had been stored away. If they could fuck things up enough, the Magician would call several meetings or one large one with his advisors. According to the chief enforcer, that was the only time they saw their boss. Didn't matter. AJ would be there whether it was one or many meetings.

"So, basically I have no story. We have to keep our information quiet in order to bring them to justice later. This sucks." She crossed her arms across her chest.

He smiled. Was that a pout? No, but it got his blood running faster.

"You do have something. You have two enforcers with a dealer in action. Get the enforcers' names and photos out, and we cripple them. It'll take away some of the heat off our backs." He grinned. "They are a little understaffed right now."

She straightened. "Oh. Are they the ones after us? What about others?"

"Yeah, they're the ones after us. There are rules for Magic Shop, and one is that Damian and his group take care of problems. Anyone taking it upon themselves is dealt with harshly."

AJ picked up another photo and handed it to her.

Looking at the photo, she smiled proudly. "I have them in several photos. They just hung out a lot, so I disregarded them."

"I have an informant who observed them as the last people seen with Carlos Martinez, the dealer who disappeared two weeks ago. They were also the last people seen with Treyvon Stewart, who disappeared last week." AJ shrugged. "Disappearances happen all the time for one reason or another. One may have nothing to do with the other, but you can have people start to question things while doing us a favor."

She beamed at him. Good. He'd provided her with enough to hold her over until it became time to tear those assholes apart.

"You have other dealers in there you can expose. The more you break these little things the next couple of days, the better." He shifted through the photos and pointed at several people providing her with their names.

"What about for Victoria? Would any of these help her?"

He shook his head. "No. We'll need her for everything to work, but I don't want you sharing anything with her except what she needs for her story."

"But we'll need to bring our stories together."

AJ stood, pulled the phone from his pocket and handed it to her. "And you will. When the time comes. You can use the burner phone to confirm anything with your sources. You'll have to trust me on what my sources know. Let them have the new number and return it to me when you're done."

She absentmindedly nodded, already dialing. He'd lose her for most of the day now.

****

"Are you sure you want to take her down there?"

"I don't have much choice. If I'm going to do this, I have to get out there. I can't leave her alone either." AJ had been reviewing his plan with Jesse, soliciting his feedback. He hid in the bathroom so Megan wouldn't overhear him.

"I think it's risky, very risky. I'm not sure I'd do it,

even with Kate. Listen, baby brother, things don't look good. I've used every FBI contact I can, and the answer is still the same. Turn her over to the FBI or become wanted for kidnapping a material witness in a major murder investigation. If you can get here, I can buy time until we solve this. I'd hate to see you as a fugitive."

He pushed the shower curtain aside and sat on the side of the bathtub. "Jesse, you know as well as I do there are dirty agents in the FBI. Besides, she won't go. And don't think for a moment she'd sit still if you had her. I'd wager I'd see her on the street within a day."

Jesse chuckled. "Oh ye of little faith. Seriously, must you do this right now? Can't you wait until the team is here? We'll help you."

"Would you wait if the fucker tried to have you or Kate killed?"

Silence reached him from the other end of the line.

"That's what I thought."

"Okay. Since you've made up your mind, make sure to keep her safe. She's innocent in all this."

AJ didn't need to be reminded of that. It stood in the forefront of his mind. "I will."

"It's your game, AJ, but don't forget I'm here when you need me. Todd let me know he's available to help protect you until the boys come home. I know you trust him. Do you want him to help?"

He wiped his hand over his face. "Now that I'll be a wanted man, I'd rather my friends not get involved. No one needs to go to jail helping me."

Jesse cleared his throat. "AJ, I don't like this, but I understand why you think you must do it. I still encourage you to wait. I love you."

A large lump formed in his throat. He hadn't heard his brother say that in years. Sure he knew Jesse loved him, but to hear him actually say it made things too final. No, he would do this. When his brothers returned, he'd work with them. But he wouldn't wait and let that fucker squirm out of this. "Thanks for understanding." He couldn't bring himself to say he loved them. What a pussy!

"You'll have whatever you need when you need it. Dev's found an account. It's only one, but you know Dev, it won't take long to find the rest and tie them back."

AJ smiled. "I'd best go. She'll be finished writing soon."

"Don't let her interfere and distract you. It could mean both of your deaths. Oh, and no cherries and whipped cream."

AJ laughed. "I can't promise that."

His brother wouldn't let him forget the night Jesse had walked in on him and Stephanie. He'd just opened the jar of cherries to top his whipped cream coated dessert sitting on his table when his brother walked into the house. AJ had lost track of time. For Christmas the past two years, his brothers supplied him with cherries, whipped cream, and a watch with an alarm.

At least Jesse didn't lecture him about getting involved with Megan while protecting her. Jesse could no longer push that rule since he'd broken it with his new wife, Kate.

AJ sighed. Again, things were different with Megan.

She glided toward him as he exited the bathroom. "I'm finished. Did you want to read it before I send it?"

Her excitement tugged at his heartstrings. His little dove.

"I'd love to read it." Grinning, he smacked her on the ass and strode to the desk.

"Hey." Megan rubbed a hand over her butt cheek, but a smile grew on her face.

She immediately drew the reader into her story and the desire to continue didn't stop with that great opening paragraph. Pride streamed around his heart at her talent.

With Alex and Trey exposed, they'd be out of the picture for a little while. Hopefully long enough to keep them off the streets while he and Megan were there. And she hadn't mentioned Jimmy. That had to be killing her.

"It's another good article." AJ stood.

"It's not a front-page story, but I'm happy with it."

"It should get good placement. Which photo are you sending?"

She picked up the photo he'd suggested. "This one."

"Good. That'll also take another dealer off the streets. A few more and Jimmy will have to step up. He won't be hard to find then."

"This is going to work out. Let me send this so we can do laundry."

****

Megan stepped out of the bathroom wearing flannel pajamas.

"What the hell are you wearing?"

She glanced down at her clothing, and then back to his lust-filled eyes. "Pj's."

"Well get those things off and get over here." He

flipped the covers on the bed to the side, exposing his naked body.

She tilted her head and raised her eyebrows. Fun AJ had stayed around. Time to play. "But I thought after what we did in the shower earlier, you'd be done for the night," she cooed.

Him taking her from behind in the shower while she'd leaned against the wall, water spraying over her, may have been quick, but it had been explosive. How could he be ready for another round already?

A growl reached her ears. "Don't make me come get you."

"Just give me a moment, I'll be there." Displaying what she hoped was a sultry, seductive look, she reached for the bottom button of her shirt, and ever so slowly unbuttoned it. She made a show out of slowly licking her lips. She reached for the next button on her top.

Before she could unbutton it, he stood before her.

She giggled. Actually giggled. "What's the problem?"

That turn-her-to-putty grin spread across his face. "Enough." He ripped her shirt open, buttons dropping on the carpeted floor. "I hope it wasn't a favorite."

Her lips parted in surprise, her sharp intake of breath bouncing around the bedroom walls, setting her pulse rate into overdrive. AJ kept things interesting and fun, in and out of bed.

She threw her arms around his neck and pulled herself close. "And what if it was? Will you buy me another?"

His lips hovered over hers, his words whispered on her lips, "The hotel room has a sewing kit."

Before she could laugh, his lips crashed down on hers, frantic and hungry. She opened to him, and their tongues fought for control. Their battle sent pleasure skipping across the nerves throughout her body, centering between her thighs, throbbing and wet.

"You still have too many clothes on."

Within moments he'd stripped her.

Dropping to his knees, his hands slid over the curve of her bottom, his lips kissing her stomach, leaving a trail of goosebumps in their wake.

Threading her fingers through his hair, she opened her legs for him, her head falling back against the wall.

The torturous strokes of his hot, velvety tongue between her thighs pulled a soft cry of his name from her lips when she came. The room disappeared around her, leaving weightlessness and bliss in its wake. Her legs weakened, and she'd have fallen if AJ hadn't picked her up and carried her to the bed.

Still reveling in her climax, she hadn't noticed him leave her for protection. She didn't protest as he slid her to the edge of the bed, put a pillow beneath her backside, and pulled her legs up to his chest, her feet resting on his shoulders. She purred deep in her throat, anticipation pulsing through her.

He guided himself against her throbbing heat and eased inside her. His deep reach set another cresting wave of excitement racing through her body.

Each stroke, each kiss he placed on her ankles and calves, reached all the way to her soul, breaking into the fence she'd built around her heart.

"You're so fucking beautiful," he said between his erratic breaths.

She slid her hands over a shimmer of sweat on her

flushed skin, stopping to caress her breasts, her thumbs blindly circling the sensitive little buds before she pinched them between her fingers.

His strangled groan told her she'd achieved the desired result. His eyes locked on her hands.

"Ready for Sexy Scissors?" he asked with raised eyebrows.

This man knew more positions than she'd thought possible. She smiled as he promised to buy her a Kama Sutra book. That set up hope they'd continue to try positions after this was over.

He slowly crossed her legs in front of him, and she involuntarily squeezed around him, so tight his groan sounded painful. Closing her thighs sent erotic pleasure drifting through her.

AJ uncrossed her legs and opened them wide, shoving in deeper. He generated delicious pleasure with the changes in each movement. Her hips moved of their own volition to take every inch until she felt his sac resting against her.

He kept the movements steady, teasing her, leaving her ready for climax before he moved again. Suddenly he tossed her legs back on his shoulders and thrust faster, reaching between her thighs to rub her nub.

She moaned, arched her back as ripples of red-hot bliss cascaded through her body, leaving her relaxed, limp and sated.

He thrust deep and threw his head back, his body jerking with his own release. He pulled out from her and collapsed on the bed beside her. A few seconds later, he stood and walked into the bathroom.

AJ returned with a cloth and slowly, sensually wiped her. "You are the most incredible woman, Megan

Rogers." He kissed her in a slow, languid kiss.

She closed her eyes against the realization that in the middle of searching for the Magician and running for her life, she was falling in love with a man who was wholly unsuitable for her.

Chapter Twenty-One

Megan woke with a wide smile, a sweet feeling of contentment curling inside, knowing AJ would have the newspaper and coffee waiting for her. She could start every morning like this for the rest of her life. She hadn't fallen in love with him yet, but with the way her heart fluttered when he was near, it wouldn't be much longer before those three words came to her. The same three words that had caused her hurt in the past.

Could she risk it and trust him? In the last week, she'd come to know him, his likes and dislikes, his attitude in politics, life in general, and stories of his childhood. However, learning why he'd become a man who worked for a crime lord had been impossible.

The man she'd come to know had become someone to have fun with, spend hours talking with, and build a life with. Her heart warmed at how much he'd relaxed around her. He would remain faithful. If his behavior recently were any indicator, he'd be a good husband and father, showering them with his love and attention.

A heavy sigh escaped her. But he wasn't always that man. The dark side of him returned whenever they discussed Magic Shop, or whenever she asked the wrong question about him, such as why he didn't join his brothers.

Something had its nasty claws digging into his

soul, dragging him deeper into a despair he wouldn't fight. That man would laugh at monogamy.

Megan came no closer to her answer on trusting him. Before she could open her heart fully, she had to know the true man, the real AJ. Would he always be different people, or could she help him remain as he was?

She reached her arms over her head, enjoying the slow stretch of her muscles and then reality crashed in. No matter the explosive attraction between them, they lived in different worlds. Worlds in the same city, but those worlds were too far apart to cross. Even for love.

A vise-grip clutched her heart. Would the police find out AJ was a murderer? Heck, he planned to kill Damian and, as far as she knew, would also kill the Magician. She didn't want him in prison. She wanted him by her side.

Impossible.

They had more time together. She wouldn't ruin it with the craziness in her head. She wanted to continue to enjoy it while she had it. She could live off the memories for a long time after they saw the last of each other.

She grinned. AJ liked her in his shirt and nothing else. She'd greet him in one when he exited the bathroom. Maybe she could convince him to spend the day in bed and deal with the rest of the world tomorrow.

Enticement first. She hopped from the bed and unzipped his bag.

Before she reached into it, the secure cell phone at their bedside rang. She hesitated and looked toward the bathroom, doubtful he'd heard it in the shower. He'd told her this phone was their lifeline, and after their last experience when called unexpectedly, she knew it had to be answered, and quickly.

Her fingers shook. What could it be? Had they been found again? With deep foreboding, she hesitantly said, "Hello."

Silence greeted her.

Odd and unnerving. She moved to disconnect the call when a man cleared his throat on the other end of the line. "Ms. Rogers, this is FBI Deputy Director Arthur Hall."

Her heart stopped. Why would the FBI call AJ on his secure phone?

If that man thought he could have his fun with me and then drop me off with this Arthur man while he hunted the Magician, he had another thing coming. A shift kick between his legs would be a good start.

"Ms. Rogers, I don't agree with AJ on this assignment. This isn't how we keep witnesses safe."

The only thing she heard was assignment. What did he mean? Her blood pumped fast. What was happening? She swallowed the lump in her throat. Thankfully it pushed the bile rising back down. "Is…?" She drew in a slow breath. "Is AJ working for you?" Her voice quivered.

Another long pause. Did this man ever just speak or did he have to take the time to put together every single word? She wanted the answer now!

"I think you'd best talk to him about that. I'd like to send someone to pick you up and place you into protective custody. Where are you staying?"

AJ working with the FBI? But he'd left the bureau. Why would he be talking with them now? Why would they have a criminal working for them?

Questions flew through her mind. Was he undercover? Could it be? Who was he really? She wasn't sure she wanted to know, but she had to find out. The possible answers cleaved her heart in two. If he was an agent, then they had a chance at a relationship, but if he was, he'd lied to her all this time.

"No. I won't go with you. I'll let AJ know you called when he gets out of the shower." What the hell did she just say? Stay with him now? Unless he spoke with this man to turn her over, he'd lied. How could she still trust him?

"Ms. Rogers, please reconsider FBI protective custody."

"Goodbye, Mr. Hall." She ended the call, frozen to the spot.

Her blood heated and rushed through her veins at lightning speed. Anger raged within her.

How could he?

****

AJ strode into the bedroom with a towel wrapped around his midsection. His gaze landed on Megan, standing beside the bed, absolutely nude. His heart did a little flip and his dick stirred.

Smiling, he walked toward her. "Good morning, my little dove." He brushed his lips lightly over hers. "We have another snowstorm coming in today, but it's not expected to be as bad and should pass quickly."

He knew how he wanted to pass the time and in their current state of undress, it wouldn't be hard to manage.

"FBI Deputy Director Hall called for you."

The smile melted from his lips. A knot of dread

materialized in his stomach.

Fuck! Fuck! Fuck!

"Megan."

Her angry glare had the knot tightened enough even a sailor couldn't unravel it.

"You son of a bitch! Look, you've set me to cursing. Did you think that pretending to be the bad boy would give you an advantage? Did you want me that badly? I gave you everything, and you've been lying to me. Who are you really?"

He hadn't wanted her to find out this way. Find out from someone else. He'd planned to tell her at some point but much later.

He stepped back. In an anguished voice, he responded, "I'm FBI Special Agent AJ Hamilton. I've been working undercover in Magic Shop for the past few months."

She crossed her arms over her chest. "Why did you need your cover with me? Why would you lie to me?" She poked her chest.

The heat emanating from her eyes had turned to pain, knifing through his heart with precision.

"Megan, I didn't want to lie to you, but I had to. I couldn't afford for you to accidentally let it slip. We're already risking your communicating with your boss. Could you imagine what would happen if she heard that? We finally have a chance to stop this criminal organization once and for all."

"So you don't trust me after all. Is that what you mean?"

He hesitated. What could he say? He hadn't trusted her to keep the truth quiet, not purposefully anyway.

She hurled the phone at him, grabbed her bag and

stormed into the bathroom.

Why did he fuck up every good thing in his life?

He ran a hand through his damp hair and dropped on the bed. Things had been good between them. He had to tell her everything. It was the only way. He couldn't afford for her to leave him and rush out on her own. She wouldn't survive. And he cared too much for her to let her run to her death.

Guilt and regret tugged at his heart as he prepared to face the inevitable.

Great fucking timing, Arthur.

****

Megan leaned over the sink in the bathroom with her chest aching as she gasped for air. Fiery anger barreled through her. She dropped her head.

This can't be happening.

Had everything been an act? Was she falling for someone who didn't exist? Someone who only took advantage of their situation? Someone who adjusted his acting to be the person who kept her in line? Kept her from searching out Magic Shop's bosses by herself to prevent her from taking away his arrest?

She wiped away the single tear that escaped and trickled down her cheek.

This should be pleasant news. He wasn't a criminal. They could be together after this. They could try a relationship and see where it led.

No. She couldn't live a life with someone who would deceive her. She'd never trust him. But she cared for the man she was on the run with, the man who had protected her, made her laugh, and shown her great pleasure. She wanted that man and hoped it was the true AJ.

What would she do if she'd been spending time with a good actor? How different would he be? Would she continue to share his bed?

She had to face him. He had a great deal of explaining to do.

Needing to give him a chance, she dressed, willed her body to calm, and left the bathroom.

****

Megan walked straight to the table and sat where AJ had placed a plate with an omelet for her. She didn't look at him or speak. With the intensity she held her fork and cut through her omelet, he'd say she was still angry. He deserved that and more.

He sat but didn't touch his fork. "Megan, I'm sorry I didn't tell you." He didn't know what else to say. He didn't think anything he said could make this right.

She glared at him, her eyes smoldering with fury. "Why didn't you tell me?"

The anger in her voice told him he had a lot of groveling to do. He needed her forgiveness, and he wanted to be on her good side. They had little time left together, and he wanted to enjoy every moment of it.

Arthur had ripped into him about keeping her from the FBI. AJ didn't want to hear the man once he found out AJ had been sleeping with her. That crossed a major line he'd be disciplined for. But it had been worth it.

Something about her held him captive. He couldn't pinpoint it, but he'd never wanted to love and protect a woman more than he did Megan. Her love for life was contagious. Even the determination to find her brother's killer hadn't taken that light from her eyes.

Now he'd ruined it all. So goes the fucked up life of AJ Hamilton.

She closed her eyes. "Are you different from the man I've been sleeping with?"

"I'm the same man you've been holed up with here. I'm not the man you met the first time. That's who I was on the street, undercover."

"Was I part of your cover?"

Pain radiated from her. God, he was such a bastard. "No. I wanted you. Still want you. That had nothing to do with any of this."

"Then you should have shared!"

"No way. I have a responsibility to protect this mission. Lives depend on it remaining secret."

"Have you really killed people as an enforcer?"

This is where he could get into real trouble with Arthur, worse than bedding her, but he had to explain it to her. He wanted her to know the truth. "No."

"How is that possible? You worked for him for months. He would've asked you to get rid of people."

He sighed. "Megan, I can't talk to you unless we're off the record. Everything we talk about, including my identity, can't be shared." Her jaw tightened, so he quickly added, "At least for now. Later I'll ensure you have an exclusive. I promise."

"How is it possible you didn't kill people for that vile man?"

"Are we off the record?"

Her short, tight nod spoke volumes of her reluctance to agree.

"The people I supposedly killed are in Wit Sec and will be testifying against Magic Shop. I made Damian think I was the best hitman he had, so they sent more people to me than anyone else. I was grateful to save lives, even criminal ones."

Once someone learned a hit had been placed on him or her, they quickly offered to testify against the organization.

"Why didn't you stop the rest of the murders?"

She meant Kevin. "I didn't know about them. The order went from the top to Damian to the enforcer. No one else was privy to the information. Believe me, I tried to find out and take over."

They hadn't been able to wiretap Damian's phone. Not being able to listen to his calls was the one thing that had disturbed AJ. That was why his ability to jump into the enforcer role had been the best thing that happened to the task force. They'd needed someone to get close to the chief enforcer so they could keep an eye on him, in case any of them were ousted.

Hesitantly she asked, "Is my brother in witness protection?"

"No. He's not," he said in a regretful tone.

Her eyes misted.

"I'm sorry, Megan." Her sadness broke something in his heart. He wished he could provide her with an answer that would please her. An answer that would take away her heartache.

Her eyes dried and slowly filled with torment. Putting her emotions aside to learn everything from him took strength.

"It's okay. It had given me a brief flicker of hope."

He itched to pull her onto his lap, hold her and soothe her. He was smart enough to know that now wouldn't be the right time. His time in the doghouse was far from over.

"How is it that you're so close to catching him when I've heard the FBI and DEA have been trying to bring him down for years?"

He had to hand it to her. She knew the right questions to ask. "We're still off the record, right?"

She nodded.

"There is a task force that has been in place for years. When the enforcer role opened, it was too good for the FBI to pass up, but no one already undercover could gain the spot. That's when I was pulled into the group and into that role. I'd been in that area undercover before as the ruthless AJ Sands so it stood to reason I could slip in the easiest.

"The team is ready to bust all of his advisors except one. The Magician is into more than drugs and prostitution." He hesitated. "Megan, he also breaks convicts out of prison and gives them new lives where no one can find them. That's why I'm involved. No one has been able to get close enough to that team or gain the information to locate the escapees."

She gasped. "I knew there was a relationship between all the prison breaks."

Of course she did. The woman was damn good at her job. "It took the FBI years to link the breakouts to Magic Shop. I'm here to help pull the last piece together to help find out who the Magician is."

She tapped her finger on her chin. "So, he sells drugs and women plus breaks convicts out of prison. I think he's into extortion too, but neither Victoria nor I have been able to prove it."

"I can prove extortion. Add to your list money laundering. Just go with plain ole racketeering."

Megan frowned. "So let me get this straight. You have everything on his top men, evidence and witnesses, and I can't do a story on this."

Self-disgust weaved its way up his spine. He'd dangled the story of her life in front of her, only to disappoint her by forcing her to put it on a shelf out of reach. "I'm sorry. A leak will drive him away. If we don't take him down when we take his top men, he'll just start all over somewhere else because it's doubtful they will turn on him. And most importantly, there will still be a hit on you."

He wanted the crime boss for that reason more than anything else. She couldn't live in fear for the rest of her life. She deserved to live a normal life, marry, and have kids. A burning sensation throbbed in his stomach and sweat covered his palms. Why did that thought create a pain in his heart? He'd never had a problem loving them and leaving them before. Sex was his escape mechanism. Escape from the pain he'd caused his family.

Besides, the two of them could never be. Their futures were slated in different directions.

Megan pushed her breakfast plate away from her and leaned forward on crossed arms. "What can I do to help you bring him down?"

"We need to go through the plan. The task force has agreed this is the best way to finally draw him out. To finally identify him. You'll be a big part of that plan, and it's almost time to put it into action. To get our final piece, I need to get back on the street. Which means we'll be at risk. The FBI has wiretaps on all of the Magician's advisors except Damian. He keeps changing burner phones, so we don't have one on him. But we haven't stopped trying."

"Who are all of those men?" She pulled out her notepad and pen.

"You know who Carl and Damian are. Aaron runs the prostitution and the whorehouses." AJ glanced at her, and then continued, "Paul is the head of the prison escape group, and Lawrence is in charge of money laundering."

A frown chased her features. "How are you planning to bring them down?"

This part shouldn't be shared, but he'd already broken every other rule. "I mentioned a task force earlier. It's FBI, DEA, and the U.S. Marshals Service. We weren't sure how deep the Magician's pockets were and didn't want to risk leaks that would get anyone killed, so only the Director and Deputy Director of each group are privy to the mission. Arthur decided to out me to my new partner, Todd, when Magic Shop tried to kill me.

"The team is waiting for me. I've heard a new prison escape is due soon, and I know where to get the information on the escapees, but it's not that simple."

AJ rubbed the back of his neck. "I did participate in a prison break but, unfortunately, I had no idea what the mission was until I stepped on the plane and met the gang. It allowed me to identify the members of the team. However, I didn't have enough time or privacy to coordinate an arrest. Plus, I'm not letting the Magician get away. He's the mastermind behind all this and needs to be behind bars if not six feet under."

She gasped and covered her mouth with her hand, her eyes widened. "You broke someone out of prison?"

"Well, yeah," he answered nonchalantly. He held up his hands palms out. "We had someone watching him. When given the signal, he was to be arrested. Unfortunately, something happened, and the rookie jumped the gun. Hank and I were blamed for Denzel's capture."

She drew her brows in, squinting. "So that's why they tried to kill you?"

"Yes. They thought we had something to do with it. Damian was right, but he killed the wrong man." He couldn't feel bad about Hank's death. Hank was lethal and enjoyed hurting people. If it weren't for AJ stepping in, he would have beaten several people to death.

"It's a good thing you wore a bulletproof vest."

AJ laughed. "No vest is bulletproof. Believe me. Mine has the hole to prove it. They help stop the bullet to keep it from hitting you. It does the job. Most of the time. Devon added one for you in our toy bag. It's one of Kate's so it should fit fairly well. And you're going to wear it on the street."

"You said this was secret, but didn't the other FBI agents notice you were missing at work?"

The way her mind cycled through this amazed him. She didn't miss a thing. "I staged a big blowout and handed in my resignation."

"Hmm." She tapped her chin with her index finger. "What's next?"

"We'll move close to Magic Shop's turf. We have to find out what we can. I need that info on the prison break. If we miss this one, who knows how long it will be until another one? He's never conducted this many so close together before. We can't count on that luck again."

"Do you think it's okay for us to be that close to them?"

"Not really. We shouldn't be there. You shouldn't

be there. We'll have to be extremely cautious and stay vigilant. Even though Kate and Jesse are watching our back, our business will be accomplished swiftly, so we're on the streets as little as possible."

Megan nodded. "I can get my sources and Victoria to meet me where it's safe."

AJ took a moment to decide. "We'll use her for information, but no one knows about the prison breaks, and she doesn't know I'm undercover."

"We can trust her."

"No."

She huffed and snapped her arms across her chest. "Fine."

"Good." He searched her eyes for a moment. "Megan, maybe you should go with my brother. He'll keep you safe. We'll be facing danger on the streets. Danger that could get us killed."

She narrowed her eyes. "AJ Sands! I mean Hamilton! Quit trying to get rid of me. I know what we face, and I want to face it with you."

He stared at her. He'd made his choice long ago even though he kept telling himself it might be the wrong one. But then again, neither could keep her completely safe. "Okay."

"When are we moving?"

"Tomorrow."

That meant they had one night before all hell broke loose.

****

Megan exited the bathroom dressed in flannel pajamas covered with flamingos. Not a good sign. Still, AJ stood in the living room, his arms crossed over his chest, watching her. Did she want him in her bed?

They'd had a good time together the rest of the afternoon.

She hadn't forgiven him, but she hadn't closed him out.

He held his breath as she stopped, slowly turned and looked at him. She smiled. He dropped his arms and walked toward her, never breaking eye contact. He engulfed her in his arms and lightly touched his lips to hers.

She moved her arms around his neck and leaned into him. He groaned, and his heart expanded.

He pulled her tight, whispered her name softly in her ear before his tongue brushed it.

They made love slowly and passionately. When AJ entered her, he knew he was finally where he belonged.

Chapter Twenty-Two

"I have to leave you alone, AJ. Kate is on her way to the hospital with Jason," Jesse said. "Stay alert and stay put until one of us is able to return."

AJ stood at the chilled window. The sun's direct glare turned the powdery, soft carpet of snow into blinding whiteness. Gazing up, a bright blue cloudless sky greeted him. "What's wrong with him?" He'd been undercover when Kate and his brother adopted the teenager after the kid's parents had died while he'd been in the hospital battling leukemia. AJ's stomach turned over at the thought of his new nephew back in the hospital for any reason. He wanted a chance to meet him.

"It sounds like a broken arm. That's not the point. Do *not* leave this hotel until Kate or I return."

"We're moving."

"Dammit, AJ! Stay the fuck there!"

His brother had to know that wouldn't happen. The time had come for him to complete this journey to regain his and Megan's lives. Much to his dismay, their couple's retreat had come to an end.

"You'll know where to find us."

"Let me just check on him, and I'll be there. At least stay put once you get there."

"Give the family my love."

AJ turned to Megan. Her beauty, both inside and

out, made him yearn to pull her close. His heart ached because for her safety, he'd eventually have to leave her.

He cleared his throat. "Are you ready?"

"Of course, where are we going?"

He chuckled. He should've expected that question. "To a little place near where I stayed when undercover once. That'll put us close enough to get our information, but be able to stay off the streets as much as possible."

"Do you think they'll be watching your old place to see if you return?" she asked nervously.

"That place is probably already rented to someone else. So no, I doubt they're waiting around to see if I return. They've already searched that area. They won't expect us to move right back into the hornet's nest."

****

Entering their temporary quarters, the strong leftover scent of cigarette smoke and body odor assailed his nose, burning the hairs in his nostrils. He had to get them into a better place soon. She deserved better than this.

Megan dropped her bag and circled. The one-room apartment came about as run-down as they do in this neighborhood. The color of the walls faded into several shades of white from chipping, peeling, stains, and age. The red plaid couch could almost be called silver with the large amount of duct tape used to hold in the stuffing.

He locked the door and closed the faded navy curtains that somewhat matched the blanket on the sagging bed at the back of the room.

"I'm sad people have to live like this."

"Some people can't afford anything better than this, Megan," he replied solemnly.

"It just angers me that the landlord doesn't even try to provide them with a respectable room. I may have to do a series on derelict landlords in the near future and start here."

He laughed. His little spitfire. Her fire grabbed hold of something inside him and he didn't want her to let it go. When he exhaled, that emotional response to her painfully blasted out of him, returning him to the reality their time together would soon come to an end.

"How long will we be here?"

"Until I think it's time to move. If what I'd heard before was correct, we have less than a week to make this plan work.

"You may as well get comfortable. We're safe." He placed their bags by the door in case they had to leave in a hurry.

The secure phone rang.

"Hamilton."

"We've got a problem. Someone broke into the GPS computer system. Hundreds of records were hacked."

"Yeah, and?" Why was Devon bothering him with this shit? Computer issues were his forte.

"Your SUV was one of them. Someone with your codes could track you through the GPS in the vehicle."

"Why the hell didn't you stop this? I thought your system was top notch. Fuck, Dev."

"Don't ever doubt my system. It was the manufacturer's system that was hacked, not mine. It'll never be mine."

"Fuck me."

"Just in case it was yours they were after, you need to ditch the SUV far away."

AJ ended the call. *Fuck!*

Megan hesitantly sat on the couch. "Problem?"

"Yeah. I need to move our wheels. In fact, we'll lose them all together." This would mean stealing a vehicle until Dev had something ready for him. Arthur will love that.

Another fucking choice where he could get her killed either way. Take her with him. But, then she'd be on the street with him longer than he'd like. Too long in fact as he'd have to park miles away and might not find a car right away. Or, leave her here. No one knew they were here for all of five fucking minutes. If they'd hacked into his system, they'd see the truck move and follow it, which was another reason not to take her with him.

His stomach rolled making this decision. The best one was to leave her. Jesse would be here soon. AJ had to do it. He couldn't chance them following the SUV and finding them both. If they captured him, his brother would take her to safety.

"Megan, I need to leave you here."

Her eyes widened to large saucers. "W-What?"

"I have to park the SUV a long way from here. Someone hacked into the system, and many codes were compromised. We don't know if it's ours they were after, but we aren't taking a chance. This just happened, so there is time to move it without them realizing we were here.

He raked his fingers through his hair. What a damn mess. "If they somehow follow me, I don't want you there. It's too risky to have you with me. You'll be safe.

We just moved here. No one knows we're here."

She inhaled loudly. "Okay."

Fuck! "Do you have your gun handy?"

She moved to pull it from the jacket she'd dropped over her bag by the door.

"Good. Keep it with you." He reached into his pants pockets and removed both phones. "Here. Keep these phones with you. Don't make any calls on the secure phone, but you could use this time to speak with your sources on the burner phone."

"What will you do without a phone?"

"There are more burner phones in the SUV. If Arthur, Kate, or my brothers call, do what they tell you, no matter what they say, Megan. If they say run, you walk away as fast as you can. Don't worry. I'll find you."

His heart pounded. He gathered her into his arms, holding her tight. *Please let me have made the right decision.* He pulled back, gave her a warm kiss, and stepped away. "Thank you for forgiving me. Now, lock this door behind me. I'll be back as quickly as possible."

****

Anxiety hijacked Megan's body, making her insides quiver and her heart race. *Kevin, I'm close to making them pay.*

She jumped at every loud noise. AJ had to hurry. Even with his brother keeping watch, her bravery only went so far. Her pulse skyrocketed when the burner phone rang. His words stuck in her head of what to do if Arthur or his family called.

With shaking hands, she answered, "Hello."

"Megan, it's Tyrone."

Her sigh of relief relaxed her body. She'd forgotten her sources had the new number. AJ's changing them so often was a bit obsessive. Weren't burner phones used because they weren't traceable?

A quick shiver of excitement blasted through her body. "Tyrone, what's up?"

"I got something to tell you, big stuff. When can you meet me at the usual place?"

"Is it something you can just tell me over the phone?" She wasted her breath with that statement. Tyrone never revealed information over the phone.

"Nah-uh."

"How long will you be around?" Maybe he'd wait until AJ returned, and they could both meet with him.

"Things are hot on the street. I'll be around for ten minutes." He ended the call.

Dang it all to hell and back! They couldn't pass up good information at this point.

The door opened, and Megan brightened. She whirled to the door and froze. Her hands shot out up to chest level, and a bolt of terror screamed through her. *Oh God. He's going to kill me.*

Chapter Twenty-Three

Megan couldn't believe this. They were supposed to be safe. "How did you get in here?"

"The manager owes us money." Alex Childs, a Magic Shop enforcer, pointed a gun at her.

She scanned the room. She'd never reach her gun before he could grab or shoot her. Where was Jesse? He must have seen Alex slip into the room.

"Don't even think about fighting, lady. I have no problem blowing out your kneecap." His voice rang with sincerity.

Her gut clenched. "What do you want with me?"

Instead of answering her, he pulled a cell phone from his pocket. His gaze leaving her long enough to dial. "Hey. I need a favor. Can you have the Harrison house opened up right away? I'll need a babysitter for a while too. I've got a special package." He shoved his phone in his pocket. "Come on, pretty lady. You're coming with me." He waved his pistol toward the door.

Where the hell is Jesse?

After two deep breaths in and out, she swallowed the nearly choking lump in her throat. "Are you going to kill me?"

She walked on unsteady legs out of the room, replaying his short conversation on the phone. He must be taking her somewhere to kill her, this Harrison place. Why would he need a babysitter? What exactly did he plan to do with her? The heartbeat she'd just calmed spiked. *Please, Lord, not rape.*

She assessed him. They stood about the same height. His short, curly black hair and baby face would fool anyone into believing he was harmless. Like the other enforcers, he had broad shoulders and toned arms. She'd never overpower him.

"Where are we going?" She winced, hot tears fighting for release from behind her eyelids. She'd asked AJ that many times. It had almost become a joke.

"You, pretty lady, *is* my bait to catch that bastard."

She knew he meant AJ. If they drew him out, they'd kill him and then her. She knew it might come to this, but she'd expected it at the end. She didn't want to be the reason he died. He'd fought to keep her alive, and now she'd be his downfall.

"Cross the street here."

His words yanked her out of her thoughts. There had to be a chance to escape. She'd find it and take it. Keeping him from shooting her would be the challenge. She doubted he had AJ's attitude toward killing someone. This brought her thoughts back to when he'd held her at gunpoint, kidnapping her. She smiled. That seemed a lifetime ago.

"Turn here."

She looked around to get her bearings. She hadn't been in this part of town where every building looked alike, and the street signs were absent. If she escaped, she needed to get back to familiar streets, back to AJ.

"Stop. We're here."

Alex ushered her up the steps of a run-down house with bars covering the windows. Once her eyes adjusted to the dimness, she surveyed the home. A cheap round dining room table with four chairs, a worn couch, and a faded chair were the only furniture. No end tables, coffee tables, or anything else that made a place a home.

He dragged a chair from the table and moved it to the center of the room. "Sit. By the way, there's no need to scream. Even if someone heard you, they know to mind their own business," he said proudly.

She hadn't screamed on the street for the same reason. It would have been a waste of breath, not to mention he may have shot her right there.

A toilet flushed and then another man walked into the room. She bent her head back to see a dark-skinned giant, a rather thin one, probably in his late twenties. He looked her up and down and smiled. Her heart dropped to her stomach.

The earlier thought that they might rape her returned. That wouldn't be the last thing that happened to her before she died. Anger turned her blood to heat in her veins. She'd fight with every last breath in her body.

"Hey, man," the giant said.

"You up for this?" Alex asked.

"Piece of cake."

"Megan Rogers, this is Jermaine. He's gonna make sure you stay put." Alex turned to the giant. "Tie her to the chair."

Her new babysitter grinned. "With pleasure." He picked up handcuffs and rope from the table. "Who is she?"

"She's my ticket to AJ Hamilton."

It took a moment for it to click. He'd called AJ by his real name. *Oh God. They knew.*

Jermaine pulled her arms painfully behind the back of the chair and cinched the handcuffs tight. Then he wrapped the rope around her body and the back of the chair. He made sure to brush her breasts.

She glared at him. No way would this sick pervert get the best of her.

"There we go. Not goin' *nowhere*, are ya?" He turned. "Done."

The writer in her wanted to correct Jermaine's grammar. Slang drove her nuts. What a stupid thing to be considering with Alex moving toward her.

"Where is he?" Alex asked through narrowed eyes.

No way would she give AJ to them. Besides, she wasn't sure exactly where he was.

The enforcer backhanded her. Her head snapped sideways. *Holy hell that hurt!* She slowly turned her head back around and stared at him. Oh, how she hated this man. She had to ignore the stinging pain and fight her watery eyes. Alex wanted to kill the man she cared deeply for. A man who'd come to matter in her life.

"Where is he?"

She remained stubbornly silent. Her palms clammy and her heart thudding so loudly it almost deafened her were the only signs of her fear. She didn't care if he backhanded her again. She would never give up AJ so he could be murdered.

"Loyal thing, aren't you? You must be fucking him. No woman would be that loyal if they weren't fucking."

She continued to stare at him defiantly. If he'd been close enough, she'd have spat in his face.

"Well, if he's as loyal to you as you are to him, he'll come to us. He'll believe that we'll do an exchange and spare your life." He laughed and backhanded her again.

Something warm slid down her chin. Blood. She wanted to jump from the chair and beat the crap out of him. She hoped AJ really hurt him. She'd never been so bloodthirsty until the Magician ordered her death. She believed in justice but had come to learn death was the only justice these men understood.

He raked his eyes over her. "You're one hot piece of ass. If you fuck as good as you look, he'll come running for you. You can make it better on him if you tell us where to find him. I'm sure you'd hate for him to walk into our trap while trying to rescue you."

Trap? Oh God, AJ. Be careful.

"Yes, we think he'll try to rescue you. Don't worry. I'll be waiting for him when he does. I'll be the one to kill him. The Magician will reward me."

"Don't hurt him."

"Oh, she does speak. How about you use that voice to tell me where he is."

She shrugged as best as she could with the ropes around her shoulders. "He left me where you found me so I can't tell you where he is. You're wasting your time. We're over. I doubt he'll come for me."

"I don't know about that. He's gone out of his way to help you so far, saving you from Joe, keeping you one step ahead of us. I'll wager that he'll come. He seems to have some protective streak when it comes to you."

She couldn't argue with that. "You're wrong. We had a fling. It's over. He left. End of story. AJ won't come."

"Well, pretty lady, you'd best hope he does."

She knew he'd come. He'd rescue her. If he didn't step into their trap. She wanted to ask Alex why they hadn't just waited in the room for AJ, but she feared they'd actually return and do that. If they thought she and AJ were through and that AJ had left her, that worked better as far as she could tell. Then again, she didn't have an evil mind that would conjure this situation, so she could be wrong all around.

Alex turned to Jermaine. "I've got to get the word out, so I'm leaving her here for a while. She's not to be harmed."

Her babysitter frowned.

After the two were alone, the giant pulled a handgun from the back of his pants and placed it in front of him on the table. After turning a chair around, he straddled it, staring intently at her. Would he listen to Alex? The way he looked at her left no doubt he wanted her.

"You sure are pretty."

She looked away.

"I wouldn't mind a piece of ya."

She snapped her head back in time to notice him licking his lips. She twisted her head away in disgust. All she had to do was survive until AJ or Jesse arrived.

She tried to block her babysitter from her mind. The red chair in the living room was worn and faded, but it looked more comfortable than the chair she was tied to, plus he couldn't tie the rope so tight. She could escape. "May I sit in that chair instead?" She motioned her head in the direction of the chair.

He turned around, looked at it, and then laughed.

Okay. That must be a no. It was worth a try. She'd try it with whoever watched her next.

If only one person watched her at a time, they had to sleep at some point. If she could find a way out of the rope, then she could escape. The cuffs could stay on. They'd prove a serious challenge, but living would help her find a way.

She attempted to shift her body. The rope was too tight.

A thought occurred to her. "I have to go to the bathroom." Maybe it had a window where she could escape. Why hadn't she thought of that before?

"Can't it wait?"

"No." She crossed her legs, bouncing them like she couldn't hold it. They stupidly hadn't tied her legs. If she could loosen the ropes enough, she could use them to fight them off. Or something like that. She'd figure it out later. Right now, glee slid down her spine. A chance to escape stood before her.

He left his handgun on the table and untied her. With his hand holding her forearm tight, he shoved her down a hallway. "Here it is. Don't try nothin' funny."

"I need my hands out of these cuffs. I can't go with my hands behind my back."

He narrowed his eyes at her and then pulled a key from his pocket. "Turn around."

She had a chance. Could she overpower him? He didn't have his weapon on him. That was when she noticed the knife attached to his belt. Unless she could get that from him, she'd be in trouble. Not to mention he outweighed her by a good fifty pounds.

She rubbed her wrists. "Thank you."

Rushing into the grungy bathroom, she closed and locked the door. A strong urine smell knocked her back. She pinched her burning nose. Why couldn't men aim in the toilet?

Megan looked around. Dang it all to hell and back! No window.

At least she could find a weapon of some sort. Maybe a razor blade to cut the ropes. Her hope skipped at the empty medicine cabinet.

She took advantage of the bathroom break. Who knew when she'd have another one?

The rapping on the door startled her. "Long enough."

She could rush him. He wouldn't be prepared for that. She opened the door and put everything she had into it. All she did was bounce off him. He roughly grabbed her arms.

"What the hell is wrong with you?"

She let out an exasperated sigh of despair. This had possibly been her last chance before AJ walked into their trap while attempting to rescue her.

He shoved her back to the chair and proceeded to cuff and tie her up.

"How long are you going to keep me here?" Could she never shut off her need to ask questions? No. It calmed her, centered her. Something she needed. Besides, it wasn't like it'd hurt any. They planned to kill her anyway. Maybe she'd learn something that could aid her escape.

"Don't know. You have to ask Alex. This is his party."

"So, Alex is your boss?" Could she create dissension amongst the ranks? If she did, she'd try to sway him to her side so he'd release her.

He chuckled. "Naw. I'm just helping out."

"Why are you helping him?"

"You're that journalist, aren't you?"

She nodded. "That's me. What do you do for Magic Shop?"

He leered at her. "None of your business."

"Have you ever met the Magician?"

He shook his head. "Of course not. I'm not important enough."

"Doesn't that bother you? Not knowing who you work for?"

"I work for Jimmy. That's who I work for. The rest are just names."

Ah ha. Another dealer. "Jimmy let you off the street to watch me?"

He smiled. "You're smart. Nah, Jimmy don't know I'm here. Alex wouldn't get to be in charge if he did."

So much for gaining his assistance. They would kill her after AJ exchanged himself for her. No, he'd rescue her, not give in. He'd know they'd lie about letting her live. She had to keep telling herself that. It didn't stop her from trying to work the knot on the back of the chair. Dumbass tied it right by her hands making it easier to grab.

****

AJ returned to an empty room. Horrible possibilities of what happened to Megan flooded his mind. They all ended with him holding her, blood running through his hands, watching her gasp her last breath.

He had to find her.

Dammit! It'd taken him longer to get back than he'd wanted. He had no idea how long she'd been gone.

With fear expanding in his chest, he answered the ringing burner phone.

"It's Javier."

"What do you have for me?" he asked Javier Marshall, one of his informants.

"There's talk on the street to get a message to you. They *got* your girl."

AJ curled and uncurled his fist in his empty hand. "What's the rest of the message?"

"Harrison House."

"Anything else?"

"Something about her fate's in your hands."

"Thanks, man." He ended the call and hurled the phone across the room barely registering it smashing into small pieces.

Fuck! Fuck! Fuck!

Pinching the bridge of his nose between his shaking thumb and forefinger, he dropped his head and took a deep breath. He had to calm down so he could think rationally. His only hope was that she remained alive until he rescued her.

He closed his eyes and developed a plan. Surveillance time.

AJ suited up in black cargo pants, a black turtleneck sweater, and his tactical vest then picked up the black bag of toys he'd brought back.

Even though it was only a few blocks, he drove the Buick he'd stolen earlier to better conceal himself while he observed Harrison House, a piece-of-shit house on an almost deserted street.

They would expect him to attempt a rescue so he'd have to be smarter. This actually wouldn't be too hard with the nimrod enforcers.

The street was lined with cars, mostly abandoned, but not many people traversed up and down it. The bright sun, uninhibited by clouds, melted most of the snow from the sidewalks. The sound of crunching snow under his boots could be a problem.

Searching for the best path, AJ caught Trey leaving the house with a heated look on his face. Alex must be leading the show and not sharing the credit with his partner.

Surprisingly Damian never showed.

AJ had seen no one else coming or going so he had no idea how many people were already in the house, how many he'd be up against. No matter. He'd take care of as many as he needed to get his little dove back. He rubbed his hand over his left breast.

He couldn't examine his feelings for her at the moment.

Dusk turned to darkness. He'd go in when they were most likely sleeping. They'd best not have harmed her or put their hands on her. She was his.

A tall man with a hood pulled over his face walked toward him. AJ turned off the dome light and unlocked the car.

"It's about time you made it," AJ said to Jesse.

"I'm sorry we weren't here to keep her out of trouble."

He felt for his brother. Jesse had placed all the blame on himself when it belonged on AJ's shoulders.

"Don't worry. It wasn't your responsibility. What've you got?"

"There's too much information about you on the street. Dev thinks he's found most of the money. It's just a matter of whatever the hell he does to find out who owns it. It's, of course, offshore under a bogus corp. He said he doesn't need much more time. That's how confident he is about it."

AJ nodded. "Good. Dev will come through. Anything on Jake?"

"No. Speaking of brothers," Jesse cleared his throat, "I told the twins, and they're on their way home, pissed at you."

"They'll get over it." He constantly pissed his brothers off or disappointed them in one way or another. How would this be any different?

"Those two?" His brother chuckled. "Are we talking about the same Matt and Brad?"

AJ nodded to the house. "I don't think Alex or Trey told anyone she's here. There aren't enough men waiting for me."

"I'm here for backup."

He shook his head. "No, Jesse. This will be easy." Plus, he couldn't put his family in any more danger.

Chapter Twenty-Four

Based on the number of men that trekked in and out of the house, there were at least two men with Megan. Two were easy. If all went well, no one would get hurt, and AJ would have her back.

He reached into the bag and retrieved a lock pick kit and a few other items. The beating of his heart skyrocketed. He took two slow, deep breaths to calm it.

No more waiting.

The empty, quiet street greeted him. He'd witnessed Alex setting his trap, which consisted of him hiding around the corner. Fucking idiot.

AJ planned his path to avoid the pockets of snow and any possible noise. Ducking down, staying behind the line of cars, he slowly made his way to the enforcer hoping Trey hadn't decided to set his own trap.

He peered around the corner. *Are you fucking kidding me?* Of all the times for a hooker to be hitting on Alex.

"Get the fuck out of here. I'm busy." The man's angry voice floated to AJ.

"Come on, baby. I need one trick tonight, or I'm in big trouble. We can do a quickie, right here against the wall."

Glancing around the corner again, AJ considered his options but then realized the woman looked familiar.

Alex howled, convulsed, and dropped to the ground.

AJ walked around the corner. "Why hello, Kate."

She threw her hands on her hips. "What's this I hear you planned to do this alone?"

"Now's not the time." He removed Alex's weapons and cell phone, dropping them into a pocket of his cargo pants.

At the unmistakable metal-v-metal sound of a bullet sliding into the chamber of a handgun, he swung around. "Kate, you are not—"

"Hands up, you two."

His heart skipped a beat. Fuck! Trey.

The clatter of both Tasers bouncing on the sidewalk pushed a sense of foreboding through AJ's veins. Dammit.

"The Magician is going to be happy with me for catching you and the girl. Who's this?" He tilted his head to Kate.

"Look, man. I just came here for some action and this yahoo tried to get me like he did the other guy." She licked her lips seductively. "I only pulled mine in self-defense. Can I go now? I have to find a John tonight."

"Turn real slow and head around the corner. Don't tempt me. I'm low enough to put a bullet in your back."

AJ faced him, shadows playing across the man's face. "Why can't you let her go? She'll run, and no one will ever hear from her again." Where the fuck is Jesse? He would never let Kate do this alone.

Trey laughed. "You expect me to fucking believe that?"

AJ could take him, but the bullet in the chamber

could end up in Kate. The enforcer planned to kill him anyway. He'd put himself between the gun and Kate. He wouldn't go down without a fight.

He shifted his weight, preparing to spring when Trey jerked and screamed.

The enforcer dropped to the ground, and Jesse appeared from the darkness. "I love these things. Dev had been right to add them to our kits." He grinned, holding a Taser. "Much quieter than gunfire, no blood and no crap from Arthur."

Kate narrowed her eyes. "Where the hell have you been?"

His brother reached for his wife. "Sweetheart, you know I had to hide around the block."

Their lips touched briefly, and the slight pull in his heart brought Megan's face to the forefront of his mind.

"Thanks, Jesse." There weren't enough words to thank his brother for saving his life. This time he'd freely admit he'd needed him and, sure enough, Jesse had been there.

"Well, we figured you'd need backup, no matter what you said."

Alex moaned and moved.

Kate dropped a knee on his back and removed flex-cuffs from her jacket pocket. "I've got these two. Go ahead. I'll be along shortly."

AJ smiled. His old partner hadn't lost her touch. He nodded and the two men cautiously turned the corner. Good Lord, Alex was more than an idiot. He'd either left the front light off at the house, or it didn't have a light bulb.

AJ slipped up the stairs, and Jesse turned to face the street. He put his ear to the door. Blessed silence. At three in the morning, he'd expected nothing less.

Someone having his back stopped the slight trembling of his hands as he went to work on the lock. In less than thirty seconds, he'd silently opened the door six inches.

Peering in, he made a sweep of the room. The two guards slept in the living room to his right. A soft glow of the television illuminated the area with the sound of porn filling the air. He turned and gestured to Jesse using hand signals his brothers had taught him from their time in Special Forces.

Quietly sliding into the house, he searched for Megan. She sat on his left, tied to a chair, her chin on her chest. Even in the dim light, the darkening bruise across her cheek was visible. His blood boiled. He wanted to kill the bastards but immediately tamped down his anger. He needed control.

AJ pulled weapons from his pocket and soundlessly moved to the living room where he angled himself between the two men, raised both arms and pushed the buttons on two Tasers.

Both men jumped. He only needed them out of commission for a short period of time.

****

Megan jerked awake to men's high-pitched, almost feminine screams. Her heart pounded. *Oh God. What's happening?*

She searched the room, and her gaze locked on AJ. Her fierce warrior aimed something at each of her babysitters. He'd come for her like she knew he would.

Jesse entered with a handgun and moved swiftly through the house.

When her babysitters stopped twitching, her hero

disarmed each of them, flipped one and cuffed him before searching his pockets. Kate slipped in and did the same to the other man. His brother returned to the room, nodded and moved to the door.

AJ rushed to her and dropped to his knees. His right hand cupped her cheek, his thumb lightly caressing it. Tingling in her muscles flowed from his touch all the way to her toes.

"Are you all right?" he asked in a strained voice.

"I knew you'd come for me." She smiled at him, love and gratitude for him surged inside of her. Yes, she'd actually fallen in love with him. She probably had been for a while, but this solidified it. After all they had been through, even with his undercover lie, she trusted him wholeheartedly. He wouldn't cheat on her. He'd love and cherish her and their children. They both worked odd hours so they'd have to figure out something with their jobs when they had little ones.

His job. Could she deal with him living like this? Going undercover and risking his life on a daily basis? A shiver drilled down her spine. She'd rather be with him than without. He'd explained to her the danger in the business his brothers owned. Maybe Kate could help her. If nothing else, she'd find out how she held herself together when her husband went on a job.

Great plan. When to speak with her was another matter altogether.

He cut the ropes tying her to the chair. "There's no way I'd leave you with these bastards." He pulled something from the pocket where he'd added the items from her babysitters. The click of handcuffs unlocking put her into action.

She launched herself into his arms, squeezing

tightly.

After a minute, he pulled back, tipped her chin up and examined her cheek. "Who hurt you?" he asked softly.

The emotions in his eyes flickered from concern to anger. "Alex hit me when I wouldn't tell him where you were."

He leaned down and brushed a light kiss on her cheek.

"It's time for you to leave," Jesse stated.

"I owe you."

"Don't worry, we'll collect."

"Let's move." AJ took her hand and led her out of her temporary prison. He hustled her down the street to a beat-up car. She didn't even question it. Didn't care as long as it helped them escape.

"Get in. We don't have time to waste."

"Thank you." The words, I love you, stuck in her throat.

He reached over and took her hand in his. "Anything for you." He threaded his fingers through hers and held tight.

****

They entered the new room AJ had rented, hoping he and Megan wouldn't have to move again.

Reaching out, he crushed her against him. The adrenaline still hot in his veins battled the surge of relief that he'd rescued her. He needed her. Needed to feel that she was truly alive.

After her experience, what she'd need was him to soothe her, calm her fears, and reassure her that he'd protect her with everything he had.

Instead, his mouth swooped down on hers,

possessively, demanding. A rumbling groan erupted from deep within, their kiss now a brutal clash of lips and tongues.

His cock burned to be inside her. Deeper than ever before. And he needed her now.

He impatiently tugged at her zipper.

She stepped back. "Let me." In mere moments, she'd shed her pants and reached to remove her jacket and sweater.

He ripped off his jacket, body armor, and shirt and then roughly pulled her to him, one hand behind her head, not willing to let her go.

She reached for his pants and released him. Her hand wrapped around his hard member. Every nerve ending in his body sizzled.

A primal growl ripped from his throat. He turned her around and lightly pushed her forward until her hands rested on the edge of the bed. He touched her only long enough to find her hot, wet, ready.

Pushing his pants down, he positioned himself, grasped her hips and filled her in a swift thrust. He stilled and gritted his teeth at the pleasure threatening to erupt from his cock surrounded by her heat.

He moved, his thighs slapping hard against her, thrust after thrust. Each one harder, faster and pushing him deeper into a slippery friction snatching away his fears, allowing him to focus only on her and the fact she was alive and with him.

Keeping his hands on her hips, holding her while he stroked in and out, he leaned forward and spread kisses on her back. He felt Megan quiver and heard her moan, dropping her head down.

This would be quick, and he couldn't help it this

time. He couldn't hold back. That fear and excitement of the evening ballooned in him, ready to pop at any moment. Feeling her tight around his cock was what he'd needed. Now he needed for them to burst into a euphoric state.

Releasing one hand, he moved it around and staged an assault on her clit. She moaned and pushed her heat closer into his hand. He gave her tight friction, adapted to each of her moves and soft, erotic sounds.

Between kisses on her back, AJ murmured, "You feel so good, so right."

Sweat broke out on his brow. His cock was ready to explode. He set his jaw tight in an attempt to hold off his orgasm until she came. But damn, being this deep inside her, with his balls slapping her, he had to fight harder than ever.

She arched her back, her breathing frantic.

"Let go, Megan."

She cried out his name in a hoarse voice, her body trembling, her legs almost buckling.

Her sweet sound of ecstasy ruptured the last of his resolve. His balls grew tight, and he drove into her once more before pulling out. Semen from deep inside him exploded in hot, wet spurts on her back.

She collapsed forward. His legs threatening to give out on him, he dropped beside her.

Holy shit! He willed his muscles to work but hated the pleasure that claimed them to disappear.

AJ turned his head to Megan. "Are you okay?" Had he been too rough with her?

She smiled and murmured, "Perfect."

He stood, went to the bathroom and returned with a cloth to clean her back. Shit. He'd forgotten.

He cleared his throat. "Megan, we… uh… we…"

"Don't worry. We're okay."

"Does that mean we don't have to use protection? I'm clean."

She turned to sit on the edge of the bed. "I am too. Is that what you want?"

He tossed the towel on the floor and gathered her in his arms. "I'd like that very much." He kissed her on her nose. "Come on. It's well past time for us to sleep."

Lying in each other's arms, she whispered, "I'm sorry, AJ."

He placed a finger under her chin and tilted it until their eyes met. "You didn't do anything wrong. I'm sorry I didn't think to tell you that Jesse had left, and no one was keeping watch."

"Oh. I forgot. Tyrone has something big for me. He won't know what to think when I don't show up. I have to call him."

AJ caught her as she attempted to launch herself from the bed and pulled her back to him. "Megan, it's almost five in the morning. I think he'd prefer you call him at a normal time." He kissed the top of her head.

"Now. We both need to get some sleep. We've got a big day tomorrow." He wanted her again. Blood had already surged to his growing erection. But, she'd been through too much. They both needed rest more than they needed more sex.

Chapter Twenty-Five

"Okay, this is our first real foray into public together. I want you to keep your scarf up over your face and your hat pulled low."

AJ's stress twisted his gut. After what happened with Alex, AJ didn't feel as safe as he'd like taking Megan with him. Thankfully, he was certain their backs were covered.

He'd wasted his breath attempting to convince Megan to remain in their room with Kate while he hurriedly sought out what they needed. Wow. He'd thought she had fire before. She refused to stay put, stating she was also seeking justice. Then a flutter whipped through his heart when she'd worried if she kept his sister-in-law, no one would have his back.

To have someone as unique as Megan as his would be better than he'd ever imagined. No matter how much he loved her, they'd be separated once this was over. Loved her? What the fuck?

Yes, he loved her with a fierceness that ripped his heart apart knowing their future.

"Okay. No one will see anything but my eyes. Will that work?" She pulled her hat down to her brow and pulled her scarf to her nose. Her beautiful blue eyes twinkled playfully.

He conducted one final check on her Kevlar vest before he zipped her jacket. She readily agreed to keep her handgun and a phone in her pockets. Although, she didn't like that he said the phone was in case they were separated.

"Let's go. We should arrive just in time to meet with your source."

They approached a nervous Tyrone, shuffling his feet, his eyes darting around and his hands stuffed in his thick Baltimore Ravens jacket. When he noticed AJ, Megan thought he'd bolt.

"Who's he?" her source asked.

"He's okay. He has the same goal as I do. You said you have something for me."

He looked anxiously at AJ before turning to her. "They have a big buy coming in a few days."

What the fuck? How had Byron, the DEA agent on the task force been unaware of this information?

Uh-oh. She had that look he'd come to know all too well. That joyful, "I'm going to do something that will get me in trouble and make your life harder, AJ" look.

"That's awesome! How confident are you about this?"

"Very."

She hugged the man. The green-eyed monster ripped forth.

"Bye, Tyrone. Thank you, again."

"Keep your head down," AJ growled.

He had to speak with Byron about this. A thought occurred to AJ. He pulled the secure phone from his pocket. Sure enough, he'd missed a call when he'd been rescuing Megan.

"This is good, isn't it?" she asked.

He kicked a chunk of ice that hadn't melted in the

sunny, warmer weather. "If it's accurate, it would be extremely helpful. What the agent had to use for our plan had been weak."

They silently continued down the street. She hadn't asked it yet, but he knew what the next question from her mouth would be. She'd be sorely disappointed with his answer, but she'd remain alive.

He decided to head it off. "You're not going to watch the buy." He cringed at the dictatorial tone of his voice.

"You've got to be kidding me. This is too good for me to pass up."

"We need this bust." He watched her tense. "You know we need him pissed off at each of his advisors for screwing things up and losing a shipment is far better than what we'd planned for Carl."

"I thought you didn't want to catch him or Jimmy. How can you avoid it?"

AJ shook his head. "They're paranoid bastards. They send someone else to their buys, someone expendable. No one has the balls to cheat the Magician. It keeps the two of them out of it. Keeps their hands clean."

"Well, I still want to witness it."

"Not happening. DEA won't allow it. I won't allow it." He put his foot down. She would listen and obey him this time.

She stopped and jammed her hands on her hips. "Won't allow it? Who do you think you are?"

He stopped. "Megan, it's not safe. There could be gunfire."

"How will I get the information if I'm not there?"

"I'll have a DEA agent call you after the bust. He'll

provide the details."

She hugged him. "Thank you. Thank you." She pressed kisses all over his face before his lips captured hers.

A loud, vulgar comment reached his ears from where his sister-in-law stood halfway down the block. He'd remember to return the language when Kate was with Jesse in a similar embrace.

He took Megan's hand in his. They were on their way into the thick of things. He held it tighter. He'd keep her alive. He had to.

****

"We've had enough for one day. Let's head back. Keep your head down. We've been very lucky no one has recognized you." People still feared AJ from his time in the enforcer role, so he'd been safer than he'd expected.

Two blocks from their room, Kate shouted, "AJ, get down!"

He spun around, pulled his weapon, and shoved Megan behind him as several shots rang out. He spotted Trey dropping to the ground. Kate rushed past them, kicking Trey's weapon away.

Confident they were safe, AJ turned to Megan with shaky hands. "Are you okay? Are you hit?" he asked with full-blown panic. He traced his hands over her. When he found her uninjured, relief coursed through him, and he hugged her tight. Thank God Kate had been on the ball.

"AJ, you've been shot," Megan exclaimed, pushing back and pointing to his left leg.

He looked down at the blood soaking his pants. Funny, he hadn't felt the pain when he'd been worried about her.

Heat and sharp pain made an appearance, radiating down his leg. He removed her scarf and tied it above the wound with shaky hands.

"Let's get back to the room. Now." His gravelly voice shocked him. He needed to get off his feet before he landed face-first on the sidewalk.

"You need a hospital, AJ," she protested, the unmistakable look of fear in her eyes.

"No. Get me back to the room." She didn't understand. He couldn't go to the hospital until they had more protection. Someone who had witnessed it might get word to Damian. They'd check the hospitals and while they removed the bullet, she'd be vulnerable.

Kate jogged up to them. "Shit."

"Don't argue, Megan. I need to get back to the room."

"He's right. Let's move." His sister-in-law put an arm under his left armpit for support.

He took Megan's trembling hand and pulled her along.

As soon as they entered the room, AJ dropped into the closest chair, warding off the dizziness that assailed him.

Kate pulled out her phone. "Megan, see to AJ."

"Get the first aid kit from my bag." Sweat trickled down his temple at the intense throbbing at the site of the wound. Having a red-hot poker shoved in his leg would hurt less than this.

Though the bleeding had slowed, he experienced another wave of lightheadedness. He couldn't pass out. He had to even out his breathing, focus on something besides the pain. Not fucking possible.

"Don't you dare yell at me, Jesse Hamilton! I told him to get down. Like you, he doesn't listen."

AJ chuckled at his old partner's angry voice. He missed it.

Megan returned with the first aid kit, opened it and panicked as all the items fell out on the table. "Oh no."

"Don't worry about it. I need your help. We have to stop the bleeding." He lightly grasped her hand. "Can you do this, Megan? Can you help me?"

She nodded.

He held on by a thread. Kate had to hurry. His body couldn't tolerate the pain much longer and remain conscious. "We just need to clean it up."

Splotches of tears on his pants attested to the care and concern she had for him.

"Quit worrying, Megan. Let Kate work her magic and then we'll leave for the hospital."

Kate returned. "Let's go."

****

Megan and Kate used every bit of strength they had to move a semiconscious AJ, who could barely put weight on this leg, into the SUV. Megan fought to keep him awake while his sister-in-law raced to the hospital.

Twins in jeans, turtlenecks, leather jackets and weapons holstered on their right sides walked toward their vehicle, a menacing look about them.

Her heart raced. "Please tell me these men are here to help us and not kill us."

Kate smiled. "Relax. We're safe. They're the good guys."

That didn't help her relax one bit.

The twins pulled AJ from the vehicle and managed to support him as he hopped past two fierce-looking men guarding a hallway labeled Employees Only. She gazed at the men warily, bit her lip, and followed Kate.

They halted in front of a group of men who rallied around AJ.

A beehive of activity, a medical group preparing for something, his surgery maybe, took her attention away from the group.

"Ms. Rogers, we'll move you to the private room he'll have after surgery. If you'll follow me," the twin wearing the dark blue turtleneck said.

She wrapped her arms around herself and looked at AJ. His pallor had turned gray. How he still stood, well not that he actually stood on his own, amazed her.

"Megan, it's okay. They'll take care of you while they're removing the bullet. You don't need to worry about me. I trust these men and someone will be outside my door. Now go. I'll see you when I wake up."

When she didn't budge, he leaned in and brushed a light kiss across her lips. "Mm. I want to taste more of that stuff on your lips when I wake up."

A delicious shudder skittered through her at the touch of lips, but worry slipped right behind and washed it away at the thought of his having surgery.

Unaware of the fear nestled inside her, AJ introduced her around the group. She went through the motions and then followed Brad, the twin who had attempted to lead her away before, to the fourth floor. He opened a hospital room door, and a man walked out. They nodded at each other. "This is a safe place for you to wait. I'll be outside your door."

"Wait. Can't we see him in ICU?"

He shook his head. "He won't be in ICU. A private nurse is on her way. The doctor reluctantly approved AJ to come straight here as long as she stayed."

After she walked into the room, he closed the door behind her, leaving her alone.

AJ had been shot. He had to be okay.

Her gaze roved around the bright room and spotted the couch. She sat. The intense pain in her heart unleashed her tears. She could've lost him today. She knew she might lose him someday, but she didn't want to lose him this soon, or to death.

Startled, she opened her eyes as Kate sat next to her. "Come here." She opened her arms and Megan fell into them.

"I love him," she said through another flow of tears.

"I know."

****

Kate returned home, leaving Megan pacing the room. How long would this take? She looked at her watch. Time passed so slowly.

The forgotten phone in her pocket rang. "Hello," she said through sniffles.

"Megan, are you okay? You don't sound well," Kristen asked.

"No, I'm fine."

"I was worried when I didn't hear from you yesterday or receive a story."

Megan hadn't thought about a story last night. "Well, I was taken hostage yesterday," she informed her boss.

"What?"

"An enforcer used me as bait."

"I take it your hero saved you since you're talking with me now."

Her face split into a wide grin. "Yeah, he saved me."

"I talked to your mother yesterday and told her you were safe. She's worried sick about you."

Megan's stomach turned on itself.

She missed her family. Her mother didn't deserve this. Megan understood the need for caution, but she wanted to be the one telling her mother that she was fine. She wanted to speak with AJ about allowing her to contact her but didn't want to push her luck. He already let her communicate with her boss and Victoria, but she knew that was because they were useful to him.

Her friends must be frantic. Kristen would keep them informed, but it wouldn't be the same. Victoria didn't need the stress of worrying about her. Kelly would wear a hole in the carpet, pacing, fretting. And Merissa. Well, she wouldn't miss Megan.

She fought the onslaught of new tears. "Thank you for doing that, Kristen. I can't communicate with her personally, and it's killing me."

"She seems to understand, although I'm sure she'd prefer to be speaking with you."

"Well, I'm surprised I was able to speak with you at all."

"Code blue room 328, code blue room 328," bled over the loud speaker.

"Megan, what's that? Where are you? Are you at a hospital?"

Her heart skipped a beat. What could she say? "Kristen, don't worry about me. I'm safe."

"Hold on, Megan. Merissa, what do you want?"

Her boss covered the receiver so she couldn't hear the conversation. Had the journalist been eavesdropping on their conversation? She wouldn't put it past her.

"Okay. I'm back."

"What was that?"

"Nothing. Do you promise you're safe?"

"Yes. I promise." She couldn't imagine being any safer than with the Hamiltons. Kate explained the team had returned and their priority was to watch AJ's back. It had been a shame they hadn't been there a few hours ago. They'd recently landed when they'd received the call to head to the hospital.

"Okay. I'll trust you. Now, tell me what you're writing next. Have you figured out who the Magician is yet?"

She hoped the task team's plan worked. She'd had enough of all this. "I have a few things coming up that you'll really like."

"Care to share?"

"Not yet. I'll let you know when they happen."

"Megan, that's not how we work. I'm your editor. I get to know what you're writing, and actually, I assign it. I gave you this project because you would've done it on your own anyway. It's gone too far. It's time you stopped and let the police finish this. I want you safe."

"Kristen, I know that I'm asking a lot from you. Letting me do this from afar. Letting me do the daily articles that I want. And I appreciate it. You have to trust me these articles will be worth it. We think they'll bring the Magician out of hiding."

"Dr. Robertson to room 328. Dr. Robertson to room 328," came over the loudspeaker.

"We'll do this for a bit longer. You're to stay safe. Think about leaving him and going with the FBI."

"Thank you, Kristen."

"Will I see something from you today?" her boss asked.

She hadn't thought about an article for two straight days. Very unlike her. "No. I won't have anything for you."

Wow. She never thought she'd put a man before her writing.

****

AJ's surgery had progressed well, and they expected him in the room in less than half an hour. Nurse Laura arrived and began issuing orders to the floor nurses. Megan convinced Brad and Matt to allow her to walk, with them in tow, to the cafeteria for coffee. They made no comments or gave her any looks of pity about her red, puffy eyes.

She stepped off the elevator and shock enveloped her. Marcus stood there. His black, probably Armani, business suit fitted him perfectly. She used to find him sexy dressed like this. Now, she felt nothing.

His disheveled look surprised her. Dark circles under his eyes, untamed hair, and an almost week-old beard were completely opposite to the man she knew. In his sick way, he still loved her and had a hard time with this. But it was only because he wasn't the one taking care of her.

He spotted her and rushed over.

Before he could reach her, the twins blocked her from his view.

Matt stepped forward. "Look, buddy. Back away."

"That's my fiancée. I want to see her," Marcus demanded. Although well-built, Marcus had nothing on the twins' large, muscled, well-toned bodies.

Brad turned to her and raised an eyebrow in

question.

She almost asked him to deck Marcus. From behind the human wall, she said, "Marcus, I'm not your fiancée any longer."

"Megan. I'm just glad you're safe. May I see you?"

She stepped from behind Brad as best as he'd allow. "Here I am. How did you know I was here?"

He motioned down the hall. "Becca is on the nurse's desk. She saw you and was worried something was wrong since two men were guarding your room. She wasn't aware that we'd broken up when she'd called me."

She'd hoped Becca hadn't seen her when she'd slipped into the hospital room. The last time she'd seen the nurse had been at her and Marcus's engagement party.

She moved her arms across her chest. "There's no reason for you to be here."

He reached his hand toward her, and she was pulled back. Brad and Matt closed in around her again.

"I'm here to take you away."

"As you can see, I have enough protection."

"Who are they? May we talk without them?"

"They're here to protect me. Marcus, I don't want to speak with you any longer. Leave," she said forcefully.

"Baby, please come with me. I can't take this. Look what it's doing to me."

Matt spoke up, "She said for you to leave. You should listen to her."

"I'll leave you now"—he glared at Matt before turning back to her—"but I'm not giving up." Anger laced his voice and almost had her taking a step back away from him.

He turned and marched away stiffly.

Brad turned to her. "You almost married that weasel?"

She nodded. "Yeah. I obviously wasn't in my right mind."

Chapter Twenty-Six

"AJ is fine and on his way to the room," one of the men guarding the room notified them when they returned from the cafeteria.

Megan almost collapsed to the floor with the weight of fear that had been lifted from her body. He would be all right.

After he'd been wheeled into the room, everyone except the nurse left them alone. She reached down and held his hand. "How are you doing?" Tears pushed over the rim of her eyelids and slid down her face, landing on his hospital gown.

"Don't cry, my little dove. I'm fine. I'm actually pretty good with the drugs they've put into my system," he answered groggily, his eyelids heavy.

"I was so worried."

"It's over now." He yawned. "Have my brothers stayed with you?"

He'd been shot, had surgery, and he still worried about her safety. That meant he more than cared for her. Maybe he was coming to love her. She could hope. Kate said he had feelings for her, but Hamilton men were stubborn about seeing the truth.

She nodded, swiping at tears with the back of her free hand. "They've been with me."

"I'm glad. They'll be with us while I remain here which won't be long."

His eyelids closed, dropping him into a drug-induced sleep.

She dozed in the chair next to his bed but jerked awake at a knock on the door. A low groan came from AJ and then the whirl of the bed being lifted into a sitting position.

Expecting someone from the family to enter, she stood and stepped back to provide them with more space. Instead, a tall, somewhat handsome man with short, brown hair walked into the room.

He wore a brown bomber jacket, a familiar side holster and an FBI badge prominently displayed on his belt.

"Arthur told me, so I came to check on you," he said then looked at Megan.

"Megan, this is my partner, FBI Special Agent Todd Powers."

The man extended his hand. "It's a pleasure to finally meet you, Ms. Rogers." He turned to AJ and crossed his arms across his chest. "Are you finally done?"

"Not a chance." He gestured to his leg. "This is nothing."

"You do realize you're wanted by the FBI, don't you?"

Megan's eyes widened. How could the FBI want him? She thought he was FBI? He'd even just introduced the man as his partner.

AJ narrowed his eyes. "Are you here to take me in?"

"Of course not. Arthur is keeping your location under wraps. We want Ms. Rogers." He gave her a quick once-over and smiled brightly at her.

She slipped closer to AJ's side. AJ reached out a hand, snagged hers and pulled her beside his bed but not before she heard a growl. "She stays with me."

Todd's eyes bounced between them. "You know that I shouldn't do it, but for you, I'll ignore seeing her today. I know your brothers have set this up for you, but I'll help however I can."

"Thanks, Todd. I'll finish this by myself. The fucker tried to have me killed. Besides, I'm still undercover and as you reminded me, wanted. I can't have an FBI agent hanging out with me."

His face fell. "Let me at least take Ms. Rogers into protective custody. The Deputy Director can only cover for you for so long."

AJ's hold on her hand tightened. She glanced down in time to see a shot of anger briefly flashed across his face.

"She stays with the Hamiltons," AJ ground out, jaw clenched.

A sly smile grew on the agent's face. "So, that's how it is."

He nodded. "That's how it is."

She had no idea what they were talking about, but it put a huge smile on his partner's face.

"I won't stay. You need your rest. Call me if you need anything," he said with a note of amusement in his voice. He turned to her. "That goes for you too, Ms. Rogers. Remember, we'll put you in protective custody when you're ready."

Megan smiled. "I'm staying with AJ. Thank you, Agent Powers."

"Todd, please."

"Only if you call me Megan."

They closed out the conversation, and he left.

"So what's this about you being wanted by the FBI?"

****

"Don't worry about it. Just a misunderstanding. Who's outside the door?" AJ sat up in the bed, tossing his legs off the side, swaying. The nurse rushed over.

"Matt and Brad are now. I don't know what happened to the two men there before."

"Would you ask Matt to come in?" He stood and collapsed back on the bed, biting back a shout of pain. He couldn't let her know how much his leg burned and throbbed, or she'd fight to stay. They couldn't.

Megan did as he asked but kept glancing back at him.

"We need to bug out. No one is to know. I mean no one," he told his brother as he entered the room.

"We're already on it. It's been damn Grand Central Station here." Matt tossed clothing on the bed. Then he spun on his heel and left the room.

Nurse Laura began disconnecting AJ from his IV and machines.

"What's going on? You can't leave. You're still recovering." Megan's voice rose frantically.

He sighed. "Megan, someone knows we're here. It won't take long for others to know. We can't stay."

"But it was just your partner. He's one of the good guys."

"But he may tell someone else, who may tell someone else. Or someone could have followed him in hopes he'd lead them to us. Do you see what I mean?"

A horrified look appeared on her face. "Oh God. But is it safe for you to leave?"

"It has to be."

He handed her clothing. "Change into this. Did you call anyone while we were here?"

"No. Kristen called me," she answered. "Oh, Marcus came here to see me."

His gaze snapped to hers. "What?"

She told him about their visit.

He couldn't help it, he saw red. Flat-out jealousy. She had loved Marcus enough to agree to marry him. Did she still have feelings for him? She'd stayed with AJ, but was that only so she could catch the Magician? He shouldn't care, but he couldn't help himself.

Once Megan had dressed, Matt and Brad rolled a gurney into the room while one of the men escorted the nurse out.

Megan looked at their emergency medical technician attire and then down at herself. He barely stifled his laughter. She'd been so worried she hadn't noticed what she now wore.

He took a deep, fortified breath, stood, and limped the few steps to the gurney. Swiping the beads of sweat from his forehead, he covered himself with the sheet to his chest.

"You're leaving on the gurney? Where will I be?"

"Right beside me." He flashed a sexy smile and gave her a wink in hopes of calming her. "Just put your hair in the hat and pull it down low over your face."

Once on the first floor, they exited through the emergency entrance. His brothers loaded him into the back of an ambulance and then helped Megan climb in. Matt and Brad walked to the front of the vehicle, and they left the hospital.

"Why did we leave like this?" she questioned.

"They would've been waiting for us to leave by the front or a side door. It was best not to chance it."

"Where are we going?"

He chuckled and pulled himself into a sitting position.

"Are we going back to our room?"

"No. They'll drop me near a new place, and you're going with them." He needed her safe, even if it wasn't with him. He had to do what was best for her.

She shot him a scathing look that singed his skin. "I may be a bit scared, but you're not pawning me off on your brothers. I'm going with you, AJ Hamilton. We have something to finish, together."

He expelled a heavy sigh. He knew she'd argue. "Megan, you're safest with them. I've told you that I can do this alone and now it's time that I do."

"Well, you've got another thing coming. I'm not leaving you." She crossed her arms over her chest.

He dragged a hand through his hair and then cupped the back of his neck. He knew he wouldn't win this argument. "Okay, they'll drop us." He leaned forward and gave her a light kiss.

He hoped he was right.

Chapter Twenty-Seven

This was the first morning AJ hadn't met Megan with a newspaper and a cup of coffee. Instead, his arms were wrapped around her waist, her body curled next to his. He looked down at her. She was lovely even with the messed-up hair.

He'd collapsed in the bed the moment they'd entered the room, sleeping the remainder of the day and through the night, but remembered waking groggily for short spurts to tell her that she needed to go with his brothers because he couldn't protect her enough himself. Jesse, who had stayed in the room during the evening as what he called extra protection, laughed at him. Damn brother.

AJ had woken to his brothers coming and going, and to the smell of coffee brewing. Megan's face had lit up when she'd seen there was a separate bedroom with a door, providing the two of them a bit of privacy.

"Good morning, my little dove." He smiled down at her sleepy eyes.

"Good morning. How do you feel?"

"Like I've been shot."

"That's not funny."

"Well, it's true." He tightened his hold on her and kissed her forehead. He didn't want to let her go, but he couldn't stay with her. He had to fix things with Jake and Emily. He wouldn't be whole again until he found his foster brother and reunited the two of them. He had to repair the damage he'd done to his sister's life before he could live a full one himself. Megan didn't deserve a broken man. And he'd remain broken until he resolved this.

He'd kicked Jake out of their home, threatened him if he returned, not realizing Emily loved their foster brother. He'd later found out she was pregnant, turning AJ's world into a whirlwind. He couldn't locate Jake. He had to return the man to Emily. It was past time Amber knew her father.

"What's our plan for today?" She reached up and brushed her lips against his.

"We're going to lay low today and allow me to heal. We'll meet with my brothers, and then we'll begin to piss off a crime boss."

****

"Where are we going?" Megan asked.

AJ chuckled. "To HIS headquarters."

"Where is it?"

"Between Baltimore and Silver Spring," Brad, their current bodyguard and driver answered.

She leaned on AJ's shoulder in the backseat. He wrapped his arms around her.

Megan had held back telling him she loved him. Kate had said he cared for her but listening to his brothers' joke with him, it became blatantly apparent that he was a ladies' man, not a man to settle down with one woman. The elation in her heart evaporated. Would her love be enough for AJ to become a one-woman man?

How could she break down the barrier Kate told her he had? Heck, he'd been shot putting himself between her and a bullet. Plus, he'd allowed her to stay with him. That had to mean something. Didn't it?

Marcus never would've protected her in that manner. Actually, he wouldn't have allowed her to continue her pursuit of the Magician. He'd have expected her to put aside her need for justice. He didn't understand. Probably never had understood her. Even if it hadn't been about her brother, she'd have still wanted to help Kevin and the police remove Magic Shop from the streets.

But AJ wasn't Marcus. He understood not only her need for justice but also her need to finish this story. To find the answers the public wanted. To do her job. A job she admitted she should've stopped before things became dangerous and she'd been shot at. But that burning desire to see this through trumped anything else.

In the middle of nowhere, they stopped at a remote, rustic house with a light dusting of snow on the roof. Smoke escaped the chimney. The cozy look had her eager to explore.

Kate and a Dalmatian met them at the door, welcoming them to her home and headquarters.

Megan walked into the large, open living room, her eyes zeroing in on the men with guns. She'd met most of them at the hospital already. AJ, leaning on a cane, introduced her to them again. For some reason, she immediately knew these men would do anything to protect her and AJ.

A man who looked similar to AJ and his brothers, but had longer curly hair and a softer, more sensual appeal, walked up to her and introduced himself as Devon. She'd almost laughed out loud. She'd expected a computer geek look. She should've expected another handsome man. Their father, U.S. Senator Blake Hamilton was an appealing man. His boys were younger versions of him.

A squeal erupted, and a flash of red passed her and threw itself at AJ. Devon reached back to keep him from falling on the floor.

"Uncle AJ! You came! You came!" A beautiful dark-haired child with an angelic face of five or six wrapped her tiny arms around him, holding his legs tight and eliciting a muffled groan from him.

Kate lifted her daughter. "Remember what I told you. Be careful, he's hurt," she whispered to the little girl.

"I will, Momma." The child's attempt at a whisper failed.

AJ smiled and kissed the girl on the forehead after his sister-in-law handed her into his free arm. "I had to come see you, Reagan. I've missed you."

She pulled back. "Guess what?"

"What?"

"I have a new brother. And guess what?"

He raised his eyebrows. "What?"

"He's hurt. And guess what?"

"What?"

"I'm babysitting a cat. And guess what?"

The room erupted in light chuckles at AJ being assaulted with the "Guess what," question the child had mastered.

"What?"

"You missed Amber's birthday. She turned three." In her attempt to display the number, she held three tiny fingers up with one hand and used the other hand to hold her thumb and pinky down.

His smile faded, and his body visibly tensed.

"Reagan, meet Miss Megan."

The little girl smiled and stuck out her hand for a handshake. "Are you Bob's mom?"

Grasping Reagan's small, soft hand, she responded, "Hi, Reagan. I am. Is he around?" Megan hadn't thought of her cat in days. Kate had told her about his antics, but he'd slipped her mind. Megan's thoughts had been filled with the man before her. She had to get her head screwed back on correctly.

The little girl squirmed away from her uncle and ran off.

"Hey, doll."

Megan turned and gave a small squeal of her own. She threw her arms around her old bodyguard. "Trent, you're okay."

"Not as okay as AJ. My bullet hit bone, so I'm out of business for a while." He waved down to a brace on his leg.

Her heart sank. "I'm so sorry. I'll pay you for the time you can't work. It's only fair."

He chuckled. "Doll, you aren't paying me. It's a work hazard. Besides, you were worth it."

"Trent, let her go," AJ demanded.

She swung around and caught the challenging look AJ cast his friend.

"Hey, AJ, jealous much?" Trent taunted.

The muscles in AJ's jaw twitched. Disgust at the male macho territorial bullcrap going on made her want to scream. She'd had quite enough.

Before she could give them a piece of her mind, Reagan returned struggling to hold Bob. "Here, Miss

Megan."

She hurried to retrieve her cat before he fell to the floor. Although cats supposedly landed on their feet, she never was one for testing the theory. Hugging him tightly, nuzzling in his warm, long hair, and listening to his loud purr, calmed her. "I missed you, big boy."

"You should've seen it. Bob hissed at Dottie, and she barked at him. And later they were friends. They played together. They played with me. Bob really likes chasing the red dot." Reagan snickered.

"Everyone's here, let's go," Jesse said above the noise in the room.

AJ leaned to her and placed a light kiss on the lips. "Stay with Kate. I'll be back soon."

Megan's hands stroked Bob faster. "But I thought we were doing this together?"

He ran his hand through his already disheveled hair. "We are, but—"

Kate interrupted. "It's okay, Megan. We'll find out what they said soon enough without dealing with all their male bullshit. Besides, AJ hasn't received his ribbing yet today." She winked at him.

Looking back and forth between the two, Megan bit the corner of her lower lip. She'd come to trust Kate. She'd saved her and AJ. If she said they would find out, then she believed her. But what was this about him getting ribbed? "I'll trust you, AJ, but I want to know what Kate is talking about."

He dropped his head and laughed. "It's nothing. Don't worry about it." He and Trent brought up the rear each leaning on a cane.

"Come have a drink with me. This will take a while," Kate said.

Megan set Bob on the wood-planked floor. "I'm right behind you." A photo on the mantel caught her attention, and she picked it up. It showed one beautiful girl and six handsome boys. Five of the boys looked like their father whom they all surrounded. The sixth boy and girl looked different from the rest. And different from each other. Different mothers maybe? But she'd read the senator had only been married once, and his wife had died of cancer.

Kate smiled. "I picked up the same photograph my first time here. Perfect looking family, isn't it? Before you ask, the girl is their baby sister, Emily. The boy is their foster brother, Jake Cavanaugh."

"I hope I meet them someday." It would have to be soon unless she could convince AJ to share his life with her. She'd love to be a part of this family.

Kate took the photo from her and placed it back on the mantel. "Emily moved to New York, and Jake is a long story. One that it's best AJ tells you."

****

AJ and Megan waited for the phone to ring. Everything had to go as planned. They needed this drug bust.

Matt, their current babysitter, lounged in a chair watching TV. AJ knew he remained fully alert and listened to everything said. His brother rubbed his own leg, and AJ sighed. He loved him and wished he could make everything normal again. AJ's leg would be fine in a few days, but Matt's wouldn't.

"Why hasn't he called?"

AJ chuckled at her impatience. "He'll call when he's able. Now, did you call your boss and tell her you'd have a front-page exclusive for her?"

"Yes. She kept pushing to learn what it was. She threatened not to take the story if I didn't let her know the basics right then. I told her that I'd submit it to her and if she didn't print it then I'd submit it to other newspapers. Dang, I wish I could've been there to take photos."

"You'll have to suffer with just an interview. The phone should ring any minute." Although Byron couldn't participate in the bust since it would blow his cover, he'd selected an agent to brief Megan. The DEA appreciated positive news articles about their success with the war on drugs.

She glanced at Matt and then back to him. "Tell me about Jake."

AJ's heart seemed to stop. How could he explain it to her without him appearing as a monster? How could he tell her that finding Jake was what held him back from a real life? She loved her brother so maybe she'd understand AJ's need to find him. She wouldn't understand his part in his brother leaving. Knowing that, she'd blame him for Emily's heartbreak like the rest of the family did.

The ringing phone saved him. She'd ask again, so he needed to prepare himself.

"Hamilton."

He handed the phone to her and knew he would lose her for the next hour or so. Holding the phone with one hand, her smile widened with every note she wrote. His heart lightened at her visible pleasure. She was in her element.

There was no doubt that Megan would insist on attending the meeting his team expected the Magician to have with his advisors who'd failed him. As a reporter, it would be too good of a story for her to pass up. Plus, there was her own agenda in bringing down the criminal. But, she wouldn't be there, end of story. No way would he allow her to be nearby when all went down.

Typing away on the keyboard, Megan seemed oblivious to the world outside her. It didn't take long for her to go from listening to taking notes to writing a full-blown story.

As for the unveiling of the Magician, he'd be her source for her article. The person who'd conducted the arrests. The person who'd finally brought down that son of a bitch. Somehow he'd have to make her see reason in it all. He almost chuckled aloud at that thought. How he'd broach the subject without her threatening to go it alone, escaped him. The only hope was to get HIS involved in keeping her out of it as well.

This was his damn fault for not handing her off from the beginning. Had he done that, he wouldn't be considering the problem. Then again—

Megan broke into his thoughts.

"I'm finished. Do you want to read it before I send it?" She turned beaming at him, almost bouncing out of the chair with excitement. "I can't believe he sent me a photo to use."

AJ trusted her. She'd proved herself and joined the elite few that he did trust. "Go ahead and send it. We need it to be in the morning paper."

And just like that, step one of their plan had been set in motion.

He rose and walked toward her, pulling her into his arms, his kiss hard and fast, her tongue meeting his halfway. His need for her took hold of him and wouldn't let go.

A throat clearing slowly brought him back.

"There is a room with a closed door," Matt informed them.

Megan giggled as AJ dragged her there while hobbling, slamming the door behind him. With her help, he pulled her sweater and bra off. He leaned down and took her breast in his mouth. He pulled back. "I'm sorry to say my injury will limit my ability to make love to you."

She reached under his sweater and slid her hands over his chest. "We already know that you being on your back doesn't limit us."

Which was all he needed to hear.

****

In bed naked, AJ kissed Megan, feasting on her mouth with his lips and tongue as a heated passion flowed between them. Her taste made him lose focus on everything but her. While he could kiss her like this forever, he wanted more.

From the beginning, there had been something about Megan that told him things wouldn't be easy, but they'd be worth it. Now, shaking with lust, he needed her more than ever, needed everything she could give.

She moaned, sexy and throaty, and arched into his hand, rushing heat to his heavy erection that painfully throbbed with the need to be inside her, to fill her, to feel her come around him.

Raising his mouth from hers, he gazed into her darkening eyes. He brought his slightly trembling hand to her face and lightly stroked her cheek with the back of it. She was beautiful, inside and outside. He'd been lucky she had been thrown in his path.

Having her beside him, her lips wet and swollen, her hair splayed over the pillows, and her eyes clouded with lust would be a snapshot he'd never forget. "I can't get enough of you."

What had she done to him? They were in a dangerous situation, and he'd willingly turned their protection over to his brothers so he could be inside her. And it wasn't the first time. If it had been the olden days, he'd think she'd bewitched him.

"I feel the same." Her voice was breathless, and her body trembled. She pulled him down for a hot, demanding kiss, her tongue invading his mouth, her nails cutting into his back. He groaned. His little dove wasn't shy and knew how to push him to the edge.

AJ slid his lips from hers, kissing across her cheek, teasing the sensitive skin along her jaw, grazing her earlobe, and then his lips explored, ever so slowly, along the silky expanse of her neck, pausing at a rapidly beating pulse that matched his own.

She whimpered softly as he continued his path toward her breast.

He took the puckered bud into his mouth, sucking, teasing, nipping until she moaned and writhed beneath him. Her body's passionate response urged him forward. Moving his hand down, his fingers crossed the beginning of hair growth on her mound. Maybe she would let him shave her? That erotic vision flitted through his mind. He tamped it and the other dozen fantasies down. Later.

AJ slid his fingers across her slick folds, nudging a finger inside her core, finding her hot, drenched... ready. Her hips strained to meet his touch. Groaning, he gave her clit an idle flick before slipping two fingers inside her. He loved the small, erotic sounds she made.

Sounds that made his cock scream to be inside her, needing release.

Megan glided her hand down his chest, teasing along the way, playing with the curly hair, tweaking the nipples before slipping to grasp his erection. His breath caught, and every muscle in his body clenched. Her touch left a trail of fire in its wake that only she could extinguish.

Grasping him tight, she stroked his length from shaft to tip, her thumb teasing the crown when she reached it, wiping away his precum. After several minutes of torture, she clasped his testicles and gave a light squeeze.

His body jerked, and his groan sounded animalistic. Her touch set his body on the edge of the floodgate, ready for the dam to break. There was only so much he could take.

Maneuvering above her, their bodies aligned, he rested on his forearms, unsure if he could string any words together. "Minx," he rasped.

"What about your leg?"

"What leg?" He tamped down the pain. He needed to be in control.

A slow, sexual smile grew on her face. "Hmm." She wrapped her legs around his back and guided him to her entrance.

AJ looked down at Megan. The heat in her eyes seemed to mirror the hunger raging inside him. With sweat forming on his forehead, he gritted his teeth and nudged his way inside her until he fully seated himself. A look of pleasure reflected on her face.

She lifted her hips off the bed and rocked against

him until he could move and they fell into a rhythm they had perfected. Their bodies were in exquisite harmony with each other.

He leaned down, his lips caressed hers, nipped at her bottom one, and sucked on her tongue. Her kisses made him feel alive and exhilarated.

Megan's breathing changed, and she wiggled beneath him, arching closer. He knew her, knew her body. She was close to orgasm.

Sweating, his heart thundering, he balanced himself on his left forearm, reached down with his right hand to cup her ass, and buried himself into her as deep as he could go, pulled out and plunged into her again, ensuring every thrust made the root of his cock graze her swollen clit.

She responded immediately. Her body tensed, her inner muscles drew tighter around him, and her moans became frantic. She came with a cry, ecstasy on her face.

With a long drawn-out groan, he surrendered, pleasure tore through him as he exploded hot, fast and strong inside her.

He had no idea how much time had passed as he lay on top of her waiting for his floating body to return to earth. Slowly he rolled off her, pulling her with him so her head lay on his chest.

Megan snuggled into him. "I love you," she whispered.

Her declaration slammed into his midsection harder than the force of the shot at his chest. AJ tensed and then went into flight mode. He pulled from under her, jumped from the bed, and raced into the bathroom, locking the door behind him.

He cleaned himself, wiped off the small bit of blood leaking from his wound, and then leaned over the sink, his head down. A deep sigh escaped. A sigh of despair.

She loved him.

How the hell did he deal with that? He didn't deserve her love. He didn't deserve anyone's love.

Where did he go from here? Pretend he didn't hear it? No. He expected she'd say it again.

Why the hell had he let himself get involved? He was supposed to protect her, not steal her heart and then rip it apart. They'd have no other option. They would end when this was over. Maybe he should tell her that so she could get used to the idea before she fell deeper in love.

No. He couldn't tell her now. She'd beg him to stay with her and he couldn't.

He looked up at his reflection in the mirror. He couldn't stay in here forever.

What sucked was that he still desired her. He wanted her under him and beside him. He loved her.

He wet one of the rags in the bathroom and steeled himself for her reaction to his running off like a chicken.

He had no plan. There was no playbook for how to handle this. He'd figure out what to do as he went along.

AJ carried the damp rag with him from the bathroom and reached out to clean Megan.

"Tell me about Jake."

His body stilled. Why not fuck up what had been great sex with her admission of love and his sharing what he'd done to Jake? AJ had come to expect all good things in his life must come to an end. He'd just hoped for more time.

Reaching forward he handed her the cloth instead of cleaning her himself and then stepped back. "Are you sure you wish to know?"

She tilted her head and drew her brows in. "It seems to be something important to you, so yes, I'd like to know."

He pinched the bridge of his nose between his thumb and forefinger. The hands twisting his heart in two ripped it open. His soul dove deeper into the darkness. He'd held on to this for a long time. He'd held in the pain and the heartache. She'd been his last chance. And it would be over shortly. Why the hell not?

He sat on the edge of the bed but couldn't bring himself to look at her. He forced breath into his constricted lungs. "Jake was brought into our family when he was ten. We're the same age and quickly became best friends. I had someone else to help me stand up to my big brothers who picked on me and left me behind." Envisioning the fun he and his foster brother had, brought out a smile that immediately disappeared.

"We'd just graduated from college. We'd left one party and were headed to another. Jake decided he'd rather go home. Since he'd had too much to drink, we dropped him off and continued on with our sober, designated driver."

He didn't want her to think he'd been irresponsible enough to drink and drive or let Jake do the same. Not that it mattered with the whole of it. He'd just needed to tell her.

"I arrived home early in the morning and had

something to tell Jake." He waved his hand as if to brush something away. "I went to his room and, as usual, opened the door without knocking."

He stood, let his head fall back, and took a deep breath. God, how he'd fucked up. He dropped his head and turned back to her. "I found Jake and Em in bed together. She'd just turned eighteen that night, at midnight. We were due to celebrate her birthday the next day.

"As you can imagine, in my inebriated state, I went ballistic. I pulled him from the bed and began pummeling him. He didn't fight back, just attempted to protect himself, like he knew he deserved the beating. At the time, I hadn't realized he'd never thrown a punch.

"Em's screaming finally broke me out of a red haze. Tears streamed down her face, and she kept crying out that she loved him, and it was none of my business." He heaved a heavy sigh. "She was right, of course. But I wouldn't listen. All I knew was that someone had slept with my sister, and it had been my best friend. He'd betrayed my friendship and the love my family had for him.

"He and I had been packed to move into our own place closer to the FBI office we'd be assigned to after training. For some reason, I remembered that and gave him fifteen minutes to be out of the house and never return, or I'd tell our father what had happened. That didn't seem to bother him so I lied and told him that I'd tell them it happened before she'd turned eighteen. Dad happened to be on a campaign tour at the time, so he'd have no idea when things happened.

"I don't know what made me say I'd tell the lie. I

311

knew I'd never actually do it, but it shot out of my mouth. I grabbed a naked Em by the arm and dragged her out of the room. She kept screaming for Jake, but I brought her to her room and blocked the door until I knew he'd left. I never gave him a chance to explain or say his peace. Or worse, say goodbye to the family."

He and Emily had kept quiet in the beginning about why Jake had disappeared. Then his guilt became too heavy. Plus, he wasn't having any luck in his search for him. He'd needed his brothers' help.

"After dealing with a broken-hearted Em for a few weeks, I felt like an ass and knew I had to do something. I arrived at the FBI office, assuming he'd have done the same. He hadn't. He never showed up at the apartment we'd rented. His cell had been disconnected.

"I pushed Dev, who was CIA at the time, to do whatever it took to help me find him doing what he did best. I even checked John Does to see if…" He turned as a tear slid down his face. "…if we'd find him there." AJ swiped a hand over his face, turned, and sat down, his back to her. He wouldn't let her see him cry. He was the monster here, not the victim.

"It's like Jake disappeared off the face of the earth. I've spent every free moment searching for him. I've used every resource I have, and I can't find him. It's tearing me up inside."

AJ had dealt with almost four years of pain and grief about what he'd done. But during that time, anger at Jake for not fighting for his family raged within him. It had torn holes in his soul, left him lost, adrift only to surface for short periods of time before vanishing again.

"You haven't had a chance to meet my sister and

niece. Amber is Jake's daughter. He has no idea she exists or that my sister still pines for him. She says she's fine, but I can see that she's not the same…not as happy as she was before. She and the family say they don't blame me, but I know deep down they do. They said that Jake knew he could've contacted one of them if he'd wanted, but chose not to. My dad took it hard that he'd just walked away without a goodbye. To this day, he doesn't know what happened. I can't bring myself to tell him."

A soft hand slid up and down AJ's back. The warmth of her touch filled him, soothed him.

"Is that why the tattoo? I looked up the translation. It's Latin."

AJ looked down at his chest and nodded. "*Never give up.* I can't give up, Megan. I've failed my family in the worst way. I won't be whole again until he's back with us."

She spoke softly. "I've seen how much your family loves you. They don't blame you. If anything, they seem to want to help you. I've heard the worry in their voices. I've seen them try to drag you closer to them. But you refuse. You allow yourself to be like this. To bear this entire burden. AJ, Jake has just as much blame here as you do. You have to release this guilt and live your life."

He finally took a chance and looked into her eyes. His heart jumped. Her love lit them. Something turned over in his chest. He'd ruined two people's lives. Not to mention left a hole in plenty of others. He slowly reached up. With the pad of his thumb, he outlined her lips. She was just too good for him.

She knew the full truth.

"Now can you say you still love me?" Dread filled his belly at what her answer would be. He shouldn't care, but he did.

He felt her words on his thumb. "Yes, I still love you, AJ Hamilton."

Chapter Twenty-Eight

Megan emerged from the bathroom to find a newspaper and cup of coffee on the small desk. She smiled. Just like old times. She loved this man more every day.

"Good morning, Devon." She pressed a quick kiss to AJ's lips and sat at the desk.

Devon chuckled. "Good morning, Megan. Great article."

She turned to AJ. "Do you think this will do the job?"

He nodded. "It's perfect. Carl will be blamed for losing the product, and Damian will still be in the shithouse since you're alive."

Just a few more days and, if their plan worked, this would be over. They'd have the Magician. Unfortunately, it meant her time with AJ would end. She'd told him she loved him, and he gave her nothing in return. Not even hope. Maybe if she helped him find Jake, AJ would reconsider a life with her. But maybe he was too broken to fix. She had to get her own life back on track first and then figure out what to do about him.

"What's the plan for today?" she asked.

"We'll be keeping an eye on Paul. We need something from him."

"What? And how will we get it? I'm guessing he's not just going to open the door and hand over what you want."

A mischievous look covered AJ's face, and a twinkle appeared in his eyes. "We'll break in when he leaves, and Dev will collect the information we need."

"Don't you need a warrant for that?" Now that she knew he was FBI, she was aghast that he'd break into someone's house, especially without a warrant. Even she knew that the evidence would never stand up in court.

"Trust me, my little dove."

She studied him for a moment then went back to reading the newspaper.

****

AJ, Devon, Megan, and their trusted bodyguard and driver, Brad, had been parked near Paul's house for three hours. "We're moving again tonight," AJ informed her.

"How many more times will we move?"

She liked the current place. She'd become comfortable there. He hated snatching it away, but he had to. They'd have a separate room again for privacy so he hoped that would settle her since it would be another dive.

He threw his arm around her and pulled her close. "As many as it takes to keep you safe." He kissed her temple and inhaled the euphoric fragrance surrounding her. The perfume was aptly named.

She wrapped an arm around his waist, and his heart pounded. He wanted her now. Good grief. He had to control his lust for her.

He and Brad exchanged piercing looks in the rearview mirror. His brothers best not say one goddamn word. AJ had heard enough. He wouldn't push her away because they said it would be the only way to keep her safe, to keep his focus. Fuck them. He'd done a good job of keeping her safe thus far. Besides, he had his brothers protecting them now.

Megan looked out the window. "What do you think Carl did today?"

AJ snorted. "I imagine he tried to think up an excuse and a fall guy for the bust."

"Do you think he can get out of it?"

"Not a chance." He looked down and smiled softly.

"You sound confident. How do you know?"

He shrugged. "Trust me."

"Do you think he had to meet with the Magician one-on-one instead of in the big meeting we want?"

"I don't know, but I'll ask his tail every place he visited and who visited him."

She loosened her grip. "You have a tail on him?"

"Of course. We can't afford for him to run. We have a tail on all of them."

She looked around and frowned. "Where's Paul's tail?"

Devon looked up from his laptop and turned from the passenger seat to glance at her. "You won't find Danny."

"I have to say that this sucks," Megan whined.

AJ pulled her close again and tightened the blanket that covered her full body. As men, they just sucked it up. He wished they could've kept the car running for her warmth.

"Did you let your boss know you'd have another big article for her tomorrow?"

"Yes. Again, she threatened to stop taking my articles if I didn't tell her what they were about before I submitted them. She fluctuated between worry and anger. I've never seen her like that before."

Journalists, with the exception of Megan, bothered him. He'd never trusted them and still didn't. No matter what they said, they couldn't keep their mouths shut. "You didn't tell her what was happening tomorrow, did you?"

"Of course not."

"Don't let her push you into giving away our plans. We can't afford for her to tell the FBI."

"You are the FBI."

He gave her an incredulous look. "Technically I'm a wanted man for not turning you over to them."

His secure cell phone rang before she could respond.

"You're good to go. Well, gray area good to go. I'm still not comfortable with this," Arthur said.

AJ nodded to Devon who went to work with swift fingers across his keyboard. "This is an anonymous group poking their noses in where it doesn't belong. I'm officially fired."

"Like I expect anything less from your brothers. What are you doing?"

"We're watching his house, waiting for him to leave. Is my team ready for tomorrow?"

"Yes. That's the tricky part. Someone may find out you're no longer part of us."

It didn't matter as long as the evidence didn't get tossed out by a rogue FBI agent. "If they do, they have to follow your orders."

"Do you plan to tell me what they'll be doing?"

"No. I'll tell them right before I need them."

His ex-boss huffed. "I don't like that you've

become tight-lipped with me. I hired you for this. I thought you trusted me. I trust you by allowing you to use these valuable resources without my knowledge of their task that goes against everything we do. My boss will have my ass if he finds out."

He did trust Arthur. But, AJ hadn't identified all the leaks in the FBI so he wouldn't chance someone knowing the task ahead of time.

"This is your show, AJ. Just don't fuck me over or you'll regret ever knowing me. Oh, and remember you're wanted. Consider turning her over so I can clean this bullshit up before it gets beyond my ability to help."

AJ tilted back his head and sighed. "I appreciate you covering for me. She won't go, and I won't force her, even if it makes me wanted and most likely fired."

With a grunt, Arthur ended the call.

The worst part was that no matter which choice AJ made, keep her with him or turning her over to the FBI, he might not be able to keep her safe. His gut clenched. He had to have made the right choice. "Megan, I have to leave the car for a few minutes. I need you to stay here with Brad and Dev."

A stricken look appeared on her face. "Why? What are you going to do?"

"I'm just walking right over there." He pointed to Paul's SUV. "I need to put this on it." He showed her the slap-on GPS tracker he'd pulled from a new black bag that Devon had brought.

Brad turned to them. "And how the fuck do you plan to do that? Don't you think a man hobbling on a cane might be noticed?"

AJ glared at him.

His brother reached back. "Hand me the fucking thing."

Task completed, they settled back in to wait.

Megan finally spoke up, "This is boring. Isn't there something we can do?"

Brad grinned, but AJ wouldn't allow him to suggest one of the raunchy games they played when stuck in the car. He opened his mouth to say the first thing that flew out, but Devon got in the first word.

"Jimmy's making a visit."

Interesting. He had no reason to visit Paul unless he happened to be passing a message from Carl. AJ wished he'd been able to bug the place.

Megan looked in Jimmy's direction and smiled. "He's going to be pissed tomorrow."

The brothers chuckled.

AJ kissed her cheek. "Yes, he is."

****

Paul left his house, and Megan's pulse rate shot through the roof. Even with her nosing around to get a story, she'd never broken into a building. Fear and excitement welled within her. Her hope was they didn't get arrested.

Brad handed AJ a device that looked like a smart phone. "It's good to go."

"I thought we couldn't have regular phones?" she asked.

"It's our GPS tracker," AJ explained.

"That's cool."

"Yes, it is. Now come on. We need to get a move on."

Devon calmly stood in front of AJ, scanning the area, acting as if he belonged there with someone kneeling behind him, picking a lock. He held an electronic device he'd explained cracked security alarm codes. Impressive.

Her job was to hold onto the GPS tracker and monitor Paul's movements, letting them know when Paul was returning. She repeatedly glanced at it, worried the man would turn around, come back, and catch them.

The door opened. "Okay, let's go." AJ used his cane to stand, and Devon slid inside.

"What are you looking for?" she whispered, entering the house.

"Records. They supposedly keep track of their clients, their new identities, where they settle, etc."

He didn't wait for his brother. He tugged her behind him as he briefly peeked into each room. All she caught were glimpses of brown everywhere.

"Here."

AJ pulled Megan into a room with wine-colored walls, dark furniture, and one large window that provided a view of the front yard.

Devon walked in and sat at the computer. He snorted. "The idiot didn't log off before he left."

"What do you want me to do?" She glanced at the tracker.

Without even looking up at her, AJ answered, "Look around for anything that has information on the prison breaks. But, more importantly, keep an eye on the GPS."

She nodded and tugged at her gloves.

"Leave those on," Devon told her. She hadn't even realized he'd been cognizant of anything except the computer screen.

She knelt and opened the dark wood two-drawer file cabinet while AJ rifled through the loose papers on the desk.

"Bingo. For such a smart man, he's not careful with this information." Devon pulled a thumb drive from his pocket, plugged it into the computer, and began copying files.

She sifted through documents in the file cabinet.

AJ looked over to her. "Anything good?"

She shook her head, disappointed she hadn't found anything helpful. "Not really. It's normal things, house deed, car title, tax returns."

He ducked his head and opened a file folder. "Where is he now?"

Megan gasped. She had been so lost in flipping through the files that she'd forgotten about checking the GPS. "Oh God. AJ, he's coming back! I'm sorry."

AJ sent a text on his secure phone. "How long, Dev?"

"I need two more minutes. I've got a few files left, including one on officials they have bribed and blackmailed."

"We don't have that long. He'll turn on this street any moment." Her heart beat faster. If she didn't make them hurry, then they would get caught, and it would be her fault. They'd trusted her with this one thing, and she'd let herself get sidetracked snooping.

She wondered what Paul would do. Would he kill them outright? He was sure to know there was a hit on them, and now, Devon had been caught in their fight.

AJ smiled at her. Actually smiled! He was enjoying this. "Look at the tracker again."

She looked down and furrowed her eyebrows.

"He's stopped at the corner."

Devon grabbed his thumb drive and stood. "Done."

AJ took her hand and rushed her to the front door. "Now it's time to go."

She looked at the tracker. "He's still not moving."

The three of them filed out of the front door. AJ propelled her forward without his brother.

"Don't look. Just keep walking. He'll catch up," he told her.

"Brad's gone. What will we do?"

AJ stepped toward the gray car slowly approaching them. "Danny will give us a ride as Brad's busy with a broken-down car at the intersection."

It took her a moment to process what he'd said. She'd wanted to applaud the brilliance of these men. "Do you think he'll know we were in his house?"

He shook his head. "I doubt it. He didn't have his deadbolt locked. That would've been our only giveaway since we wouldn't have had time to lock it."

"And, unless he's computer savvy, which I doubt based on what I saw, he won't know that I was there," Devon added.

"Did anything identify the Magician?" Fingers crossed in her mind he had found something to help them.

"Not that I noticed, but I've quite a few files to review. Don't count on his being named. Even Paul is smarter than that."

A devilish grin stretched across AJ's face. "We'll find out. We still have plenty of cards up our sleeves."

Chapter Twenty-Nine

"How will you do this? You didn't even bring your cane to help you walk?" Worry reflected in the furrowing of Megan's brow.

"Why do you think the twins are tagging along?" AJ smiled cheekily.

"We do have names," Matt retorted.

"Yeah. The twins." AJ chuckled. They'd picked on him his entire childhood. Not only had he been the youngest Hamilton brother, but he was also an April Fools' Day baby. They never let him forget it. That love of poking at him had bled over to the HIS team. Even with the ribbing, he knew without a doubt they had his back. He and Megan were safe.

A grunt sounded from one of the twins in the back seat and Megan giggled. Ah, a smile looked much better on her.

They had to move to his plan B to learn the date of the prison escape. This had a chance of tipping their hand, but they had to do something. They needed that bust. This group couldn't slip through their fingers. They'd just set up elsewhere with their excessively large bank accounts.

They found a parking space across from Tony Mather's house, a driver on the prison break team. AJ dialed a number on the secure cell phone. Before anyone could speak, he said, "I'm here," and then hung up without waiting for a response.

The four of them cautiously approached the door. With a nod to his brothers, he confirmed they were ready.

His pulse rate increased as adrenaline shot through his body. He'd never tire of this.

Ignoring the doorbell, he pounded his fist on the door three times and then removed his weapon. He glanced back to witness the twins placing their hands on their weapons but leaving them holstered as they tightened their coverage around Megan.

He didn't expect this to be dangerous, but one never knows how a suddenly caged animal would react. With his brothers protecting her, he could keep his attention on the task.

A tall man with shaggy, sandy-brown hair opened the door and gasped when he saw AJ and the weapon pointed at him. After scanning his uninvited guests, the man straightened, changed his demeanor and acted as if someone held him at gunpoint daily.

"AJ," Tony said with a nod.

"Inside," AJ demanded, waving his Beretta.

Following instructions, the man turned and walked into his house, the group in tow.

"That's far enough. Let's go to your dining room."

Tony was prodded to a red leather chair pulled back from his dining table.

"Have a seat. Matt, put the cuffs on him."

AJ's brother walked forward.

"Put your hands behind the back of the chair and don't try anything. I've been shot and am not in the mood for any more shit."

He breathed a silent sigh of relief when Matt

returned to protect Megan.

Tony shot AJ a furious look. "There are a lot of people looking for you, especially now that they know you're not who you said you were. You're a Fed," he spat out.

AJ holstered his Beretta, taking in Tony's words. So, they found out about him. Later he'd find out how. At least it worked to his advantage right now.

"Good. Then you know that I'm about to bust you." He turned a chair around and sat across from his prey.

A panicked look struck the man's face. "W-What?"

"You heard me. I'm having you arrested. You're the first of Paul's team I've come to see, so I'm giving you an opportunity to help yourself. And, you will go to prison today unless you help me."

Tony flattened his lips and shot a venomous glare at AJ. "Are you kidding me? I'm not telling you anything. I don't want the Magician on me. I don't have a death wish."

AJ shook his head. "Tony, Tony. You don't understand. Even the Magician will go down this time. Your entire team will soon be arrested. The first one to talk has a chance at protective custody and a new life. If you don't want to be the first to talk, then I'll go to someone else on the team. One of them will see the writing on the wall and spill their guts."

"What do you mean the Magician is going down?"

AJ shrugged nonchalantly. "I'll be arresting him too."

"Do you know who he is?"

AJ allowed a cool, confident smile to curve his lips. "I will."

His brothers had visited the night prior while Megan slept. They'd discussed the information gathered to date on the investigation being quietly conducted by the HIS team. Putting together their facts, they created a short, solid list of possible suspects. Megan wouldn't like any of them, so he hadn't shared the information with her. At some point, the two of them would need to discuss it, but he didn't want to see the pain it might cause.

"How?" Tony asked.

AJ stood and walked around the man. Without the cane to hold some of the weight off his leg, pain pulsed through it with every step. "Don't worry about that. Here's what's going to happen. We'll arrest you for your part in the operation. Taking me with you on a mission was a mistake." He stopped in front of him. "After I arrest you, I expect Paul will have you sprung. Unfortunately, the Magician will think you spilled the beans to either me or the police and will put a hit on you."

Tony's eyes widened again. "What?"

AJ assessed him. This could be easier than he thought it would be. He'd expected some fight from Tony and truthfully was disappointed not to get it. AJ needed to take his anger out on someone. They'd shot at him and Megan.

"The Magician won't take the chance that you made a deal or talked. We can keep you alive with the Witness Protection Program if you become our source of information and testify against Paul and your team."

The man visibly trembled. "I don't want prison, and I don't want to die."

"You really should've thought of that before you

joined Magic Shop. I'm not in a position to promise you anything but the chance to live."

Tony dropped his head, and a loud, defeated sigh emanated from him. "Are you sure the Magician will put a hit out on me, or are you just saying that?"

"I'm one hundred percent certain he'll do it. He's had people killed for less than that."

Tony swallowed audibly. "Are you sure you can keep me alive?"

AJ contained his triumph. He had him, hook, line and sinker. "There's a Deputy U.S. Marshal on the way here. He'll take you to prison or into protective custody. That's your choice, Tony. It's a live-or-die decision. It should be an easy choice."

"What about my girl? I don't want to go without her."

That was the reason AJ had chosen Tony first. The question had been expected, and AJ had already cleared the way if the man asked. "Are you ready to marry her?"

He nodded. "Yes."

"Then I think we can work something out."

Relief shifted in the depth of Tony's gaze. "Okay, I want protection."

AJ smiled, returned to his seat, and sat. "Good choice. Now, how about you give us some information?"

"What do you want to know?" The man's voice broke betraying his nervousness.

"When is the next prison break?"

"Tomorrow."

Shit. He'd known it was soon, but fuck, he'd have to work fast.

Tony answered all the questions to AJ's satisfaction. Another person's life he'd saved.

A Deputy U.S. Marshal walked through the door, and AJ stood to greet him. "Protective custody and no one knows except your protection detail."

****

AJ paced the floor waiting for the secure cell phone to ring. He hated sitting on the sidelines. He hated waiting like this. He needed to be involved, injury or not. He had a slight gait, but nothing that would've prevented him from participating in a raid or arrest. Maybe he'd bust a stitch or two, but who cared? That could be fixed. Hell, he'd already had a few stitched again after his and Megan's escapades in bed.

"Calm down, baby brother. He'll call."

He gritted his teeth and swung around on Brad. AJ hated it when any of them called him baby brother. "Fuck you."

Megan's giggle lifted his spirit, sending a shot of happiness bouncing around inside, relaxing him. He needed that in his life. Fuck. No use thinking that way. It was almost time to tell her what her future held. She'd fight him on it, but she would lose. And, in the end, so would he.

He checked the phone to ensure he hadn't missed a call. His head back into work, her laughter forgotten, his muscles tightened into knots worrying something had gone awry. They couldn't afford that to happen. They'd selected the right people. He was sure of that.

Tomorrow would be the biggest day. Besides the prison escape, they'd add hitting the brothels at the same time.

After today, striking out at Carl and Aaron's

business should be the final straw. And the final card in their deck. This had to be the right approach to capture the Magician. It had to be. Everything agents had done over the years to identify him had failed. This had been a gamble. Adding Megan's articles to the plan had been his brilliant suggestion and had strengthened it all.

He jumped at the ringing of the phone in his hand. He answered but remained silent.

"It's all done," Arthur stated gruffly.

AJ let out a heavy breath. "Any issues?"

"Nothing they couldn't handle. No one expected them. You could've told me what the plan had been, soon to be ex-Special Agent Hamilton."

He nodded even though the caller couldn't see it. "Yes. I could have."

Arthur cleared his throat. "I've added the deputy marshals you requested for tomorrow. Dammit, AJ! Tell me about this one. I had to pull a lot of strings for you."

"Can't, Arthur. I don't trust the phones anymore."

"Yours is secure and so is mine. What's the fucking problem?"

"There's a leak, and I'm not willing to chance it. This is too important to me."

His pseudo ex-boss cleared his throat. "I never should've allowed you so much leash on this one. When you come back, we'll discuss your choice to keep the girl with you over your career and possible jail time."

He couldn't care less what happened to him after this ended. He'd go back to his lonely life tearing apart every potential lead he had to find Jake. His heart clenched. *Where the fuck did you go, brother?*

"AJ?"

Shaking his head to clear his thoughts, he stated, "I'm leading the team tomorrow."

Silence. "Is that what you really want to do? You could blow your cover."

"I found out my cover has already been blown, not that it mattered anymore since they attempted to kill me. I couldn't have slid back into the organization. So I'm not sitting out tomorrow."

"How's the leg?"

He absently stopped pacing and rubbed the wound. "It won't be a problem."

"What about the girl? How do you plan to protect her when you're playing federal agent?"

He had no choice in the matter. If he left her, she'd find a way to get into trouble. The team already had a weak spot for her. Her bubbly personality was contagious. They all wanted to be around her. Which pissed him the hell off. He'd kill any of them who touched her. He feared she'd somehow sweet-talk one of their warriors into breaking protocol. If anyone could do it, it'd be her. So, no choice.

"She comes with me. HIS will be there to keep her safe."

"Maybe you can convince her to leave with the marshals."

Arthur had no clue how adamant she was about that topic. No was her only answer, never hesitating. She stayed with him, her faith unwavering. He didn't deserve it. He still held important secrets from her.

He ended the call and gave Megan the go-ahead.

"AJ, I forgot. When Alex held me captive, he used your real name. They've known for a while who you really are."

He shrugged to assure her it was no big deal. The more he thought about it, the closer he came to the rat.

She moved to the desk, pulled her hair back in a clip, her face serious, and began typing. Knowing at the end she'd stretch.... *Fuck.* Brad would see her perfect breasts push out, asking to be suckled. AJ would have to distract him at the right moment. No way would he have his hound dog of a brother salivating over what was his.

Today had been a good day. They'd captured Jimmy and picked up twenty Magic Shop dealers. She had another front-page article. It had to burn the Magician reading her articles, when she should not only be dead, but also she more or less flaunted his failures.

His eyes honed in on her long, silky neck. Blood pulsed and flowed to his groin. He looked away. He couldn't get enough of her.

His burner phone rang.

"Hello."

"Did you create this chaos?" Blade asked.

AJ smiled. "What makes you think that?"

"I've come to know you. You're trying to seriously piss him off, aren't you?"

He ignored his question. He'd protected Blade on the bust, but the dealer didn't need to be aware of that or any of his plans. "What's the word on the street?"

"There's talk the dealers arrested are on their own. That's pissed off the ones who were lucky. They were hot after Jimmy until they heard he got arrested too. An escaped convict. Huh. The dealers want Carl now. They refuse to go on the street until he can provide them protection from DEA."

"It's very unfortunate things are as they are." AJ wanted to fist pump. The dealers revolting made this all the better.

His informant chuckled. "You're good."

AJ's smile broadened. He couldn't be more pleased with the day's results. "I don't know what you're talking about."

"Okay, whatever you say. Thanks for getting Jimmy for me."

"I told you a long time ago, you help me, and I help you. Stay off the streets for a few more days."

"Gotcha. Keep it up." Blade ended the call.

Carl was in a bigger shit storm than they'd planned. The dealers refusing to work helped their cause.

They'd made good progress. First had been Damian. He'd allowed them to live and Megan to publish her articles. The two of them had made Magic Shop lives hell. AJ couldn't be prouder of the work she'd done. He couldn't see the big boss appreciating his advisors' failures.

Next had been Carl. Losing that shipment had been a big hit. Real big hit since the drivers freely shared the transportation routes. Then, he'd lost twenty dealers and quite a bit of money and product. The bonus was that he'd lost Jimmy, which had to make him squirm since he also was an escaped convict. But he'd have to go on the streets to straighten out his problems. Problems he would have a hard time explaining.

Tomorrow would be Aaron and Paul's turn. With Tony's disappearance, the escape might be canceled. If so, AJ had been told by his task team leader that was it. They were done. They'd get what they could and get out. The other agents were getting antsy.

The secure cell phone rang. Who knew he'd be such a popular guy. And when he wanted to lay low. "Hamilton."

"Hey, AJ. I hear you've got something going tomorrow. I want in," Todd said.

Fucking Arthur. AJ should've known he couldn't put a team together without others finding out. "I've already got it covered."

"What's going on? It must be big because everyone is tight-lipped, and I hear it's a joint agency venture."

"That's because they don't know what they'll be doing yet."

"Is it big? You know I want in. I promised to protect your back."

AJ chuckled. "Don't worry, Todd. It's not big, and it has nothing to do with what I'm entangled in right now. This is a favor for my brothers. Besides, you'd be bored being a part of this. I'll make sure to let you know when I finalize things here so you can be a part of it."

He hated lying, but he couldn't afford anyone, including his partner, to know the plan. He liked Todd, but the man liked to drink, which led him to say more than he should. AJ had carried him home on more than one occasion.

"If you say so."

"Bye, Todd."

Megan swiveled around the minute he put the phone down.

"I'm finished. Did you want to read it?"

Megan's excitement in offering to let him read her articles first, made him want to reach for her, enclose her in his arms and run away.

He cleared his throat. He needed to stop thinking such foolishness. "No. Go ahead and send it. Make sure to let your boss know that tomorrow you'll have a story that's so big you'll need most of the front page."

His time of living in hell was finally coming to an end. But would he just move to another form of hell without Megan at his side?

Chapter Thirty

Megan wanted to squeal like little Reagan had when she'd spied her Uncle AJ. He'd allowed her to watch the takedown of the convict and the team. To make it even better, Devon had provided her with a digital camera to use.

She stood in an airport hangar watching Deputy U.S. Marshals, or DUSMs, and half of the Hamilton brothers' team suit up in assault gear and prepare many, many weapons. AJ had checked with her five times to ensure she'd worn her vest and to remind her she was not to leave Rob's side. She doubted Rob enjoyed the fact he had babysitting duty instead of participating. The man took it seriously because more than a few inches never separated them.

From their hiding spot, they watched two SUVs drive up the tarmac and stop near the hangar, just as Tony said. Walt and Ben were the names of the two men who stepped from the vehicles. They made new identities and set convicts up in new locations, new lives. She fought a snort. The marshals should use them to help set up people in Wit Sec program. Heck, they'd hid escapees for years without being located. They definitely had skills. Unfortunately, they chose to use them on the wrong side of the law.

The men silently swept from the hangar. The united team was an impressive sight. Her heart swelled with pride at the image of AJ leading the men.

They rushed the men waiting for the plane to land, MP5s and AR-15s pointed in their faces with DUSMs yelling, "Police! U.S. Marshals! Let me see your hands!" They had to repeat it before the men did as instructed. Having all that firepower shoved in her face would've frozen her to the spot also.

Two marshals returned with their cuffed prisoners. The remaining four blended with AJ, Brad, Matt, and Ken, the HIS team leader, and filled the waiting SUVs.

Ha! Criminals shouldn't get tinted windows. It made it easy for them to get closer to where the plane would taxi. She'd expected some elaborate special ops plan, but his was simple and made sense. She witnessed a few grim faces in the crowd. Maybe they'd have rather been the ones in the SUV.

Anticipation seeped into her every pore. She would see everything unfold before her. The only glitch to her achieving full giddiness was her concern that AJ could be shot again. She should've fought for him to stay with her. She'd asked, but he'd quickly told her that he wouldn't miss making the arrests.

Hopped up on adrenaline, she had a hard time standing still. She would watch a big part of Magic Shop destroyed. And, she'd have the exclusive on it. This would surprise the public. Who would've thought the Magician, or really anyone, would do something like this for a living?

Thanks to the data Devon had retrieved from Paul's computer, Deputy U.S. Marshals had been watching the escaped convicts around the nation that Magic Shop had helped escape. To avoid leaks to their plan, AJ and his brothers had personally coordinated with the marshal they trusted in each area where a convict now resided. They waited for the signal to arrest them. It had to be a synchronized event so there could be no tip-offs.

She held her hands over her ears at the noise from the private airplane taxiing toward the hangar and then stopping in front of the SUVs. Three men walked down the stairs of the jet. Once they'd stepped on the tarmac the doors of the SUVs burst open, and men ran from the hangar. "Police! U.S. Marshals! Let me see your hands!"

Megan peeked around Rob, who blocked her view of the scene, snapping photos. She heard gunfire as someone shoved her to the ground.

She remained still until the man on top of her spoke, "Are you okay?"

"I can't breathe," she struggled to say.

The weight lifted from Megan, and strong arms pulled her up and into a warm, tight embrace. Taking in AJ's scent, she clung to him.

A warm breath washed over her ear. "Thank God you're okay."

Large hands rubbed themselves up and down her back and arms, soothing her, warming her blood and calming her.

"You've been shot." The emotional pain in his voice slammed into her.

"That's not her blood." Rob stood beside them, holding his arm.

"Let me see, Rob." Megan reached for his arm.

"Don't sweat it. It's just a scratch."

She knew better but wouldn't argue. Let him do his macho stuff and act like it was nothing while he suffered.

AJ nodded, and Rob walked away.

"Megan, I think it's time for you to go home with Jesse and stay there with Kate until this is over."

She looked up at him. "What? After all I've been through, you want me to hide? You've some nerve. I told you we're finishing this together, and I meant it."

A smile slowly crept up his face, more of a satisfied smirk. "Don't you have an article to write and a deadline to meet?"

****

AJ dreaded the expected phone call. He'd have pissed off plenty of people. Not only had he organized the captures of twenty escaped convicts plus prison escape secret team, he'd done it as a wanted man by the FBI. His brothers had a lot of pull. They'd kept the marshals from dragging him and Megan away earlier.

He heaved a weighted exhale when the phone rang. "Hamilton."

"What the fuck?"

He had to move the phone away from his ear at the volume of Arthur's voice.

"You're capturing escaped convicts all over the nation and keeping it from me and the marshals' office. Even though it was a win for them, they have been up my ass the last hour that I didn't clue them in on the mission."

AJ waited for his deputy director to finish his tirade. He'd certainly earned it. He'd truly be fired this time.

"Son of a bitch! You should've told me!" A fist slamming loudly on a desk exploded through the phone.

He still remained silent.

"Well, what do you have to say for yourself?"

He'd witnessed the man rip into agents. This had been child's play compared to those sessions. "Arthur, I had to keep it quiet to ensure we captured all the convicts. I've told you before that I don't trust your phone."

"Did you acquire this info from your search of Paul's home?"

"I did. We walked away with much more. Look, it's a great day. We've cleaned up the streets, captured a bunch of criminals, all the good guy stuff. With the success of the past few days, the FBI, DEA and U.S. Marshals look like heroes."

So he hadn't completely followed the book, but he wasn't FBI—according to the law.

The escaped convicts were captured, no matter how they'd acquired that information. They could fight it all they wanted. No judge would release them based on that. For them, captured was captured. The marshals accepted tip-offs all the time, and HIS happened to be the ones to anonymously tip them off this time.

They'd figure out how to use or not use the remainder of the information they'd found. He'd leave that to his brothers and the FBI. It was good information, but they didn't need it to be successful.

The man chuckled. "It's a great day. Congratulations, AJ. You did a good job."

"Thanks, Arthur." The man didn't praise people often, so this meant a great deal to AJ. Maybe this could keep him from being arrested when he eventually turned Megan over.

"It's time for you to come in. We have enough to put them away. Your cover has been blown, and you've been shot. Megan Rogers is innocent in all this, and we need her alive. Get out now, and get out alive."

AJ tightened his grip on the phone. "I'm not stopping without the Magician. I want him out of commission and behind bars. I just need the time the task force has allowed me. If I can't bring him in by then, they can make their arrests, and I'll walk away as directed."

"I think you misunderstood. Get your ass back here and bring the girl. That's an order."

He dropped his head and rubbed his forehead with his hand. "Then I guess we part ways here because I'm not quitting and I'm not turning her over." The man tried to have him murdered, was responsible for so much carnage and pain, and his boss wanted him to walk away. AJ thought Arthur knew him better than that. Wasn't that why he'd chosen him for the mission? He'd said something about his inability to back down.

"You have three days. After that, you're on your own, and I won't stop the law from chasing you."

Hell.

It was what AJ expected… it was what he would've done. But he would see this through till the end, no matter the consequences.

Chapter Thirty-One

AJ accepted the newspaper and coffee from Jamaal through the crack in the door, slamming it shut after the smartass asked for his tip. It was humorous, but he wouldn't let him know that.

Jesse laughed from the dining table.

"You have some asshole employees."

His brother's dark brows rose. "They could be your employees also."

AJ had checked it out a long time ago and knew Jesse had added all the brothers, including him and Jake, as owners of the company. Jesse kept that information to himself.

AJ tossed the paper on the desk. Adding the coffee, he set it down so hard that the cover popped off and hot liquid sloshed over the rim. "We've been through this before, and the answer is still no."

Megan walked into the room. "The answer is no to what?"

"Nothing. The newspaper is on the table. I didn't read it, but I did see an interesting headline." He laughed when she vaulted across the small room and snatched it up.

Her excited squeals brought a smile to Jesse's face. "Is she like this every time she has an article in the paper?"

Warmth flooded AJ. He'd love to have had a

chance at a life with her. He forced a chuckle his brother must see through. "Mostly."

They turned to the breaking news on the TV.

Megan walked up behind him and wrapped her arms around him. "The busts are all over the news. You should be proud. The footage is outstanding. This will be big news for a while. The deputy marshals look like heroes. I can't wait until the other charges are added to these men."

Jesse cleared his throat. "AJ didn't do it by himself."

She released him and beamed at his brother. AJ's hands curled into fists at his sides. For a moment, he thought she planned to kiss Jesse, but she continued past his brother to the desk. Picking up the newspaper, she returned to him. "The photo turned out much better than I thought it would."

Thank God for Rob. She'd captured that picture right before she'd been shot at. Having the escaped convict on his knees front and center set a slight tremor through AJ thinking about how he could've lost her.

"I think this article made things up to Kristen." Megan's smile broadened. "She's breathing down my neck for what's next."

"You did a hell of a job on that article," Jesse said.

"I couldn't have done it without you. All of you. Thank you for taking me with you and providing me with the exclusive." She stood on her tiptoes and kissed AJ.

Fuck it. I'll tell her later. "I need more of a thank you than that." He tugged her to the bedroom, her laughter bouncing off the walls.

Jesse chuckled behind him.

AJ didn't care. He knew how he'd spend his last few days with her.

****

AJ grinned and pulled Megan closer. He reached up and brushed her full, pink bottom lip with the tip of his index finger. "You have the softest lips." He leaned down and gave her a teasing kiss and then straightened. "Are you sure?"

"Yes, I'm sure. I'm starving. Besides, your brother is in there and knows what we've been doing for the last hour or so."

"Who cares what he knows? It's not like he's a blushing virgin."

She laughed, slipped out of his grasp, and raced to the living area.

He slowly followed, stopping when the secure cell phone rang. "We're not through, Megan."

"Give it a rest," Brad growled from where he lounged on the sofa.

When the fuck had his brothers changed shifts? Shit, whenever Megan got naked, AJ lost focus on everything but the two of them. He'd never been like this. He'd never allowed his professionalism on a job to slip this far. Then again, he might not have a career to return to so what did it matter?

It mattered because he'd given her false hope. She'd told him she loved him several times, and he'd refused to return her sentiments. He'd told himself it was to make things easier when they split. His love for her, knowing they'd break, had ripped his heart out. He could only imagine how she would feel.

He snatched up the phone. "Hamilton."

"AJ, you said it wasn't big."

He knew his partner would call sooner or later. "The FBI wasn't involved. Only deputy marshals. Besides, locally it was small, only one escapee."

"Damn, but that would've been fun. I heard she was there taking pictures."

Todd's interest in Megan disturbed AJ. No, it ate at the jealousy he held for any man who looked at her. She was a beautiful woman. Of course men would look at her. Besides, he had no hold on her. "She was."

"Don't you think it's time she comes with us? Arthur thinks I can talk you into it whereas he hasn't been able to. It's time. Tell me where you are, and I'll get together a team for her."

No fucking way would he hand her over to Todd. It had been hard enough watching her with Trent. AJ and his brothers would continue to keep her safe.

"She won't go with you."

"That's what her Marcus has been pushing."

AJ growled. "He's not her Marcus."

"Are you going to let me come help you?"

"No. I'm good for now."

"Come on, AJ. You need me at your back. Besides, I'm fucking bored looking at our old cases. They can all wait while I help you with this."

He chuckled. Todd preferred action to paperwork. He'd chosen the wrong profession because their jobs involved more paperwork, research, collecting evidence and interviews than heated arrests. "Maybe later."

"Found out who the Magician is yet?"

"Not yet, but I will," AJ answered determinedly.

"What can I help do here? Do you have any thoughts?"

"Some."

"Want to share? As much as I hate it, I can do research for you. Just give me specific cases."

"Nah. I've got it." He needed to work the information he'd received out in his head. Devon had found what he thought was all the money under dummy corporations. He now dug into the lives of several people suspected of having ties to the crime boss, or being the man himself.

"Well, I can't say I'm not disappointed I don't have to sit behind the computer. Are you sure you don't want me to come get her? I need something to do."

"When she's ready to go, I'll call."

"That works. Just don't forget me when the action starts."

He hated to tell him that no one but his immediate circle would be involved in the takedown of the mastermind behind Magic Shop. They were the only ones he fully trusted with Megan's life. He hadn't been partnered with Todd long enough to truly know the man.

AJ returned the phone to his pocket.

Flashing his most charming smile, he walked toward Megan. "Now, where were we?"

He captured her gaze, love sparkling in her eyes.

"You're about to get your fucking ass kicked with all the mushy shit," Brad tossed out.

Clearing his throat, AJ addressed his brother, "Do you have the new information Dev wanted me to review?"

That was where his mind should've been instead of attempting to quench his thirst for her before he no longer had the chance. As much as he'd like to spend the time with her, the woman who helped him see light, who helped him have hope, he couldn't prolong this mission forever.

Brad slid a quick glance at Megan. "I think you'll find his latest research extremely interesting."

"The happy couple is here." Brad didn't move when a knock sounded on the door.

Fucking Brad. AJ snagged Megan around the waist before she opened it. "No. I've got it." He removed his weapon and cracked the door.

"Let me in, AJ," Jesse boomed.

Kate leaned forward and whispered, "I'm sure you won't like the results of Dev's research, but I'm here to prevent Megan from reading it. We can't chance her spilling the beans, as reporters like to do. By the way, you were right about the Magician's identity. Great work."

AJ put his gun away and smiled. Yes! His computer whiz of a brother never failed them. He must've linked the money back. Then he thought of Megan. How would she react?

His ex-partner jerked her thumb at her husband. "The men are waiting for you to decide how you want to do this."

That would explain Brad's irritation at AJ playing around with Megan instead of ending this.

AJ opened the door wider. "Come on in, oh great sister-in-law of mine, plus my brother."

"Megan, I'm here for some girl time."

"But I wanted to," she said, pointing to the paperwork on the table, "go through that."

Kate waved her hand. "It'll be there later. Come on. We're having a mani-pedi, facial party." She touched Megan's arm and guided her to the bedroom, closing the door behind them.

AJ had almost snorted aloud when his old partner told Megan what they'd be doing. Kate was not a pampering princess, but it had worked. He grinned at Megan's reluctance to leave the room. Her eyes had been glued to the file on the table in front of Brad. Beating her curiosity would be difficult.

"Let's hurry. I'm not even sure my wife knows how to do that mani whatever she called it." Jesse removed his jacket.

The brothers laughed. They loved Kate. She'd been good for his oldest brother. Just like Megan had been good for him.

Before he could torture himself more, his secure cell phone rang.

"Hamilton." He paced the floor.

"Agent Hamilton, FBI Special Agent Tom Martin. I'm on your wiretaps."

AJ halted and looked toward his brothers who sported quizzical expressions. "Yes. And?"

"We picked up a call on Paul's tap from Carl. In what he must've assumed was cryptic, Carl informed him of a meeting with their boss tomorrow. Although he never said it outright, it was easy to discern the meaning. I believe this was what you were hoping for." Pride came through in the agent's voice.

"It is. Great job, Agent Martin." AJ considered his options. "Have you told anyone else about this?"

"No. I was told by Deputy Director Hall to call you first when we had something worthwhile."

"Who else knows?" He could contain this. He could control it.

"Only me. My partner was on a lunch run when the

call went through. He hasn't returned."

"Good. Don't tell another soul about this, not even your partner or Deputy Director Hall. Do you understand?"

The agent took a moment to answer. "Um. Is it that important I break protocol?"

"Deadly." His tone should've conferred to the agent the seriousness behind his answer.

"Since the deputy director sent me straight to you, saying you were in charge, I'll do this. But, I won't erase it, and I won't bring it up when my partner returns. But, if I'm asked by Director Hall I won't lie."

"Thank you, Martin. What did you decode on the specifics of the meeting?"

He listened intently, ended the call, looked at his brothers and smiled. "We've got him."

****

After they finished dinner, Matt left the room. AJ clasped her hand and led her to the couch. "Megan, we have to talk."

She gazed at him and tilted her head. "You're so serious. What's going on? If you think you're keeping me from being at the meeting, don't even try. We've been over this. I'm going with or without you."

Jesse had taken the file with him when he and Kate left, but AJ told Megan about the meeting, letting her know what was basically in the file. Tomorrow she'd finally know who the Magician was and witness the arrest. She'd finally close this out and find justice for Kevin.

She mentally crossed her fingers he wanted to have a relationship. He knew she couldn't go to her home so hopefully he'd ask her to stay with him. Could he be ready to admit that he had feelings for her?

He looked deeply into her eyes. "Megan, once this is over, you're going into protective custody with the Marshals Service."

Her heart beat a little faster in her confusion. "Why? It'll be over? I thought we'd be safe once the Magician was arrested." She caught the pity in his eyes. "Is this about me telling you that I love you?"

"No. This is about you being a material witness for the government. You need to testify against Damian. He might try to prevent you from making the trial. We can't take that chance."

She nodded. "Okay, so I go into protective custody until after the trial. I think I can live with that. Could I go with your brothers instead of with the marshals? Kate told me they sometimes take protective custody jobs."

Megan had been so driven lately on identifying the crime boss, she'd forgotten about the murder she'd witnessed. She had pushed it to the recesses of her mind. This murderer would be put behind bars, and she'd help. She'd promised Kevin and her mother.

But being away from AJ for so long tore at her heart, at her entire being. Didn't some cases take years to go to trial? She didn't want to be away from him that long.

After listening to his brothers, she'd discovered that he may have ruined his career by choosing to protect her versus handing her over to the FBI. She didn't want to be the reason he'd lose his job, but she was glad he'd made the choice he had. She'd survived, and she'd fallen in love, finding her soul mate.

"Megan, it's more than that. You'll go into the Wit

Sec. You'll be relocated and provided with a new identity. No one, not even your family, will know where you live, and you won't be able to contact anyone. You won't be able to write for a newspaper anymore either."

Her heart stopped. *No. No. No.* This couldn't be happening. She wouldn't leave everyone and everything behind. She loved her life, her friends, her job and this man.

She jumped up, her expression mutinous. "No! I won't do it!"

AJ stood beside her. "Megan, you have to if you want to live. There's no other option."

"But once the trial is over, he won't have a reason to kill me. Why can't I go back to my life?" There had to be another option, one that involved AJ.

The sadness in his eyes and his drooping mouth answered her before he spoke. "Nothing is bigger than revenge, Megan. You'll help ensure he lands in prison for a long time. Crime bosses don't forgive or forget."

"Do I really have to do this?" She couldn't walk away from her parents especially after their loss of Kevin. Her mother would never be the same.

Nervously she asked, "Will you go with me?"

****

AJ turned away from her. The pain in his heart tore at his entire body. From the beginning, he'd known this would be Megan's life once everything was resolved. Letting her go wasn't supposed to rip apart the soul she'd helped him repair. He'd fallen in love and couldn't do anything about it except tell her good-bye.

He had to find Jake and right the wrong he'd done to Emily. If he left with Megan, he'd no longer have the

351

resources at his disposal. Yes, his brothers could do it alone, but this had been his fuckup, and that meant he had to clean it up. Which meant he couldn't leave. Even once he found his brother, he couldn't be with Megan. Arthur might cross some lines with him, but he'd never allow AJ to know where she'd moved, or what her new identity had become.

"No," he answered softly. He turned back to her. "I can't."

Tears slid down her cheeks. "I won't get to see you again, will I?"

"No. I won't be allowed to be involved in your relocation, know where you go, or what your new identity will be." He wrapped his arms around the woman he loved, hugging her tightly as she wept on his shoulder.

When she looked up at him, the same need that held him together showed in her eyes. Without speaking, he released her, took her hand and led her to the bedroom. His brother knew what AJ had needed to do tonight and wouldn't come back. Matt would keep his vigil out in the cold.

"This is our last night together. We won't waste a moment of it." He needed to savor the feel and taste of her. It had to last for a lifetime.

"Then stop talking and make love to me."

They relieved themselves of their clothing and tumbled on the bed, ready for each other, ready to be one.

A silent consent passed through them to bypass foreplay.

AJ held himself above Megan. "Look at me, my little dove," he said in a gravelly voice. "I want to remember."

He entered her slowly, his strokes slow and deep, her liquid heat enveloping him. Their two hearts beating as one, he trembled with his need to stamp his memory on her. To make every moment count for both their lives.

Soft, loving kisses passed between them along with deep gazes into each other's eyes. Love, loss, and pain slid over her face.

He flipped over, placing her on top. They didn't speak, both lost in the sensual feelings of being together. They explored each other's bodies leaving emotion-filled imprints that would last a lifetime.

He gritted his teeth, holding onto the pleasure, holding back his release. He belonged inside her.

They surrendered completely to the passion that flowed between them.

She shifted their rhythm, a moan of ecstasy slipping from her lips, a sheen of sweat covering her flushed body sending a tremor thundering through him.

As she climaxed, she whispered her love for him. He bit his tongue to prevent himself from telling her he loved her when he came deep inside her, shuddering with bliss.

He could never say it aloud, but she would remain in his heart and soul.

He'd never anticipated his life would change when he'd been sent to threaten a pesky reporter.

An unchecked tear escaped down his cheek.

Chapter Thirty-Two

The day had finally arrived. The day for Kevin. The day for her family. They would have justice. Tiny pinpricks scurried across Megan's neck and down her spine. Everything had to proceed as planned today. This could be their only opportunity.

Earlier, she'd argued with AJ and his brothers about her and Victoria's participation. This was both of their stories. They'd both dug into it and had brought valuable information to light. They'd both helped make this plan a success. They'd share credit for the article naming the Magician so it stood to reason they should also be included in person this time.

The men didn't agree. They kept talking about security, blah, blah. She'd follow AJ's orders this time to prevent herself from ending up in the situations she had recently. It was the most dangerous thing she'd done to date. His brothers reluctantly backed down after AJ stood up for her, reminding them it wasn't their decision to make.

Then he and his brothers battled about how things would be handled. AJ wanted to attend the meeting without them, but Jesse said AJ had no choice. The problem had been that he refused to provide his brothers with the location of the meeting. Her heart skipped a beat. She understood his need to catch the crime boss, but why did he have to push his brothers away at this stage? They needed them.

Things became heated, and words were spoken they'd each come to regret, and Jesse slammed the door on his way out, calling AJ a few names she wouldn't repeat. She worried that his family relationship might be irreparable.

She'd never expected his brothers to leave AJ to handle the meeting by himself. But they had. It felt like when they'd first started. Just the two of them. He'd returned to the broken man she'd first met. The man who still lived in anguish, caring nothing for himself, who had to do things alone, and the one who had broken her heart.

After today, she'd never see him again or feel the safety and love in his arms. She'd miss that tingling through her nerves when he looked at her with lust in his eyes.

Her life, while it would be new, would be over. She didn't think she'd ever recover from this heartache. How would she put the thousands of shards of her heart back together?

She had to push those thoughts away to another time.

At least the weather cooperated. The beautiful blue sky lit with the blazing sun, small clouds drifting swiftly through the air, which meant no more snow.

"Why didn't you let your brothers help us? We could use it."

He'd said that only one of the men at the meeting would be armed. That'd be Damian. The man who had ruined her life.

"Megan, quit worrying. I can handle this. My only concern is that you'll be there." AJ pulled her into his arms and kissed the top of her head.

And she'd never let anything happen to him. She'd be his backup if needed.

They arrived forty minutes early to meet Victoria and find their hiding places. With the entryway plowed, they didn't have to trek through the three feet of snow behind the warehouse. Megan kept looking over her shoulder, certain his brothers had secretly followed, but no cars appeared.

She took a calming breath, telling herself that luck was with them. Sure enough, at the warehouse, they had large piles of snow, pallets and stacks of scrap metal to hide behind. She and Victoria hid together behind a large snow bank that AJ had selected.

He moved close to Megan and touched her lips softly with his. "I'm not happy about you being here, but I have no other way to keep you protected since Jesse left." He dropped his forehead to hers and sighed. "You promised to do what I said. I want you to promise that no matter what, you'll stay put."

What did he mean by no matter what? A slight trembling grabbed her body and let loose. "I promise." If he thought she'd stay hidden if his life was in jeopardy, he didn't know her very well.

Reaching up, he removed his glove and lightly stroked her cheek with his palm. She leaned into it.

Victoria cleared her throat. "Sorry to interrupt but I'd like to be ready before someone shows up and decides to shoot us."

He hugged Megan tight and whispered, "Trust me."

Her blood turned to ice. What did he have planned that he hadn't shared?

Wearing snowshoes, AJ walked across the deep snow around the back of the building to the far side of the warehouse.

Settling down to wait, she and Victoria brainstormed on how to pull the story together. Victoria had a sharp mind. The two of them worked well together. They had wanted to split up, but AJ had refused, saying it would be easier for him if he had to worry about only one spot.

"I could sneak to that pile closer to AJ without his knowing," Victoria said. "It's a small stack, but I can sit instead of crouch."

If anyone moved closer, it would be Megan. And there was no way she'd sneak there without AJ knowing. "No. Let's just stay put. Do you have your phone ready?"

"My recording app is open."

"Great. I'll get photos. Either you or AJ will hear what's happening and be able to record it. We'll get what we need for our article and finally catch this evil man."

"I wish Kevin was here," Victoria said. "He wanted to break this story."

Megan dropped her head and closed her eyes. Victoria had had a crush on her brother. Sadness welled briefly inside her before anger took over. The Magician would pay.

After AJ had arrested him and the marshals arrived, who AJ had purposefully told the wrong time of the meeting to so he could handle it alone, she would walk out and face the man who took something precious from her and her family. She felt the gun in her pocket. No, she wouldn't kill him, no matter how much she'd like to do so.

Megan wished she'd had the phone number for that FBI director guy or brought Kate's number. The more she thought about it, the more she worried. *Great, now I have heart palpitations to deal with on top of everything else.*

The first vehicle arrived, and her pulse raced. "I hope they don't check behind these things."

Victoria waved her hand. "Your man said he'd keep us safe. He's kept you alive, so I trust him. Look, here comes two more."

Knowing someone else trusted AJ filled Megan with pride. He'd die before he allowed someone to hurt her. The thought sent a shiver snaking down her spine. He would not die.

It was time this mystery was solved. The Magician had kept his identity secret for too long. Kristen had reminded her that as a journalist, she had to remain open-minded. It was a long shot, but the Magician could be a "she" and not a "he."

Of course, they parked near AJ. He knew they would which was why he hid her back here. But he'd share the recording.

Kevin, it will finally end today. I just wish it would bring you back.

She peeked around the snow as the occupants exited their vehicles. She snapped photos. She'd seen a photo of everyone except Lawrence, and well, the big boss. She moved from person to person. She reached one face and gasped. It couldn't be. That couldn't be the Magician.

****

Anger and hatred rolled through AJ's stomach.

This son of a bitch had attempted to kill the woman he loved. There would be no mercy.

He turned on the recorder Devon had provided. Sitting still long enough to collect incriminating evidence would be difficult. His hands itched to slap cuffs on the no longer elusive crime boss.

An extra person had arrived. He'd been right about that particular man. Thank fuck he hadn't trusted him with any information.

"What the fuck is going on? Can't you control your business?" the Magician yelled. "With the exception of Lawrence, you're all lucky I haven't put a bullet in you. Thankfully my money is safe."

Lawrence stood taller.

AJ caught himself from laughing out loud. Right now, Devon was draining all of the Magician's accounts in the US and abroad. Lawrence wouldn't be standing tall much longer.

A finger pointed at Damian. "You let two people slip through your fingers. They've been making our lives hell. Why are they still alive?"

The chief enforcer shuffled his feet, his hands shoved in the pockets of his jacket. "We're doing everything that we can. Since you can't get the information, we have to rely on the word on the street. Every time we've located where they were staying, they'd moved by the time we got there. We're going to catch them though."

"You'd best because I can't find out where they're staying from my contacts. We can't afford any more of their trouble. I want more people looking for them, people ready to pull the trigger."

The Magician turned to Carl. "And how the fuck

did you lose a shipment, Jimmy, and twenty dealers?"

The man blustered. "We usually get a tip when the DEA is planning a raid. We didn't get it this time. We never expected they'd hit the dealers so hard."

"We pay well, but there are times when you won't get a heads-up. You need to have a plan to keep my money and products where they belong. If you think you can't do it, then I can find someone else."

"No, I can handle it," Carl said nervously. "I'm working on getting business back to normal."

"You'd best. You're lucky you didn't get picked up when Jimmy did. I'd bet they know your true identity by now."

Carl shrugged. "Maybe they're not that smart."

The Magician shot him a scathing look. "They're both smart. With an FBI agent and an investigative reporter out there, you'd best watch your back."

"I already am," Carl responded.

The Magician turned to Paul. "How the hell did you lose your entire team and an escapee? You're supposed to be the best there is, yet you fucked up with Denzel and now this one. What the fuck happened?"

AJ could almost feel the heat radiating off the crime boss.

"I think they got to Tony. I thought he'd just skipped out on us. He kept talking about a girl back home. It didn't occur to me that one of my own would be used against us."

Oh boy. This kept getting better. How the hell had these assholes been so successful? They were fucking idiots.

"You lost an employee and didn't think to amend your plans? Didn't think that your mission might be in jeopardy? Are you taking one of our products or something because going ahead was the most fucked up decision you've ever made? And they had to have collected the info on all the escapees from you. Except for me, no one else has all that data. We fucking lost our entire setup."

Paul hung his head, his fists at his side.

The Magician looked at Aaron. "I don't even want to hear it from you. You never should've hired the Richards brothers as pimps."

Men shuffled and looked anywhere else except at their boss. "Here's what we're going to do. We will focus all our energy on finding those two problem-makers, and then we're getting back to business."

"Problem," a voice whispered.

****

"Get up." Megan turned with her finger to her lips for quiet and froze. Her heart skipped a beat. She looked into the barrel of a gun.

"I said get up," Victoria repeated.

Fear sent a shiver surging through Megan, leaving her body shaking. She took a deep breath and attempted to speak over the pounding of her heart in her ears. She swallowed and forced out her words, "Victoria, what are you doing?"

The journalist stood. "Get up and put your hands up. I know you have a gun in your pocket. Reach for it and you die."

Megan did as told. This couldn't be happening. It wasn't part of the plan. Did AJ have a backup plan? She should've pushed him to use his brothers. The marshals. *Yes! The marshals.* When would they arrive? Would it be in time to save them?

Victoria removed Megan's gun, taking away her hope of fighting back. She could take the woman but not the rest of the men. How could she have been so wrong about someone she called her friend? What had changed Victoria? She'd work just as hard as Megan to get to this point. "Now move. The boss is waiting for you."

She walked on wobbly legs. They had told Victoria everything. That meant AJ's plan had been exposed, which meant they knew he was here.

"Honey, look what I have here." Victoria smiled and walked to the group.

Revulsion burned the back of Megan's throat and curdled in her stomach.

"Well, well. I knew if we put out the bait, you wouldn't be able to pass up watching this meeting, thinking you could capture me. That's why Victoria was on the story. To keep an eye on your brother and then you."

Oh God. They had been set up. They'd been lured here.

The Magician smiled, and it sent a cold chill through her. "It's good to see you, Megan. But someone is missing from the party. Where is your boyfriend? Where is AJ hiding?"

Victoria pointed to where he hid.

Megan looked around the group. Detective Cooper walked up to her, pointing his weapon, relieving Victoria. He was supposed to be a good guy. Megan had trusted him.

"We have your girlfriend. Come out, AJ, or we'll shoot her. Do you want her death on your conscience?"

Silence. She held her breath. What would he do?

AJ slowly walked from behind the metal pile with his hands up, his Beretta hanging from a finger, his gaze on her. Damian moved forward to retrieve the weapon. He searched AJ and removed his backup weapon, handing it to his boss.

Despair gripped her as all hope fled. What chance did they have now?

AJ's gaze moved to the Magician. "You must be Marcus Bryant, Megan's ex-fiancé."

"You don't seem surprised."

AJ casually strolled to Megan's side, turning to her, his gaze holding her captive with an expression she couldn't read. He shifted. "My brothers and I unraveled it piece by piece until we had the final piece—you. You and this bunch you call leaders did little things wrong here and there. Nothing noticeably incriminating by itself but put them all together…." His voice trailed off.

A hard, evil glare from her ex met the eyes of each man present.

"It struck me as odd that you kept after Megan when I heard you had a new fiancée. I didn't know it was Victoria. Good job on keeping that secret."

AJ had known who the Magician was and hadn't told her? A spike of anger fought its way through her fear. How could he have not told her? They were a team. After everything, he still hadn't trusted her.

Too many competing emotions swirled through her. This bit of news took last place compared to what they currently dealt with. Staying alive took first, and AJ's demeanor worried her. How could he be so calm in the face of death? Did he really think he could overpower these men by himself?

Marcus pulled Victoria closer, leaned down, and

brushed a kiss on her lips. "We're leaving after we dispose of you. We'll be enjoying drinks on the beach on some remote island."

AJ lowered his hands. "Well, about that. We found your money here and in offshore accounts."

Marcus turned and glared at Lawrence who hunched his shoulders and stuffed his hands in his jeans pockets.

"Of course, we weren't sure if you were just another layer or actually the Magician. But, you screwed up with the hospital."

"Oh yeah. How's that?"

"You sent Todd. He's been under surveillance for months now. He called and gave you the specifics of my guards. Not only did he use his FBI phone, but he also called you on your personal cell." AJ grinned and shrugged. "It's hard to find good help these days."

"How'd you know he was mine?"

"When I kept him in the dark, we had successful raids against you. Plus, he talks too much when he's drunk."

Marcus's expressive, dark eyebrows rose in query. "And Allan?"

AJ shrugged. "I suspected him after Megan was shot at." He grimaced. "The first time. You really should've taught them how to hide bribe money better. Allan and Todd gave us the stepping stones to your fortune."

"I'm impressed. You're a top-notch investigator. How you managed to infiltrate my organization without my knowledge was ingenious, but I won't lose sleep over ridding myself of a federal agent."

He glared at Damian. "You're still alive because

someone fucked up. We'll remedy that now."

Megan gasped. He freely admitted to having people killed. Who was this man? How could she have been fooled? She'd never questioned his extravagant spending on her. She'd noticed his two phones but hadn't thought anything of it at the time.

"Why me?" Fear made her voice tremble.

He leered at her. "You were a means to an end. I had to keep tabs on you and your brother before Victoria was assigned to help. He started nosing in my business long ago." Marcus raked his gaze over her. "Pity. We had a good time."

Victoria's narrowed eyes filled with hatred at Megan.

Megan sniffed and wiped away a tear that silently slid down her cheek. She'd failed Kevin. She'd failed her family. Her mother would have to deal with both of her children disappearing not knowing if hope existed.

A part of her had believed she'd survive this investigation. Especially after she'd paired with AJ. They hadn't done anything stupid except for trusting Victoria. Okay, maybe they'd done a few other things they shouldn't have, mostly what she shouldn't have. But, in the end, she knew she'd have justice for her family. She'd end this crime boss's reign.

"Why? Why did you do this?" Megan asked.

"Why not? I plan to retire soon and in style. I certainly can't do it off the shitty pension the bank pays. I needed money and lots of it. Drugs were a no-brainer to start with. You'd be surprised what you can get past the DEA." Marcus shook his head with a look letting them know he held a secret.

"It was making me money but not fast enough. I

decided I needed to expand my business, and I needed more of a challenge. Who better to lead my business in other states than other drug kingpins?" He laughed. "It was exciting breaking them out of prison and watching everyone scramble to find them. You can't believe the rush I felt when we succeeded in keeping them hidden."

"Since you're planning to kill us anyway, why not tell us everything? Let Megan and me at least die knowing the truth," AJ requested.

Her stomach plummeted to the ground. Had he resolved that they'd be murdered? No way would she accept that. She had to find a way to save them. Fighting Victoria from the beginning and bringing her in, as a hostage would have been an excellent start. Hindsight. *Think.*

"Oh, you mean that I am the Magician"—Marcus pointed a finger at his chest— "and I am a drug lord and, oh yeah, I break criminals out of prison for money. Something like that, AJ?"

"Yeah, something like that. How did you decide who to break out of prison?"

"I guess it doesn't matter if I tell you. It's not like in the movies where the police are coming in to save the day. There is no cavalry. I had Allan and Todd make sure of that," Marcus said, looking around. "Your desire to bring me down alone has been your downfall, yours and hers." He gestured to Megan.

"How were clients selected?"

He had to be buying time in hopes the marshals arrived early. Thank goodness he hadn't trusted Victoria enough to tell her about them.

"I chose our clients personally. Ones who could pay and would add to my empire. My services are costly."

"How did you contact them?"

"Oh, AJ. It's so easy to blackmail or bribe someone to bring messages in and out of prison. We just had to find the right person, and then we had a line to our client. I assume you know the rest."

He nodded. "Yeah, I figured it out. It's remarkable how you pulled it all together. You've used some ingenious ways to break them out of prison. At least you accomplished it with as few people injured as possible."

"Why, AJ, it almost sounds like you admire me." Marcus's face hosted a boastful grin.

AJ's face remained impassive. The same as when he'd looked at her that first time. His earlier words returned to her about how he expected to die finishing this. But he'd sworn to protect her.

"Admire you, no, despise you, yes."

Her ex chuckled. "AJ, AJ. You do make me laugh. You're about to die and instead of begging for your life, you insult me."

Keep him talking, AJ. Interrogating Marcus answered questions her reporter curiosity had held. It wasn't the time, but if he kept talking, they'd stay alive long enough for the cavalry to arrive.

"What about the hits? Did you order all of them?"

"Of course, the hits came from me. That reminds me, what happened to those you killed? I'm sure you didn't actually murder them, so where are they?" Marcus's face pinched as the light came on.

AJ nodded and smiled. "They're all in Wit Sec and have turned on the organization. People don't take too kindly to someone wanting them dead. We have a host of witnesses awaiting your trial."

Marcus threw his head back and belted out a laugh. "What trial? These are the only people who know my identity, and they'd never turn on me because they'd incriminate themselves. And you and your girlfriend won't be alive to tell the police nor lead them to my men. My inside men will drive the Feds in circles while they continue to look for the Magician, especially knowing he was responsible for your disappearance."

Marcus turned to Megan. "And, you won't get to print another front-page story about me, no more exclusives, baby. You're a talented writer, but I'm tired of all the negative publicity." He looked her over. "It's a shame you wouldn't listen. You're just like your brother."

She dropped her arms and fisted her hands at her sides. Something snapped in her. Rage overtook her senses. "You ass! You had Kevin killed and act like it's nothing. I'm glad I dumped you."

His hostile glare told her she'd stepped over the line. Marcus turned to Detective Cooper. "Do it."

Allan pointed his weapon at Damian's head and fired. The man she'd once dubbed ape-man dropped with a loud thud.

A scream worked its way to her throat, but no sound passed her frozen mouth. She and AJ were next. She looked at the love of her life. As if feeling her gaze, he turned. She could've sworn love was the emotion flaring in his eyes.

"I want her." Victoria's voice carried a murderous lilt.

"By all means, baby." Marcus gestured her forward.

Detective Cooper told them to get down on their knees.

"Kill her first," the man she once thought she loved said to Victoria. Then he turned to AJ. "I want you to watch her die."

Victoria moved to Megan, and Detective Cooper tried to force AJ to his knees.

AJ swung to her with a wide smile, winked, and said, "Playtime."

Shots echoed, and both Victoria and Detective Cooper fell. Then all hell broke loose.

"Police! Drop your weapons! Get your hands where we can see them!"

The HIS team, dressed in all white, appeared from the snow and formed a tight circle around Megan, pulling her back. Federal agents filed out of the warehouses on each side of them.

She moved and leaned down until she found a tiny gap where she could see from behind the white wall of HIS men protecting her.

Detective Phillips stopped at Detective Cooper's body, a look of disgust on his face. He turned to her. "I'm sorry, Ms. Rogers. I had no idea."

From inside the Hamilton team circle, she sighed before replying, "I trusted him, too."

AJ and Marcus still faced each other. Marcus attempted to raise the gun, but AJ launched himself at the man, knocking them to the ground.

Her protectors caught her peeking and closed the opening. She moved around until she found another small spot to observe AJ and Marcus.

The two men wrestled for control of the weapon. When AJ broke it free from Marcus's grasp, he tossed it out of reach.

Now, why would he do that? He should've used it. Not to shoot, although it wouldn't hurt her feelings if he did, but to control the situation.

Next thing she knew Marcus had rolled them until he was strangling AJ, gripping his neck tightly.

One of the men shifted in front of her. She pushed him without budging the man. "Move! I can't see."

He ignored her. She continued to shift, hearing grunts and the distinct sound of fists connecting with flesh, until she found a sliver of open space.

Was that AJ on top? *Yes. Yes.* Her heart leaped. It was him. He'd pinned Marcus down, drove a fist into his jaw, and with the swiftness she'd witnessed before, flipped him, planted a knee in his back and pulled his arms back to cuff his hands.

He did it! She tried again to get around the men surrounding her to no avail.

"Where is she?" AJ's voice carried to her.

Suddenly, the men stepped away but stayed within reach, allowing Megan to see AJ stagger to her, sweat running down his temples, blood on his lips, and crimson running down his leg.

He engulfed her in his arms, his forehead resting on hers. "Are you all right?"

She pulled back. "Why did you do that? Why did you risk getting shot? And why the hell didn't you tell me about your brothers? And why did you fight Marcus?"

Gathering her back against his chest, he tucked her head under his chin and kissed the top of her head. "He raised his gun, but I wouldn't let him go down with death by cop. He has to face justice. As for my brothers,

I had a feeling they'd show up anyway. I found an earpiece at my spot."

He loosened his grip as she pulled back. Reaching up with a surprisingly shaky hand, she wiped blood from his mouth. "Are you okay? Your leg is bleeding. Maybe you busted your stitches."

Instead of answering, he leaned down and kissed her deeply. A kiss filled with passion that turned into desperation. She leaned back. Something was wrong. There was something he wasn't telling her.

She brightened. "You saved me like I knew you would. I love you, AJ Hamilton."

He reached up and pushed her hair behind her ear. "Megan," he said in a tortured voice, "it was almost too late. Victoria wanted to shoot you. I didn't think our sharpshooters would make their shots in time. I've never been so terrified."

Megan loved this man. AJ might not tell her he loved her, but he did. With everything that happened, they could make a life together.

"It's okay. I'm okay. And since Detective Cooper shot Damian, I don't have to leave." Elation filled her. She stood on her tiptoes and placed kisses all over his face. Things had been set right. Kevin had justice, and she had AJ.

Her mom would be glad to see her finally settled down. And in time they'd give her grandchildren. Megan sighed, contented.

He cleared his throat. "Megan, Damian may be dead, but you witnessed this. You heard his entire confession, so nothing changes for you. If I'd known they'd kill Damian, I'd never have let you come, and you'd have been free. I'm sorry, but they're still taking you into protective custody from here. The Department of Justice will want you as a material witness. Without Wit Sec, you won't survive to testify against Marcus or his men."

This couldn't be. Things should be right. They should be together. "No, AJ. Don't say that. I want to stay with you." He couldn't be saying goodbye. Couldn't be leaving her. "Can't the others here testify instead of me?"

"It won't matter, Megan. These assholes will have you killed if you don't leave. I don't want you to die. We've worked too hard to keep you alive."

"What about you? Won't they try to kill you too? Can't you come with me?" He couldn't do this to them.

"Megan, don't worry about me, I'll be fine." His hand lightly rubbed her cheek.

No! "I don't want this. I don't want to leave you." Her voice cracked. She fought to keep tears at bay. She'd finally found her other half, and he was walking away. A knife sliced through her heart.

"Megan, you know you have to go. You can't stay with me."

She stepped back and wrapped her arms around herself. Their time together meant everything to her. How could it mean so little to him that he could just walk away?

He couldn't do this. She threw her arms around his shoulders and pulled herself tight to him. "No, AJ. Don't leave me. I need you."

He leaned back and lifted her chin with two fingers and then lowered his head for a soft, slow kiss that she put all her love into. He loved her. It came through in his kiss.

Matt interrupted them. "AJ," he said, touching him on the shoulder, "it's time to go."

AJ lifted his lips from hers. Megan no longer attempted to hide her streaming tears. This couldn't be goodbye. It just couldn't. How could he not feel this pain?

He wiped a tear from her face. "Don't cry, my little dove. This is for the best. I need you to live."

"I love you, AJ. Why can't you come with me? Why can't you be with me?" She didn't care that she begged. They belonged together.

"Someday, you'll find someone to love, and you'll forget about me."

She'd never forget about him and the heated awareness when he was around, the tingling paths he burned over her when he touched her. Nothing could be more painful than this split. How could he just rip her heart out like it was nothing?

"No. No. That's not true. Don't do this to us, AJ."

He dropped his arms. "It's time." He lifted his hand and with his thumb wiped more tears from her face. "Have a great life, Megan Rogers. I'll never forget you." He turned, walked away, not looking back.

Megan fell to her knees, sobbing uncontrollably.

Chapter Thirty-Three

Five months later – Ogden, Utah

"Miss Sykes. Miss Sykes."

Megan chuckled. Of all her students in the summer English class she'd been substituting, Brandon never went a day without seeking attention.

"Settle down, Brandon. What can I do for you?"

"Do we really have to finish *The Adventures of Tom Sawyer* before summer school is out?"

His pitiful frown made her want to laugh. It had almost worked on her the first week she'd filled in. Thankfully, she'd been warned about his antics.

"Yes, Brandon. You were supposed to have read it this past school year."

"But, but, there's not enough time. Summer school is almost over."

"I promise you, Brandon, there is enough time. You just have to make this a priority. If you don't, you can't move up a year. Is that what you want? To stay back while your friends move up?"

"Hell no!" His sheepish look faded under her stern, teacher stare. "I'm sorry, Miss Sykes. No, I don't want to repeat this class. But I have too much to do to read."

She rose from the uncomfortable chair behind her desk, stretched, and moved to her student's desk. "Brandon, this is a decision you have to make. You keep telling me you're an adult now. Well, it's time to start acting like one. An adult does what they *have* to do first not necessarily what they *want* to do."

When he looked at her with a blank stare, she continued, "That means you make the time to read this book. Nothing else is more important. Do you understand?"

The class bell rang, saving him from attempting a feeble response.

Loudly, she called out, "Class, take advantage of the rain expected this weekend to complete your reading assignment. One more week. I'll see you on Monday."

The teenagers almost fought to be the first out of the door. She didn't take it personally. Not everyone enjoyed this course or summer school. Becoming an English substitute teacher hadn't been what she'd imagined she'd be doing, but she enjoyed it. She hoped a full-time position would open this coming school year. Rumor was the teacher she filled in for might not return. She kept her fingers crossed. This is what she'd been retrained to do since she couldn't return to journalism.

Megan had been angry when she'd first been set up in this town. Even with the agents who attempted to help her acclimate, loneliness had consumed her. The only other time she'd made a big move, Kevin had been there to help her settle in. She didn't have anyone this time. She didn't have anyone anymore.

AJ's handsome face flashed in front of her. She quickly pushed it away. She'd worked hard to force the memories they'd made down as far as possible. They flooded back up more than she'd like. Sometimes she let them stay for a while, remembering the joy and love they'd shared.

Before they'd forced her to her new life, she'd been allowed to submit one final article naming Marcus as the Magician, and detailing the meeting she'd witnessed. Well, as much as the police would allow her to report. At first, she'd read Kelly's follow-up articles online. Now, she didn't search them out. The agents kept her informed enough.

In the beginning, she'd prayed AJ would come to her with the agents and tell her he loved her. Her prayers had gone unanswered. If he'd really wanted to know where she was, he could've found out. It had been five months. He was back to his old life, without her.

She had been settled in a cute little three-bedroom, two-bathroom cookie-cutter house in a friendly neighborhood. When she'd moved in, most of her neighbors came by to introduce themselves, bringing cakes and pies. They'd made her feel welcome. She'd slowly begun making new friends.

After a short drive home, she parked in her driveway. She waved to her neighbor, Carla, as she strode to her mailbox. It was a Chinese food night. She'd finally found a place with great cashew chicken. She'd called in her order as she'd left the school so it would be delivered right after she arrived home.

She greeted Bob. He'd made a few feline and human friends in the neighborhood. One little girl, two houses over, came by to play with him several times a week.

A knock sounded on the door.

Good. The food had arrived. She'd missed lunch,

and her stomach let her know about it. She picked up her cash, went to the door and opened it. Her breath caught in her throat.

"Hello, Ms. Sykes, Ms. Laura Sykes."

She couldn't find her voice. She stood rooted to the spot, her heart pounding. He was here. Megan inhaled much-needed air into her oxygen-deprived lungs. "How… how did you find me?"

"Tsk, tsk, Megan. Aren't you going to invite me in to sit down or offer me a beverage?" he asked, a killer smile spreading over his face.

That simple statement made her heart skip a beat.

"May I come in?"

Before she could respond, the delivery boy rushed to her door. "Hello, Miss Sykes. Here's your order."

The boy looked back and forth between her and the man standing on her doorstep.

"Is everything okay, Miss Sykes?" His usually chipper voice now serious.

She forced herself to smile. "It is Derrick. Thanks for asking. Here. Keep the change."

"Thanks, Miss Sykes," he said over his shoulder as he hurried back to his car.

"Now may I come in?"

She'd replayed this scene in her mind hundreds of times. But she couldn't remember a single one of them.

"Sure, AJ." She moved to allow him into her home. She wanted to rush into his arms but held back. Why was he here? Why now after so long? Had her prayers finally been answered? Or was he here to break her heart again?

Her body burned as his gaze roamed over her. The power behind those gorgeous eyes touched her all over.

When his eyes returned to hers, he cocked one brow in question.

****

AJ's pulse raced. He'd missed Megan as soon as he'd walked away from her. That had been the stupidest thing he'd done in his life. But, he'd thought the longer they were separated, the less he would think about her. He'd been wrong.

With everything he did, he wondered if Megan would like it. No woman had ever remained with him like she had. He'd been miserable without her.

After a swift kick in the ass from his sister-in-law, he finally decided he couldn't live his life without Megan. He only hoped he wouldn't be too late. That she hadn't fallen out of love with him.

As she walked by, he grabbed her and pulled her close to him. He looked into her eyes. "I love you, Megan Rogers, aka., Laura Sykes." He took her mouth in a slow, sensual kiss. A fiery storm drove itself to his groin.

Her arms made their way around his neck, and he tightened his hold on her. He lifted his head. "I missed you," he whispered, brushing butterfly kisses on her face. "I missed you, my little dove."

"AJ. Why are you here?"

"Later," he rasped and then claimed her mouth again in a deep, hard, demanding kiss. He lifted his head, attempting to catch his breath. He had to have her.

"Where's the bedroom?"

She pushed him away. "Are you kidding me? You let me go, AJ. Let me go! How can you walk in here like nothing happened?"

Kate had warned him he would need to grovel. "I love you. I never should've let you go."

Megan raised her eyebrows at him, her eyes brightened. "You love me?"

"Yes. I was stupid. I thought you'd be better off without me. I didn't realize the mistake I made. I can't live without you, Megan."

"Upstairs." Her breathless voice notched up his desire.

He led her up the stairs. In her bedroom, he pulled her against him. He needed her now. He struggled with the zipper at the back of her green sundress. Of course, her pulling his shirt over his head and running her hands on his chest didn't help. Plus, his hands shook.

He finally pulled the zipper down, and her dress fell. AJ caught the flicker of amusement in her eyes after he'd looked up from her stomach, his eyes wide.

"You can't hurt the baby."

He gulped. A father. He'll be a father. "Are you sure?"

"Yes. We're fine."

"You're so beautiful." He dropped to his knees and kissed her stomach. "Thank you."

Her hands played with his hair. "I should be thanking you. You left me something to always remember you by."

He hugged her and laid his head on her belly, chuckling.

"What's so funny?"

"I guess we won't need the box of condoms I bought on the way here."

****

Megan's head lay on his chest, her hand playing

with the sprinkling of curls, her touch a slow torture. He'd take that any day over not having her.

He ran his fingers through her silky hair. "Megan. Paul is dead. Word is Wilkes had him killed for failing on his escape."

"Oh."

"In fact, all of the Magic Shop bosses are dead one way or another." AJ wouldn't go into the details of their deaths. How dealers they'd let rot in jail turned on them. How Carl had committed suicide. How gruesome Marcus's death had been. Both convicts and people he'd blackmailed had a hand in it. Or so the rumor goes.

She looked up at him and drew her brows together. "What does that mean?"

"It means you're no longer needed to testify. You won't have to face them again."

Pushing herself to a sitting position, she turned to him. "Does that mean I can go back to my old life?"

"Don't you like your new life?"

She frowned. "It doesn't have you."

That was the answer he'd hoped to hear since he'd decided to chase after her. "If it had me, would you want to stay?"

She bit her lower lip. "What are you saying?"

He sat up beside her. "I thought living with my wife might be the right thing to do."

"Your wife?" She looked down. "Are you doing this because of the baby?"

"Megan, I decided I wanted to marry you before I knew about the baby. I gave up everything to be with you, if you'll have me." He slid off the bed on one knee. He hadn't expected to propose to her naked or with her pregnant.

She gasped. "You'd give up everything to live here with me? What about finding Jake? It was important to you."

"I've already given up everything. I'm just sorry I didn't do it before now. I was wrong to let you go." He sighed. "I spoke with Em. At this point, she doesn't care if we find him. She's moved on. But, my brothers won't stop looking. You're more important to me. Can you forgive me?"

Her face lit up. He loved the brightness in her. "Of course, I forgive you. I'm glad you're here now. You get to see our baby grow up."

"Does this mean you'll marry me?"

"Yes. Of course, I'll marry you."

She reached down and threw her arms around him. He stood pulling them back to bed.

Megan pulled back and drew her brows in. "What about all of that work you did? The person you had to be?"

"What do you mean?"

"You worked hard to bring them down, and now there's no one. You wasted your time."

He placed his hand on her cheek, and his thumb traced her lips. "I wouldn't say that. I did meet you."

She smiled. "Can we go back?"

He knew she'd ask. He almost hadn't told her she wouldn't need to testify, but she'd hear from a marshal this week. Going back to Baltimore. He didn't know. Arthur would never approve. But the FBI didn't manage this program. The U.S. Marshals did. "Is that what you would prefer, Megan?"

"I want whichever life has you in it."

"Well, luckily for you, any choice has me in it. You won't be rid of me." He loved this woman and couldn't believe he'd let anything come between them. He'd had to make a lot of tough choices to be with her. Once he had his head screwed on right, his choice had been easy. There was only Megan for him. Life without her wasn't a life he wanted.

She kissed him. "I'm glad to hear that because our little one and I need you."

He held her away by the shoulders. "Is it a boy or girl?" Excitement filled his voice and his body. His heart finally beat whole. Now he'd have a family of his own. A family to love.

"I decided to wait and be surprised. But we can find out if you'd like."

"It doesn't matter as long as he or she is healthy. I wish I had been with you during the first five months."

"You'd have hated the morning sickness bouts. I'm just glad you're here now."

"So am I."

****

"Are you ready to head down to dinner, my little dove?" AJ asked affectionately.

Her heart did a flip-flop hearing him call her that again. As Megan met his gaze, that wonderful tingle erupted in the pit of her stomach. This man had given up everything for her, which accounted for their staying at a hotel in Baltimore instead of his old home. He'd seen to everything, including somehow upgrading their flight to first class.

Allowing them back to their old lives had taken a great deal of work. Since there was no way his brothers would let him fall off the face of the earth, he'd called them first. They'd done some magic and the hits on them had been removed. It seemed the new drug lord appreciated Megan opening the door for him by taking out the old boss. That hadn't been her intent, but she hadn't planned on telling him that. He did leave her with a threat. No nosing into his business, or he'd change his mind about canceling the hits.

It still took a month to get approvals, paperwork, and identifications changed. He'd had to pull Arthur into it to smooth the way and speed up the process, as the U.S. Marshals weren't happy or cooperative. She'd had some trepidation at the beginning, but having AJ at her side, knowing he felt safe enough to move back, washed it all away. The life she'd worked so hard for would be hers again. This time it would include the love of her life.

AJ had told her they'd needed to check in with the marshals in Baltimore before they flew down to see her parents the next morning. She was so excited about seeing them again. If only they hadn't have had to stop over. It sounded odd, but she trusted AJ to make sure they did everything right.

She laughed. "You're always trying to feed me."

He reached out and lightly rubbed her swollen belly. "You're eating for two. Plus, you bug me for something every few hours."

She couldn't argue with that. He'd been amazing taking care of her and the baby, constantly running to the store to purchase something to satisfy her weird cravings. He rubbed her feet and back daily. How had she survived this pregnancy before he'd arrived? "Now that you mention it, I could eat."

He chuckled and led her from the room. "I didn't

expect any other answer."

On the ground floor, he guided her to a closed door. "This is our private dining room." His eyes danced merrily.

"You reserved us a whole room by ourselves?"

"Yes. I wanted to be alone with you. We've been apart too long." He opened the door, took her left hand and ushered her into the room.

"Surprise!"

Megan's breath caught, and her right hand flew over her racing heart. Happy tears sprang to her eyes. AJ placed an arm around her to steady her. He'd organized this for her. He'd known how important these people were to her, how much she'd missed them and couldn't wait to see them again.

She loved him more each day.

Kristen came forward and hugged her. "I'm so glad to see you. I've missed you."

"I missed you too, Kristen."

"I won't keep you. There are a lot more people here to say hello." Her old boss's smile turned serious. "We'll talk later."

"Okay." What could it be? Her fingers were crossed it was a job offer. She wanted to return to her old job. It'd been a long time though. She had no idea if her position had been filled. AJ had reminded her there was more than one newspaper in Baltimore, but she'd loved working at *Baltimore News First*.

"Megan!" Kelly approached her and engulfed her in a tight hug.

A single tear slid down Megan's face unchecked. Dang hormones. "I'm sorry I didn't listen to you and go to the FBI."

Kelly waved her hand. "Don't sweat it. Things turned out fine. You got the hunky man out of it."

Megan laughed. She did have the hunky man.

"We have so much to talk about, but everyone will kill me if I tie you up as soon as you arrive." Kelly glanced over her shoulder.

Megan looked in that direction and gasped. She turned to AJ. A playful wink accompanied his sexy smile.

"Mom. Dad." Megan flew into her father's arms.

"Hi, sugar pie." Jeffrey Rogers kissed the top of his daughter's head. "It's so good to see you."

His familiar smell reminded her of times long gone by when she'd sought comfort in these strong arms.

He handed her off to her mother. "Oh, honey, I've missed you so much."

"Oh, Mom. I missed you." Tears of joy rapidly streamed down both of their faces, dropping on each other's shoulder, leaving behind a damp spot filled with love.

She surveyed her parents. They'd changed since she'd last seen them. Her father's hair was grayer and a little thinner. Her mother had lost weight. She figured losing two grown children would do that. She'd have to ensure she and AJ made regular visits to see them. It would be good for their little one to grow up knowing his or her family.

"Your sister sends her love. She's due to deliver any day and couldn't travel." Her mother wiped tears from her face and looked down at Megan's belly. She clasped her hands together. "Megan, honey, you're finally giving me grandbabies."

She laughed, remembering all the times her mother

asked when she'd have them. "Yes, Mom. AJ and I will be parents. We had a sonogram and asked the doctor not to tell us the gender. I'd heard of this fun way to find out. We brought a sealed envelope and planned to hand it to a bakery with the specification that they'd make a cupcake in either blue or pink. I hated waiting, but AJ convinced me that it'd be more fun to do it with you. I can't wait much longer." She cast a loving glance at AJ.

He took her hand. "Mr. and Mrs. Rogers, your daughter has agreed to marry me. Your grandchild will have my love and name."

"Well, it's about time you found her then," her mom said.

Butterflies bumped around in her stomach at the loving look he cast her. "Yes. It was about time."

****

AJ kept an eye on Megan as she moved around the room greeting colleagues, family, and friends. He loved seeing her happy. They'd made the right decision to move back. She never would've had a fulfilling life being unable to write. He knew Kristen planned to offer her a place back on the team. Minus one Victoria Bell and one Merissa Attenborough, who had also been planted by Marcus. Merissa had found out about Victoria and turned on Marcus, telling the police all she knew. Apparently, Marcus had also proposed to her, and he'd promised to take her out of the country. The same promise he'd made to Victoria.

Megan made her way back to him. He pulled her close.

"Megan, I'd like you to meet FBI Deputy Director, Arthur Hall.

"Hello, Ms. Rogers. It's good to finally meet you. Highly unusual, but good. I'm glad to see AJ. Although I wished he'd return to us instead of joining his brothers, I understand family comes first."

Her smile broadened. "I'm glad he can work with his brothers. Whether he admits it or not, he loves them."

"I do believe he loves someone more. He walked away from everything and everyone."

AJ spoke up, smiling, "It doesn't matter who or what I love more, but I'd go to the ends of the earth for this woman."

"So, I'm guessing I'll be attending a wedding," Arthur said with a twinkle in his eye.

"You bet. She's agreed to be my wife, and I'm holding her to it." AJ turned and kissed her temple. They couldn't get married fast enough for him. Kate and Megan had spoken at length, and his sister-in-law had taken care of things here to speed up the process.

"We're under time constraints, so it'll be real soon." She placed her hand on her belly.

Arthur laughed. "Yeah, well, that can definitely do it."

Megan walked over and kissed Arthur on the cheek. "Thank you for helping us stay alive and for letting AJ find me."

With a reddening face, he cleared his throat. "Well, um, I'll take your thanks for one and tell you that I know nothing about the other." He winked at her.

AJ turned her to face him, holding her shoulders. This had to go well. It was one of two surprises he had for her today. "Megan, you know how sorry I am for not being there to save your brother."

She closed her eyes and bit her lip. She opened them up and looked at him. His gut clenched at the pain in them. She nodded.

"I was able to save someone else."

A woman walked up behind Megan, and he smiled. "Megan, I'd like to introduce you to Teri, your niece."

She spun around, almost losing her balance. "Oh my God! Jenny! You're alive!" Megan reached to hug her but stopped when a baby was placed before her.

Holding the baby tightly, more tears slid down her face. The woman never ran out of them now that she was pregnant. In this case, he understood. Then the moment he feared. She turned back to AJ with narrowed eyes. "Why did you lie to me?"

He took a deep breath and knew this would come. No matter his answer, he'd be in the wrong. "You only asked about Kevin, and I couldn't volunteer the information on Jenny."

She opened her mouth to retort, but he beat her to it.

"I've another surprise for you." He hoped doing this without asking would be okay. He'd hate to sleep on the floor in their room.

Kate moved forward. "You'll need to give the baby back and follow me."

She reluctantly released Kevin's daughter, and they followed his sister-in-law to a table. He pulled out a chair for Megan. She looked up at him inquisitively.

Reagan bounded forward, followed by Mrs. Kessler, the woman Jesse had hired to help take care of his daughter before he'd married Kate. The family loved her so much that they kept her on after the marriage. She kept his brothers in line. She'd also created this surprise.

He held his breath as the older woman placed a cake in front of Megan who gasped, her hands flying to her mouth. She looked back up at him. "Is this what I think it is?"

He nodded. "It's up to you, but if you'd like, we can cut this cake and find out if we're having a boy or girl."

"Guess what, Ms. Megan?" Reagan bounced beside her.

Megan looked at the little girl with a wide smile. "What?"

"Mrs. Kessler made the cake, and she let me add the color to it. But she said I can't tell you what color I used." The girl huffed. "She says it's a surprise."

AJ leaned over her and spoke to his niece, "Well I guess we'd best open this surprise."

She giggled. "Uncle AJ, you don't open it. You cut it."

He widened his eyes in fake astonishment. "Really? Okay. Let's cut it." He turned his gaze to his little dove, hoping she wanted to do this now. He'd lied when he'd told her he could wait until she gave birth. He wanted to know now.

"Reagan, where's the knife, please?" Megan asked.

The girl heaved a heavy sigh. "Mom has it. No one would let me carry it even though I'm big enough."

A round of feminine giggling and male chuckling filled the air. It was good to be home. Megan and his family were his future. They'd manage anything together. It'd taken this special woman to help him open his eyes and see what was before him.

Kate moved forward and handed him the knife.

His glowing fiancée reached for his hand. "Cut it together?"

His heart expanded. He nodded, closed his eyes for a second, praying the family hadn't played a trick on them and colored it yellow. Together, they held the knife over the cake with shaky hands. He wasn't sure whose hand trembled more. The silence of the room didn't help his nervousness.

They'd just made their first slice into the cake when Dev raced into the room. "We've found Jake!"

The quiet room exploded into cheers and people attempting to speak over each other. AJ froze, his body tensed, his mind spinning. Had Dev said what he thought he'd said? Could it be true that finally, things would be right? He opened his mouth to speak, but nothing emerged.

He closed his eyes tightly. He had a great deal of groveling to do with Jake, but he'd do whatever it took to repair their relationship and bring him back into the family fold.

Megan pulled him close. He hadn't noticed her stand. She whispered in his ear, "Now your life is complete. Now you can live fully."

With her at his side, he knew he could do anything. He reached his arms around her, holding her tight. He felt something in his hand, looked at it, and smiled

Blue.

A word about the author…

Sheila Kell writes about the romantic men who leave women's hearts pounding with a happily ever after built on memorable, adrenaline-pumping stories. Her debut novel, His Desire (HIS Series #1), launched as an Amazon #1 romantic suspense bestseller, later winning the Readers' Favorite award for best romantic suspense novel.

As a Southern girl who has left behind her days with the U.S. Air Force, and as a University Vice President, she can usually be found nestled in the Mississippi woods, where she lives with her cats and all the strays that magically find her front door. When she isn't writing, she has her nose in a good book, is dealing with the woodland critters who enjoy her back porch, or is wishing she had a genie to do her bidding.

https://www.sheilakell.com